THE FIRST HERESY

First published in 2022 by
Ely's Arch Books
an imprint of Liberties Press
libertiespress.com

Distributed in the UK by
Casemate UK
casematepublishers.co.uk

Distributed in the United States and Canada by
Casemate IPM
casemateipm.com

Copyright © Eddie Hobbs, 2022
The author asserts his moral rights.
ISBN print: 978-1-912589-25-8
ISBN ebook: 978-1-912589-26-5

2 4 6 8 10 9 7 5 3 1
A CIP record for this title is available from the British Library.
Cover design by Baker @ Plan B Associates
Cover illustration 'Magdalena' by Eve Ventrue

This book is sold subject to the condition that it shall not, by way of trade or otherwise, be lent, resold, hired out or otherwise circulated, without the publisher's prior consent, in any form other than that in which it is published and without a similar condition including this condition being imposed on the subsequent publisher.

No part of this publication may be reproduced or transmitted in any form or by any means, electronic or mechanical, including photocopying, recording or storage in any information or retrieval system, without the prior permission of the publisher in writing.

The First Heresy is a work of fiction. Any resemblance between the characters in the book and actual persons, living or dead, is coincidental.

THE FIRST HERESY

EDDIE HOBBS

Author's Note

The First Heresy was written during the first Covid-19 lockdown, as an escape from it. The story is pacy yet detailed, so be prepared for it to move at a clip. It draws upon historical figures, events and practices relevant to the time-period in which it is set. It also creates some fictitious lead characters, while delving into early Christian history and mysticism to blend the story together. Most of the action takes place in fourteenth-century France and Ireland, but the back-story covers Roman Judaea and early Christian history.

The appendix is split into natural slots: fictitious characters, and historical figures and events. Each is marked with the chapter in which they first appear, so there is a quick reference-point to each figure, battle or event.

I really do hope you enjoy the yarn – and pick up some history along the way.

Eddie Hobbs

Medieval France

CHAPTER 1
Alexandria, 415 AD

Venus, the Morning Star, was all that remained of the night-canopy as the sun rose from its berth over Alexandria. Leon looked towards Hypatia, his heart springing open like petals in the early sunlight; she seemed to be both smiling and frowning at her bittersweet triumph. As he watched, her back arched in her high-backed chair. Her eyes, pools of green under greying walnut hair, strained over her star-taker, her astrolabe, as she completed her final calculations.

The garden, he thought, was a fitting place for her to fix the date of the Vernal Equinox; here at the house of her father, the cradle of her knowledge, the birthplace of her gnosis. Here, there was the certainty of knowledge but outside, the streets of Alexandria boiled, caught in the jaws between Cyril, Bishop of the Church of Alexandria, and Orestes, the Roman prelate.

Both men, Leon knew, wanted to claim the right to set Easter: one for the Christian God, one for Rome. Both put Hypatia at the centre of their struggle for power, a struggle between state and church, between imperial Rome, humbled by the Visigoths, and Saul's surging Christianity.

Orestes was in love with her, so he didn't expect any harm from that quarter. Besides, she gave the Prelate proof of the date he craved. But Cyril was a different matter. He despised her independence as a woman, her mastery of mathematics, her philosophy. He circulated rumours that she used black magic, that she consulted the stars to divine the future, that she was a necromancer. He loathed her popularity. She openly taught everyone, Christian or Jew, it mattered not to Hypatia. Everyone listened. They loved her. But Hypatia in love? Hypatia was a servant to knowledge, never to man.

The thought amused Leon. Over the course of fifty years, he'd known her mind like no other. From as far back as he could remember, he had known that her curiosity about the world was boundless, absorbing and exclusive. There was no room except for knowledge and the pursuit of it, and he loved her for it. Hypatia now swivelled gracefully, eyes flashing with mischief – which they always did when she had added to her store of knowledge.

'It is done, Leon,' she said, then added wistfully, 'but my time is fast fading.'

Barefoot, she moved towards him, her small frame silhouetted against the sunlight filtering through the vines of the roof garden. Leon gasped quietly, transfixed, as always, in her presence. She had aged and greyed, but rich sallow skin was still drawn tightly across her high cheekbones, which were set by deeply penetrating eyes that fired with intelligence, curiosity and energy.

'Leon, I fear the next era will be challenged by a dark impulse that seeks to poison knowledge, alienate the mind of man, and convince all that we must rely on interlocutors in order to talk to the gods. I feel it is driven by an ancient being, one which cannot be named until it threatens incarnation and is confronted by mankind. All must be prepared for that confrontation, because it will set the course of man, either for the stars or back to the caves. It is why we now do what must be done.'

Leon trembled visibly. He knew she was asking him to sacrifice her.

He had watched over Hypatia since they had played together, boy and girl, student and teacher, slave and mistress. She placed her right hand gently over his heart, her left cupping the back of his head, fixing him with her full attention. 'Leon, your breathing is shallow. Draw it in slowly and deeply, and leave it there, to rest, and escape at its own pace.'

He complied, pulling in great gulps of air through his nose, and slowing the heart-rate in his failing body.

'How do you feel now?' she asked.

'Mistress, even though you have predicted this day, and prepared me for it, I cannot control my fear for you – a fear which threatens to overwhelm me, a fear that feels so old, avaricious, anti-life. It is what I have sensed before.'

'Breathe, Leon.' Hypatia inhaled with him until both were in harmony, two old friends in the twilight of life, swaying in unison to the sound of their breaths. 'Whatever comes to pass today, Leon, you must promise me that you will not look back. You must not look back. You must proceed. Everything depends on you, now. My work is done. Yours is yet to be completed, at Usna. Do you promise?'

His eyes stung with salt as he gazed into hers – so close now that he felt her heart beat in rhythm to his own. 'Yes, mistress, it is promised, even though what you ask of me – to let you go – will be the hardest task of my life.'

Hypatia slowly nodded, gazing as if through his eyes and deep into his mind.

She knows that what she asks of me screams against all the decades of my training, the root of my person, and my love for her, he thought. But I must remain strong, must hold. It is the only way. He forced his mind to return to his list. 'The master mason, Marcus the Ebionite, flees far south in search of the Mandaeans, to the ancient lands of Sumer. He will look for the teachings of the Baptist, never to return, but his craftmanship remains. His legacy is exquisite. No trace remains of the vault within. I have seen it so.'

Hypatia nodded, acknowledging the truth. She had carefully selected both the mason and his task. 'The ancient line of knowledge must not be broken if man is to be saved, Leon. You must complete it; preserve the secret knowledge that was once in the custody of the Nasoreans and is now with us. It runs long and deep, far into antiquity, beyond the Pharaohs, before the flood, and before it could be written. Since the burning of the Serapeum, the great library, we've been barely holding onto Alexandria as the sanctuary for knowledge and a cradle of learning. Our duty to discovery must not end; not here, not like this, succumbing to Cyril's dark hunger and the brute ignorance of his minions, the Parabalani.'

He blinked slowly, acknowledging the truth she had told him many times before, knowing what was to come, but helpless to prevent it.

Whispering now, as if she could be overheard, Hypatia ended, 'We must trust in future histories to fulfil the sacred purpose to preserve that which has been entrusted to us: the secret knowledge of the Ebionites, which fled with them after the fall of Jerusalem to Titus.'

Leon's heart-rate began to settle as he controlled his breathing. He held Hypatia low at her waist, moving with her as she began to sway, the energy flowing between them. He held her gently as the sun rose, not wanting to let go, knowing this was their final goodbye.

He knew that no amount of persuasion could change her course once she had made up her mind to advance a breakthrough in learning, even when it challenged the most powerful. He had watched what was left of the great Library of Alexandria burn, and had stood by helplessly as the Jews were evicted, their goods and homes stolen by Christians who blamed them for the death of the Christ. The city was already boiling when Hypatia told him that she alone would name this day the Vernal Equinox, because the universe had revealed its knowledge to her.

He knew that Hypatia adored knowledge and was, above all else, a lover of wisdom: a philosopher who drew her inspiration from the legacy of Alexandria's library, her discipline from Plato, and her adherence to truth from her father, Theon of Alexandria. She had already taught openly, contrary to the Christian creed, that the sun did not rotate around the world, but the world around the sun. She had confided to him that she believed everything spun – the world, the sun, the stars – that everything was connected, and that, in time, the universe would give up its secrets to man. These things, he reasoned, could be posited as arguments of teaching, but fearlessly setting the date of Easter at a time not approved by Cyril and the Christians?

That was a point of no return.

As Leon observed her, he sensed Hypatia's mind turning to what she must now face. She slowly broke from their embrace, turning her back to allow him to drape the *palla* over her shoulders. She swivelled one last time, lifting from her chair a silver casket, and passed it firmly to him. 'Remember, Leon, no looking back. Head to the harbour, no matter what unfolds. The streets are black with Parabalani. They must not connect you to me. Not today, of all days.'

With that, she stepped out through the porch into the bustling street, Leon trailing some way behind – just enough to keep her in view, without being swallowed by the crowds. He watched the street darken with Cyril's teeth, the black-clothed Parabalani – ten, twenty, fifty – until there were hundreds of them. He recognised their tall leader, Peter the Lector, Cyril's infamous henchman. They surrounded his mistress like a swarm. Peter was clearly goading her, shouting at her, gesticulating to his men. Outside the Caesareum, on command, the swarm suddenly unleashed its power upon Hypatia.

They lunged at her, stripped her of her clothes and dragged her by the hair into the building. The significance wasn't lost on Leon. This, which had once been a pagan shrine, now a Christian church, was where they intended to sacrifice her. He was nauseous, but her orders were clear: use any attack as a diversion to get to the harbour. He moved quickly with the mob that gathered, and followed in the wake of the Lector's men. Parallel to the doors, he saw the Parabalani grab broken shards of tiles, and heard Hypatia scream as they went to work on her writhing body, knowing instantly that they intended to scrape the skin off her while she was still alive. Frozen by Hypatia's screams, interspersed with the sound of men grunting with the effort of flailing their prey, bile rose to Leon's mouth. His body shook in waves, the top of his head tingled, alert with expectation. As his mind reeled from the sudden violence, his senses were overwhelmed by a cold and malevolent wave of energy which exploded from the church, nearly knocking him senseless. His mind yelled a command: *run*. Hypatia's warning echoed through his head, over and over. *Move as fast as you can. Don't look back. Get to the harbour.*

He clutched the casket and staggered from the scene as Hypatia's screams faded to a loud death-wheeze. All the most cherished moments of his life, when his heart ached with his love for her flooded his mind, each memory drowned by the horror and loneliness of her death.

He turned into a narrow side-street, bent over, and vomited up the contents of his stomach. In that moment Leon loathed himself for not being there for her, to hold her hand, to comfort her, to die together. When he had recovered, Leon edged past the tide of people pushing their way towards the Caesareum, making eye-contact with no one. Despite the heat, an icy dread reverberated through his spine, his senses screamed that a predator stalked nearby, seeking him. Its presence hit him in waves. His mind blanking out the horror behind him, Leon's journey to the harbour was made in a daze, his old legs wobbling, his stomach heaving. Within sight of the sea, he collapsed in shock and lost consciousness.

He awakened to the sound of seagulls, the smell of the sea and a cool breeze on his skin. As the wind snapped into the sail, and the boat left the lee of the land, he pulled himself up, seeking the city of Alexandria, away to the south-east. In the distance a fire was burning outside the city at the Cinarion, black smoke catching the breeze as it climbed.

He knew. The Parabalani were burning his mistress, the last great pagan philosopher, to purge the city of her knowledge. As Hypatia feared, she had become an offering to their God. Alexandria was theirs; the old days had passed. Tears welled and his chest ached with grief. As he started to wilt again, pale, freckled and muscular arms reached to support him. Turning, Leon took stock of the crew, his eyes widening in amazement. He had never seen a race of men so tall, so different from the Alexandrians. Their countenance was at once alien but familiar, their words strange but comforting, like an echo across time.

'Usna?' he asked them, directing his gaze to the largest of the men, who had a full red beard, curly flaming hair, and radiated with controlled wildness. Pointing north-west towards the Pillars of Hercules, the man nodded vigorously, grinning from ear to ear. 'Uisneach. Uisneach.' It was as if he were teaching a child to speak its first word.

The crew burst into laughter, one stooping to return to Leon the casket they had rescued with him, another passing him a pigskin of fiery honey-water, which warmed his throat and settled his stomach.

As Alexandria drifted over the horizon, Leon marvelled at Hypatia. She must have planned this ever since they had stormed the Serapeum. His heart skipped a beat as he made the next connection: his new companions had pale skin, freckles and red hair, just like his. Hypatia had kept one last secret. As the boat surged forward, the tail-wind whispered to him: Leon, you are going home.

CHAPTER 2
The Room of Books

Snapping the book closed with long, slender fingers, a tall young man with sparkling blue eyes set in a chiselled, rusty face, watched the last air rush out in a small puff of dust. It wavered briefly in the violet-trimmed light of the lectern-lamp, then drifted, as if escaping the seas off Alexandria to seek fresh ground. Closing his eyes diminished the unsteady feeling of tilting in the seas, and eventually the snapping of the wind in the sails and the melodic rush of the waves under the bow faded. His last recollection was the murmur of the sailors, whose words curled into phrases he was sure he had heard long ago. He experienced a sense of completion, a connection across time that felt right. He chose to accept it fully. Now is not the moment to consider this deeply, he thought. Now is the time to absorb, without analysing.

Then he was back on land, in the library. The room was high-vaulted, every shelf crammed with leather-bound scrolls, the lanterns warming and welcoming, marching through the length of the corridor. He felt at peace here, accepted, connected. He walked slowly back to the shelf, where the librarian had first directed him to the glowing book, and replaced it gently, caressing the cover as he did so, silently promising to return. '*Au revoir*, old friend.'

He turned his attention to the desk by the door, to the librarian who had been watching over him. The old woman beamed a knowing smile, nodded silently in acknowledgement, and with a thin hand, lined with veins, indicated towards the rosewood door. It was time to leave.

He pushed against the heavy door, which was carved with a wooden likeness of an open book, and stepped into the corridor. Instantly he knew something was wrong. His sense of calm evaporated, replaced by a sudden feeling of familiar dread. Before him, one by one, the lights in the corridor were consumed by a sentient darkness, an anti-light, seeking him with ravenous, alien fingers of blackness that seemed to pulse, curl and rush up from the walls of the corridor. It felt very ancient, a dread beyond mortal fear; not the stuff of dreams but of a deeper shared memory. His mind screamed in alarm. This has pursued me through the Pillars of Hercules, through the sea, through time itself. I can spend no more time in this place. Flee!

He turned to run, trusting in his youthful energy to create distance, but his long legs were turning to stone, his movements slowing, as if he were pushing into a gale. He was being dragged backwards. The harder he struggled, the more his movements slowed. He was trapped, yet the thought of turning around to face the predator consumed him with horror. Instead, he curled up in a ball and put his hands over his ears, pressing his elbows together, trying in vain to block his sight.

The blackness had filled the corridor, and beyond it he perceived a vast expanse of despair, a nothingness of hate. He could smell its breath. It reeked of ancient decomposition, of rot. Skin recoiling in horror, he awaited the doom he assumed must surely follow. Moments passed. Nothing. Lifting his gaze, it dawned on him: it could not pass the light from the Door of Books. But it was so cold, and stank of a need beyond comparison, beyond appetite; a vast well of desire to ingest its prey for eternity, in its home, in the abyss.

A rasping low voice pulsated from the dark, its words clear: 'Return that which has been taken by the Nasorean. Return what is ours.'

The command throbbed repeatedly throughout the corridor, not diminishing in intensity. As the curls of blackness neared, he felt he was being pulled back along the mosaic tiles towards it, as if the corridor itself was trying to consume him in its maw. Inch by inch the gap closed as he desperately fought for a fingerhold in the tiled floor. It tilted against him. He was to be devoured, and he knew that when the darkness touched him there would be no hope, nothing but dread, despair, anti-light. The icy, rasping voice was now commanding. 'Return. Return. Return.'

He dug his fingers like claws into the cracks between the tiles, desperate to prevent himself from sliding further down the corridor. His legs kicked violently, seeking a foothold, while his mind erupted with the astonished realisation that he was being eaten alive. His lungs filled with air and he screamed, every organ of his body rising in unison, in rebellion against this fate. A triumphant primordial howl echoed in reply, mocking him, coiling and uncoiling around the corridor.

Suddenly the dark energy swivelled its attention towards the Door of Books, vibrating with amplified rage, frustration and hate, the words sharp and clear. 'Golgotha shall not triumph. The will of man is weak. All will fall to my kingdom. There is no water here for wine, Amesha Spenta.' The name spat from the darkness in a surge of primal hate.

The Door of Books had opened, and a dazzling light blazed a wall of colours across the corridor, red, orange, yellow, then pulsating green, followed by blue, indigo and violet. For an instant he sensed the depth of its pain before its connection to his mind severed as the darkness withdrew swiftly backwards from the display of colours. Dizzy with relief, he gulped in air to steady himself.

Just at that moment he heard his name, Cormac, being called over the crackle of a fire, and felt its warmth curl about him. He was free. Slowly opening his eyes, he'd returned to the dim light of candles and fire and brought his attention to his hands. They felt like stone affixed to their resting place over his knees. He knew he had gone deep, his hair matted in sweat from the violent spasms that accompanied his confrontation in the corridor. Heat from the fire contested the early morning chill. He was in Duncannon, in northern Europe, far from Alexandria, and after crossing nine centuries, back in his own time. He had survived. His eyes shot open, fixing upon the intense gaze from his guide and companion.

CHAPTER 3
Paris, 1307

The bed-canopy, affixed by lines to the arched oak ceiling-trusses, blew outwards as if a breath that had lurked beneath it had spent its fury on the occupant before escaping into the autumn night. Inside a small figure twisted and struggled, muttering her protest in several languages, her voice rising and falling before the grip of half-sleep was finally broken.

Suddenly she threw back the bedclothes, her heart pounding and in a cold sweat, and jumped out of bed. Trembling from the heavy weight she'd felt squat on her chest, she stared back into the bed, repelled. Gathering her senses, she took in great gulps of air, shed her wet nightclothes and scrubbed her skin violently, as if fending off a feasting of lice.

When her breath finally calmed, she pivoted towards the loft door that opened onto a narrow roof terrace, and stepped out under the Parisian night sky, scanning it for the constellation of Orion. There, she stared in the direction of Betelgeuse, the fading of which she knew was associated with the prophesy of a dark incarnation. She considered defiance in Hebrew, Persian, even in Arabic, but instead chose French, the language of the streets below, filled her lungs and bellowed into the night sky, 'Vas te faire foutre.'

Satisfied, she sat down, forcing herself to calm her heart-rate, to return to the physical world, to reason, by slowly taking in the panorama of the rooftops across Paris. From her perch over the silk merchant's shop on Rue de Jardins, her eye came to rest on her lifeline to knowledge, the College of Sorbonne, which lay across the Seine in the Latin quarter.

Behind her she heard familiar light footsteps approaching and felt a blanket fall over her shoulders, felt loving older arms wrap around her from behind, rocking in rhythm to her breathing: two women, young and old, gently moving in a comforting unison.

'More dark memories, another pursuit through the corridors of your dreams?' the older woman asked.

'No, Marguerite, and I'm sorry to have awoken you,' said the younger woman, 'but this was no mortal pursuit from my childhood, no blood-crazed Mamluks scaling the walls of the citadel, no savagery in the narrow streets, and no waking at the moment of capture. This was an assault on every part of my body while I was pressed down at the chest, unable to move; half awake, half asleep. It was not Acre, Marguerite, nor was it the memory of the tales of my people escaping the Mongols at Baghdad before finding sanctuary in Cyprus. This was different, something ancient, powerful and knowing. I was awake, Marguerite. My eyes were open. It felt as if I were being skinned.'

She shuddered. Marguerite wrapped her more tightly from behind while she caressed her temples, signalling her to go on, knowing that she needed to talk it out before she could find sleep again, and before sunrise would bring the bustling noise and rancid smells of a city awakening to a hot summer's day.

'In this moment when I need to heal, I envy you so Marguerite, I seek refuge in reason, but you find God within. You touch Him, are part of Him, move forever closer to return to Him. I see your unshakable faith every day in the way you love the women in your care, even the poorest of the creatures; the night-women who were cast aside, alone, isolated. You do not need books and endless enquiry to find the interface with God. For you there is no discovery. It just exists, inside.'

The two women sat silently for a moment. It was a conversation they'd had many times since Marguerite had first opened the door to her and found a place for her among the community of women, that she might continue studies which challenged the very foundations of the practices of the faithful. She'd listened to her recount the words of God spoken through Gabriel over twenty-three years to the illiterate Prophet Muhammad. She'd been fascinated to hear how the great Islamic philosopher Al Biruni reported on common ground across many religions: Hindu, Buddhist, Christian, Jew and Muslim. Marguerite held that their meeting was not chance, that they were destined to blend sure and simple *knowing* and love of God, with her journey to find him in the physical world.

Marguerite had come to hear how Islamic philosophers, the young woman's heroes of its golden age, had advanced the teachings of the Greek and Byzantine schools of learning, before Hulagu Khan punished the hubris of Caliph Al-Musta'sim by destroying Islam's greatest city, Baghdad, before trampling the Caliph to death, wrapped in carpet, under the hooves of the Mongol cavalry.

The fall of Baghdad ended her parents' study at the House of Wisdom, the great library of Baghdad. The Tigris had run black with ink from its vast quantity of books during the Mongol frenzy of massacre and destruction that followed, in the confusion of which the young couple had fled north towards the Levant. It had been a long journey over several generations from the seat of her ancestors in ancient Bactria at the foothills of the Hindu Kush, through which Alexander had marched sixteen centuries before, to the capital of the Frankish kingdom, Paris.

But here she was, this feisty scholar, steeped in a remarkable inheritance of study and free thinking, living a life of pure learning. She fed off borrowed notes and manuscripts from the Sorbonne, from which she was excluded on grounds of gender. Few grasped the power amongst them, save for a sect of Templars with whom she quietly studied under their master of knowledge.

'Marguerite, try as I have, I do not feel as you feel. Unlike you, I must venture to the very edges of philosophy, mathematics, and astronomy in pursuit of Him. I don't know if there are enough great thinkers and books in the world, nor enough time for me to reach them, to ever know how you feel.'

'Perhaps you are closer than you think?' Marguerite whispered into her ear.

'Why, what makes you say this?'

'Firstly, you found your way here to this community of simple souls, dedicated to finding God within, not without; secondly, it is here you have been targeted this night. Why so? Is this not to deter you from your direction of inquiry at the edges of the physical world? Use your reason, child of God.'

Silence returned to the two women as they watched the night sky. The great womb of the universe, known to the ancient Greeks as the Milky Way, towered over them, as if listening to their thoughts.

Marguerite broke the silence. 'Go back to your fountain, tell me again, tell of Avicenna the Muslim, tell me of his test of the soul's existence that has so marvelled you.'

She knew Marguerite was distracting her, guiding her back to her seed-corn, but loved her for it. She smiled, took a deep breath. 'Look up to the stars, Marguerite, consider a woman has just appeared above us, created by God, with no memories, mind blank, naked and suspended in the air. She has no senses, no hearing, sight, smell, taste, she cannot feel her outstretched limbs, she is devoid of all senses even on her skin. Can you see her?'

'Yes, I can see her.'

'Now Marguerite, here's the test: can you feel like her?'

'I think I can.'

'That's it, you think. Look up at her, feel as her. She is aware of her existence, that she exists. She is self-aware. That awareness comes from what you know as her soul. It is separate to her body, from which she has no sensation. We are self-aware even when asleep, Marguerite. Often, we are not conscious of being self-aware, but we cannot see or be aware of things without first being self-aware. Avicenna gave me a bridge to the existence of the soul Marguerite. The woman above us doesn't know that her body exists, but she is self-aware, so these two things cannot be identical. This has fired my mind, not just because it breaks from Aristotle, but that it provides a reasoned argument for the soul. Does that make sense to you Marguerite, that the soul is separate?'

Marguerite paused her rocking briefly as she considered her reply. 'I think the soul is divine, part of God, that it isn't simply separate, but is our essence. I feel that we are on a long journey back to Him, a journey towards a state of divine grace, and when we unbecome and are united with Him, when our souls will be annihilated. That is what I know the soul to be.' The older woman paused for a second, then started to giggle. 'Naturally, that is not how the Church would rather I see things.'

'Leave nothing out in that book of yours, in the common tongue for all to read. I can just see row upon row of red hats pouring over the manuscript, great blobs of black ink poised over any aspect that echoes what they most fear: a free spirit, especially that of a woman.'

Both women started to giggle, then flooded into uncontrolled laughter as each visualised the stern brows of Church leaders facing the possibility that the route to God was not, after all, through old men in gowns.

Memories of the night slipped away as their laughter rose to meet the first rays of sun on the horizon to the east. Paris bustled to life.

CHAPTER 4
Duncannon, County Wexford, Ireland

'Holy Mother of divine Jesus!' Cormac declared aloud. 'That is not a place I'll be going back to again in a hurry.'

Across the small room, Guiscard Carrel, a giant, white-bearded monk with a girth to match his booming voice, laughed aloud. 'Well, Cormac lad, that looks like one of your more eventful night walks. You were rocking about like a hen on a cracked egg. Let me get out my quill and parchment. This promises to be the most exciting tale of derring-do since the Saladin fled from us at Montgisard.'

Outside, the south-westerly beat the rain-squall that had travelled across the breast of the north Atlantic upon the roof of Dun Cannon castle, as if drumming its impatience for Cormac to start the report to his mentor. As the young man's heart rate slowed, he began to recount his experience to the old monk. He'd followed Guiscard's voice, first visualising floating in a dark void, feeling calm, rocking into a gentle trance, before arriving at an endless, high-vaulted corridor, dimly lit by lanterns.

Walking the corridor, he had passed polished rosewood doors left and right, pausing only at the Door of Books as Guiscard had guided him. He pushed the heavy door and stepped through to find the librarian sitting at her desk as Guiscard had described. He recalled feeling serene and asking the librarian for the book of his lives, before following her as she gracefully left her desk and brought him to a glowing and heavily bound book on a shelf some way down into the library. He lifted the book from the shelf. It was heavy. He remembered that it smelled like a very old manuscript. He placed it at the nearest reading bay, guarded by a lantern shimmering white and violet light. He opened a page in the middle. It seemed to be in a script that he didn't at first understand but that quickly resolved as his mind found a way to read, found a way to Theon's house in Alexandria, to 415 AD. It felt familiar. Nothing had surprised him; it felt like home, another home.

Guiscard listened attentively, pausing and asking him for detail that the old warrior monk seemed to think important, but letting the young man fully describe his experience outside in the corridor, without interruption.

Guiscard was busy writing furiously.

When he'd finished, the old monk went silent, squinting intensely at his notes, his breathing heavy as if he were reading a rollcall after battle. Cormac, he knew, welcomed the silence; he was exhausted, confused and numbed. But Guiscard asked him to go through it again and again until he'd extracted every last morsel of detail, committing all to his parchment.

'Cormac, this is very important. We know of Hypatia from our records, but the rasping words spoken in the corridor, are you certain that it said Nasorean?'

'It couldn't have been clearer to me. It was as if it was speaking into my ear, searing my mind with its intent. Why is Nasorean so important?'

'Because, my dear boy, it is a term from another time, from antiquity, first prophesised in the Old Testament. It is a long-forgotten term to describe the earliest followers of the Christ. The voice didn't identify which Nasorean, which is interesting,' Guiscard mused aloud, before returning to his notes, going quiet again.

'The last sentence, *There is no water for wine*, was not addressed to you, Cormac. It was addressed to something called Amesha Spenta. There is an intervention here, and the reason for it is extraordinary. You say you felt in mortal danger, that you'd lost hope, and just at that moment of greatest peril outside the Room of Books, to whom did you call out?'

Cormac was surprised by the question. Puzzled, he shrugged his shoulders, signalling to the old monk that he couldn't remember.

Guiscard put down his quill and said reprovingly, 'Cormac, there is no shame in calling out. I've witnessed grizzled warriors, both Christian and Muslim, call not for their battle colours with their final breath, but for their mothers.'

'I have no answer, no memory, but a strong feeling that I did call out. I just can't remember to what or to whom.'

The old monk was sympathetic. He knew that he was pushing the young man, and in danger of getting a wrong reply if pressed. 'It may reveal itself to you in time but this whole episode will need greater study from better minds than mine. I fear that it is of huge importance, Cormac. Not a single word of your vision must be spoken. This you must promise me, as solemnly as you promised Hypatia that you would not look back. Can you do that?'

'It is so promised, Guiscard. But what of the casket. What does it all mean?'

'I feel that is part of a bigger tapestry, and best not for discussion now. There is much here that needs to be interpreted, so I will consult with the

Grand Master himself in Paris. There are things here beyond our knowledge, maybe beyond the wisdom of the Order, but we shall see. The sun is rising. Let us walk the long sands, and with bare feet, reconnect to God's earth.'

With that, both men stepped out, the older man wearing the white Templar's tunic, emblazoned with the cross of red, the young man wearing a plain brown smock. Dawn was breaking from the east, chasing away the overnight squalls, illuminating the huge lighthouse at the most south-easterly fingertip of the peninsula, which marked the mouth of Waterford harbour.

The morning cleared to a fine summer day as they stepped onto the long beach. In the distance, the great lighthouse, built by William Marshall, Earl of Pembroke, had stood for over a century. It sat on the site of an older beacon, dominating the skyline, rising a hundred feet out of the rocks to face Normandy to the south-east, the Frankish power that dominated Europe. Cormac squinted in the bright morning light, pushing his mind off the events of the night. 'Directly to the south, Guiscard, in a straight line stands the oldest lighthouse in Europe, the Tower of Hercules at Corunna. Did you know that?'

The monk glanced sideways as his much heavier footprints more deeply marked his path over the wet sand. 'No, I can't say I knew that. Why is that in your mind?'

'Well, because the Galician lighthouse is modelled on the great Lighthouse of Alexandria.' Cormac beamed. 'Imagine that!'

'Our lighthouse is not as pretty, Cormac. It's thick and squat, designed to battle the north Atlantic where it meets the Irish Sea.'

Guiscard knew the story of the peninsula, where the Normans had first fought to retain their foothold in Leinster before spreading north and west, cutting a swathe through light-armoured Gaelic resistance; but he was bothered by older matters. What link in the chain is missing? The connection was just beyond his reach.

As they came to the end of the strand, the two turned to go back along the path they'd etched on the beach, when Guiscard had a sudden thought. He put his hand on Cormac's arm to slow him. 'Cormac, is the lighthouse in Galicia the only connection you've made?'

'No, the sailors in the boat looked like the wild Gaels of the West. The Pillars of Hercules lie to the south of Spain, where the Mediterranean meets the Atlantic, and Uisneach is here, Guiscard. It is the ancient centre of Ireland. Back in those times, this land remained outside Rome and the Church of Rome, many miles from Constantinople, from Antioch and from Alexandria.'

Guiscard grimaced but nodded at the logic. 'A good spot to hide something, then?'

'Yes, but it must be something extraordinary and terrifying to have travelled this far.' Cormac paused as he teased out his thoughts. 'Whatever it was or is, it's not something that the early Christian Church could tolerate. My sense is that this why Hypatia was butchered, and why that vile presence I encountered in Alexandria, followed me here, to this time.'

Guiscard had turned to face his young companion, visibly shaken, aging in a moment, his head throbbing with a growing sense of menace. 'That's the connection I was hoping you weren't going to make; it is my worst fear. This news must travel on the next tide to Paris. I sense that there is not much time, that whatever is coming is not so far away. Cormac, I believe that we may be under siege in the spiritual realm.'

'And as above, so below?' Cormac asked softly.

Guiscard briskly nodded as both men quickened their pace, a fresh squall darkening the skyline to the west.

CHAPTER 5

Above the fires lit by the line of circular torches, the Iron King, Philip IV of France, stood completely still, like a bird of prey, content that, to those below his perch, he was unseen. He'd designed the balcony meticulously, shielded from the light of the tower, accessible only through his private quarters. He welcomed the familiar rush of excitement that travelled from groin to crown, tingling with anticipation.

Here is where heresy comes to perish, he thought, here at my hands, not the hands of the old men bartering power and favours behind closed doors in their flowing robes, red hats and false piety. Two years it took them to elect that cave-hermit as Pope Celestine V. The old man lasted five months in Naples before fleeing the papal court for his cave, then the fools elected that two-faced weasel, Cardinal Benetto Caetani, to succeed as Boniface VIII, imprisoning Celestine, and opening the time of two popes. How I loathe that creature.

He visualised digging up Boniface for denigrating Christendom, to make an example of the Pope who dared challenge the King of France. I could bring his corpse to Paris for inquisition, trial and punishment. I could burn the *Ausculta Fili*, the papal bull which sought to make me subservient to Rome's power. I could stuff the ashes into its empty maw before crushing his dry bones into the blood-drenched earth that screamed for it. He spat out the name, clutching the iron balcony rail as if he wanted to strangle it by force of will and intention.

Boniface, heretic and sodomite, you escaped the wrath of God. I should have had you killed at Anagni when I had you in my grasp. Still, it only took a few weeks before fevered death strangled you, and it won't be long before my puppet pope will put you on trial. What delicious irony that the puppet Clement V, neither Italian, a red hat, nor resident in Italy, is in Poitiers, in my kingdom, under the shadow of my power. Before all Christendom they will see how I am the true instrument of God. I will inflict His judgement on popes. The fools think the route to salvation for kings is to be found fighting Muslims for Jerusalem, but it isn't, it is here in Christendom rooting out heretics and sodomites among the faithful, especially those at the Holy See.

Below him, the tall, gangly, pockmarked Brother Bertramnus, his favourite Dominican, hand selected from the Toulouse Inquisition, nodded reverently towards the ceiling of darkness above him. The Dominican sensed the presence of his temporal master before returning to his task, smiling. Philip understood the Dominican's appetite. The king had Bertramnus moved to Paris so both of them could practise their common lust for crushing heretics, undeterred by the niceties of the papal bull which, for over fifty years, had allowed inquisitors to torture, provided any blood-spilling was left to secular authorities.

Below the king, stretched before Bertramnus, face down, naked and restrained, lay the delicate, pale white and bloodied body of the heretic. A real prize, the king thought, one of the last of the Cathars; an old woman preacher, a *perfecta*, found hiding in the mountains of the Pyrenees. The monk checked the wrist-binds of the *strappado* that bound her at her back to the pulley affixed to the crossbeam eight feet above. In Latin he ordered the first lift, the pulley creaking, blood and saliva dripping to the ground as the king observed curiously: 'A light one, this. She will last long under Bertramnus.'

Just then a soft voice over his shoulder whispered, 'Your Majesty, de Nogaret has returned from his investigation of the rumours from the Villeneuve du Temple. He awaits at Your Majesty's pleasure in the antechamber.'

In the circular room below, the elevation of the *perfecta* continued, searing pain into both shoulder-joints as the full weight of her body left the floor in stuttered movements practised by the Dominican's attendants so as to inflict most agony.

The king looked down, unmoving, his heart-rate even, unconcerned as if looking at something already dead. Slowly he turned away, reluctant to leave the quarry solely to the Dominican. 'Pity about the timing. I was so looking forward to a rare contest between my Dominican and a Pure One. It will have to wait.'

With that King Philip took the squire's candle and ascended the spiral staircase that led directly to his quarters. 'One of the *perfecti*, a leftover from the Albigensian Crusade,' he sighed. 'What glory to have been at the feet of their last nest, Castle Montségur, when two hundred of them were offered to the flames.'

He visualised the *Prat dels Cremats*, the field of the burnt ones, as line after line of pyres made from faggots, straw and pitch committed nearly two hundred *perfecti* to a great conflagration of purification while the clergy chanted psalms. Sick and wounded, men and women, they had walked willingly on to the pyres. The image filled him with cheer as he bounded up the stairs to his private chambers, reciting the words of the Cistercian Arnaud Armaury a hundred years before at Béziers, when he had ordered the deaths of twenty thousand Cathars, including Catholics. '*Caedite eos. Novit enim Dominus qui sunt euis.*' Kill them all, for the Lord knows who are His.

King Philip signalled for his guest to belay the report while he crossed the room to the water basin, to wash his hands as if wanting to cleanse himself of his moment at the balcony. The two men who stood facing each other couldn't have been more differently made. The Iron King towered over his subjects, tall and handsome but wooden, chilly and reserved, born into wealth, privilege and responsibility at Fontainebleau. A member of the Capetian line which had held the Frankish throne for over three hundred years, Philip traced the kingdom back to the Carolingian dynasty, to Charlemagne, against whom he measured himself. He saw his father as weak and soft, and chose to model himself on the stern piety of his grandfather. In Louis IX he saw a devout, uncompromising Catholic king, a leader in two Crusades in his thirties and his fifties, and a prosecutor of the Albigensian Crusade against the Cathars.

Philip knew that his grandfather saw himself as an officer of God on earth, a hater of usury, and hammer of the Jews, whose lending he outlawed, and whose books he burned. He died aged fifty-six from dysentery, far away in Tunis, when Philip was aged two. He had witnessed his grandfather canonised a saint in 1297 by his nemesis Pope Boniface. Philip's own father Philip III died leading the ill-fated Aragon Crusade, which left Philip with a legacy of crushing war debts. His father also contracted dysentery after becoming infected in Girona, forcing him to retreat over the Pyrenees with his stinking, enfeebled and shrinking army in 1285.

Philip IV chose to be different to his predecessors. He promoted powerful civil servants rather than nobility to his administration, men handpicked not according to bloodline or marriage but for the talents and appetites he wished to exploit. He had selected Guillaume de Nogaret as he picked his lead hunting hound, with meticulous care, both sharing the uncommon ability to see the ground differently, to seek out their prey, to kill without compunction, to obey without hesitation, one his God, the other his king.

Guillaume de Nogaret was born to be a hunter of men. A lawyer by profession, he came from deep in Cathar country and studied in Montpellier before being called to the king's court in 1296, where he came to royal attention for his cold, ruthlessness, and strategic cunning as a spymaster. Both men understood each other. Their relationship was forged by de Nogaret's bold move to recruit a mercenary force of fifteen hundred men and capture Pope Boniface at his palace in Anagni, where he humiliated, assaulted and tortured the seventy-nine-year-old pope, leaving him without food and sleep for three days before retreating. The affair infuriated Boniface who, before he died, issued a papal bull excommunicating both the king and his Hound.

De Nogaret was small and squat, built from the ground up, his hands and mind calloused from climbing out of landless obscurity. His memories of childhood ranged from the harsh beatings he received from his mother, the calculated disdain of his father, and the cold indifference of the local Cathars. It was rumoured that he slowly garrotted the king's enemies, revelling in the task, whispering into the ears of his most hated victims his plans to have their children raped, so as to sculpt fresh horror into his collection of death-masks.

Philip saw in the lawyer a sharp counsel, a mind free of the corrupting influences of noble family bloodlines, legacies and agendas. He relied upon de Nogaret because the man understood the same currency that Philip did: that men are best bought and not trusted. Philip believed that power extended from the purse and not the heart; that nothing was without its price, and with enough gold and silver he had the capacity to be the most powerful force in Europe since Charlemagne.

He despised the whisperings across Christendom about his lack of crusading energy, as if this was the true measure of a Catholic king. The legacy of his father's disastrous Crusade, his crushing defeat by the Flemish at the Battle of the Golden Spurs, from which he had bounced back, and his costly war with the English, had taught him that money equalled temporal power, that nothing other than God stood higher than gold and silver, even his family.

He promised his young daughter Isabella to Edward Prince of Wales, despite knowing him to be a sodomite, because it secured peace and put his bloodline onto the throne in England. Philip, coming from a long line of Capetian kings, saw his line as divine, springing from God and closer to Him than the corrupt electoral processes of Rome, where powerful Italian nobility warred among themselves for the spoils.

Philip distrusted any clerical power not under the direct command of the King of France, and that included all Catholic Church property and commerce in his territory. Unlike his grandfather, his appetite for gold was rapacious, a craving that overwhelmed all other senses. He crushed the Jews not just to eradicate the pestilence of usury, as his grandfather had done, but also because of his thirst for their precious metal and property.

In his sights, however, he had the biggest prize in Christendom: the assets of the Holy order of the Knights Templar. Although the Order had financed his wars and once protected him, providing refuge from a Parisian mob after he had debased the currency of the realm of its silver content, he despised the idea of a state within his state, answerable only to the Pope. Philip had shared his grand plan with de Nogaret. He would put a puppet pope in Poitiers, who would answer to the pulsating power of the king; secure peace with England through marriage; and appropriate all Jewish wealth within his kingdom. The coup de grace would be to annex the wealthiest and most famous military arm of Rome: the Knights Templar.

Boniface, by challenging Philip's taxation of Church revenues, and by issuing a bull which sought to make, by decree, the Capetian king a servant to the pope, had stood in the way of his grand strategy. It was why de Nogaret had been unleashed against him at Anagni in 1303, why Philip had rewarded him with lands and stood by him against vengeful papal successors. Both men had much in common, but only one was convinced he spoke to God, that his actions were divinely sanctioned, putting his soul beyond reproof. De Nogaret held no such views. He played along, kneeling childlike in prayer in a convincing display of piety whenever required, but the Hound was only interested in money and power.

The king fixed de Nogaret with his customary chilly, thin smile. In truth he rarely experienced warmth. At banquets, audiences and tournaments, he'd learnt from an early age to take his emotional signal from others, quickly seizing on the mood and mimicking it. He neither understood nor cared for humour or gossip, and his well-known loyalty to his wife, Joan of Navarre, was born out of his overwhelming desire for a male heir.

He was interested in women only for breeding and performing royal duties. Joan of Navarre, whom he'd married aged eleven, had died the previous year in childbirth after bearing four children for the royal line. The Queen had understood her husband's indifference from the outset, content to play her part, although fretting that their only daughter, Isabella, was a copy of her father: beautiful to look at but dangerous to touch and vindictive when crossed. The king indulged Isabella, sensing the predator beneath the beauty, and prepared to launch her into the heart of the English bloodline like a weapon.

At length the king spoke. 'Word has reached my ears that you have important findings about the Templars, not shared with the pope. A serious matter that warrants our attention?'

De Nogaret had carefully rehearsed his report, leaving out no detail, and embellishing nothing, for he had witnessed his master's capacity to see through appeals to vanity, attempts to manipulate the royal favour. The king, he knew, believed in the doctrine of his absolute right to all property in his kingdom, and that included what you knew. You handed over everything, and the Iron King decided what to give back in payment, if anything. The Seine flowed with the memories, de Nogaret knew, of the dismembered bodies of those who failed to understand that nothing withstood the king's power in pursuit of God's agenda.

'Word has reached me from my sources within the Templar hierarchy, close to the Grand Master, of the arrival of a hard rider with a message from Waterford, the Norman stronghold in Ireland. Its importance was determined by the fact that the message was delivered in person by the same Templar Knight who had sailed with it. It appears it was not committed to parchment, nor trusted to be heard, except by the ear of their Grand Master, Jacques de Molay.'

King Philip chose to sit, calmly folding his long, silked legs, and sighed. 'The Templars have much to concern them. Since the fall of Acre, they've been bottled up in Cyprus, their usefulness spent, except for meddling in the affairs of kings, and trying to raise another Crusade. I don't see what Ireland has to offer the Templars. It is a lawless land of warring kingdoms, and a wild church. Besides, thanks to your delicate handiwork at Perugia, I expect our new pope will find his way shortly to merge the order with the Hospitallers; then I can annex it.'

De Nogaret glowed with this unexpected praise from the king; he recalled his pleasure at news of the death of Boniface a month after he had been captive at Anagni, but his proudest moment was poisoning the next Italian pope, Benedict XI, at Perugia. De Nogaret had learnt of Benedict's regular enema for a bowel complaint. He had gone to work, first bribing a papal assistant to swap the doctor's potion with odourless cyanide embellished with monkshood, and then later despatched his agent to hell in what appeared to be a common street robbery. De Nogaret had left no evidence, no line of enquiry, just the suspicion that the otherwise healthy Benedict had died suddenly. The monkshood wasn't necessary, but he hadn't been able to resist the delicious irony, not after the pope had unwisely excommunicated him for his part in the affair at Anagni.

After the enema had been administered by the papal doctor, Benedict suffered nausea, vomiting and palpitations, complaining of numbness, clammy skin and breathing difficulty. The poison worked quickly through his bloodstream. His death came swiftly when his lungs and heart collapsed, clearing the way for a French pope at Poitiers. That indeed was my finest work, de Nogaret mused.

He revealed the slightest trace of a smile across his fat lips, his narrow eyes fixing the king with a slight bow in acknowledgement. 'Your Majesty. This, I believe, has nothing to do directly with the scheming of the Holy See. It brings a new player onto the board. According to two reports, which I have cross-checked for accuracy, the message concerned the vision of a Norman Irish youth mentored by a Templar Knight, under whom he is being taught their inner ways.'

The king shifted his sitting position, putting his head to the side. 'Why should these visions so concern us?'

'Because, Your Majesty, they relate to a new treasure that the Templars seek and, evidently, a treasure convincing enough for the Grand Master to call the Septum to counsel.'

If De Nogaret expected a startling reaction, he got it from the normally implacable king. Philip sat bolt upright. 'The Septum is called? So, it is true then? This inner society of theirs is true?'

Philip was amazed, excited and hungry, now, to learn more. He'd long known of the legend that the first Knights Templar, led by Hugues de Payen, had excavated a treasure from under the Temple Mount during the reign of King Baldwin II of Jerusalem, that from 1120 they'd been mining under the Temple of Solomon beneath the Al-Aqsa Mosque, that they'd found something and had it secreted out of the Holy Land, and that it was the foundation of their vast wealth. How else could a small band of French knights rise to become the most powerful and influential Order in Christendom? It stands to reason that whatever they found would be held tightly by an inner group. It was how he would have proceeded.

'Indeed, the Septum exists. That is so, Your Majesty, but there is more. The vision spoke of a secret knowledge hidden by Hypatia, the last pagan philosopher at Alexandria, nine hundred years ago, a knowledge that runs contrary to the foundations of the Church, to the inheritance of Charlemagne and Louis.'

The king shot out of his seat, to pace around it like a predator, drinking in the meaning of the extraordinary briefing. De Nogaret held his tongue. He knew well not to interrupt the king when his mind pivoted from information to strategy.

'Weigh the answer carefully. This philosopher of whom you speak was pure pagan, not Christian?'

The Hound nodded.

'Are you telling me that the Knights Templar are engaged with heresy? Because if so, we have finally found the weakest point in their portcullis, and what is rotten cannot be reinforced.'

'The detail will only be shared within their inner society, Your Majesty, so we can but watch their behaviour to guess its origin and purpose; but yes, they are dirtying their hands with Hypatia, unbeknownst to the pope; that much is a reasonable conclusion. I do not believe that this knowledge is widespread within the Order. There is no evidence of it except that within it lies this inner circle which holds the keys to Your Majesty's ambition.'

De Nogaret watched his words have their intended impact on the king, whom he knew had long been waiting for the stroke needed to topple the Templars. 'Then we must act swiftly but without scaring our prey. They must not be alerted to our royal eyes upon them, while we continue to play at diplomacy, as if no knowledge of this is held here. We must wait in the long grass, de Nogaret, and then strike as lightning with all our temporal power. We will strike only when the time comes to do so – the time when it will be clear to all Christendom that God speaks, not through the Templars, not through the pope, but through the King of France.'

De Nogaret beamed and bowed slightly in assent to the king's Orders.

'Leave no trace, just like in Perugia, but find this boy. Find out what he knows. Use any method you deem fit, to run this heresy to ground.'

The king gestured downwards with both hands to underscore his will, then turned towards the blazing hearth and filled his goblet with red wine, his back towards de Nogaret. His mind was already moving on, consumed with the import of finding heresy at the heart of the Templars. This changed everything. He was not just going to annex Templar power by having it amalgamated with the Hospitallers, he was going to expose it as the anti-Christ among the flock. He was going to obliterate it, sow it into the ground with salt, and cleanse all Christendom.

De Nogaret recognised his cue to go. He bowed to the king and left for the royal treasury to make plans for Ireland. His blood flowed fast, his legs shaking with energy and anticipation as the scent of a fresh hunt filled his nostrils. Life got little better than this, he thought as he bounded out of the king's chamber. *It is far from obscurity you are now.*

CHAPTER 6
East of Paris

Geoffrey de Charney chose to call the assembly at the fortified Templar farm at Coulommiers. It was away from prying eyes, and curiosity from inside the community of brothers at the Villeneuve du Temple in Paris, a day's ride away to the west. Here the Templars' second-in-command knew they could meet quietly, that they could find peace, and that approaches could be watched for strangers by those who had been hired to run the farm.

The Septum gathered at dawn to a rising sun pouring through the stained-glass windows that surrounded the rotunda. The effect was warming, flooding the circular room and its round table with a dancing array of colours carefully chosen by its designers: red, yellow, orange, green, blue, indigo and violet. The building drank fully of the sun's light, the windows not uniform, but arranged in different sizes to follow the cycle of the sun from its birth in the east, to its high apex, before descending to sinking into the west.

Over the meeting table there was a concave ceiling matching its circumference. Painted deep blue, almost navy, it glistened with hundreds of gold and silver stars that seemed to twinkle as the room flooded with sunlight. There was nothing here of Christian iconography which, to an outsider, would seem very strange for a Templar meeting room, but it marked the inner sanctum of the Septum. The effect was wondrous, calming, peaceful, preparing the mind for an altered state of consciousness by suppressing the chaotic rages of life. It was an altar to nature, to Him, but there was nothing of the Son here, nothing of the red crucifix that adorned the Templar tunic, no paintings of the saints or allegories of the Bible. Nothing Christian at all.

Sitting alone among the stars was one image, gently positioned as if watching shyly, not wanting attention, a companion for those here assembled. This was an image that transcended known history, an image from a time before Christ walked among the Jews of the Holy Land, before Moses led the Exodus, before Noah, before Abraham. It was a meaning lost to antiquity but not for those who still used it to adorn the boats of the Nile. They used it for protection, health and restoration, knowing that its parts represented a descending geometric sequence.

It was the Eye of Horus.

On cue, as the first rays of summer started to light up the small rotunda, seven Knights Templar walked in. Led by Grand Master Jacque de Molay, they were in jovial form, voices murmuring greetings and excitement at meeting each other again. After his extensive travels between Cyprus, England and France, Jacque, now in his sixties, was delighted to reduce his pace and enjoy the company of his closest friends in the quiet of a French countryside in full bloom. He'd been happy to let his close friend, his second-in-command, lead.

Geoffrey de Charney, a few years younger than Jacque, had grown up in the ancient tribal lands of the Arverni. His youth echoed with tales of Vercingetorix, the Celtic leader who had united the tribes and defied Julius Caesar before his capture at Alesia in 52 BC. Geoffrey, forty years before, had been accepted into the Templars by one of his other boyhood heroes, Amaury de la Roche, whom he had idolised as the perfect knight and who had been a close friend of King Louis since the Eighth Crusade. De Roche had presided over the young Geoffrey's initiation at the Templar chapel in Sens.

Geoffrey, at a nod from Jacque, gestured for everyone to be seated.

Guiscard, red faced after his journey from Ireland, sat heavily, his huge frame letting out such a loud smack on the heavy oak bench that it was greeted by a burst of laughter from the assembly. The old monk glowered before joining in the amusement he had caused among the younger men, his laughter hiding his reminiscing as he scanned the knights before him. Well, by heavens, I've done my bit, I wasn't always leaden-arsed, he thought. It was I who pulled Grand Master Guillaume de Beaujeu from the fray at Acre, blood flooding out of the mortal wound in his armpit, after we had hotly contested the ground against the Mamluk hordes within the walls.

Trapped in the last redoubt, the Templar castle within Acre, Guiscard had escaped the wrath of the Sultan by slipping away under cover of darkness with the Templar treasure. His small group included the next Grand Master, Thibaud Gaudin. Guiscard had led them through secret passageways from the castle in the west corner of the walled city, to the harbour and to freedom in Cyprus. He recalled his bitterness on receiving his orders to retreat from the Templar marshal, Peter de Severy, knowing that the knights who remained behind would perish to a man in a forlorn rearguard. The oath he swore, never to retreat in the face of the enemy, burned in him still. Sultan Khalil would show no mercy after hundreds of his Egyptian and Syrian soldiers, caught within the closed gate of the castle, had been slaughtered by the Templars for betraying a truce. When he crept through the tunnels beneath Acre to the safety of the harbour, he had known that his comrades planned to bring the castle down upon themselves and the enemy horde, burying access to their escape route.

Next to Guiscard sat the oldest of the monks by a decade, Astralabius Bazin, the most learned Templar in all of Christendom. Guiscard smiled warmly at his tiny and wizened neighbour, and heartily shook his hand, his bear-like grip rattling the old bones of the librarian.

Putting one of his great paws on his companion's shoulder, Guiscard leaned over and whispered into his ear, 'I suppose we'll need the talking book again shortly, but can you hold off from dipping into the red wine before starting to confuse the centuries again?' He thumped the librarian's shoulder so hard, he almost succeeded in propelling him out of his seat.

Astralabius, a monk with an endless store of knowledge and bottomless patience, glowed, laughing at his friend's joke, and pointed to his table-water. Although never in the field, he was revered throughout the order as a tireless teacher and researcher, and rather enjoyed his simple nickname, the Librarian.

With everyone settled, and the sunlight dancing across the room causing some of the brothers to cover their eyes, Jacque stood and opened the Septum. 'Brothers, I've called the gathering in response to the report from Brother Guiscard, for reasons which will become clear in a moment. The purpose of this meeting is to elicit your collective wisdom about the implications of what has been revealed, and what we ought to do next. What we discuss today will, by necessity, reveal more to you than you already know. I say this to prepare you. Now over to you, old friend.'

Guiscard rose, his great frame casting a shadow across the table. He had considered his words carefully and chose to be concise and to the point. 'Brother Templars, I have been teaching a young initiate, Cormac Fitz Stephan, the Way, having sensed his talent for it from a young age. The boy has a remarkable gift, not just for the Way but for knowledge itself. This event about which I will speak tells us why this may be so.'

Around the table the warrior monks leaned forward, signalling Guiscard to continue without pause, their excitement mounting. 'Cormac followed my guided meditation to the Room of Books, therein to experience a past life. This past life we believe to be that of a companion, a slave to Hypatia, the great pagan philosopher of Alexandria, until the day of her death. It is clear from Cormac's recall that this day was seared into his record because Hypatia was flayed alive by the Christian mob under the orders of Cyril Bishop of Alexandria. Cyril was later made a saint for his troubles.' He paused and looked around, winking at Astralabius. 'As you all vividly recall from your studies.'

All the monks laughed at the timing, except Astralabius, who was clearly disappointed that his charges had so easily forgotten his lessons. He spoke up as the laughter subsided. 'We think Hypatia died at around the age of sixty. Let me remind you of your lessons. She was the leading mathematician, astronomer and philosopher of her time, and its greatest teacher. People travelled great distances to hear her speak and she was much loved. Her death, and the manner of her slaughter, was intended to shock the Roman Empire, and it worked. It marked, I believe, a turning point. Even though Hypatia was tolerant of all creeds, including Christians, they were not tolerant towards her. The Church had become the aggressor, those who differed, the heretics, and the new measure was Constantine's Nicene Creed.'

Astralabius let his words settle as the group considered the impact of how the Catholic world would react if the greatest living teacher were a woman who popularly held open discussions with all religions. The idea seemed preposterous, after hundreds of years of blood-spilling Crusades in France, Spain and the Holy Land.

'Aye,' Astralabius concluded, 'the time between has been called the Dark Ages for good reason, for in truth we have not travelled in much light, or that far, have we?'

The group sat in silence, contemplating the Librarian's pithy comment, before Guiscard continued his report. 'The boy has a crystal-clear recall of being given a small chest by his master, with instructions to secret it out of Alexandria. But there is also a mention of some other item hidden by a master mason, under Hypatia's orders.'

Fabian D'Airelle, who was ten years a monk, sat bolt upright like a falcon with his eyes popping about, and raised his hand swiftly. The monk had joined the Order in Cyprus, eager to apply new military strategies and inventions with which to improve battlefield tactics, the performance of Templar cavalry, and its defences when under siege. He had studied the histories of Caesar, Hannibal and Charlemagne, and was fascinated by the tactics used by the Mongols to capture an empire that ran from the Karakorum to Baghdad. 'Brother Guiscard,' he said, 'why should we be concerned about the secrets of a pagan teacher hundreds of years after Christ? I don't see the connection.'

'Because, Fabian, you haven't heard what follows. There is reference to an ancient line of knowledge hidden by an Ebionite.' Guiscard recaptured their fullest attention. 'Yes, an Ebionite Brother, in Alexandria, four hundred years after the Christ.'

Split by a Roman nose, eyes rolled in the weathered face of Jean du Fay, known in the group as Le Grincheux. In practice, while everyone knew him to be prickly and short-tempered, he was admired for his instinct for sensing coming trouble. Jean had hauled the Knights Templar out of many predicaments in the past, without leaving a trace, for he was Jacque's spymaster: the eyes and ears of the seven within and without the Templars. Jean's thin nose was twitching with a sense of hidden meaning. 'Perhaps, my dear Guiscard, you are corpulent with further insights that could now be shared with these young fellows?'

The double meaning was not lost on Guiscard. He attempted to suck in his great belly as the group chuckled. 'Well, who among us is unfamiliar with the meaning of "Ebionite"?'

He cast his eyes about and came to rest on the youngest among them, Rostan D'Arcy, who yawned in reply. All the monks knew Rostan by reputation. The youngest, smallest and most agile of the monks relaxed with effortless ease, almost as if he did not require to breathe, his face calm. His manner was affected, for it disguised the lightning-fast reflexes of a weapons master who had schooled in all the martial academies that dotted England, France and Italy. He was there for two purposes: his knowledge of combat and his ability to protect. There was no equal among the Templars for speed and deadliness. Without speaking, the young monk gently cocked his eyebrow towards Guiscard, who accepted his gesture to press on.

'Here we enter informed speculation. Firstly, we know from the scrolls that Jesus Christ was *Ebionim*, meaning *the poor*. It means this Jewish sect must have survived four centuries, having moved location to Alexandria from Jerusalem to escape the wrath of Titus.'

Astralabius nodded vigorously, taking his cue from Guiscard. 'Alexander's city was chosen because it was the beacon in those days of chaos, the legacy of the Great Library. Alexandria was the receptacle of ancient knowledge, and the safest place to go to escape the ravages of the Judean-Roman wars. My conclusion is that this connection suggests that much more of the knowledge held by the Ebionites, the teaching given by the founder of Christianity, is intact and awaits discovery.'

The room went completely silent at the implication, each monk considering what it would mean if the knowledge held by an arcane Jewish sect, rather than the Nicene Creed, was the true foundation of the Church. It was now clear why they had been called, and why Guiscard was happy to let Astralabius interrupt: the old librarian had already been briefed.

'Aye, and Brother members of the Septum, he is referred to as a master mason, so what has been hidden was hidden with great skill. The slave also bore a small casket through the pillars of Hercules, which means to the north-west. This also makes sense because it goes to the farthest regions beyond the reach of Rome, to Uisneach.'

He paused to let the assembly absorb the meaning.

De Charney, who had already been briefed, smiled at the puzzled expressions around the table, at the mention of Uisneach. 'Are you going to put them out of their misery? Tell us of this place, Guiscard.'

'Uisneach, in those days, was the centre of pagan Ireland, a hill that predates the Celts, a place of worship by earlier tribes, a place upon which the people lit the first fire of *Bealtaine*, the fire of summer to welcome the sun. It is from here that fires would be lit in hills throughout the land, each taking their fire from the next. Be clear my brothers, Hypatia chose this place for a reason.'

Astralabius stirred again. '*Beal taine* in the old language of that country means "bright fire", the day held sacred as a time of fertility, of birth, of renewal. It is a ritual to the god of light, to Lugh, to the ancient people of this land. You will recall that the old Roman great city of Lyon to the south of here was originally called *Lugdunon* by the Gaul? That is derived from old Irish *lugh*, meaning "*light*", and *dúnon*, meaning "fort". *Bealtaine* is thus a celebration of light and so a rejection of the god of darkness. This duality echoes through history, and throughout the ancient scrolls the Order unearthed under the Temple Mount. The dual nature of God has run down the centuries and is shared by the Cathars.'

The meeting visibly gasped at the Librarian's conclusion, for here was a link in a chain of information held sacred and secret to the Septum. It meant that what was unearthed under Herod's Temple was part of a longer chain of knowledge ready to be reassembled when the time was ripe.

Guiscard continued, 'Astralabius is correct, not just because of the pagan influences of the early Irish Church, but because Cormac's last memory describes Celts. It is clear he also was one, likely a child captured and enslaved by raiders along the western seaboards of Ireland. This opens to the mouth of its great river, a river that leads to the interior, to the Hill of Uisneach.'

Rostan spoke up softly, barely moving in his seat. 'Why should we concern ourselves about any danger in Ireland from discovering whatever Hypatia's slave did or did not conceal from the early Church?'

The room went silent at the young monk's intervention. Guiscard breathed in slowly and deeply. 'Because, young Rostan, of what happened after Cormac left the Room of Books. Cormac was confronted by what I believe to be the Adversary, by the same being that he sensed just as Hypatia's mortal body failed. His description, which he could not have known – and I have been his lifelong teacher – comes straight out of our records of the Adversary, the overwhelming dread. This is nothing like battlefield fear; it is an ancient, icy, ravenous dread. Cormac could not have known these as its characteristics, not without experiencing it.'

The room lapsed again into deathly silence, each monk drinking in the import of what was being said, until Guiscard spoke again. 'There is more.

The Adversary addressed him directly. It sought to recover what had been stolen by the Nasorean – which was the term it used, Nasorean and Ebionite being interchangeable names. This links directly to the Christ, It tells us that what was secreted out of Jerusalem after its fall to Titus, is a threat to the Adversary. That's why this is so important.'

The group gasped. Astralabius said, 'Brothers, this means that the Order has skirmished with our great spiritual adversary. It further means that the Adversary is missing something it values, something it wants returned; something that Christ's intervention robbed of it; and finally, it evidently believes we are close to discovering it. This is the question I have been considering at length. But isn't there more, Guiscard?'

'Aye, there is,' Guiscard replied. 'Cormac was saved from being consumed through the intervention of something the Adversary directly addressed as Amesha Spenta.'

The monks now turned in unison to Astralabius.

Fabian asked the question everyone was thinking. 'What in heaven's name is Amesha Spenta?'

From the shade next to the largest window, hidden from view by the strength of the light pouring through the stained glass, a clear female voice rose sharply in reply. 'Templars, the Amesha Spenta is a very ancient name. It is from Persia. It is familiar to you Christians as "Archangel."'

The word hung in the air like a great chime.

The monks spun around in shock to see a tiny woman walk slowly towards them, as if materialising out of the sunlight itself. Astralabius, well versed in the Latin Code that forbade the company of women, was first to speak. 'Esi, your timing is excellent. I've lived to see this group struck dumb.'

Guiscard guffawed, took two giant steps towards the woman, lifted her up in his bear-like arms and spun her around, dancing with joy. 'Esi, it has been so long. How I've missed you. You haven't lost your sense of mischief, I see.'

The big monk held her out as if weightless, and looked her up and down. 'How you've grown to womanhood! Astralabius, you old rogue, what have you been filling her head with?'

The older monk grinned. 'I'm the teacher no longer, my old friend. I am the student. She surpasses me on every score and draws knowledge from the Sorbonne like a master.'

Sensing he was losing his audience Jacque raised his hand for calm and forbearance as Esi hung tight to Guiscard, whispering into his flowing grey beard, 'Old Bear, I've missed you too.'

Guiscard's chest swelled, tears rolled in his eyes as he spun Esi around again, to the astonishment of those at the table. 'Brothers, let me introduce you to Esi Akiba, now known as Esi Benoit, the greatest treasure in the Levant. You'll come shortly to understand why for yourselves.'

Guiscard let out a bellowing laugh at the faces of the monks. When calm returned, Jacque rose and gestured Esi to take his seat. Standing behind her, the Grand Master placed his hands on both her shoulders and faced the astonished monks. 'Esi's parents did not survive the siege of Acre: she was selected to take the last boat, under direct instructions of the Grand Master, who died fighting the breach in the walls of the city. Guillaume de Beaujeu closely interviewed young Esi during the siege, and became convinced of her value to the Order as a celibate and scholar. Her father's engineering skills had helped bolster the walls and her mother taught brilliantly across a wide range of subjects, but Esi had come to our attention in her own right as a master scholar at a very young age.'

The monks, who held the Grand Master of their last redoubt in the Holy Land to be one of the greatest leaders of the Order, stared in shock at Esi. Jacque continued his slow delivery, to firmly establish Esi's credentials for the group, knowing that he had to lay a strong foundation to have her accepted, and for what she would impart to them. 'Esi's esoteric knowledge astonished the Templars at Acre. This brought her to our attention not because of the extent to which she had been taught but because of her specific use to us in interpreting the scrolls. It is why she was selected for the last boat, brought to France from Cyprus, and placed with Astralabius here, under whom she has studied ever since.'

As Jacque filled in the gaps, the group stared at the woman. It was hard not to, even for monks. Esi had long dark flowing hair, bronzed skin, and deep-set emerald eyes which seemed to dazzle with mischief. She returned their astonishment with a warm smile, knowing that of all the creatures to walk into their secret world, she was the most unexpected. And also, because she knew more about the Templars than they did of themselves.

CHAPTER 7
Paris

The chapel was sparse: a small altar under a grey stone arch, poorly lit by the candles that circled the room, its walls hung with drapes no sunlight could penetrate. It was designed so. Its sole penitent, the King of France, was sitting on its single bench, surrounded by scenes he had selected, most of them from the Old Testament, each capturing moments when the God of Thou-Shalt-Not intervened in the affairs of man. Philip preferred these moments of direct action, which left no doubt about God's intentions.

Over the altar a plain crucifix hung, to its right an image of Christ's suffering on the Cross, the moment when Longinus, the centurion, speared His side with the *lonchē* to determine if *crurifragium*, the Roman practice of breaking legs to hasten death, was required. It was not. To the left hung the Greek letter Chi traversed by Rho, forming ☧, the first two letters of the Greek word Christos. Philip had commissioned the work to portray the Lance of Longinus drawing blood and water: blood signifying His mortality, water His divinity as Son of God, as it was ordained by the first Council of Nicaea.

The Roman Emperor Constantine, the architect of Nicaea, was a favourite of the king. He was drawn to Constantine's having ascended to the throne, selected by God, on the eve of battle at Milvian Bridge in 312 AD. He warmed to the vision of God lighting up the midday sky over Constantine's army. *In hoc signo vinces. In this sign, conquer.* It was here that God had propelled Constantine to drown Emperor Maxentius in the Tiber, together with his army, after Maxentius had marched out of Rome to confront him. He visualised Maxentius sitting with his cavalry to face Constantine's army, whose shields were adorned with his newly found emblem, Christos, the Chi Rho. He warmly approved of the fact that Maxentius' pale corpse was later fished out of the Tiber to be decapitated, his head paraded through the fallen Roman capital and then to Carthage. It was God's message from the new empire to remnants of the old, to the pagans.

In Constantine the Great, he saw a brother, a fellow regent to whom God spoke, one who had conquered the Roman empire from his capital at Trier, from whence he had first ruled Britain, France and Spain, before extending his power over the five-hundred-hour march to Byzantium. He visualised his place in history with Constantine on his left, Charlemagne on his right, each of them canonised by the Church.

After first washing his hands incessantly in water, King Philip remained motionless, sitting alone in the stone chapel for hours, breathing slowly and deeply. His heart-rate slowed; his eyes closed. He waited for the voice of God, the God of the Old Testament, which he knew would come. He was about to become one of the great regents, selected by God like Charlemagne, King of the Franks, Emperor of Rome, Father of Europe. He silently acknowledged Charlemagne's order to ritually behead 4,500 Saxons at the meeting of the Aller and Weser rivers, for refusing conversion to Christianity. Charlemagne had drawn inspiration from David's slaughter of the Amalekites under the edict from God. He mentally recited his favourite words from Deuteronomy, as he had so many times tha it became a prayer. *'Therefore, it shall be, when the Lord your God has given you rest from your enemies all around, in the land which the Lord your God is giving you to possess as an inheritance, that you will blot out the remembrance of Amalek from under heaven. You shall not forget.'*

Your will be done, the king told himself as he sat alone facing the altar. I will blot out the remembrance of all pagans who do not convert, and all heretics who fail to renounce. His head dipped, gently swaying in short circular movements as the time of trance arrived, and dizziness finally took hold. He prepared to hear once again from the emissary of God. Ahead, behind, all around, darkness. He was floating, spreading himself in any direction his mind favoured; effortless, calm, relaxed, he waited.

His body began to spasm, at first imperceptibly, but quickly spreading, his head shaking, the tremors moving through his shoulders, arms and legs. He welcomed the familiar sensation, for he knew it to be the harvest of hours of contemplation, without food, water or movement. Pure stillness, his breath the only sound echoing within the low stone arches of the chapel.

Philip saw in his contemplations the gateway to heaven, believing himself to be in the legion of saints, blessed with access to the Lord God. His vibrations suddenly stopped, like a candle blown out by a gust of wind, and the darkness in his mind gave way to a dim light through which Philip perceived the outline of a man, a face in shadow but carved out of the greyness. It is the Guardian of the Gate, he thought blissfully, the emissary of the Lord God.

He leaned forward, as if straining to hear the low rasping voice within. The words came slowly but the message was clear, a message known to him. He recognised it instantly as the *Capitulatio de partibus Saxoniae*, Charlemagne's edict on the Saxons – revised to be aimed at the Templars.

'If any one of the race of Templars hereafter concealed among them shall have wished to hide himself unbaptised, and shall have scorned to come to baptism and shall have wished to remain a pagan, let him be punished by death.'

The king drew in a deep draught of stale air, nodding his understanding, his acceptance, his duty. 'Thy will be done,' he said aloud reverently. 'The Templars are thus unbaptised, outside the sight of God, unless repentant of their heresy. The route back to You comes only through the King of France.'

The grey light faded but Philip remained swaying in reverie on the bench, slowly rising out of his trance, sensing the cavernous walls of the chapel. His eyes opened, drinking in the low candlelight, remembering where he was, remembering his task, his divine instructions, his revelation. He rose to his full height, energy surging through him. Regaining the strength in his legs, he strode to his hand basin at the exit to the chapel, where he paused to wash his hands vigorously once more.

He turned towards the altar. 'I am ready, ready to do what must be done, but first I must consecrate the bare ground with the blood of heresy to honour this place of divine instruction.'

He swiftly left the chapel, striding through his chambers, and returned through the passageway to the narrow stairs, to his balcony. Below him the Dominican had continued the intermittent torture of the *perfecta* with periods of rest interspersed by ever greater elevation on the *strappado*. He whispered into the ear of the *perfecta* as she moaned in pain, elevated five feet off an earthen floor sown with the human ashes carted from the field of flames below the limestone hill of Montségur. The Cathar's shoulders were screaming in agony, sending sharp pain throughout her back, arms and wrist, her body contorting and convulsing.

Bertramnus spoke. 'Old woman, below you lie the poisoned blood, ashes and bones of the last of your kind, from the field of flames. You will join them unless you renounce. Do you renounce your heresy?'

The *strappado* was jerked to rhyme with his question; the room reverberated with fresh groans, then silence. Bertramnus crouched closer, his ear resting inches from her mouth.

Her weak voice, croaking through blood and spittle, spoke back in clear words. 'Dominican, the Church of Wolves has no dominion here. I lie above the sacred ground of my ancestors. They entered through it after the sacrament of Consolamentum, our gateway to the Divine God. Happily do I follow, cleansed and ready to be with Him.'

Bertramnus reeled, propelled backwards by the realisation that the *perfecta* welcomed her passing, craved it, that nothing could be done to win her soul back to the Catholic Church. He looked up, sensing the king's presence.

The king had listened silently in the darkness, his mind throbbing as he drew and redrew possibilities, each ending with his mission fulfilled: to cleanse Christendom of heresies, to purify it in a great flame or wash it away, in blood. Below him the Dominican signalled with an open-hand gesture that he could make no further inroads with the Cathar. The king nodded and left as she was lowered to the floor but remained tethered from behind while the Dominican rested to consider what new torture to apply.

Suddenly the door to the chamber was pushed violently open. To the astonishment of the Dominican and his attendants, it was the king. Each of them knelt, but the king snapped his fingers, gesturing them to their feet. Stunned, they observed the King of France engage with the heretic. This was a contest no one had never been seen before, for no king would soil his office so, not without extraordinary cause. The king's eyes blazed with intent: Here I am the instrument of God, here the battle to rid the kingdom of the last heresies begins! God calls for blood and He will have it.

'Old woman,' Philip began, haughtily, 'do you know who I am?'

The *perfecta*, rolling on to her side, looked past the pupils of the king's eyes as if addressing something inside. 'I see you, ancient one, I know you for what you are, Rex Mundi, for your loneliness is without end, but know this: you too will be redeemed by Divine God when your task is done.'

It was not what the king had expected. In shock he staggered backwards as the words of the *perfecta* crashed through the walls of his mind. He tried to command, but no words would come. Faint and disorientated, he held on to Bertramnus, swaying in the centre of the room until his strength and calm returned. Gone was the confidence and certainty of control from the Dominican's crew. All were silent, flabbergasted by the impact of the woman's words on the king. The room remained in deathly silence except for the heavy breathing of the old woman as she fought for breath through the agonies left by hours on the *strappado*.

Philip, after struggling to regain his balance and composure, faced the woman again and shouted, 'You hold the Lord God of Abraham to be evil, and you believe yourself to be ready to enter the kingdom of another. How is this so?'

She paused, fighting for breath to deliver her response. 'Because, mortal king, we know the Divine God directly, for we are part of Him. You rule over the mortal kingdom of the Demiurge, wherein our divine spark lies captive. No one may leave and enter this place unless they are clean.'

In a gesture of mockery, King Philip held out his hand for the wash basin, cleaning his hands slowly before drying and holding them out to the perfecta. 'I have spent my life clean in body and in soul. You, on the other hand,' he gave the faintest smile at his pun, 'hold that carnal knowledge between men and men, and women and women, is clean, but between men and women is unclean?'

She smiled through her agony at the opening the king had given to her response. 'We are all angels, neither man nor woman. All believers can become pure ones, as you call us. The baptism of *consolamentum* is open up to the moment of death. We hold women to be the same as men, because there is no such difference among the angels. You believe yourself to be other than us, in unique converse with the Divine. Truly, how is this so?'

Taken aback at being challenged, especially by a woman, the king chose to end the exchange. 'Woman, you have cleaved the Lord God in two. You will die unclean for it; I will make it so.'

He gestured to the attendants to strap her by both ankles. She was jerked upside down, legs spread-eagled into position, waist high to the king, who stood back to make space for Bertramnus and his team. At his gesture they moved the large two-handed crosscut saw into position and held, awaiting orders.

'In the name of the Lord God,' Philip announced, gesturing upwards, 'I spill the blood of this heretic into this ground. You will be halved as you have halved the Lord God. You will be defiled, and you will be made unclean.'

The *perfecta*, knowing that the blood rushing to her head was designed to keep her conscious longer, grimaced in defiance. 'The road spirals to the Divine God until it is clean. I may return, king, but never through the structures of man, nor oaths to popes or to kings of the material world.'

King Philip gestured for her death to begin after he left, not wishing to be sullied with her blood or smell. He ascended the stairs, visualising a similar death for unrepentant Templar heretics. Perfect indeed, the king thought, as he reached his chamber's wash basin, just perfect. He waited in silence to hear her screams. None came.

The certainty of her faith and the manner through which she had addressed him, rattled the Iron King long after her remains were committed to the sewer and into the Seine.

CHAPTER 8

The Septum broke for a short spell to allow further seats to be brought into the rotunda, then reconvened quickly, the members eager to hear more from their surprise guest. Each monk knew that this moment was like no other in the history of the Templars, that after the gathering, nothing would be the same. They were now engaging the ancient enemy. With everyone settled, Esi began, her accented French betraying the cultivated tones of a polyglot.

'Templars, know first that I am not one of you. I am neither Christian nor Muslim. Though I have studied many creeds, I do not abide by the structures of faith nor worship in those ways. I worship only wisdom but, like all, I seek to know the Divine God. I say this so that you do not believe that what I tell you is captive to the conventions of man, his politics, or his times.'

The monks were astonished by Esi's opening remarks. Uttered in any other setting, her words would have been enough to have her burned as a heretic.

'Under the guidance of your librarian, I have studied the material of the Order, most particularly what is known of the scrolls secreted out of Jerusalem by one of the first Templars, one of your two knights-on-horseback, Geoffrey de St Omer, in order to be examined by the great cartographer, the Benedictine scholar Lambert Canon of St Omer.'

Astralabius rose and gently interrupted his student. 'Esi, perhaps you ought to begin with the Amesha Spenta, and outline what connections may be spanning such a great river of time? We can then, Brothers, consider how to proceed from the facts, and the wisdom drawn by connecting them. This is how Esi has been taught – although, in truth, I continue to find new depths to her not of my creation.'

Esi acknowledged the guidance from her teacher and recommenced. 'The Amesha Spenta in Cormac's meditation comes not from any recent religion. It predates Christianity and Islam by two thousand years or more, perhaps before writing, and before the Great Pyramids of the Two Kingdoms of Egypt were constructed. It is unknown how old it is, because records only begin around the time that Pythagoras, Aristotle and Plato taught at the great Greek schools. Amesha Spenta is from what may be the mother of the great religions, from Zoroastrianism.'

The group snapped to attention as Esi drove the meeting into territory which was, unknown to most of them.

'The people of ancient Persia followed the teaching of Zoroaster, the prophet. They held that there was one uncreated divine artisan of the universe whom they called *Ahura Mazda* and which we believe to mean "wise lord", supported by the *Amesha Spenta,* of which there are seven.'

Fabian was quick to interject, joking, 'Brothers, there are seven here also.'

'Indeed, Fabian,' said Astralabius. 'Seven is a number that echoes through the ages: seven titans of ancient Greek cosmology; seven from the Great Fall; seven archangels.'

Esi continued. 'The significance in Guiscard's report is that the *Amesha Spenta* is not named, so it could be any one of the seven, or all of them. What is of concern is the unknown being, the *Amesha Spenta*, interrupted in the struggle. Zoroastrianism holds to dualism, that there is an anti-god, the *Angra Mainyu*, a being of chaos, deceit and disorder in perpetual conflict with both the spiritual and material world. If that sounds familiar, it should. What it also means is that what happens above, happens below. Thus the Order itself, which guided Cormac Fitz Stephan's meditation, may be in extreme danger.'

Esi paused to let the monks ponder her words before continuing. 'Zoroaster taught to love nature, all of its plants, animals, humankind, and that the route through life was through good deeds, words and thoughts, that these held the energy to keep the *Angra Mainyu* at bay until the end of time, when the spirits of the dead would join *Ahura Mazda* in the divine dominion.'

Fabian, warming to the connections like a series of signs on a map through time, shifted in his seat and asked, 'The End of Days?'

'The End of Days indeed,' Esi acknowledged, 'but during life Zoroastrianism taught that there is a duty to engage in the conflict between the competing energies of the Good God and the evil opposite, between what they called *asha* and *druj,* positive and negative impulses. At risk is what we term the soul, the *urvan*, which wants to reunite with *Ahura Mazda,* of which it is a part.

Jean pointed his finger in the fashion of a challenging student. 'So, Esi is trying to tell us that Christianity, Islam and Judaism are merely constructs of a religion that rushes out of the mists of time to greet us here, from a place of no records; that these religions are merely copies with evolutionary steps, not original creations?'

The meeting was shocked by the spymaster's blunt conclusion.

'No Jean, I'm merely recounting what is written; it is up to you to draw the parallels. Zoroastrianism, according to some writers, may be as much as five thousand years from our time. This places it before the pharaohs, before the Two Kingdoms of the Nile. If so, it echoes throughout history and all the cosmologies that come afterwards. Remember, this religion taught about the free decisions of men and women, about heaven and hell, and about the last judgement, about everlasting life, long before Abraham spoke to Yahweh.'

'I think,' said Geoffrey, who had been quiet since the meeting began, 'that whatever the genesis of this teaching, these two words *Amesha Spenta* have transcended time and geography, thousands of years and thousands of miles. This is significant and relevant. That this being has appeared in the meditation of a Norman Irish youth unschooled in profound matters of faith is what should most concern the attention of the Septum.'

The group nodded, acknowledging the wisdom of bringing the discussion back to the inescapable.

'So Esi,' Geoffrey continued, 'can we move on to the implied connection with the Temple Scrolls?'

Esi took a breath. 'The Temple Scrolls were located by the founders of the Order during the nine years in which they excavated under Herod's temple. They clearly date from the sack of Jerusalem. In the Jewish archives, the Testament of Moses makes reference to the end of days and the need to preserve books of knowledge within, it specifies, *"Earthen vessels in the place which He made from the beginning of the creation of the world."* This can only mean in the Holy of Holies, which lies beneath Herod's Temple. That explains the find, and explains why they would be placed there, but not by whom.'

Guiscard, who had been listening carefully as Esi unfolded her learning, was amused by the idea of Templar monks trying to read ancient documents by candlelight, underground and in a foreign tongue. 'Indeed, Esi, there is much we don't yet know. The scrolls were written in a language unfamiliar to the Knights Templar, most of whom would have struggled even to read French,' Guiscard said. He paused. 'Much like many of the owls around this table.'

The room echoed with laughter, Guiscard's timing and accuracy serving to break the tension, allowing Esi to gather her thoughts before pressing on. 'What stands out to me from the scrolls is what they do not contain. There is no reference to the Son of God, no attempt to convince early readers of His divinity. It is as if it didn't matter at all. You will know from your studies that this echoes with Arianism, which, by the time Constantine assembled the heads of the Church in Nicaea, was deemed a heresy – even though it was widely shared across the early Church and was central to Gnosticism.'

'So, let me see if I can follow where you are going,' said Jean, their spymaster. 'Hypatia chose to send secret knowledge out of Alexandria to pagan Ireland, where it could seed in more fertile soil?'

'Precisely Jean. The Arian heresy held that the Son of God was begotten by God: that He was *of* God, but not God. This belief, although named after Arius, a Church leader in Alexandria in the third century, was widely shared throughout the Roman Empire by those who believed that Jesus the Christ was a man. It was also the belief held by the Ebionites, the Jewish sect from whom we believe that Jesus the Christ came, that he lived and died an Ebionite, a Nazorean.'

Esi's eyes twinkled as she drew breath and gazed around her attentive audience of warrior monks. 'The drawings Lambert made of heavenly Jerusalem, copied from the original scroll, make no reference to the Son of God. Instead, they show two main pillars, each named Jacob, not Jesus, and at the centre of the plans are squares and compasses, which echo the great constructions of history. Templars, it is what is missing that is important.'

Esi went silent. She had thrown the group a challenge, and they knew it.

Fabian was first to respond. 'So, what we have are documents, hidden in what was regarded as the site of the Holy of Holies, within a short number of years after the Crucifixion of Christ, by his own Jewish sect, which have no reference to the Cross, the suffering, or the Lamb of God, or to Jesus. What does this tell us, Brothers?'

Esi simply nodded. She was content to let them digest what had been revealed so far.

'Well, I have had the opportunity of being briefed in advance and so have the advantage,' said Astralabius. 'The Nicaean Creed postdates the sacking of Jerusalem by nearly three hundred years. There, in 325 AD, Constantine made himself the centre of the synod of Church leaders. The synod narrowly voted against Arianism in favour of the Trinitarian view of God. This was decided by man, not God. That is the point.'

Esi took up the argument. 'The greater point, Astralabius, being that the Church was not founded on the teaching of the Christ as recorded by Him but on how it was written, many years after his death. What Constantine achieved at Nicaea was the political act of deciding upon the opposing theologies of the Christian Church within his empire. Immediately after his victory at the battle of Milvian Bridge, at the doorway to Rome, he did not worship at the Church of the Lord but at a pagan shrine. On the eve of death, twelve years after Nicaea, Constantine sought to be baptised by the Arian Bishop of Nicomedia, Eusebius. What does that tell us?'

No longer able to contain himself, Fabian D'Airelle stood up. 'My ears burn and my heart trembles. The implication is that for 1,300 years we have been following false doctrines! That Constantine only sought baptism on the eve of death makes him a Cathar, all of whom were burned at the stake or otherwise put to death. This is the Nicaean Creed for whom millions of lives have been ruined, countless numbers executed; in whose name then?'

Complete silence descended at Fabian's outburst. Gesturing for the monk to regain his seat, Jacque addressed the group. 'Brothers, we have known since the discovery of the scrolls that Divine God is within, that we are of Him and He of us. Our route has been to experience Him directly. Although we continue to adhere to Church rules and the practices of man, we no longer see in man's rituals the only connection to God the Divine. It is also evident that we have much yet to learn, and that we face both temporal and spiritual danger here.'

Looking towards Jean, the Grand Master nodded a silent assent for his spy to speak up.

'King Philip intrigues with Pope Clement in an unequal struggle for power. The pawns on the board are the Order of Knights of the Hospital of Saint John of Jerusalem, and our Order. In short, the king is pressing the papal court in Poitiers to unite both military orders now that the Holy Land has been lost. Not, as we fear, to lead a new Crusade, but to weaken and plunder under a new leader, the King of France. This is his intent. We are already countering with argument to Pope Clement to maintain the separation of the military orders, and strengthen the resolve to retake Jerusalem. While Philip maintains a diplomatic show, there is already a silent and bloody war under way in the alleyways of Paris, between my agents and de Nogaret's. I believe it is a harbinger of what is to come.'

The Templars bristled at the name of the king's Hound, knowing him by reputation to be savage, brutal and effective, posing a real threat, financed by the royal treasury to bribe informants, hire mercenaries and end lives.

Sensing the ongoing conflict between the Templars' vows of loyalty to the pope and the development of their knowledge, Esi spoke up, her voice almost a whisper. 'Templars, it is with great difficulty that you struggle to reconcile God the Divine, which you experience in the Way, and the oaths to the pope. You are not alone. I have studied all the great teachers, religious and philosophical. Among them standing tallest in these times is Thomas of Aquino, whom you can expect to be made a saint by the Catholic Church, as is its way. Thomas tried to reconcile the teachings of Aristotle with that of the Church. His direct experiences have visibly manifested in ecstasies and levitations. This is hardly the stuff of dogma.'

Esi paused and looked around slowly, directly into the eyes of each monk. 'Know this, Templars. After his last ecstasy, Thomas Aquinas abandoned his holy works. He declared to Reginald of Piperno, his Dominican companion, *mihi videtur ut palea:* that all I have written seems like straw to me. He died a few months later, never returning to complete his works, not after he had had that last direct experience of the Divine.'

After the monks had drawn breath, Jacque gestured to let Esi's summary sit for a few seconds. The Grand Master knew that by choosing to end with Thomas Aquinas, she had chosen well. The prolific Dominican philosopher lived within a generation of the group. Much of his time was spent in Paris, and he was widely revered throughout the Order.

'Brothers,' he began, 'we have heard enough. I believe the road ahead is clearly mapped. Geoffrey, you and I will base ourselves at the Enclos in Paris, to deal with the affairs of pope and king; Astralabius, you will remain in Paris as well, ready to interpret anything that is found; Jean, you must plan strategy but stay in the field, adopting a mobile role to keep us linked. Fabian and Rostan, you go with Guiscard. Return to Ireland, find what is hidden, and report back to the Enclos, but be discreet in following the pathways that open before you.'

Esi was stunned by the effect of her words, and the speed at which the Grand Master had moved. Her heart sank with the realisation that she was not a Knight Templar, merely a custodian of knowledge, and that she was expected to return to her books.

Sensing her concern, De Molay winked at Guiscard and smiled. 'Well, Esi my child, we have fashioned light armour to disguise your gender among us monks. I suppose you will have to go along and make sure we don't make a mess of whatever we find.'

Esi clapped her hands, shrieked with delight, and threw her arms around Guiscard, nuzzling his beard. 'At last, old bear, we have another adventure together! We go to mystical Ireland!' The old monk reddened with delight; the Septum laughed its approval. None of them guessed that it was the last time they would all meet, or that they faced the ultimate foe.

CHAPTER 9

After making hurried preparations, the company was ready to set off towards Paris, thirteen leagues to the east. The warrior monks took to their mounts with graceful ease at the entrance to the farm stronghold, and awaited Esi's exit from the stables. She had shouted out a few times through the stable-door that she was nearly ready, as Templar fingers drummed impatiently on their saddle-pommels.

Geoffrey selected a pony for their small companion, with a saddle made for a teenager, and had anticipated her having difficulty keeping up with the knight's war-horses. After several attempts which ended with Esi upended on the ground like a crab on its back, she was eventually secured in the saddle with the help of the stable-hands, out of sight of the monks. When she finally emerged into the autumn sunshine, it was clear that the Templars thought the wait worth it. Gone was the confident, commanding and formidable scholar and out from the stables came a parody: a wobbly, diminutive and unbalanced knight with glistening breastplate, whose shoulder, arm and leg armour was offset with an oversized helmet. What started as a stifled chuckle amongst the monks cascaded into hoots of laughter as Esi coaxed her horse to an ugly turn and nervous trot towards the gate.

Unfazed by all the attention, Esi paused, loosened the reins, smiled mischievously and kicked the horse with her heels, trotting past their position as if she had been born to ride. Guiscard laughed loudest, calling after her as she led out, 'Esi, it was far from war-horses you were reared but I'll grant you, you are making a good show of it here in the slow mud of the farmyard. We will soon see, young woman, if your wit on that yoke matches your gob.'

Esi, already feeling chaffing from the weight of her armour through her clothes, sniffed mockingly, but silently accepted the challenge, putting aside the meaning of the word 'gob' for the time being.

The fields were in full green hue, splashed with bright yellows and orange, and with movement as teams of serfs sickled crops that ran in every direction over the low rolling hills to ancient woods. Every third field lay fallow; they grew barley and beans in the spring, and wheat and rye for bread in the autumn. Occasionally a field-worker would stop and wave at the Templars as they passed, but for the most part the company was ignored as labouring backs bent with the effort of mowing with scythes, harrowing with rakes and coaxing oxen through the deep furrowed fields. Where fields were fallow, cows wandered about, separated from the sheep, which since shearing in June, now occupied the higher ground.

Jacque had moved out to the front with Geoffrey, and the two were locked deep in conversation, while Esi rode, protected in the middle of the company. Rostan took up a defensive position at the rear, spinning effortlessly in his saddle, eyes scanning for movement from behind. As the riders looped around a small hill between a copse of woodland, Jean emerged from the dense undergrowth, and moved at speed towards them. The Templar spymaster had galloped ahead to scout out their path to Paris, which they had hoped to reach by nightfall. Jacqui raised his hand to signal a short stop, gesturing the group to dismount while he and Geoffrey conferred in quiet tones with Jean.

At length, Jacque addressed the group. 'Jean reports that there are king's agents in the village ahead. From their bearing, they are clearly not local. Their horses are in good order even though they are not attired in the manner of royal soldiery. His assessment is that they are scouting, looking for some or all of us, so we have a change of plans, to take advantage and sow some confusion. Jean will explain.'

The Templars gathered more closely, forming a circle around the spymaster.

'My assessment is that they are gathering information, that the group will be instructed not to engage with Templars in combat, under any circumstances except in mortal defence. Nevertheless, it does indicate that the Hound is hunting, that he already has intelligence that puts us in this region. We are to continue forward, showing no concern, indicating no knowledge of their presence. We will skirt the village at a sufficient distance for them to see us and count our numbers, but get no closer. We can then use this to our advantage when we reach Paris.'

The monks, bred for combat, were used to being guided by the nose of Le Grincheux. They nodded in agreement and remounted. This time Esi did not find it quite so amusing. Sensing the group's tension, Rostan's right hand caressed the high polished pommel of his sword, as if calming a great cat. Guiscard moved closer to her as the group tightened.

'Eyes to front, middle trot, no talking, look unconcerned,' Geoffrey barked as they set off swiftly.

Some hours later, with the sun visibly beginning its slow arc in the skies to the south-west, the group reached the outskirts of the most populous city in

Europe. Split by the Seine, King Philip's capital was walled in by a league of defences that included seventy-five watchtowers. Pulsing with power, it was home to a quarter of a million souls, and the most formidable fighting force in Christendom: the French army.

At the centre stood the Île de la Cité, the redoubt once used to protect against the Saxon and Viking invasions, and later expanded by King Philip into the majestic fortress, the Palais de la Cité. To the north-west of the city stood the Knights Templar enclosure, overlooked by its twin turrets the Grosse Tour and Tour de César, a reminder to the covetous French king, every time he gazed across the rooftops of Paris, of the powerful state within his state. Here he could see the headquarters of an organisation of warrior monks who reported not to him but to the papacy, and whose vast wealth extended from Dublin to Famagusta. It rankled with him.

The fires of Paris had begun their flickering dance across the gathering night sky when the spymaster called the group to a slow walk up to the doors of a large barn that lay within an arrow-shot of the city walls. Jean dismounted, opened the doors and beckoned the group inside while he disappeared hurriedly into the night. The monks and Esi rested, quietly sharing bread and cheese they had saved for the journey from Coulommiers, and whispered in low tones, awaiting the return of the Templar. Within an hour the door opened softly, this time to a group comprising three men and a teenage boy led by Jean.

In a low voice, he called for silence. 'Brothers, as you have guessed, we let the Hound's spies see us on our journey, precisely for this moment. You will exchange outer garments here.' Seeing her confusion, Jean added, 'Esi, you will be pleased to know that you can now discard that armour and proceed from here disguised as a common squire.' Esi almost yelled with relief and delight, thrilled to be rid of the weight and its burns and bruises, and never so happy to jump into a boy's sweaty clothes.

'Guiscard, Rostan and Fabian, and then Esi, will be guided to the Beguinage, where instructions have been left with Marguerite before your onward journey by daybreak. The rest of us will make a show of a slow entrance through the streets to the Enclos du Temple in the precise numbers identified by the King's agents. It will be days before De Nogaret realises he has been duped. That ought to buy you time, Guiscard, to get to the coast unhindered and undetected.'

'So, my brothers, this is goodbye then?' asked Guiscard, raising his bulk to its full height and clasping the arm of the Grand Master. 'I wish you great fortune, Grand Master, in grappling with that beast and his minion in Poitiers. There are grim trials ahead for all of us but we will take them head on without retreat, as is our way.'

Jacque replied warmly, 'Come, let us say our goodbyes quietly and quickly, and get you through the back-streets, to the Beguinage.'

Esi, despite her aches, hugged Astralabius furiously, almost choking the old librarian with her fierce grip. 'Astralabius, what can I say? All the times you stood over me, candles burning to the quick; all the patience you showed; all the times you guided me to my cot bleary eyed from study; all the times you brought me breakfast to prepare for the next day. No words can say how much you have meant to me, how much I love you, the father of my youth.'

The old monk's eyes filled with tears, flowing freely down his cheeks to his thinning white beard. 'Esi, it was never a labour, always a joy and a preparation for what we now do, but, in truth, I will miss you as a sunflower misses the sun. You have made these last times of my life bearable and adventurous. Thank you for the gift of your time with me. I will pass through this life, feeling like a father who has loved. It is beyond compare.' She dried his tears gently with her fingers and through her own tears clung to him. Both sensed that they would never see each other again, that they held each other one last time. At the centre of the barn the monks exchanged farewells in their custom, through the kiss of peace, then vigorously shaking arms, silently accepting whatever fate awaited them.

Rostan checked outside before beckoning Guiscard's party to exit quietly, walking their horses. The walls of Paris rose steeply over the group, the city towers standing sentinel in the darkness as the party wound its way through the narrow streets outside the walls to a less-used gate into the city on its north-western approach. Fabian had advised Guiscard of this gate because of its nearness to the Gibet de Montfaucon. This was the hill of death, which few Parisians would wish to visit at night. The group passed silently below the imposing stone building, much of its forty-five gallows stinking with the corpses of men and women in various states of decay, each creaking in feeble protest, a macabre orchestra of the dead as the breeze caught them. Fabian had chosen well, even if the sight, as had been the intention of its architects, chilled the bones of all who passed it, a visceral reminder of the wrath of the king for anyone who dared transgress his laws.

Guiscard signalled the group to dismount. He walked slowly to the gate guards, in his hand a bouncing bag of livres. The soldiers, bored since curfew, eager to bolster their thin pay after the king had devalued the currency of the crown, perked up at the sight of the new polished coins, each worth three times what the old ones had been. Guiscard's modest bribe was quickly put out of sight as the party passed through without a sound, the guards looking away as instructed.

The night smells of the city immediately assailed them; its walls confined a great cauldron of humanity and livestock densely packed between narrow streets. Each street was little wider than a horse's length, overarched by narrow town houses that seemed to bend towards each other at the top, the cobbles below running rivulets of sewage.

Bustling during the day with noise and street merchants shouting their wares – garlic, vegetables, fish, milk and clothes – the winding streets were eerily quiet at night, faintly dotted by the grey shadows of the poor, beggars and prostitutes, each desperate to survive the night air, fouled by urine from emptied chamber-pots. The air was mixed with the smell of charcoal and burning wood, while through the city centre the mother Seine flowed, washing out the mélange of offal, waste and decay that ran downhill into large open pits.

Esi had taken the lead as the group wandered further into Paris, coolly guiding them through the maze of streets using hand-signals, while the monks stayed on high alert. They had listened to Le Grincheux's warnings to watch for the Hound's assassins, those skilled at quietly despatching his enemies in the back streets of Paris without leaving a trace back to the king. The monks were under orders from the Grand Master to evade, not engage. It was essential, he had told them, to steal through Paris and not alert the palace to their presence. De Nogaret had the capacity to shutter the city in minutes, trapping his prey while he turned it over to find them, using silver livres, threats and torture.

Esi turned to the monks, signalling that they had arrived. The modest single-storey cloistered building comprised the living quarters and workspace of the Beguinage trade, which made silk clothing for the elite of the city, using the proceeds to feed and clothe the poor. Esi guided them to a narrow door at the side of the Beguinage, knocking rhythmically and whispering softly through the keyhole.

The door opened, a candle revealing the grinning face of Mistress Marguerite Porete. 'Welcome back, Esi my child. How I have so missed our little conversations!' She reached out and put her index finger on Esi's lips. 'I have revised the book, Esi, the Mirror of Simple Souls.'

Esi's eyes lit up. She skipped in the air and clapped her hands, almost entirely forgetting her companions, before recovering her poise. 'Marguerite, I must see it, I must, but first to hide these three worn-out monks, and rest our horses. We leave by dawn before we are discovered, before we compromise the security of the Beguinage, before we bring the Hound to your door.'

'Don't fret about him my dear, our many eyes and ears throughout the city report a great movement of his spies to the Enclos du Temple, covering every street. De Nogaret himself stalks the circle of his creation, so his attention is not here. No, you are safe, at least for a few hours. Come.'

Esi and the monks followed Marguerite through the pristine corridors of the mother-house, passing Beguines in common plain habits finishing their work of spinning, weaving and illuminating, their children running playfully about. They entered a long kitchen lit by candles. It was high vaulted, and dominated by a long table, with a blazing hearth at its gable end, near which the monks took their seats and offered quiet prayer before meal.

'Your companions must be hungry,' Marguerite announced once the monks had finished prayers. She beckoned the cooks. 'Our food, which we share with the poor of Paris, is plain but nourishing. Isn't that so, Esi?'

'Indeed, it is so, Templars, but it is not the most surprising things you will find here. There are no cords to bind us, no constitution. Sisters come and go freely from this life of sharing and giving. You will find the most remarkable women here, from scholars to former women of the night, from rich families and poor, each sharing the same devotion to God, each believing in direct experience of Him, elevated by how they serve the poor, how much they love others. Here they lead the *vita apostolica*, the life of service to Him.'

Breaking from his fresh-baked bread and cheese, Fabian raised an eyebrow. 'Such service must come with gifts from the citizens. You cannot be popular with the Church authorities, diverting funds they presume to be theirs, and bringing God to the people rather than the people to their cathedrals of stone.'

Marguerite smiled. 'How observant you are for so young a monk. Unlike the religious orders, we take no vows here. We meditate much, but we also dance and sing. We practise direct experience of Him and believe that our souls crave to be reunited, that we are part of the Divine, that our purpose is to find our way home. In this task none of us needs an interlocutor to find God. He will find us and we will find Him within us, not within temples.'

Fabian nodded in understanding, returning Marguerite's smile, his exchange catching a deep interest from the monks as they ate. 'Then Mistress, perhaps like us, you too walk a tightrope across the princes of the Church, who believe that it is their exclusive right to interpret His laws. So, how do you hold your balance?'

Placing her book on the table near a candle, Marguerite carefully considered her reply, clearly warming to the young monk's crisp mind. 'As Esi will attest, I have long debated theology with the scholars of the Church. Relying on Saint Francis of Assisi has been helpful, and I have consulted Church scholars. What I think aggrieves them most is that I have written the Mirror of Simple Souls, not in Latin but in French.'

Esi laughed aloud. 'So, Marguerite, you took my counsel and shattered the glass. Good for you! These Beguines believe in personal experience, with Christ as a lover and sufferer. To them, purgatory is not a place of punishment, but of love and purification; that the only pain is a longing to be reunited with Him. Let me say it, Marguerite, for you will not. The relationship the sisters foster with God is not just a matter of religious envy for the princes of the Church, but a poison to their manhood. There, I have said it, at the heart of this is jealousy because these Beguines live a life of chastity, in love with God alone, something that the male Church finds deeply unnerving, for reasons they seek to explain from scripture but not from their loins.'

Fabian and Rostan visibly winced. Guiscard, used to Esi's fire, hooted with laughter at the young monk's discomfort, slapping his big arms across both monks' shoulders, and addressing Marguerite. 'Tell us more of this marvellous book you write.'

'Well, after much debate with Esi, I decided to write it in the current fashion, teasing through our beliefs as a conversation between players, reasoning that it is better to experience God rather than try to define Him, for that cannot be done. When our souls are fully united with God, we are in His grace, beyond sin. This is our true journey.'

'Saint Francis indeed is a useful shield, mistress,' said Fabian, as he thought his way through her strategy. 'He too came from a wealthy silk merchant family, but swapped his fine clothes for that of a beggar. Aye, and his stigmata, which can only come from direct experience of God, protects you more than any act of mortals, for he is canonised.'

Marguerite was impressed. 'You reason quickly, young monk. Esi, you will have a match here someday,' she added playfully, 'but it is getting late, and you have an early start. Use the bedding here by the fire. We will wake you before dawn.'

As the tired party settled to catch some sleep, Esi, who was flicking through the book by candlelight, sighed. 'Oh, this is so beautiful. She has a lovely flowing style. Before I blow the candle out, sleep, my Templars, with this wind-chime she uses from John the Apostle for your dreams: *I am God, says Love, for Love is God and God is Love, and this Soul is God by the condition of Love. I am God by divine nature and this Soul is God by righteousness of Love. Thus, this precious beloved of mine is taught and guided by me, without herself, for she is transformed into me, and such a perfect one, says Love, takes my nourishment.*'

Before Esi finished and blew the candle out, the snoring had already started. Well, well, the little puppies, she thought. I shall have to improve my timing, maybe work on them in the saddle, alert, and on empty stomachs!

CHAPTER 10

Jean and Geoffrey crouched low; they had wrestled their loads through the narrow tunnel. Their candlelight flickered in the weak draughts of air, and cast poor light on the uneven ground. The tunnels smelt of stale air, rot and rat urine as they pushed through years of cobwebs and decay caused by flooding. It was a test of endurance, balance and strength, doubly so for older monks, despite all their training. They had made their way beneath Enclos du Temple, west in the direction of St Martin-des-Champs. The priory, once in a field outside the walls of Paris, now marked its inner northern edge. The tunnel, built for clandestine movement in and out of the Templar headquarters, was one of a number of subterranean routes that extended in all directions. This one, chosen by the monks, extended beyond the ring of steel that surrounded the *enclos*. The tunnel turned left, running parallel with the walled enclosure of the priory of Saint Martin of Tours, the Roman cavalryman turned hermit monk, beloved of Parisians. The route now headed towards the streetscape of the city. They had found the exit: a series of narrow steps leading up to a small stone room, the door to which pivoted when pushed. It hinged on the other side to a plain wall in a storage room.

Jean, pouring in sweat from exertion, cursed Fabian under his breath for not warning the spymaster of the difficulty in carrying the Mongol powder bags over such a distance. Behind him, Geoffrey grinned at his companion's discomfort. He was enjoying the experience of outwitting the Hound's trap, eager to see out the plan. They waited in the gloom of the storage room for the first sign of daybreak to creep across the early morning sky, then made their move. Both monks were unrecognisable, each bearing the clothing and stance of beggars tasked with clearing up the streets in the early morning light in return for a breakfast of thin gruel.

They made their way deeper into the city, towards Île de la Cité, the island that dominated its heart, stopping only when the streets began to widen near the Seine. Both travelled by gestures, feigning the manner of unskilled workers, and masked their speech from unwelcome ears, as it would instantly reveal their educated dialect, compared with the stilted language of the streets.

They reached the river, within sight of the Pont aux Changeurs, and paused. Both monks understood that here they would separate, each of them going to a different house on opposite sides of the royal grain store. This held the reserves of the city, to be handed out by the king at times of poor harvest, to stave off hunger riots. Neither Templar wished the grain store harm, but each grasped its vital importance to the king.

As Jean had expected, the nearby properties were unguarded and empty, each containing nothing of value to the king. Fabian had made the connection when planning tactics with the spymaster on the road to Paris. He had enlightened them regarding the Mongol powder, explaining how to handle the supply at the Enclos du Temple, where he had stored it. The monk had blended sulphur and saltpetre with freely available charcoal, experimenting with sugar to recreate the fire-arrows of the Mongols. He had diluted the mixtures in a little wine, then dried it into pellets for transportation. Geoffrey had the pellets arranged in neatly coloured bundles within moulds; Jean carried the heavier load – and the more dangerous of the two. Both slipped noiselessly into the empty buildings and set about their work carefully, running a trail of powder from the entrance to Fabian's inventions. They waited. When the first rays of the sun caught the high golden cross of Saint Chapelle, which towered above the royal residence, they each lit their trails of powder and hurried away into the thinning shadows.

*

De Nogaret was perched like a bird of prey on a rooftop near the Enclos, with a panoramic view of the open ground to its walls. He loved the early mornings in Paris, from whose rooftops he could survey the ground for his quarry and direct his agents to dispatch them. He maintained contact with his officers through a panel of runners to the positions in which he had placed them, ringing the Templar headquarters with eyes. He had received multiple briefings about a group of eight riders, seven Templars and a young knight passing in plain sight through the streets of Paris to the Enclos in the twilight hours, and couldn't believe his luck that they had chosen to return to their lair, within his open fist. He had quickly launched his surveillance plan of the ground to detect their next play. The royal spymaster especially yearned to capture the young Irish Norman, a gift for Bertramnus, to make a new song for the King. It was all falling nicely into place, he thought smugly, through the familiar sounds of early morning. An instant later the first fire-arrows took to the sky with a loud swoosh. Swivelling, he saw a line of fire travel up in a violently weaving pattern, then with a boom, it lit up the early-morning sky before cascading in sparks across Île de la Cité, and the king's residence.

The Hound spun on his heels, shocked by the suddenness of the sound, the sight alien to his eyes. It was quickly followed by a cacophony of bursting light and more sound, the windows of Paris flung open as residents craned outside to discover the origins of the noise and the strange lights in the sky. Just as the Hound bounded out to the street, Jean's explosion followed, sending a straight ball of thick black smoke and flame straight into the sky.

He raced towards alarmed cries that the grain store was aflame, and darted his way through the confusion of crowds, bumping heavily into a beggar running in the opposite direction. There was a general panic to fetch pails of water to save the city's food supplies. No one had yet taken command, and the royal guards mingled urgently with commoners, grimly passing buckets in the lines forming to the river, everyone terrified of what winter would be like with a shortage of grain.

Drawing a breath, de Nogaret paused. Something was not right. The grain store was not aflame: it was the building next door. Then he made the connection. *This is a deliberate distraction. The night guard from the city walls have been drawn to the mêlée, and the city gates are open. All of them! Bordel de merde*, everything was in chaos! There was nothing quite as fearful as the possibility of a winter of starvation in a city without bread, to turn trained soldiery into a mob. Just then one of his officers pointed to his back. 'Master there is a writing on your tunic. Not words, Master; a symbol.'

De Nogaret yanked his tunic about, to find pinned to it, the shape of an eye, the Eye of Horus. The Hound's heart stopped: *the beggar!* He guessed immediately that it must have been the Templar spymaster.

He turned rapidly and barked orders to the men nearest him, for them to return to encircling the Enclos, not yet realising that Jean had intended him to believe in a botched escape attempt, that the stunt with the symbol was designed to overpower his cold cunning with hot anger. It worked; the Hound was in such a temper as he hadn't felt since the retreat from Anagni. His head pounded with rage, his thoughts were out of control, focused on his prey, the Enclos du Temple.

*

Across the city, Guiscard's party left the Beguinage. Esi hugged Marguerite in a hurried goodbye, mounted her horse and, flanked by Rostan and Fabian, took off in the direction of the nearest gate in an even trot, just as Paris erupted. Along the narrow streets crowds still in night attire rushed against them, heading towards the commotion, shouts to save the grain rising through the early-morning air as panic took hold. Grinning, Guiscard led, his great horse clearing a path. Jean my old friend, you still have the gift, but now it's my turn, he thought.

Turning towards the three following him, he shouted, 'Fast trot! Let's get out of Paris before the king's favourite pet discovers he's been hooked like an eel.'

He galloped out of the gate, heading west, in a straight line towards their destination, the three riders close behind, Esi clinging on to her horse for dear life, squeezed between the Templar steeds but finding it much easier to balance without the metal armour. Rostan, low over his mount, winked at her with malicious enjoyment at all the excitement. *Merde*, Esi thought, as she clung on for dear life, I am keeping company with madmen these days.

Guiscard's first destination was the steeple of the Cathédrale Notre-Dame de Chartres, which rose 350 feet out of the plains of the Beauce, the granary of France. Late on the first day, they hastily made camp to the west on the banks of the River Eure, and watered their horses.

Esi, her shoulders, back and legs aching from another day in the saddle, drank in the spectacle of the great cathedral to Our Lady, the symbolism and geometry firing her mind. 'This Guiscard is an interesting first camp. It is a place held sacred by the ancient Celts and their druids as a place of power and mystery.'

'Indeed, young Esi,' Guiscard said wryly, 'but the real mystery is how you are still awake. It wasn't my intention to make this journey intellectually stimulating, but more of a way to get you to learn the saddle.'

'The architecture is most revealing, Templars,' Esi continued, barely breaking stride. 'There is known to have been a druidic well here, held sacred long before the Romans. It is a place where the energy of the world breaks forth to help initiates in the ancient mysteries to reach altered states and commune with the gods. Most revealing. Did you know the tradition here is of the virgin birth? It predates Christianity. Throughout the Celtic world the feast day of rebirth is the first of February, the first day of spring. It's no wonder that the Celts took to the Virgin Mary with such ease. It didn't need a fragment of the *Sancta Camista*, Mary's birth-garment, to fire the passions of the local population. See those rose windows yonder? Truly spectacular. Let me tell you about the stories they represent.'

Esi turned to find the monks already sleeping soundly, while Rostan, out of earshot, was patrolling the perimeter as the horses gently chewed grass. By God's bones, that's two nights in a row. These monks really do test a woman, she thought, and covered herself with her blanket near the fire. She was asleep in seconds.

CHAPTER 11

At daybreak Guiscard assembled them. 'The easy part is over. We now pick up pace towards the coast. Travel fast, rest late, move quickly.' Esi groaned, her chafed shoulders, thighs and legs aching. 'God in heaven, I thought that was the hard bit. I don't know if my seat can take much more pounding. Can we not take a more leisurely passage through the countryside? The casket isn't going anywhere in a hurry. It's been there nearly nine hundred years.'

Guiscard's thin smile told her otherwise. 'We have to assume that by now De Nogaret has figured out he's been duped. He won't be happy: that fellow has a nasty temper. We must make haste, as if every fast-moving soldier the king has at his disposal is on our tail. Right now, messages are probably being pinned to carrier pigeons, flying out in a great circle from Paris. Every command from here to the coast will be looking for us. What is to our advantage is that they don't know where we're heading.'

Swinging on to his horse and turning it in one swift movement, Guiscard announced, 'It is time for hard riding. We go as if the hounds of hell are on our shoulder, for they most surely are.'

Esi groaned loudly. The gamesmanship phase was over; it was time for flight.

Guiscard steered a direct course for the coast, testing the limits of endurance for both horses and riders deep into each night. They moved swiftly, forever westwards, towards the setting sun. He chose forest routes and trails, avoiding the main roads and villages. They slept in the open, rationing food; there was no time to forage. Guiscard did not underestimate the Hound. At best, Jean had bought a day and a night before de Nogaret would pick up their trail. He would send his fleetest killers, armed to the teeth, filled with revenge towards those who had made a cockscomb of him in front of the king.

From the morning of the fourth day after they had left Chartres, the fast-moving company could smell the change. The south-westerly was blowing salt air from the Celtic Sea across the Duché de Bretagne, clearing away the scent of the Maine countryside with fresh allure, offering a hint of the great blue expanse beyond, and the mysteries it might hold. Lush green pasture gave way to fields of weathered granite, lines of standing stones which whispered of an ancient people talking to their gods, in their fashion, before the great Celtic migration from the east, before the beginning of recorded time. Finally, they arrived at their destination, exhausted and saddle sore, relieved to see a steeple by the sea.

Guiscard called a halt, sending Rostan and Fabian to scout out the town. 'That,' he told the young monks, pointing to the steeple, 'is Saint Pol de Leon. You will find it a busy jumble of modest houses and streets surrounding the Bretons' largest sea market. The cathedral is built to commemorate Paul Aurelian, its sixth-century bishop. That monk, a Welsh lad, ate nothing but vegetables, they say, for a hundred and forty years. Can you imagine how regular he must have been! There is no king's command here, but keep your wits about you and join us later at Plage de Dossen, the beach just up the trail.'

Esi's spirits lifted as she rode alongside Guiscard. The old man had relaxed as they arrived, to whatever destiny awaited. She chose not to pester him with questions: he was the opposite of Astralabius, and only spoke when he needed to give commands or, after finding something upon which to comment, for his amusement. He had taken her out of the smoking ruin and terror of Acre, escaping the death-breath of the Franks. The Mamluks, she knew, did not differentiate. All non-believers, women and children, would be raped and butchered, save for those who had been selected to live out their days as slaves, toiling in rocky ground under the boiling sun of a caliphate.

'Here we are, Esi.' Guiscard dismounted and held the reins of her horse. 'You can get off now. Kick off your tiny boots, girl, and walk the beach.'

Esi looked curiously at the monk, thinking it an odd request, but did as she was told. Her feet pressed into the soft sand, while in the background the waves were breaking, white on azure, driven by tide and breeze under a cloudless sky.

Guiscard pointed along the beach, shimmering under the sun, to an approaching solitary figure. 'Go see what that lad might want, would you, Esi?' She froze for a moment, then spun around, clapped her hands and ran on the spot with excitement. 'You old trickster! That's Cormac, isn't it? That's what you've been hiding. That's why we've galloped across half of France, by God's heart!' Esi exclaimed.

'Aye, Esi, that's the lad I've been telling you about. That's Cormac. Run and say hello. I sincerely hope that you two have a lot to talk about, because you've completely worn me out of words. Young woman, you need a companion who is a match for you,' he added wistfully. 'And something tells me you two are foot and slipper.' With that, Guiscard laughed, and kicked Esi's pert, bruised bottom playfully.

In the distance, the figure waved. Esi started to run but caught herself. How undignified! Why should she run towards this stranger? But why was she so excited? Why did her heart race so? What was dancing within? I've butterflies in the belly, she thought. This isn't like anything I have felt before, not escaping Acre, not reaching Cyprus, not even galloping out of Paris.

She found herself sweeping back her hair and checking her stride to a fast walk, trying to look composed, but her eyes widened in disbelief as the distance narrowed and she could make out his features. Settle! He is just a young man, tall, as is the character of his race, still slender, still a youth. Oh, but he'll fill out nicely. No, Esi, she thought then. He's a stranger. All you know about him is what Guiscard revealed to the Septum. This echoed in her mind like a musical note.

She stopped, letting him close the distance to an arm's-length. He cocked his head, his long red hair flopping to the side. That gesture was so familiar to her. But how could it be? Inside, the butterflies were kicking up a storm. Why did she feel so – she searched for the word – so *reunited*. There is a bond, but how could there be?

Cormac paused, as Guiscard had warned him to do, keeping his distance from the alien woman Guiscard had rescued from the Holy Land. Cormac loved to hear the tale, especially the words Esi had spoken about the matters of the world, about its nature, about the character of God. Hearing the old monk recount his adventures, he felt as if he had known her since he was a child. He had always stopped Guiscard at Esi, and now he knew why. She was so familiar that she walked out of his imagination, commanding the space, the air around her, as if she was carved out of it. He studied her eyes, his head tilting to the side in curiosity.

Neither spoke, just stood there in the middle of the beach, uncertain of what to say.

Esi wondered why she felt that a common greeting of some kind seemed out of place, although they had not yet been introduced. Over her shoulder, she saw that Guiscard had given up his vigil, and was sitting by the dunes chewing a reed, squinting through the bright sunshine.

Guiscard was wondering how the meeting he had planned for so long was working out. He knew Esi to be fiercely independent, bristling when outmanoeuvred – even if this was deftly done. She loved to control her fate, and this was certainly not in her script for today. Cormac was her equal in intelligence and speed of thought, but he was very young to meet Esi unaccompanied. He might say the wrong thing, and Guiscard would have a great deal of explaining to do, to both of them. These two, he thought, are the most precious part of my life. They *must* get on. They simply must.

Further up the beach, Esi was breaking the silence. 'Cormac Fitz Stephan, I see you.' She broke into a huge smile, stepped forward, extended her right hand to clasp his, placing her left hand across their handshake, over his heart. It felt so familiar; the right thing to do.

Cormac instantly echoed her by placing his left hand over her heart. He chuckled. 'Esi Akiba, I see you too.'

They both stood there grinning, in a perfect setting as the sun-kissed wavelets lapped on to the sands. Neither knowing why, each felt strangely comfortable just being there at that moment, in that place, in that time, needing nothing more, at peace. Bliss.

CHAPTER 12

Guiscard was the first to hear the commotion. He strained his ears: approaching horses, coming fast; two, by the sounds of it. No, there's more. Many more. A pursuit! He leapt to his feet just in time, to see Fabian and Rostan rounding the end of the beach at full gallop, their horses steaming with effort, straining through the soft sand and kicking up spray.

He pivoted and ran towards the horses, rapidly untethering and mounting his, and pulling Esi's by the reins. Digging his spurs in sharply, he propelled the animal along the beach, shouting, 'Cormac, Esi, look up! We are discovered!'

Guiscard could see more men arriving at the other end of the beach, in the distance. Men-at-arms, lightly armoured for fast movement. They must have been on our trail for days, he thought.

Cormac instinctively shielded Esi, drawing his arming sword as Rostan and Fabian reached them, circling to protect them. At both ends of the beach, the horsemen slowed. No need to rush; they had their prey trapped.

'Guiscard, I know this ground,' Cormac exclaimed. 'We retreat over there to Isle de Sieck. The rocks are slippery. It will force them to dismount, to engage us.'

The old monk looked to the narrow inlet catching the incoming tide to the tiny island beyond, and turned towards Fabian. 'Well, what say you?'

'It's a dead-end, Guiscard. The tide will buy us some time, if we can fend them off. I don't see much advantage there, but to go back the way we came is to meet even more of them. We came close to this lot in the town. It's clearly a vanguard: light-armoured, fast-moving. Heavy armour is surely coming just behind.'

'These are De Nogaret's creatures. *Routiers*, mercenaries,' Rostan spat. 'They fight foul. The street-fighting of Paris is good at night, for overpowering opponents by surprise.' He grinned as he drew his sword. 'They will not be so brave in the sunshine, face to face. There are many, but not as well trained as those who come behind them.'

Fabian nodded a greeting towards Cormac. 'Aye, I agree. That's why they hesitate. They weigh the risks of proceeding now to their prize – which is presumably young Cormac, here – or laying siege and waiting for reinforcements.'

'That's what I say too,' Guiscard snorted. 'Quick, to the rocks and over to the island before they change their minds and charge.'

The party withdrew from their exposed position gradually, facing in both directions of threat. Cormac led the retreat, guiding Esi by walking their horses through the obstacles to the narrow spit of grass and sand which lay beyond. They quickly drew their lances, shields, and extra arming swords from their horses, placing them on their fighting field. Esi volunteered to act as squire to the men.

Guiscard gestured for the monks to take up position on both sides, marking the easiest exit through the rock-field, determined to thin the numbers of their attackers in the first wave of assault. He counted eighteen of them closing fast, a nasty-looking bunch in a mixture of light chainmail, hauberks and jacks, steel plates sewn into leather jackets. They were armed with an assortment of lances, swords and maces. The two groups met in front of Isle de Sieck and dismounted. It afforded Guiscard the opportunity to assess their leader.

'They listen to the large one, wearing the weathered tan brigandine with a blue-plumed helmet,' Fabian said, reading the old monk's mind. 'Take him early, Rostan, and it will weaken their will.'

'As I see it, this is an uneven fight. There are not enough of them, and they are snared,' piped up Cormac, grinning from ear to ear. He caught a secret smile from Guiscard as they drew their arming swords, the deadly double-edged, open-hilted weapon favoured by the Templars.

They took up defensive stances on solid ground, inviting the oncoming men-at-arms to meet them with slippery rocks underfoot. On the beach, the mercenaries formed a narrowed line of attack, moving carefully through the narrow channel towards the Templars, three to four abreast, led by the blue-helmeted sergeant who was barking Orders. They moved with the confidence of a hunting pack approaching a trapped prey, the only consideration being how to kill it with least injury to themselves, the outcome already decided.

Rostan, cat-like, suddenly sprang forward, swivelling low, to bring his fine-edged sword at lightning speed under the guard of the lead soldier, cutting straight through his unprotected leg below the knee. Without losing speed, his movement flowed seamlessly upwards to the sergeant behind, thrusting the sword-point through his exposed chin, the tip of the blade exiting through his mouth. The red spray marked the opening violence, sending a signal through the attackers that first blood was not theirs – that they had lost their leader.

Guiscard, wielding a long sword with a double-handed grip, used it to shatter the first shield which was offered. He turned fast, despite his bulk, to jam the pommel into the face of his opponent, felling him by dint of weight and velocity. He then swung the great weapon in an arc, splitting open the shoulder of the nearest soldier, forcing him to drop his lance. Fabian, seeing the opening, used his dagger at close quarters to thrust upwards under the soft armpit of the soldier nearest him, driving deep through to the throat.

Rostan was quickly encircled by four opponents. Alerted to his speed and deadliness, they taunted him with their spears, looking for an opening to charge in and overwhelm the young monk. Across the field, the other Templars were yielding ground under mounting pressure, isolating Rostan. He was desperately parrying spear-thrusts when Cormac made a long, loud whistle. Instantly, Rostan heard blood-curdling yells, and saw two giant, bear-like warriors emerge from the dunes, their size heightened by peaked iron helmets. These were the wildest men he had ever seen, scything through their opponents from behind with oversized double-edged battle-axes. They were shouting in an alien tongue.

'God in heaven, Guiscard, they are shouting with joy!' Rostan yelled. 'Those aren't just battle-axes, they are Viking blades!'

Guiscard nodded grimly and bellowed across the mêlée. 'Ultan and Felim, could you have left it any finer?' He turned to his fellow monks, grinning. 'Gallowglass, Cormac's bodyguard.'

The Gallowglass, with their heavily muscled shoulders and arms under leather and mail, were swinging razored steel a foot long on the end of five feet of polished wood, straight through light armour, inflicting gruesome wounds with each stroke. The effect was to send a shockwave through the attacking group. They were attempting to rally when a second shockwave announced itself in a shower of arrows from the crest of the island, quickly followed by a dozen tunic-clad warriors who charged past the Templars into the fray.

Catching Rostan's eye, Guiscard yelled, 'That'll be the *Ceithearn*! Nasty buckos in tight quarters!'

Fabian laughed, and eased off his own efforts, to watch the remaining *routiers* go down like flies, caught between the lightning-fast darts of the unarmoured Kern, in their saffron tunics and small round shields, and behind them the gruesome, grinding battle-axes of the Gallowglass.

Esi, shaking from shock, sobbed and averted her eyes, stunned by the butchery as the Kerns and Gallowglass went to work on the remaining pursuers. As tears ran down her pale cheeks, Guiscard stepped back towards Esi and put his arms around her shoulders, shielding her from the sight. He spoke quietly. 'Esi, you will know from your family's journeys, that war is brutality. It is either them or us, and what they would have done to you as a prize is not worth thinking about. This is their destiny.'

He turned as the last groans from the wounded were silenced by the coup de grace, a thrust through the throat. The water ran with blood from dripping wounds; severed heads and limbs rolled in the tide. 'It is always the same,' he said. 'The emptiness after battle. There is no glory, just ugliness and the stench of wasted lives. Introductions later; we must fly. Heavy armour comes behind – far trickier to despatch, and in much larger numbers. Follow Cormac,' he ordered.

The two Gallowglass cleaned their blades in the sea and dutifully followed Cormac, while the Kerns attended to their wounded, helping them limp along close behind, their words masked in Gaelic. Instead of heading for shore, the young man turned to the monks. 'Come follow me over the hill. Another surprise awaits.'

The Templars stripped their horses, picked up their weapons and followed. Nestling on the exposed seaward side of Isle de Sieck, in a secure anchor fastened to shore, lay a small ship.

'Well, Fabian, fountain of military knowledge, what do you make of her?' Guiscard asked the young monk, as the Kerns loaded the boat and released the Templar horses to the shore. In the background, Esi was hugging her pony tearfully, saying goodbye and thanking her for her service, patience and love, while Cormac watched, enviously.

'Never seen such a vessel, Guiscard,' Fabian replied, examining it from bow to stern. 'It has a square single sail, and a clinker hull, handy for beaching. She can be rowed in light winds; not great heading into wind, I'll guess, but ideal for coastal travel. It is a vessel of the wild Scots and Irish, so it has to be a Birlinn, a descendent of the Viking longship, like those two demons, does it not?'

Ultan responded in fluent French. '*Va te faire enculer,* monk. We are twins. And take care you don't insult the boat again, for she is better in rough seas than you, my friend.'

Guiscard bellowed with laughter. 'You have much to learn about these island people, Fabian.' He raised his voice. 'Ceithearn, to the oars. Let us leave this treacherous anchorage at haste, and catch the wind to Waterford, and home.'

CHAPTER 13
Poitiers

Bertrand de Got sat in the tight garde-robe cut into the narrow hallway at right angles to it. He had insisted on a door for privacy. He always hated the *necessarium*, the long communal latrines common to abbeys, from which he had been elevated. He sat and waited. His bowels lurched again. It was a pattern with which he was familiar. I've spent my life squatting, he thought, reaching for the bag of pressed flowers he insisted upon carrying with him for his unexpected diversions. Sitting there, he could feel the breeze whistling up his exposed backside from outside, its fingers driving the stench of waste back, while its substance crept its way slowly down the slime-green walls to the sewer, to freedom in the River Clain, which wound through Poitiers. That is, if the local farmers didn't procure it as holy fertiliser, he thought, ruefully. He visualised them selling their holy vegetables for extra prices at the local market, and chuckled aloud. The movement brought on another heave. He was nearly finished, thank God. He reached for the fresh herb-infused straw he used in preference to light wool, and wiped himself before returning to court.

While he waited, he thought back to his election, the eleven tumultuous months of politics among the factions at Perugia, and the bitterness and bile it created. The French cardinals, spurred on by Philip's intriguing, had won the day, elevating Bertrand de Got, Archbishop of Bordeaux, to the papal throne. He knew he had done well to traverse the treacherous waters between Edward of England, to whom he was a subject as a Gascon, and Philip, to whom he owed his career.

He winced at the memory of his grand coronation – not in Rome, which was preferred by the irate Italians, but in Lyons, favoured by the French king. It had been a triumphant parade until the moment he had been unceremoniously thrown by his horse, which had been spooked by the collapse of a wall. He and his new crown, the papal tiara, had sprawled into the crowds. He had gasped as he was lifted back to his feet, his silks ruined, his hands bloodied, the tiara recovered, but missing its most precious jewel, the ruby. The jewel could be replaced, but the humiliation would remain. It would be interpreted as an omen for choosing France and the French king over the traditions of the Church. He was right: the toxic atmosphere spilled into conflict in the streets between his staff and those of the Italian Cardinals. Not the start that Clement V desired.

He rose from the latrine, fixed his robes and made his way to the biggest room in Europe, the Salle des Pas Perdus, the Hall of Lost Footsteps, to face the Iron King for a fresh round of abuse. It is no wonder I go to the garderobe, the pope thought, as he made his way unsteadily back through his quarters to the babbling sounds of the court.

The high-vaulted room was dominated in the middle by a raised dais, arranged for the visit. It was surrounded, at a respectful distance, by the papal and royal courts, the red hats competing with nobles and civil servants for the finest silks and baubles. Together, at the centre, were seats for both rulers, celestial and temporal. They had dispensed with the need to have members of their courts close by, unless enquiring into points of law, both church and regal. Courtiers and cardinals strained to hear the low tones of the conversation from the two men, both known to each other from childhood; they could overhear nothing, unless this was intended by either speaker.

The meeting had been temporarily suspended to allow the pope a short break before returning with his entourage to retake his seat in a display of papal reverence, eyes cast down, hands in prayer, as if he had left to seek divine guidance, before returning, inspired.

The Iron King sat, coiled like a great serpent, unmoving, observing. Although their seats were arranged on opposite elevations, he towered over the squat Pope Clement V. The effect was marked by the pontiff's pallor, as if the weight of Christendom was pressing his shoulders into his robes, his bowels into his seat, his mind into subservience.

The king was fed a consistent stream of intelligence from de Nogaret's spies within the papal court, which included members of the *Camerarius Domini Papae*, the Papal Chamberlain. He was well aware of Pope Clement's movements, night and day.

'Pope Clement.' Philip addressed the pontiff formally. 'The king trusts that you are well enough not to sit exposed much longer on the issue before you, concerning Boniface?'

The pope grimaced at the double-entendre, grasping that the king was warning him of his weak position in his territory – and his poor health. That meant the cunning de Nogaret, the pope guessed.

The king continued, 'There remains a gap between Crown and Church which must be healed.'

That is not a question, it is an instruction, the pope thought, his face unmoving, despite his rising alarm. 'Your Highness, I have done much to relieve you of the pope's legacy. I have refreshed the absolution granted by my predecessor. I remind Your Majesty that Pope Boniface's bull, *Unam Sanctum*, which has vexed you so, has been removed from your royal kingdom. I have suitably watered down his other bull, *Clericis Laicos*. These, combined, are a clear acknowledgement of your devotion and piety. None other exists anywhere in Christendom.'

King Philip smiled thinly. 'That is acknowledged, Holy Father, but the king desires, in his devotion and piety, that the heretic and sodomite Boniface is forgotten as a pope; that his memory is crushed; and that he is remembered only for his disinterment, his burning, and for fouling the winds with his ashes. I remind you, Bertrand, from whence you came, and how that road was paved for you.'

Clement stifled a gasp. He understood the meaning of using his first name, and grasped full well what it meant to be the object of the king's hatred: he knew his character and suspected his vices. He decided to turn the discussion to internal processes which he could control, and buy some time to consider the response to what he deemed more than a subtle threat. 'King Philip, such measures ought not to be taken in haste, not without due process within the Church herself.'

The king, thanks to de Nogaret, had anticipated the pope's ploy. 'Word has reached the royal ears of the Dulcinians in Piedmont, Holy Father, led, as I believe, by Fra Dolcino, who drew inspiration from the much-beloved Francis of Assisi. He justified his defence against your Holiness' troops with Saint Paul's epistle to Titus: *To the pure all things are pure, but to the corrupt and unbelieving nothing is pure; their very minds and consciences are corrupted.* Fra Dolcino was a most cunning fellow, indeed. Very intelligent – and, just like Boniface, a *heretic*.' The king spat out the word like a poison in the air between them.

Clement V pulled back into his chair, as if the very act of distancing himself from the king would preserve him from what he knew would follow.

'But what is most interesting,' the king continued, 'is that neither he nor his companion, Margaret of Trent, were tried by the Church at all, that under your Holiness' watch, Dolcino was first castrated, before being torn limb from limb, and burned by public execution – but only after he had first witnessed the rare beauty, Margaret of Trent, mother of his child, torn to pieces before him. So, you see my point, Holy Father. *Comme on fait son lit, on se couche*. As you make your bed, so must you lie.'

It happened rarely, but Clement was lost for words. He knew precisely what the king was telling him: that nothing would protect him, neither lineage, nor friendship, nor the Papacy, should he choose to resist the will of the king. He decided to throw the beast a bone. 'Indeed, Majesty, I do understand. It is rather a matter of timing to allow for a Church Council before putting a dead pontiff on trial. Meanwhile, I am open to engagement with Your Majesty on your other request: to amalgamate the Templars with the Hospitaller knights in preparation for the next crusade.'

King Philip bristled at the mention of the Templars, distracted by the pope's ploy. Sensing his opening, the Pontiff continued. 'Outside, Your Majesty, are Jacque de Molay and Geoffrey de Charney, waiting on my pleasure. The Grand Master has been much in correspondence from his base in Cyprus since my first enquiries about this matter. Will I ask him to join us?'

The king cast a sideways glance at de Nogaret, who returned his thin smile, both men sensing the springing of the trap. 'Holy Father, we are at your disposal here in the papal court and will, of course, provide you with whatever guidance you might seek on the internal review of Church military orders.'

The pope nodded graciously, gestured for his *camerlengo*, and raising his voice, instructed him. 'Admit Jacque de Molay, Grand Master of the Poor Fellow-Soldiers of Christ and the Temple of Jerusalem.'

CHAPTER 14
Enclos du Temple, Paris

High above Paris, over the crenellated walls of Enclos du Temple, in the turret-room of Grosse Tour, rays of sunshine lit up the long wooden desk over which Astralabius had spread his work. He felt inordinately tired and exhausted, his health being in its twilight. He had been busy for days locked in the room, away from prying eyes, bent over the lengthy parchments before him, deep in calculation. His fingers worked at speed across the Arabic abacus, while his quill and ink worked up new sums on fresh parchment.

Every so often, he would leave his chair, stretch his back and straighten the old bones of his shoulders – which were rounded from a life of study. He would walk slowly around the table to recheck his sums or go to the narrow windows to gaze out over Paris, visualising the kingdom which stretched beyond, and the costs of managing it. He had already formed preliminary conclusions, and had sent a message to Jean to join him as soon as possible. The Librarian had accumulated a lifetime of records, which covered every aspect of the kingdom, mapping out its assets and its debts, and fed the information to John of Tour, the Templar treasurer, responsible for lending Templar funds to the Iron King.

Astralabius' estimates had included the remaining costs of the disastrous Aragon Crusade, which the young King Philip had inherited from his father, and the drain caused by Philip's secret pact with the Scots against the Plantagenet Edward I. The pact had resulted in a decade of war with England. It had ended with the Treaty of Paris in 1303, and the pledge of marriage of Isabella to Edward's wayward son.

The monk had concerned himself more recently not just with England but with the costs of the legacy of the king's conflict with the Flemish on his northern border. The military occupation exploded when Philip left command of his huge forces to Count Robert II of Artois, who was heavily defeated at the Battle of the Golden Spurs in 1302, the summer before the treaty with the English. Astralabius knew that the management of the French army had been beset by matters of pay, and his attention had been drawn to the overhang of debt even before the Flemish war had ended.

The defeat in 1302 ended Philip's quick attempt to quell the rebellion of the cities of Flanders, and exposed the poor tactics of the French, who had launched repeated heavy cavalry charges against the well-drilled and armoured pikemen of the Flemish militia. The five hundred spurs left by the French nobility on the battlefield gave the site its name – and lent humiliation to the French king.

It would cost Philip three more years of war, until the French fleet's victory at the Battle of Zierikzee, and its victory on land a week later, led by Philip at Mons-en-Pévèle, before he got his revenge. The Iron King forced painful war reparations on the Flemish at the Peace of Athis-sur-Orge in 1305, which included the loss of three cities to his crown. What concerned Astralabius was not the outcome of the lengthy conflict but its cost: how it was funded, and what forces the pressure from a thinning treasury might release. He was putting himself into the shoes of the French king, to determine his mind.

The soft knock on the door announced the arrival of the Templar spymaster. Astralabius opened it to Jean, ever hungry for information, and capable of working at extraordinary speed to turn it to advantage. The spymaster had obtained scattered records of the king's finances from 1305 the end of the Flemish war, and was keen to know what they might contain, compared to reports provided to John of Tour, in assessing the king's true financial position.

'It looks as if you have been hard at work again, old friend. You appear very tired. What do you have for me?' Jean asked, taking a seat and kicking off his boots.

'Well, first to the currency, which, like a skin-ulcer, marks outside what is happening inside. You will recall that his grandfather, King Louis, fathered the pure silver *gros tournier*, each worth twelve *deniers*, bringing stability to the kingdom for many years. As a young king, Philip plundered its value by raising the rate from twelve to fifteen deniers.'

'Aye. Mightn't sound like much, but that was a swing of a quarter,' Jean proffered.

'Precisely, but let me sketch it out. Things rested so until the end of the conflict with Edward, when he revalued again, this time to twenty-six *denier*, and last year to forty-one and a half *denier*.'

'Yes, a monumental swing. It is why he banned his subjects from taking the old pure silver *gros tournier* out of the kingdom, to preserve it. So?' Jean was keen to push the old monk on.

'Patience, Jean. I won't be long. The king's attack on his own currency, which has been ruinous to the people, was then partially offset by his attempt to reduce the amount of pure silver coins in circulation – as if currency was a matter of conquering territory. It is not. Forcing people to hand back their *gros tournier* in return for these poorer *deniers*, doubled the cost of food.'

'Which is why we gave the king temporary refuge from the mob, behind the wall of the Enclos. I understand, Astralabius. But where is this taking us?'

'I have been endeavouring to put myself into the saddle of the king. I have already plundered the currency of the realm, and risked its collapse, but it is still not enough. So what will I do next? Taking an old leaf from the books of Louis and Edward, I turn my piety against the Jews, and my avarice towards their assets, plundering their wealth while redirecting the rage of the mob against them. After all, they have been less useful across Europe since the coming of Italian banks. This is where I have been focusing: looking in depth at the most recent records.'

Jean shot out of the chair, to stare across the table. He didn't like where this was heading. 'Why should we be concerned about the arrest of a hundred thousand Jews, their imprisonment or deportation?'

'Because, Jean, the wealth of the Jews, which Philip imagined he could take for his treasury, lay not in their property or possessions, as the king hoped, but in the value of their book of loans, the income from their usury. My study of the records shows that the king robbed the bank, but took only its physical property, and failed to take its true wealth – the loans. In other words, Jean, the royal treasury has not been repaired. It is burst. The king is in a grim position, and you can whistle goodbye to any plans for a Crusade; that is certain.'

The room went silent as Jean paced beside the table, watched silently by Astralabius. Jean stopped and stood completely still, his hands clasping his head, as if trying not to let the thought in, as if controlling it would prevent it becoming so. 'What you tell me are three things. One, he has come away unsated in gold and silver. Two, that what he has learned is how to launch a sudden strike against a community of one hundred thousand within his realm. And three, that he has no intention of crusading. Then, Astralabius, what you leave hanging in this room is the conclusion: the Iron King found a new way to strike, but hit the wrong target.'

'Go on, Jean. Keep following. Where does it take you?' asked Astralabius quietly, not wishing to interrupt the thoughts of the Templar spymaster.

'That leaves the question: what other target to strike? Ordinarily, I hold no weight in prattling tongues – not unless there is a ring of truth to it – and I see that here, my friend.'

'To what prattling do you refer? Paris is always awash with rumours, the fables of those who cannot read words. Prattling tongues are not facts; I have never valued them much, Jean.'

'Maybe not this time, old friend. De Nogaret has a singing bird, one Esquin of Floyran, sprung from prison, who alleges that he spent time imprisoned with a Templar runaway. He sings of secret initiation ceremonies, false idols and sodomy – a vile song he sells for silver. He is a rat. In ordinary circumstances, there is no link, but I suspect that if the Hound compiles a dossier for the king, there can be but one purpose.'

Across the table, the old monk's pallor turned to grey. He seemed to age and shrink under the weight of the conclusion. 'God in heaven, Jean, since you've been gone, Jacque and Geoffrey have journeyed on command. As we speak, both are before pope and king, at Poitiers.'

CHAPTER 15
Papal Palace, Poitiers

The great door to the Hall of Lost Footsteps opened to the Camerlengo, followed by the towering figure of Jacque De Molay in full Templar regalia: a white mantle emblazoned with the red cross over a surcoat with a red cross. The assembly turned to stare at the unique sight of the fabled Grand Master of the Knights Templar marching towards the two most powerful men in Europe. The room erupted in buzzing conversation, those present sensing that a moment in history was at hand. Jacque was not armed with a sword, but in his hand he carried the Grand Master's pastoral staff, the *baculus*, its length symbolising support for the weak, its rod to strike down the vices of delinquents. Behind him, the Preceptor of Normandy, Geoffrey de Charney, walked in lockstep, their footfalls muffled by the rising murmur of the assembly echoing in the vastness of the vaulted roof.

At the dais, Geoffrey turned to sit at the front row of the papal court, directly opposite de Nogaret, who nodded, but whose thin smirk and narrowed eyes betrayed malevolence. Geoffrey ignored him, focusing fully on the Grand Master. Jacque made his way on to the red-carpeted dais, to the extended hand of the pope, and stooped to kiss the *Anulus Piscatoris*, the Ring of the Fisherman. He then took a standing position to the side of Clement V, like a sentinel.

The pope waited for the commotion to die down before raising his voice. 'Grand Master, you are most welcome to the papal court. I do regret the postponement of our meeting due to my recuperation and ablutions.'

Jacque nodded silently. The pope continued. 'I have studied your letters about the strategy needed to reclaim the Holy Land from the Mamluk scourge, as I have that of the Hospitallers. Both approaches differ in tactics, though not in scale. Theirs offers a two-pronged assault, led by naval engagement, followed by a land army. Yours has the advantage of simplicity: a direct and overwhelming land invasion to reclaim the Holy City of Jerusalem.'

The pope paused, to leave an opening for the Grand Master. 'Indeed, the Holy Father is correct. We envisage a general passage by force of fifteen thousand horsed men-at-arms, supported by five thousand of foot, while ten galleys lay anchor off Egypt, to cut off supplies to Europe. The size of the force will press them to exit the field and leave the road open to Acre, from where we can retake our strongholds, including Jerusalem. That the Mongols may attack to the rear and draw the Mamluks to defend their southern approaches will assist, but the plan is not dependent on the Mongolian horde drawing the Mamluks from the field.'

Pleased with the response from his military order, the pope turned towards King Philip. 'You will be aware, Your Majesty, that the red cross the Templars carry is a symbol of martyrdom: death in combat for Christ, assuring each monk a place in heaven. Such devotion has made the Order the vanguard of our Crusades since Saint Bernard of Clairvaux created the Latin Rule, the code of behaviour for the Templars. Indeed, King Philip, no Templar will leave the field while any Christian flags still fly. The flag on the field is such a symbol of defiance, is it not?'

Across the dais, the king stiffened at the implied reference to the oriflamme, the gold-flamed banner of the King of France, which he had lost on the battlefield to the lowly citizen militia of Flanders. The king paused, considered his response carefully, drew breath, and said in an even voice, 'Jacque, all Grand Masters bar two have died on the battlefield. This is an enviable record of service to the Church, but one sadly not reflected in the lineage of the papacy.'

The pope sank into his chair, instantly regretting goading the king, and fearful of what was coming next. 'You may be aware, Grand Master, of the king's concerns about the heresy of Boniface. Correct me if I am wrong, but in 896, Pope Stephen VI disinterred the corpse of Pope Formosus and put it on trial, sitting in court on the throne in full papal vestments, did he not?'

Jacque maintained his silence, eyes down, signalling close attention to the king's words. On opposite sides of the dais, the audience leaned forward, to catch an exchange which was clearly meant for them to hear.

The pope struggled to keep a neutral posture, but his head ached and his bowels growled as the king warmed to his theme. 'The Cadaver Synod ruled against Formosus, deeming him an unfit pope and, by *damnatio memoriae*, that all his acts and orders were annulled. Pope Stephen himself cut the three blessing fingers from the right hand of the corpse before stripping its vestments and throwing it into the Tiber. Thus, Grand Master, a dead pope has been put on trial by a strong and determined one. Is that not so?'

Alerted to the fact that he had interrupted a battle of wits between king and pope, Jacque paused to consider how he ought to reply. 'Your Majesty, as always, is highly informed, but I recall how it ended. Pope Stephen died in prison, strangled, his condemnation of Formosus overturned, and the seven cardinals who had supported the finding against Formosus, excommunicated.'

'Indeed, Grand Master, it was a confusing time, but the essential point is that it set a precedent for the trial of a dead pope, where circumstances warranted. Pope Clement here follows Boniface almost in the same timeline as Stephen followed Formosus, so there is also that similarity.'

The king let his comment hang in the air. The room went silent. Jacque caught Geoffrey's eye, who signalled him to stay silent by casually putting a finger over his mouth, as if considering the question. The pope gathered in his robes, as if checking for dust, while his mind scrambled for an elegant exit. 'Your Majesty has also shown considerable interest in leading the next Crusade to the Holy Land. Perhaps you will do so after we have completed our review of Boniface by council?'

It was a move to the weakest ground for the French king. Unlike Edward the Plantagenet, Philip had never fought the Saracen. It was the king's turn to stay silent.

'Grand Master, do continue with your report,' the pope added, summoning up all his experience and skill, to mask his growing alarm.

Jacque, relieved to be rescued by Pope Clement's skill in linking the king's demand to crusade, moved on. 'Baybars, the powerful Mamluk leader, once said that he would confront up to thirty thousand Tartars but not more than fifteen thousand Frankish knights – that, faced with such numbers, the Mamluks would retire from the field. Our plan is based on his words: to bring one large hammer-blow to bear, and scatter them before us.'

Jacque cast a look towards Geoffrey, who nodded for him to continue. They had rehearsed their defence of the Order all the way on the ride from Paris to Poitiers, both grasping that this was the key moment since the loss of Outremer. Jacque pressed on as they had planned. 'Holy Father, your predecessors have often examined uniting the military orders of Mother Church, and each time the pope decided not to do so, but I understand that it is always wise to revisit strategy.'

Opposite Geoffrey, de Nogaret stirred in his chair, leaning forward to ensure that no words went unheard by him. This was the key moment for the Crown. Jacque paused for a moment, choosing with care the words he had rehearsed. 'The Church has been well served by the separation of Orders – Templars, Hospitallers and Teutonic Knights – each bringing its own talents to bear. The natural competition between them makes for a sum which is greater than its parts. Members of each Order have pledged their lives to it, not to an unnatural compound. The different hierarchies, culture and properties would create much confusion, and to what end? ULtimately, the Holy Father requires effective fighting and administrative forces, which are sharpened by rivalry, not comradeship. If the Templars transport a large number of brothers, horses and equipment to Outremer, the Hospitallers would not rest until they, too, had done as much. If the Templars excel as a fighting force, the Hospitaller knights would respond in kind. Together, we have formed both the vanguard and rearguard of armies on crusade for generations.'

The pope listened closely, smiling, noting how the Grand Master had skilfully avoided dealing with the vast savings to be made by uniting the Orders – a point not lost, he knew, on king Philip or on the papal court.

The king was next to speak. 'Grand Master, the discipline of the Templars is renowned across the years of its service, but how do you hold that discipline together among the brothers, especially when some are in need of confession?'

It was an extraordinary question of church law, out of step with the flow of conversation. Geoffrey almost jumped out of his chair, alarmed that the smooth words of the king masked the deep thrust of his rapier. Geoffrey knew it was a trap, and that his proud friend might not sense the peril in it. He cast a look towards de Nogaret, who was now grinning openly at him.

Jacque, as Geoffrey feared, did not sense a trap, but saw instead an opportunity to reinforce the rigid rule of the monks. 'Highness, we maintain a hard discipline among the brothers, who are aware of the harshness of penance for confessions – which is why, as Grand Master, occasionally, I will hear a brother's sin confessed.'

Interrupting the conversation, and visibly uncomfortable, the pope had risen suddenly from his seat, his hands clasping his robes over his bowels, his pallor whitening. 'Your Majesty, Grand Master, you will have to excuse this old pope, but my insides growl for attention. I must away to the garde-robe and leave you. The *camerlengo* will sit for me.'

Used to the pope's sudden need to leave meetings, the papal staff moved swiftly, with practised ease, to whisk him from the audience to the privacy of his quarters – and to fresh clothing. The king also rose to leave, his court rising with him, but he paused beside the Grand Master and, as if as an afterthought, enquired further, 'Tell me, Jacque, when confession ceases, do you administer the kiss of peace in the manner of joining the Order?'

Geoffrey, at the base of the dais, overheard the king's words and instinctively raised his hand in warning to Jacque. But it was too late.

'It is a common custom, Your Majesty. And yes, it is ours as well,' Jacque responded, genuflecting towards Philip as he passed.

In that instant, Geoffrey felt hot breath in his ear, and heard a low whisper. 'Templar, for hearing confessions outside of priestly ordination, for the fire-powder in Paris, and for that last admission, the sands now fall. There is no escape, not from me, not from my king and not from your destiny. Real flames, Templar, not the trick fire over Paris.'

Geoffrey spun around, to find de Nogaret's reddened face up close, pulsating with menace. He returned the stare and growled, 'Hound, begone from here, from holy ground, deceiver, spout of lies, poisoner. That tongue will strangle you yet.'

CHAPTER 16
Royal Palace, Poitiers

King Philip bounded up the steps of the royal palace at Poitiers, eager to confer with de Nogaret, who jogged behind, trying to keep pace with the king's sudden burst of energy. Philip breezed past courtiers and staff who were lingering, hoping to gain the king's attention for their pleadings. 'Not now, later,' he growled as he strode intently through them, chin forward, eyes ablaze. De Nogaret followed, dismissing the royal retinue by gesture, and closed the doors. Both men knew that the moment had arrived. The king spun around. 'You heard him, did you not? That arrogant old fool has gifted us the Templar wealth, right in front of the pope.'

'The elegance of it is that neither pope nor Templar noticed that a trap had been sprung. The one was distracted by his innards, the other by his pride.' The Hound grinned. 'Esquin de Floyran, our source, earns his three thousand *livres* – a cheap price for which Your Majesty may extract all the wealth of the Templars in France. It was supremely well played.'

This time, the king chose to accept the flattery, for it was true. He had played his hand with great skill. The admission by the Grand Master confirmed the testimony of de Floyran, and the reports from the agents planted by de Nogaret throughout the Templar estates. It was no longer gossip, but an established admission – which he knew could be transformed to support allegations of foul relations between Templar monks. All that was needed was to move the location of the kiss from mouth to navel.

'Extraordinary, too, that the Grand Master, who is not an ordained priest and cannot hear confessions, admits to the practice in front of the pope, as if the rules of the Church held no meaning to the upper orders of the Knights Templar.'

'Do we move to the second phase of Your Majesty's plan? Do we now destroy the Templars, who are surely beyond sanctuary, even for the pope?'

Silence followed the question. King Philip paced in calculation, weighing up the risks and the timing, seeing in his mind's eye the royal treasury rooms brimming with Templar gold and silver, the blue and gold royal banner replacing the black and white Templar *baucent*, flying proudly over their vast estates and castles. His fingers twitching in anticipation, his mind raced to a France free of the state within it, the skyline of Paris forever altered. He craved an *oriflamme* flapping in the wind over le Gros Tour. 'Here is my instruction: go and prepare sealed letters for the officers of the realm, to be opened a month hence. Follow the path we dealt the Jews last summer. Let no one know what is therein contained, save us, then strike harder than we have ever done before. We will bring the full might of my realm down on these heretics, catch them asleep, and squeeze until the poison seeps from their wounds into the dirt. Use the harshest inquisitors. We must leave no room for Clement's wind.' The king grinned at his own pun.

'The inquisitors, Your Majesty, will report to William of Paris, the Dominican friar? I presume that you wish me to remind him of his duties to the king?'

'That creature knows to whom his duty falls. He will relish the opportunity to test his inquisitors on Templar flesh, but persuade him in your usual manner if he needs to be convinced. There, it is done. The trap is set. Finally, France is to be free of this disgrace to the Church: heretics and sodomites all, an affront to Christendom.'

'With what words would Your Majesty wish to grace his sealed letters?' De Nogaret was poised, pen over parchment, expecting a royal flourish in this supreme moment of triumph.

King Philip grinned like a wolf, imagining his lowly officials breathlessly breaking the king's seal after a month's isolation, and coping with the shock of its contents: the raiding and arrest of the untouchables, the Templars. He clasped his hands behind his back, considered his audience and addressed it, as if it was the full royal court. 'There has recently echoed in our ears, to our not inconsiderable astonishment and vehement horror . . . .' The king paused.

'Vouched for by many people worthy to be believed?' de Nogaret added helpfully, and received a nod of approval.

'A bitter thing, a lamentable thing, a thing horrible to contemplate, terrible to hear, a heinous crime, an execrable evil, an abominable deed, a hateful disgrace, a completely inhuman thing, indeed remote from all humanity.'

Philip paused to give the lawyer time to catch up, then chose to move to his duty to exact justice, as a Catholic king. 'Having weighed up its seriousness, we felt the full immensity of our grief increase in us, the more bitterly as it became evident that crimes of this nature and importance were so great as to constitute an offence against the Divine Majesty, a loss for the orthodox faith and for all Christianity, a disgrace for humanity, a pernicious example of evil and a universal scandal.'

De Nogaret wrote furiously, then downed his pen and applauded the king's cold fury, envisaging officials gasping at the words, their blood pumping hot, their desire to extract the king's justice screaming for release. 'That, Your Majesty,' he said with satisfaction, 'ought to set the ravenous foxes loose in the hen-house, without pause or favour.'

The king sat and let the emotion pass, his mind quickly cooling, and turning to current matters. 'Well, what fresh intelligence do we have on the Templars, from Ireland?'

'We traced the Templar party first to Chartres, then to St Pol de Leon in Brittany, cornering them at the coast – or so it was thought. I regret to report that our pursuit-party, hand-selected all, the best we had, were slain. According to local fisherwomen, the handful of Templars were joined by what I believe to be wild Gaels, and together they butchered our party, to a man.'

The king sat up. 'This tells me that a fresh game is afoot. Why would a party of Gaels accompany the Templar monk to my realm, except to safeguard something, or someone, and to return to Ireland?'

'Precisely so, my king,' de Nogaret replied. 'There was a short-haired young warrior, without the distinctive long hair of the Gaels, and – a surprise to my ears – a young woman who might be from the Levant or further south, who was being carefully protected by the group.'

'Secret meetings, Mongol fire-powder, Gaels, Templars... and now they go to Ireland?'

'Indeed, Your Majesty. Their boat was last seen rounding Ile de Batz, making towards the north-west. I had anticipated this outcome, and had already commissioned a small fleet ready to set off in pursuit. I sent a note on your behalf to young King Edward's court to seek help in Ireland, saying that the matter related to heresies, and to concerns shared by Pope Clement at Poitier.'

'Nicely played, Guillaume. I must have all of it, everything of the Templars. The treasure they seek is mine, so spare nothing in recovering it – short of trouble with England. How can we be assured that the new English king will assist, and not seek to thwart our endeavours?'

'Young Edward is informed that the heresy includes a rite to deny Christ three times, to kiss naked men on spine, navel and mouth, and to spit on the holy image of Christ.'

'Careful, Guillaume. All that kissing of men might cause my son-in-law to apply to the Templars himself.' The king chuckled. 'You expect the young king to grasp the opportunity to turn attention away from his favourite noble, Piers Gaveston?'

'Indeed, that is my expectation. Your Majesty will recall the widely reported confrontation between his father, Longshanks, and himself when the young fool had pleaded against Gaveston's banishment to Gascony?'

'Ah yes, I learned of it with some amusement – and a little admiration. Longshanks still had enough vinegar in his old bones to pull fists full of hair from the head of the brat before manhandling him out of his chambers.'

'Your Majesty is correct, but with his father fresh in the ground, young Edward now continues his extravagance towards Gaveston. Despite Longshanks' dying wishes, the king has already recalled him from Gascony, making him first Earl of Cornwall.'

'It is telling that the new King of England relies so much on nobles – unlike his father. First, we take all the wealth of the Templars, and then we secure the English Crown through Isabella. Heaven save Edward and Gaveston from the wrath and cunning of my daughter,' the king mused.

The spymaster winced as he left the king. He was glad the little viper would be at the English Court soon, and he looked forward to getting her there. The sooner this poxy wedding could be arranged, the better.

CHAPTER 17
The Atlantic

The Birlinn, under a full complement of rowers, had pulled powerfully and gracefully out of the Isle de Siecke, and set a north-westerly course away from the French coast, her square sail filling with the prevailing breeze, and spelling her name: *Briganti*. The breeze had stiffened to a wind which chased away the clear sunshine, bringing low rolling clouds which darkened the horizon to the west. Each time the boat lifted, as the force of the gusts caught her sail. Her elevated bow carved through the waves, while the boat keeled to starboard, balancing herself as the south-westerly wind slipped the head of the sail. The Kern, at the tiller, deftly helmed the seas, while barking orders in Gaelic to tighten or loosen the main sheets and braces, forever searching for perfect balance.

Under instructions from Guiscard, Fabian and Rostan rotated watch at the stern, their younger eyes scanning the horizon to the rear for any signs of mischief. Occasionally, they spotted isolated vessels a good way off, travelling either back to the French coast or northwards, on course to England.

Esi watched it all, mesmerised. She already felt comfortable with the Gaels. They had engaged with her as an equal in her early attempts to learn some of their language. She was enjoying the experience, so very different from the Mediterranean crossings she recalled. The seas to Cyprus and Marseilles had nothing like this raw wildness. Ever alert, Cormac stood close by, acting as her interpreter, and watching out for her balance as the Briganti whipped through the seas and spray.

'Cormac!' she yelled over the wind, pointing to the square sail in full belly, sheets creaking from the strain. 'What is in this name, Briganti?'

'That's Bríg, in their ancient lore. She is the goddess of rebirth. She is celebrated on February first, which they call *Imbolg*. But Bríg goes back a long, long way, before the Celts.'

'The first day of spring!' Esi shouted. 'That makes sense. But what is she doing on the mainsail of a Christian ship a thousand years later?'

Esi moved closer, linking arms and nuzzling close to the young man, to lessen the need to shout above the noise of the wind and aid her balance – or so she told herself. 'The early Irish Church was Arian. About fifteen years after the death of Hypatia of Alexandria, Pope Celestine I ordained Palladius of Poitiers to convert the Gaels and Scots. He arrived before your Saint Patrick. Did you know that, Cormac?'

Cormac pulled in his breath, cupped his hands over her ear and whispered, 'Don't mention the idea of two Patricks loudly; the saint is precious to the Gaels.' Esi lowered her voice, holding Cormac closer. 'Eight centuries later, why did an English pope want to see an invasion, if not to stamp out the remnants of paganism, and suppress the wild and independent Irish church, as Rome saw it?'

'True, Esi, it is still a tribal land. There was no Roman reform here, so the hot breath of paganism blows through into our time. Many Gael priests and abbots married and had children; not Rome's way.'

Esi hooted with laughter. 'Well, if there is one thing that most upsets Church fathers, it is the thought of some of its priests openly enjoying the pleasures of women, while they do not.'

Before she could stop herself, she elbowed Cormac playfully, but instantly berated herself for her lack of control. The young man reddened, but smiled warmly before continuing. 'Gaels still hold four days to be sacred, Esi, in their cycle of birth to death. *Imbolg*, the first day of spring, is Bríg's festival. *Bealtaine*, the first day of summer, is when fires were lit at Uisneach, then across the hilltops. *Lughnasadh*, named after the god Lugh, marks the harvest season on August first. Finally, there is *Samhain*, on the first of November. This is the Gaels' most favoured time, halfway between the autumn equinox and the winter solstice, the festival of the dead, when the threshold into the world of the spirits is at its thinnest.'

Esi took to studying the crew on the Briganti. Both Gael and Templar worked seamlessly, managing the sheets, and taking turns to helm at the tiller. There was much mirth-making and joking among the Gaels, poking fun at each other and bellowing with laughter, as if a running joke was, to them, like breathing. Their language was very different to French, holding its own strange rhythm.

Cormac gestured for Ultan to join them, making space on the low bench that spanned the inside of the boat. 'Ultan, Esi wonders about the land to which we draw near, the land of your ancestors. How would you describe the difference between Norman and Gael?'

Esi was delighted at the turn of conversation. She stared into Ultan's ruddy complexion. His great beard was matched by waist-length red hair, braided, but with the *cúlán*, a long wisp of hair combed forward over a half-shaved head, creating a cave-like effect on the face. It is like sitting next to a great wolf in his lair, she thought. She gently touched his hand closest to her, and gave it an encouraging squeeze. Ultan flashed a huge grin, filled his lungs with sea air and began, in his strangely toned French, 'We are an island people but we travel wide, keep the poems, stories nand songs of the *filí* deep within us. We pass these to our children, not through parchments but by the fireside. Our rules of custom and hospitality bind us.'

Esi clapped her hands, as she was wont to do when she was excited by new knowledge. 'That is wonderful! A tribal people who emerge straight out of the mists of time, before Rome, yet your scholar monks spread their Christianity across Europe in a conquest of education. How does the Gael differ in matters of custom and law?'

'We are a land of tribes. We do not decide succession by oldest male heir,' Ultan replied. 'We have known High Kings, but the island is divided into smaller kingdoms. Kingship is granted through our *tanistry*, so a man is elected king and a member of his father's line is elected to become *Tánaiste*, to succeed him when the king dies. All freemen can improve their lot by merit, by skill, by valour.'

Esi fixed Ultan with one of her stern stares, and came to the summit of her questions. 'How do you differ in the treatment of womenfolk? Are they the chattels of men?'

Ultan threw his head back and gave a long bark of a laugh, saying something aloud in Gaelic that caused the crew to chuckle with mirth.

Esi found herself laughing along with the Kerns, turned towards Cormac and quietly asked, 'What have I said that is so funny?'

'Esi, you clearly have not met many Gaelic women. Despite what you might think, this is not a patriarchal society, it is *matriarchal*. The Irish mother is greatly feared by hulking bears like Ultan, who dote upon them and seek wives who mimic them. Just don't say that to them. It is rather a sore point.'

Esi's eyes opened wide. 'Ultan, explain how the rights of Gaelic women are not bound to those of their husband?'

'In our ways, marriage is that of equals. While Gaelic women are dependent on their husbands, this is not an absolute. Although land must pass through the father's line, women may own cattle, horses and other things by themselves. Women may marry from age fifteen – eighteen for men. The husband pays her family a dowry, which is kept by her and her family when the husband is responsible for causing the marriage to fail.'

'What happens, Ultan, if the husband beats his wife?' Esi asked.

'A wife may seek divorce or separation just as easily as a husband, and she keeps all the property she brought to the marriage. This is why we laughed at your question. A few of the lads here were married once – except Cormac, who by Gaelic law is underage.'

Ultan slapped Cormac on the back and laughed heartily at the young man's evident discomfort. Esi looked amused, and remained wrapped tightly to him.

As the Briganti rounded the Isles of Scilly, off Cornwall, the breeze stiffened into a heavy wind. Heavy seas made the crew turn serious, as the Kerns struggled to maintain their course. At the height of the squalls, they responded like lightning to barked commands from the helmsman.

This sudden change in energy alarmed Esi, who was unused to coping with the rapid winds which roamed these waters like great beasts. Her enthusiasm when leaving the sun-kissed coast of Brittany had given way to concern as they crested each giant wave, staring into the deep troughs that followed, as if readying to swallow the Briganti whole. The Gallowglass twins laughed loudest at moments of greatest danger, taunting the Atlantic to try its worst. The storm lasted a full day before subsiding into the night. Morning light, breaking from behind, pointed the Briganti towards home, as the seas slowly calmed. Esi had managed a broken sleep, tucked up snugly between Cormac and Guiscard, her dreams full of the images painted by Ultan, imagining that the land was beckoning to her, as if completing an old promise.

Guiscard rose, his bulk blocking the bow-view, straining his eyes, seeking a dark line on the far horizon. 'Look, there she is. The coast of Ireland, still a thin line before it fills our view.'

Esi jumped up, relief spreading through her that at last she would be free of the confines of the boat, and the close company of its crew. She longed to be around other women, away from prying men's eyes, even if for a short while. Their course altered to north-west, the sails filling again, the breeze making the sheets creak as the Briganti lurched forward in reply.

All eyes looked at the horizon as it started to fill, just as Guiscard had predicted; all, that is, except Fabian. At the stern, the monk scanned the horizon to the rear, then moved quietly forward to Guiscard, talking to him in a low tone, out of earshot of the crew. The old monk stiffened, took in a large breath and sighed, before engaging in drawn-out conversation with the young monk. Esi sensed a change: something was afoot; everyone knew it.

Guiscard turned to address them, mixing French and Gaelic. 'We are being followed – or so it seems. Fabian thought he had spotted movement on the far horizon before we hit the storm, in the quieter waters off the toe of England. We hoped that it wasn't so, but the same three specks still follow us.'

Guiscard raised his hand for calm. 'It means that de Nogaret has been a step ahead. He cannot have planned a pursuit that quickly: not without information, not without knowing more than we thought he knew, from the moment I landed in France. This gives us less time than I had hoped. More cause for speed, and more reason to expect surprises. If a small French fleet follows, it can only do so with the approval of the English Court – which puts our journey through the heart of Ireland in great peril.'

Ahead, the great lighthouse loomed large at the mouth of Waterford harbour, but the mood on the Briganti had changed. Gone was the sense of adventure, replaced with the glum realisation that their odds of survival had just shortened, that they faced a cunning, informed and resourceful foe, and the certainty of a hostile reception as they travelled through the island.

Cormac, anticipating more questions from Esi as she absorbed the news, spoke to her quietly. 'Esi, remember that large parts of Ireland remain Gael. Their allegiance to Longshanks, King Edward, is no different to any foreign monarch; it is a convenience, used to gain advantage locally. Norman power wanes because the Gael have learned how to resist, and have been strengthened by their Gallowglass. Chieftains grow in strength in south-west Munster, in Connaught, in Ulster, and in the mountains of Wicklow. Normans have built cities and towns on the coasts and rivers – at Cork, Limerick, Dublin and Waterford – and we may yet dock this day in New Ross before heading towards Kilkenny. These are all strongpoints held by Norman stone – but beyond, well, that is another matter. You will see.'

Cormac pointed Esi's attention to the most south-easterly outcrop of Ireland. 'Swathes from Rome arrived through here: the Dominicans brought learning; the Franciscans work among the poor; the Benedictines brought the illumination of manuscripts; the Cistercians, improvements in agriculture; even the Templars have added knowledge of banking. But none have fully captured the mind of the Gael.'

Esi considered Cormac's words as the Briganti surged forward. Her eyes were drawn to Duncannon fort on the starboard promontory, then out past the stern of the Briganti. On the far lip of the horizon, three cogs of the royal French fleet were cutting quickly through Irish waters. *Nom de Dieu*, she thought. What more can go wrong?

CHAPTER 18
New Ross

After sailing through the great mouth of Waterford harbour, Guiscard faced a choice: to sail into Waterford city, or push deeper up country. He had been worried that they were being hunted ever since the skirmish in Brittany, and consulted with Fabian to determine the likely composition, tactics and numbers they faced on the French cogs. Together, the two Templars pored over Guiscard's maps.

'My sense, Fabian, is that they are likely to steer a course to the west once into the harbour. They will presume we are heading towards Waterford port and castle' – he pointed his finger along the narrowing mouth of the estuary – 'but if we sail our lighter boat northwards, up the Barrow estuary towards New Ross, we can quickly provision, and reach Kilkenny Castle by nightfall. What do you think?'

The young Templar studied the maps closely. 'The Hound is angry. He thought he had us in his grip, but his men failed. He will be humiliated by the loss of his hunting party. It's not as he envisaged, but he is cunning, and won't make the same mistake again. He will come here better armed and resourced, and in greater numbers. He will seek allies of the English, here, and buy help with French silver. It will include local trackers, that is certain. He will follow, but not spring at us until we have discovered our prize. It is what I would counsel in his place.'

'I agree, Fabian. We have, at most, two days' start, and can travel fast, but the countryside hereabouts, though quiet now, will become hostile once the French arrive. It also means that the corridor we take is but one way. We go north to Uisneach, but we cannot return as we have come. It has brought me to a painful decision.'

'You intend to split the group?'

'Aye, Fabian, I do. I will have need of robust fighting skills. Rostan seems to have made close friends with those two demons; they are a formidable trio at close quarters. When we get to Uisneach, we will be in a different country, in lands contested between Norman and Gael, and will need all the help of the Gaels if our project is to succeed. You, Fabian, will need to stay with the boat, with the Kern, and take her back to sea.'

'But in what direction?'

Guiscard consulted his map, drew his finger across a portion of it, and tapped. 'There. That is where you must take her.'

Fabian's eyes opened wide. 'That is a huge challenge, even for the Kern.'

'Easterly winds will help. If we follow Jean's plan, there is no other way, brother. We cannot return back south, or travel through Cork or Dublin to get to La Rochelle.'

Fabian extended his hand to Guiscard. 'It seems as if I am going to have to brush up on my seafaring Gaelic, then.'

'Lots of Gaelic swear-words will do the trick, Fabian.'

The younger monk grinned. *Snaidhm bundúin ort!'* – 'May your anus be knotted! – Guiscard bellowed. 'You'll make a sailor yet, Fabian!'

He beckoned to Cormac and Esi to join their discussion as the Briganti passed the mouth of the Blackwater to Waterford, and turned northwards towards New Ross harbour. 'Cormac, I will need you to make an inventory for a party of six to travel for fourteen days. Everything you will need may be got at New Ross: there are trades of all kinds, fresh and salted meats and fish, cloths, animal skins, horses, carts, cheese, butter, flour. But we move at speed. When we dock, the Briganti must leave immediately. We are to proceed but keep a low profile – which means talking to no one.'

Cormac nodded. He had been to New Ross before on market-days, and knew it to be bustling with trade, and a great spot for gossip.

Guiscard then turned to Esi. 'Young woman, that mind of yours has had plenty of time to think about Uisneach. What will we find there, and what will we need? We will have little time for error, that is now certain, for the French will be snapping at our heels.'

Esi considered her words carefully, knowing how much rested on her shoulders. 'Ultan talks of a hill, the ancient centre of Ireland, but the land thereabouts is not crowned with a Norman castle. This makes sense. Castles have been built at strategic points for defence. Uisneach was built for its sacred position. In its heyday, during Hypatia's time, it was thought to have had great wooden halls in circular ring-forts, common to the Gael, but at high elevation, where its grand structure was visible for many miles, just like the cathedral at Chartres.'

'So, it's a hilltop with the ground-marks of old ring-forts, distant from castles and towns. But how do you find a casket, nearly a thousand years later, in such a place?' Guiscard asked.

'I wish I knew for sure, but I have another plan, although it involves taking a huge risk,' Esi replied. 'I will figure it all out when we get there, when I see what Hypatia must have seen through the eyes of ancient travellers. I need to envisage what the Hill of Uisneach looked like, at its height, before the coming of Christianity, when tribal people venerated Lugh and Bríg and lit the fire of *Bealtaine* from its ridge.'

Guiscard sighed. 'Not a great plan, young woman, especially with the French on our heels. There will be little time to scout. We will need to get in, and out, fast.'

Esi shrugged, acknowledging the dilemma. 'We have no choice but to rely upon Hypatia's guile. She will have anticipated that the casket would need to be stored for a long time. It is why she chose a pure metal. She knew that the Church would not be ready for what it contained, not for a long time. I also suspect that whatever is inside, is also carefully crafted to survive for centuries. She was a woman of the stars, Guiscard, and understood great measurements of time. I will begin there, through her eyes. That is as much as I can give you, until we reach the hill.'

Seeing Guiscard's puzzled look as he absorbed her words, Esi added, 'I suspect we will find the casket, if it is still there, in a souterrain.'

'Very well, Esi.' Guiscard beamed, and turned to address the crew in French and Gaelic, outlining his plan, and the thinking behind it. After Guiscard's address and hurried preparations on board, the *Briganti* pulled gracefully into the bustling docks at New Ross. The crew blended in, just another sea-voyager returning after a successful trading mission. Ropes were thrown to secure the boat in the falling tide. Esi, Guiscard, Cormac and Rostan disembarked, eyes cast downwards, while the Gallowglass shoved the *Briganti* clear, joking to Kern about how to stay clear of loose women and bad drink.

Fabian, mimicking their accents, yelled back to shore, drawing a chuckle from them, '*Lá breá ag do chairde – dod adhlacadh.*'

Cormac whispered to Esi, 'He says, may your friends have a fine day burying you.'

She giggled under her hood. 'Looks as if the monk is learning the sailor's tongue a bit fast.'

Guiscard's party made their way from the docks to the town, Cormac guiding Esi through the crowds, to deflect any questions about her unusual looks. Two hours later, on fresh horses, with a small wagon full of provisions which included digging tools, tents, food and fresh clothes, the group left the walled town of New Ross and rode to the confluence of the two rivers above it. They paused to check that they were not being pursued, then headed west along the lazy banks of the River Nore, towards the huge fortress upriver: Kilkenny Castle. The riders made good progress on solid underfoot conditions across the fertile lands the Nore divided. The late-afternoon sun revealed the land's abundance in wildlife, birds and insects. The natives, Gael and Norman alike, took little notice of the small party travelling the pathways of the river, presuming them to be trading between the two cities.

They stopped to rest and water horses at Inistoige, one of the lowest crossing-points of the river. Esi, delighted with the rest, wandered to the bank of the river, testing its temperature and current with Cormac, who continued to mind her and act as her guide.

'All around here, Esi, was the first place to feel the heat of the Norman invasion. Like the Vikings before them, they followed the great rivers up from Waterford. It is why William Marshal built his castle at Kilkenny. The Normans had learned from the mistakes of their ancestors, the Vikings. This land was once the Gaelic kingdom of the Osraige. Where you stand, they routed the Vikings of Dublin in 964 in a great slaughter.'

'Hard to imagine this being a place of death, Cormac; it is so beautiful,' she replied as her pony drank its fill of fresh water.

Guiscard was first back into the saddle, anxious to keep up the pace. 'Remount: we must leave the Nore, for Thomastown, at the bend, just up ahead.'

But Esi remained on the ground. She glared defiantly at the big monk, hands on her hips, and raised her voice to address the group, as if talking to children. 'Since we left Coulommiers, in what seems like another lifetime, I've been attacked by villainous creatures on the sands of Brittany, galloped across half of France, much of it in the dark, bashed by the heaving Atlantic swells and then rushed through New Ross like a prize cow. Now, much as I fear our pursuers, I crave a swim, gentlemen – and a swim I will have! Cleanliness might not mean much to you, but it does to me. So, Guiscard, you can get your fulsome arse down off that poor steed and rest your bones because, pursuit or not, this woman is taking a bath.'

With that, Esi turned on her heel and, clutching a small bag, marched towards a grove of trees overhanging a shallow pond adjacent to the ford, where she started to disrobe. She was determined not to look back, but make her way into the waters with her most treasured possession. The Castile soap had been a gift from Marguerite at the Béguinage; she had secreted it in her bag just before their departure, advising her to apply it liberally, and never to await the nose of a man. Moments later, the soap, made from olive oil and potash, was gliding around her dusty skin like a golden eel brought to life by the soft river-currents.

Esi need not have feared a hostile reaction from her companions. Hearing a loud whoop and cry, she turned just in time to see five bare bottoms rush into the river and splash about like plucked geese trying to take flight. She swam around in circles, loving the feel of the cold current cooling her body, cleaning the grit, salt and dust that had matted on her for days. We must stink like fish guts, she thought, as she went to work cleaning and rubbing, dipping her hair in and out of the water, feeling the act purify her.

The men left the river to Esi, and dried off in the sun, happy to have had the opportunity to refresh themselves. 'Just as well we did that,' Guiscard barked as he squeezed back into his clothes and mail. 'We wouldn't stand a chance of mixing with the fine folk of Kilkenny Castle smelling like sewer rats. The inns would always take us, for sure, but castle folk? They prefer a sweeter air. So, consider this little diversion an investment in where we sleep tonight.'

The group mounted and waited at a discreet distance, to allow Esi to dress herself and comb her hair. She was in no rush to get back in the saddle, and took her time, ignoring the impatient coughing of the men. Guiscard led the disapproval, casting his eyes to heaven as she walked her horse back to the path and mounted to join them. 'Right then, Templars and Gaels, let us go. I feel like a new woman.'

Guiscard groaned loudly as the group laughed, everyone having been energised by the Nore.

Esi surprised them by pushing past Guiscard, who had been leading out the party, on her small horse, shouting in thick Gaelic: *'Má ithis, nar chacair.'* With that, she pinched her stirrups into the belly of the horse and set off at a clip, leaving the group to catch up.

Guiscard beamed his approval. 'That woman is finally learning!' he yelled at the Gallowglass.

'Indeed she is, Guiscard,' Ultan replied. 'She wished you a rich digestive experience with your next meal.'

'Did she indeed? That's so nice of her!' Guiscard roared, as he and Cormac galloped off after her.

Tears streamed from Ultan's eyes as explained the source of the amusement to Rostan. 'She just told your fat leader: if you eat that, you may not shit!'

The young warriors giggled for miles, getting much fun from the thought of Guiscard squatting and groaning with impatience while passing nothing but wind.

CHAPTER 19
Kilkenny

Under the late-afternoon sun, the group made good progress, heading across open country to Bennetsbridge, within two leagues of Kilkenny. Guiscard led them in single file to the bridge, where he and Cormac engaged some travellers in small-talk, their purpose to gather intelligence from the traders streaming out from the city, making their way home.

Guiscard spotted a group of merchants in an assembly of empty wagons, and trotted over with Cormac, guessing that their owners, satisfied with the day's trading, had taken to Kilkenny's inns before beginning their journey south.

'It doesn't take much beer, wine or mead to loosen these tongues,' he remarked to Cormac, 'but it does help.' He trotted over to the traders. 'Greetings and good trade to you,' he began. 'What news from the city of affairs with the Uí Mháine?'

The merchants, Guiscard knew, would note his use of the Gaelic reference to the troublesome region, rather than its Norman translation, Hy-Many. The nearest, a stout fellow, unsteady on his feet, his cheeks flushed with wine, took it upon himself to lead the conversation. 'Fine day, Templar. Grand stretch in it altogether. 'Tis obvious you've been away from these parts, for there has been a great slaughter at Ahascragh on the other side of the great river, beyond Lough Ree. Many were slain by the O'Kellys in retribution for the burning of townlands by Edmund Butler, the Justiciar of Ireland.'

Guiscard feigned mild interest but gently touched Cormac's arm, to alert him not to interrupt. Uisneach lay within a day's march of Lough Ree, through which the River Shannon drained before continuing on its course, more than two hundred miles, to the Atlantic. Both knew the lands to be hotly contested by the O'Kelly chieftain who had led the Gaelic resurgence in his kingdom.

'What is the outcome of the contest?' Guiscard asked.

'Many prisoners are taken in ransom after putting the Normans of Roscommon to the sword. Included in the catch is the Sheriff and many of his officers. Imagine!' The merchant chuckled at the thought, before gathering himself. 'Tis a grim tale, and surely will cause more widespread mischief than the great slaughter at Callann in Desmond, by McCarthy Mór.'

Guiscard nodded his thanks to the merchant and turned his horse towards his group, beckoning them off the path to the water, out of earshot of the travellers. 'Well, Cormac, what do you make of that surprise?'

'If O'Kelly has achieved what McCarthy Mór did at Callann, then matters have taken a major step backward for Norman power in much of the west. Callann shut down the south-west to the Normans for nearly fifty years.'

'Aye, Cormac, that is the truth. O'Kelly appears to have done the same, and so confines Norman power to the east of the Shannon.'

Guiscard eyed his group. 'This reversal opens up the lands around Uisneach for fresh contest. It means that Norman power is in retreat. Quite a turn of events – and useful to us.'

Cormac nodded. 'Guiscard reasons that we may have been granted a gift. If French and English follow us from the south, they may now face a fearsome foe.'

Rostan looked quizzically towards the big monk. 'I don't understand, Guiscard. Why should we concern ourselves with local disputes. Haven't we enough on our hands?

"Because, Rostan,' Guiscard replied, 'the lands around the Hill of Uisneach are now disputed territory. Both Fabian and I expect that the French will approach from the south, with English help. O'Kelly is one the toughest of the Gaelic chieftains, and not one you want facing you, far from your lines of supply. He could prove very handy in a fight, having many more like the twins.'

Rostan looked towards the Gallowglass and asked, 'Many more like them two?'

Guiscard smiled and nodded.

'What's your plan?' Esi asked the big monk, shivering at the memory of the bloodbath in Brittany.

'We do not avoid Kilkenny. Instead, we visit the castle, but leave a false trail. Ultan, you stay outside the walls, ready to deal with any pursuit, in case we have to leave in a hurry. Felim, you are to continue overnight, and make haste to the O'Kelly clan in Meath. Advise them to get word to their leader, Donough Ó Ceallaigh, of a French and English force likely to be coming up from the south, and to gather near the Hill of Uisneach in a few days. Go now.

'Rostan, you are to act as my second. I am known to Sir Gilbert de Bohun, who holds Kilkenny Castle. He is crafty, but his weakness is flattery, wine and spectacle. Cormac and Esi, you are servants travelling with us, and we are on a fact-gathering mission for the Grand Master of the Knights Templar, to test popular support for a Crusade to recapture Jerusalem.' Guiscard turned towards Ultan, placing both hands squarely on his powerful shoulders, and said firmly, 'Listen carefully, Ultan. There is an exit, a wicket-gate locked and lightly guarded from the inside, between the castle and the river. I will need you there. These are not our enemies – at least not yet – so do not leave a trail like the abattoir in Brittany.' The Gallowglass grinned and nodded.

As shadows crept into the evening light, the party reached the walled city of Kilkenny. Guiscard trotted towards the main gate, beyond which lay the hulking castle, with its four sturdy towers. The monk announced his party to the sergeant-at-arms at the portcullis, and was beckoned through uncontested, then escorted towards the great hall.

As they entered the heart of the castle, Guiscard muttered quietly, 'Rostan and Cormac, you I trust, but you, Esi, must promise to keep that big gob of yours firmly shut, no matter what Gilbert has to say.'

Esi glared back at the Templar, squeezing her fists tight, her brow a knot of concentration. She was fighting to suppress a sharp reply. God's bones, Guiscard thought, as the herald announced him, this is going to be touch and go. If he was expecting a chamber full of court officials and wives, bustling with servants, he hid his surprise well. Sitting at the top table was Sir Gilbert de Bohun, who rose from his chair to greet the Templars. But what drew Guiscard's attention was a knight sitting opposite him at the table. 'That knight, he is not English,' Guiscard whispered through gritted teeth. 'You do not see those fine silks in these parts. And there is something oddly familiar about him. Follow my lead, but keep your mouths firmly shut. I sense danger here.'

'Greetings, Guiscard Carrel, Knight Templar. Your presence is always welcome in my humble home.' Gilbert chuckled at his own jest, and said, 'Come, take a seat, and some food. Your companions too.' He pointed to the lower tables, then said, 'Let me introduce you to Simon du Merle. You may know his illustrious father, Foulques du Merle, Marshal of France.'

Guiscard stiffened at the news that a leading French noble was already in Kilkenny, quickly calculating that de Nogaret, must have dispatched him as a single envoy as soon as he had been alerted to Guiscard's arrival in France. 'Greetings to Sir Gilbert from the Order of Knights Templar. Indeed, I do know Foulques du Merle. Who does not, in France? Your illustrious father was appointed Marshal by His Majesty King Philip, alongside whom he fought valiantly at Mons-en-Pévèle. You are in most noble company, Sir Gilbert.'

Simon rose gracefully from his seat, bowing slightly to Guiscard, but his stern eyes belied the courtesy of his greeting as he addressed the monk in high French. 'I thank you, Guiscard Carrel, on behalf of my father's master, King Philip.'

There is indeed danger here, the Templar thought.

'Well, Guiscard,' Gilbert said. 'It has been a while. What brings you out from your hermit-cave in Dun Cannon?'

Guiscard reasoned that Gilbert's attempt at humour masked a snare, and chose to be open with his reply. 'It has not been entirely tiresome, Sir Gilbert. I have been to visit the Grand Master in Paris, at his behest, and returned to measure the desire among the flock to support the pope's call to crusade. We go north to Dublin and work our way through Norman lands, to return via Waterford, through which we arrived.'

He watched Gilbert closely for any sign of knowledge of their arrival through New Ross, and quietly breathed a sigh of relief, finding no suspicion on the face of his host.

'Simon, here, introduced me to the *Libros de los Juegos*. Have you heard of it in Paris? It is the book of games from Castille, learnt from the Arabs. Ha, it is intriguing. A game of conflict and conquest, with four colours for four seasons,' said Sir Gilbert playfully, gesturing for Guiscard and his party to sit.

'The Castilians, however, have another game, Templar,' said the French knight. 'It is a board-game played with *seven* circles in the middle.' Simon paused to let his words sink in.

Guiscard masked his surprise. So, they know about the Septum! It can only mean that we have been more thoroughly infiltrated than Jean estimated.

The Knight, rolling a piece in his hand, like a cat playing with a mouse, continued, 'This game spreads from the seven circles to the twelve symbols of the zodiac, which so fascinated the ancient world. Christians, of course, cannot play with such heresy. It would be at our peril, would it not, Templar?' De Merle fixed Guiscard with a chilling stare.

He was about to reply when he heard Esi clear her throat. Oh hell, he thought. She has not been invited to address the top table, as is the custom. 'Sir Gilbert, as a scholar to the Order, called upon to study old manuscripts, it is intriguing to learn that this game is not from Arabia or Outremer, but is more ancient. It traces to that part of Hindu India conquered by Alexander the Great. Now, there was a military commander for the ages!'

A brilliant stroke, Guiscard thought. She has shifted attention to martial matters.

Gilbert could not resist. 'Why thank you, and indeed it is so, young lady. And you are?'

'Esi Benoit.' Guiscard was quickly back, to wrest control.

'Thank you, Esi Benoit,' Sir Gilbert continued. 'Alexander is indeed remarkable, as was our own William Marshal – and of course let us not forget the legendary fighting prowess of the Knights Templar.'

Simon's face darkened. 'What they each have in common is that they are in the past, including the prowess for battle among the Templars – who, if I am correct, have been fattening themselves in Cyprus ever since running away from the Holy Land. Is it not now a feeble Order made up of old monks and their memories? I wager that none can stand against a knight of France.'

This was a clear challenge, one Guiscard reasoned could not be left unmet – at least not without raising greater suspicion from his host. He chose to use the opportunity to deflect further questions about their mission and sow doubt about their intentions. 'We do not have anyone of your rank and skill among us in Ireland, Simon, but you are welcome to demonstrate your skill with young Rostan, if it will serve you?'

Rostan turned to face Simon and feigned a nervous smile, rising from his seat awkwardly, concealing his normal feline movement.

Gilbert stood up and clapped his hands. 'Delightful! A demonstration of French technique! Clear the centre of the hall,' he cried. 'Bring us the array of ash-swords, that we may have good entertainment and cheer.'

The great hall quickly cleared, as the practice swords were mounted on stacks at both ends, to afford the combatants a choice of lengths and weights. De Merle strode purposely to his position, and chose a long sword without hesitation, his movements concise, confident and efficient.

Rostan hesitated, unsure of which sword to choose, and determined that the lighter and shorter arming sword might be easier to handle. Across the hall, de Merle swung the long sword in huge, smooth arcs, testing its handling and balance. Rostan, meanwhile, stood rooted to the spot, hardly breathing.

Guiscard smiled as he adjusted his seat next to Sir Gilbert, to face the centre of the floor. Rostan was conserving energy, playing the young fool's arrogance masterfully.

'Guiscard, what will you wager on your young Templar?' the Englishman asked.

'Templar monks are forbidden to gamble, as you know, Sir Gilbert, but what I would ask is that, in the most unlikely event that Rostan wins this contest, you will do whatever is required to maintain control over the French noble this night. I fear that his capacity for violence has not yet been tempered by noble maturity, such as your own.'

Gilbert recognised the obvious flattery, but could not resist. 'That is a fair request. I do hope that your young Templar, here, can last a few rounds, or the night's entertainment will be short.'

Out on the floor, the contest began. De Merle closed the gap quickly, moving forward with the long sword, menacingly. Rostan remained still, but repositioned his feet, the left facing forward, gliding over the floor in almost imperceptible movements while adjusting his balance, all the time maintaining eye-contact with his opponent. He placed his arming sword not in the advance position, but behind his back, as if concealing it, and his left arm forward, while keeping all his weight on his back foot.

De Merle saw this opening as a mistake, an opportunity to launch a full attack and finish off the contest. The audience gasped as he lunging with the long sword in a great arc from over his right shoulder downward across his body to his left knee. The objective on the battlefield would be to carve a path through his opponent, from the left collar-bone to the right waist, a cleaving which killed instantly, as innards flowed through the maw that opened across the torso.

As the arc passed through its midpoint, Rostan's back foot shifted at a right angle behind his lead leg. His body was forced to follow in a lightning pivot, which removed him from the space through which the long sword fell. Without pausing, he brought his raised elbow to de Merle's exposed nose. The savage speed and momentum of the blow, intensified by redirecting the oncoming force against him, caused de Merle to stagger back, eyes streaming, nose flattened, blood flowing from both nostrils.

Rostan's pivot continued in another circle, which put him behind his opponent, enabling him to mark the French knight on his exposed neck with his sword. The message was clear: in one swift movement, on the battlefield, de Merle would have been speared by the tip of Rostan's sword from behind, a blow from which no knight could expect to recover. Rostan instantly danced backwards, extending the distance between them without breaking his movement, and re-adopted his opening stance. The entire fluid movement had taken seconds, leaving the hall in stunned silence. The loud crack from the Frenchman's nose breaking echoed through its rafters.

De Merle, bloodied and humiliated, roared *'Fils de pute!'* and lunged forward, attempting to drive the sword-point home as if it were a lance. Rostan shifting his body to the left, leaving a pocket of empty air for the thrust, and repeated the pivot movement, except this time he ended behind the Frenchman, with his right forearm under the chin of de Merle, his left forearm bracing and rotating clockwise under his opponent's chin, applying painful pressure on the throat and windpipe. The Templar rolled and squeezed the chokehold, pulling his opponent backwards so that his feet could not grip the floor, cutting off the knight's air-supply. The long-sword dropped noisily as the Frenchman flopped onto the floor in an unconscious heap. Rostan lifted his arming sword and marked its point between his opponent's eyes, registering a second kill.

The great hall remained silent, stunned by the speed of movement and the swiftness of the felling. French squires ran forward to their prostrate master, to revive him and guide him from the floor. Sir Gilbert gestured his own staff to assist de Merle to his chambers, and away from further mischief.

'Nicely played, young Templar. You move like a cat.' Sir Gilbert grimaced. 'Simon has much to learn. I will see to it that he does so tonight, but advise you to be on your way early, before silver is spread for violence tomorrow. My servants will show you to your quarters. We will guard you until your departure for Dublin.'

When they had retired, and before they reached their sleeping quarters, Guiscard drew them together. 'We do not wait for breakfast. Get a few hours' rest. We leave before daybreak. We have done well to misdirect Sir Gilbert as to our destination, and have bought ourselves a little time, but that is all. He has eyes and ears everywhere. Behind us, we leave a wounded and humiliated foe. We must assume he will shortly be joined by a considerable force coming up from Waterford. Their blood will be bubbling in the heat of the hunt. We must flee.'

CHAPTER 20
Commanderie Notre-Dame-de-la-Boissière, France

Jean sent a message by courier to Jacque and Geoffrey in Poitiers to meet en route back to Paris. The chosen location was on the banks of the Loire: the Commanderie Notre-Dame-de-la Boissière, about thirty miles south-west of Chartres. The spymaster chose this Templar location because it was unlikely to contain agents who were on the payroll of the king.

Jean, after his discussion with Astralabius, took it upon himself to disperse the Order's most precious and controversial manuscripts and relics, rather than leave them to be plucked in Paris. He deemed the city to have become hostile territory, and filled wagons of precious material from the Enclos, disguising them as common trading carts, and stealing out at night with wheels oiled and heavily padded. They were dispersed throughout the Templar Atlantic fleet at La Rochelle, and onward to Templar castles deep in Portugal.

He concluded that the King of France's ambition to unite the Knights Templar with the Hospitallers had changed; that he was bent on crushing the Order. He believed the king would shortly make the attempt to breach the iron veil between Church and State, and fretted as to whether the Church was powerful enough to protect both its absolute authority and its military Orders.

Jean had commandeered the Templar house adjacent to the church and hospital and, accompanied by Astralabius, awaited the arrival of Jacque and Geoffrey from Poitiers. They arrived late in the evening, when candles had burned low.

The four members of the Septum cleared the dinner table for Astralabius' documents, and began their discussion. Geoffrey first recounted the confrontation with king and pope, going slowly over the specific questions raised by the king, ending by reporting de Nogaret's whispered threat word for word – which he left hanging in the air, ominously.

Jacque broke the silence. 'Jean, how do you assess the situation? I am of a mind that the king plans mischief, but is thwarted by the simple fact that the Order reports to the Holy Father rather than to him. Only the pope may have influence upon us. We are accountable to kings, only insofar as we breach temporal laws, and there is no breach here.'

'Grand Master,' Jean replied, 'I do not share your trust in the protection of this French pope. Firstly, I fear Clement is weak; he makes a demonstration of authority, but fears for his own life under the eye of a baleful king. Secondly, Astralabius has told us of the chronic state of the royal treasury, and the debts owed to Venetian bankers and the Knights Templar, so we have much to fear from the rapaciousness of this king. His hunger for gold breathes violence across his kingdom, and he gazes at us across the rooftops of Paris with growing need. This, I am sure of. He has already plundered the Jews and extorted the Lombardian merchants, charging them to be his subjects, yet he thirsts for more. It explains the actions of his Hound. Forgive me, Jacque, but such is my conviction that this is so, that I have already taken steps to prevent worse from happening. Our most valuable items have been spirited out of Paris rather than await the outcome of this meeting.'

Jacque was visibly shocked. 'Do you not think that an overreaction, Jean? The king, for all his power, cannot subsume the power of the Church. Even though Clement is a French pope, is he not bound by more than a thousand years of separation between Church and State?'

'Jacque, if I am wrong, all our precious items will find their way back to Paris, but if I am right, my action will have saved our most precious relics. Black rumours are swirling, not just in Paris, but throughout the land, that the Knights Templar have been engaged in heresies. This includes spitting on the image of the Christ, using pagan rituals that involve carnal knowledge between monks, and worshipping an entity, a pagan head.'

Jacque stood up abruptly. 'But Jean, this is nonsense! Any examination ordered by the pope would quickly reveal it to be so. Philip may unilaterally target the Jews of France and the merchants of Lombardy, and get away with it, but we are of the Holy Church itself. He has no grounds upon which to launch his power against us.'

Jean looked him in the eye and said quietly, 'Jacque, I fear you may be underestimating the hunger of this king, and the wiles of de Nogaret. I concur with Geoffrey: the innocent questions put to you while the pope was distracted contained a poison. He was not engaging in small-talk; he was skewering you. He was gathering evidence.'

The Grand Master turned to the Librarian. 'What say you, Astralabius?'

The old monk paused, then spoke up very quietly, his breath laboured. 'Brothers, what worries me beyond the king, the pope, and their unpleasantness, is something that Esi revealed to me before she fled Paris.'

The room went quiet. The Templars were all aware of the regard in which he held her insight.

'Well, Astralabius, out with it,' said Geoffrey, fearing what was coming.

'Esi had listened with rising alarm to Guiscard's report when he had first arrived in Paris, and asked me many questions about the personality and behaviour of the king. At the Beguinage, she had received reports, from royal cleaning staff, of the king entering into prolonged periods of fasting and meditation, alone in the dark hours, by red candlelight. Putting both together, she concluded that he has been night-walking.'

The Templars jolted at the mention of their sacred rite, assumed to be known only to a few within the Order, in which the use of red light kept walkers midway between sleep and wakefulness, that they might penetrate the veil to the spirit world.

'Esi concludes that Philip may be under an impulse. As you know, she values evidence and knowledge above all, but has arrived at her own interpretation. She shared in confidence with me that she herself was the subject of demonic attention. This coincided precisely with the moment of Cormac's experience in the corridor. This causes her to suggest that Philip may be acting under instruction from another power, not divine, as he may believe, but malign; its mission to destroy all knowledge that challenges it.'

Jean leapt to his feet. 'Astralabius, you should have shared this with me before now! It explains why de Nogaret sent mercenaries across France hoping to capture the young Norman, and why the reports of the departure of a French fleet to Ireland are accurate. We are in more peril than even I suspected!'

The Grand Master steepled his fingers and closed his eyes in thought. 'Brothers, we have done as much as we could, dispersing our valuable knowledge and manuscripts, but the Knights Templar retreat from no foe, temporal or spiritual. We never leave a battlefield; we stand to face this king with the full protection of the Holy Church. There is no other choice, no place to which we may retreat. This is our home. My duty as Grand Master is to the Order, to all of our monks, sergeants and servants from Dublin to Famagusta. We will hold, and we will defend against these pernicious slanders, trusting that our history of service will win the people and the pope. There is no other way.'

Jacque looked across the room, at Jean and Astralabius. 'Brothers, I go to Paris with Geoffrey, to continue as we must. You are free to stay in the field, to continue to act as you deem fit, whatever arises.'

'Grand Master,' Astralabius interjected, 'my bones are too old and failing, my mind too full of books, to be of much use to Jean in the field. With your permission, I will follow the main part of our library to La Rochelle, and to wherever that leads, before resting my head one last time. But mark my words: whatever the Order does, it must protect Esi at all costs. I believe that she is somehow the key to everything, that she has been drawn to us, as we have been to her.'

CHAPTER 21
Uisneach

Guiscard led the group out of the wicket-gate before daybreak, joined up with Ultan, and departed the city without incident as the early-morning sun reddened the clouds. They followed the Nore to its elbow, avoided settlements, and after fifteen leagues skirted the great Norman castle at Dunamase, taking care to stay out of sight. Built upon a natural rock-formation which rose one hundred and fifty feet above the pastures of Laois, on the site of the ancient Celtic fort of Dún Masc, the huge grey castle crouched over the landscape like a great spider.

They camped in thick woodland to the north of the castle, lighting no fire, before turning north-west at daybreak towards their destination. Excitement mounted as they forded the River Bhrosnach, which flowed from Loch Uail to the Shannon. Here they entered the lands which formed the very centre of Ireland. Ahead of them, rising majestically six hundred feet out of the flat, fertile plains, stood their destination: the Hill of Uisneach.

Cormac stood up on his stirrups, taking in the surroundings, envisaging how it must have looked before the coming of Christianity. 'So, this is Cnoc Uisnigh, the place of hearth, their fire-summit, their place of light. This is the great centre from where twenty counties can be seen. By God's bones, it is easy to see why they chose this place, is it not?'

'If you mean a druid's place, Cormac, this place is much older,' said Esi. 'The Celts adopted the cosmology of older races, so this spiritual centre once pulsed with pagan mysticism, long before the Celts got here. My guess is that they practised on this hill in the centre of the island before the Pyramids were raised. Hypatia must have learnt of it through trading routes that ran from here to the Euphrates valley. She deemed this the most northern part of the world when Rome was in full retreat from Britannia.'

Guiscard spun in his saddle towards Cormac. 'Imagine traders arriving here, Cormac, lad, after travelling up the Shannon estuary, disembarking and finding themselves just on this spot, looking up at this, the greatest Celtic hill-fort left in Europe.'

'Aye, Guiscard, I can,' the young man replied.

'Good, Cormac, because we will need you to remember quickly where that box of yours went. Judging by the size of that hill, it is going to require more than a hunch to find it! Come, let us to Uisneach.'

Guiscard urged his horse forward. But when they crested the hill and dismounted, they did so in open-mouthed disappointment. There was nothing on Uisneach, not a single structure.

Esi, seeing her companions crestfallen, broke the silence. 'By the gods, perk up! What did you expect? This site has been abandoned for hundreds of years. The great structures of wood and earth have long since been eroded by wind and rain. What we seek is their echo. Let's scout around, ask the ground to give up its memory. Look for the undulations which marked the great ring-fort, the palace. Find that, and we can begin to lift the veil of time.'

Energised by Esi's command, and respectful of her knowledge, the four set out walking slowly away from the summit, searching in quadrants, with Esi at the centre. It was not long before Cormac call out, 'Look here! There is a slight rise in the ground. It seems to form a huge circle, and beyond, a smaller one.'

Some distance away, Rostan raised his hand. 'It is here too.'

'And here!' Guiscard shouted back. Ultan merely raised his hand and pointed to the ground. They had found the centre of Uisneach.

Esi drew them to her. 'Right here marks the centre. Picture it as a great rounded palace structure, surrounded on its perimeter by its defensive wall, then outside, in concentric circles, many other constructions of various sizes, to house the population. But what we are now looking for is why they chose here. Why this hill? What is it about its features which resonated with their cosmology?'

Ultan, who rarely spoke, raised his hand. 'You mean the old gods, *sorcière*?'

The Templars laughed, leaving the big warrior perplexed. He looked towards Guiscard. 'Ultan, lad, I don't think you meant to call Esi a *sorcière*. That means a *cailleach*, an old witch!' Ultan reddened. The tension had dispersed. As the laughter subsided, the Gallowglass continued, 'Esi, there is more. Much more. Follow me.' He turned to move downhill. 'Over there is a tomb of the ancients. Little remains. It is sometimes called Saint Patrick's Bed.'

'It is much older than Saint Patrick, Ultan,' Esi responded.

'Where the water gathers, below,' Ultan said, pointing down the north slope, 'that is Loch Lugh. Next to it you will see another ring, the remains of the burial-mound of Carn Lughdach.'

Esi clapped her hands. 'So this is the spiritual resting-place of the great God of Light, their messiah?'

'In the old tales,' Ultan continued, 'Lugh leads the Tuatha Dé Danann into a great battle to the north-west, at Loch Arbhach, against their oppressors, the Fomorians, who were led by Balor of the evil eye.'

'The evil eye, I believe, refers to the third eye. The cyclops is a creation to explain those who use the third eye with malice,' Esi added, gesturing for Ultan to continue.

'In Gaelic lore, Lugh kills Balor in the battle with a stone from his sling,' Ultan explained. 'Lugh later died, below there, it is said, speared through the foot and drowned. The harvest festival on August the first, *Lughnasadh*, still bears his name.'

'How it echoes across time, Ultan!' Esi responded. 'In the lore of the Jews, David slays Goliath with a slingshot of stone in battle, announcing himself as someone selected by *Yahweh*, the God of the Jews.'

Guiscard interrupted, 'Can we concentrate on our task? We don't have much time here. If I was to conceal something at this location, it would be far from that water.'

'There is much in the ground here. On the south-west slope, facing the evening sun, is Ail na Mireann, the stone of divisions. It is here that all the borders of the provinces meet,' Ultan replied.

Esi took off in a sprint in the direction pointed out by Ultan, and did not stop until she arrived breathlessly at a great boulder which dominated the hill to its south-west. She was still breathing heavily, trying to control her excitement, when the group caught up with her.

Guiscard was first to ask the question which was on everyone's lips. 'Why is this so important, Esi? It is just an old boulder.'

'Because if you are going to bury something in sacred ground for a very long time, Guiscard, you would choose a marker which could withstand the tempests of time. This is the first reason. The second is that it marks the navel of their boundaries. Not just of the physical provinces but, I believe, also their spiritual one. This exact spot is the centre of Ireland. The place teems with spiritual markers. Remember that it was from here that the light of fire was created; the first fire of *Bealtaine*. Somewhere close to here marks the spot under which there must be a souterrain: that is what I conclude.'

'The boulder is shaped like a twenty-foot cat,' Rostan observed, as he walked lightly around the great limestone rock.

'Not surprising you'd see it that way,' said Guiscard. 'Esi, you may be right about the location, but we do not have weeks and months to spend exploring the ground. We have hours, at best. How do we find it?'

Silence descended. Esi looked towards Cormac, who cleared his throat and addressed Guiscard in a low voice. 'Since we fled France, Esi has spent much time talking to me about my vision, about how I might recall the tiny details, things that I left out when you asked me so many questions at Duncannon. Ever since we arrived here, I have been feeling strange, and that dizzy feeling of familiarity grows, as Esi said it might.'

'What do you remember, Cormac?'

The young man stayed silent and shrugged. 'Nothing much more than you know, Guiscard. That is the problem, isn't it, Esi?'

The group turned to Esi for an explanation. 'I believe that past-life visions are implanted by great emotional events in what you describe as the Book of Lives. Cormac recalled the day Hypatia died because of its trauma: he experienced a force that terrified him, and which drove him here, to the end of the world. I suspect it is here that her slave-companion gave up his life after completing his task, and that his bones lie with her casket.'

'Go on, Esi,' said Guiscard. 'There is more. Why does Cormac pale?'

The group turned to stare at the young Norman. 'Because, Guiscard, Esi's plan, when we got here, was for me to go back into the Way, to look for a detail which would help us find the souterrain, if it is here. It is our only choice. We cannot find it without an army of diggers, provisions and time – none of which we have.'

Guiscard glared at Esi, ashen-faced. 'Are you mad, woman? You are asking this boy to risk facing the Adversary, when it is alerted to him, and in a place where he risks eternal despair? I cannot permit it.'

'It is not up to you, Guiscard,' Cormac said stiffly. 'I have given this much thought. There is no other way; I must try. I think it is why I am here, to do this thing, to finish it.'

Esi shrank from the confrontation. From the first moment they had spoken about the meditation in Duncannon, she had known it would come to this. The two men stood facing each other, anger rising in both.

'Cormac, the last time, this thing nearly took you! How do you expect to return, and not find the way compromised? Don't be a fool. It is a malign intelligence, older than time. That you may be capable of tricking it, is inconceivable. You risk more than your life, boy: you risk everything..'

'I am well aware of what I risk, old man, but this creature is hunting for what was taken or lost to the Nasorean. What it craves is precious to it, and therefore a danger to us all. It seeks to restore the balance of power it had before the Christ.' Cormac was shouting across the hill now. 'I am not relying on my ability to save me, but on that of my ally. I will go again through the early-morning shadow, but I cannot do so without your guidance,' he said loudly, before dropping his voice. 'You must allow it, Guiscard. You simply must, or we are lost.'

Silence lay between the two men, as they weighed up the alternative, which was to flee, empty-handed. Finally, Guiscard spoke. 'You will need to prepare the breath like never before, to go deeper than you have ever been, with an elegance which only comes from many years of practice – and which you do not have. It is a great gamble, Cormac. You must be ready to break back, at my first call. There can be no hesitation because, be quite clear, you are entering its lair. It will come for you.'

Esi looked at the two, keeping silent, her ears prickling. It was the first time she had been exposed to manifest evidence of the esoteric knowledge of the Septum, the circle within all circles of the Knights Templar.

Guiscard addressed her. 'Esi, you will assist. No woman has witnessed the Way before, so what you see and hear, you must never speak about. Do you understand?'

Esi nodded and replied slowly, weighing her words, 'Templar, I know more than I reveal. I am here as a scholar, not a believer. I have studied the parchments unearthed from beneath the temple, and even though I am not an initiate, I already know much of what you hold to be your most sacred knowledge.'

Guiscard studied her quizzically, in silence.

'There is no cross, is there?' Esi said simply. All four men froze at her words. 'All the focus on the material world, the suffering on the Cross, the pain, torture and blood; none of it was formed in literature or imagery until the fourth century, the time of Nicaea. What we have been told, is a tale written by men for the world of men, edited to fit the agendas, ambitions and politics of empire. Even that, on your tunic, is a misdirection. The Cross, which has been carried everywhere in Christendom, from child to grave, for more than a thousand years, is itself a lie, isn't it? It was T-shaped, and there were no nails through the hands but through the wrists, the Roman way.'

Guiscard went to open his mouth to reply, but Esi put up her hand. 'That is not all. Something profound happened for mankind in the early years of the first century, among the Jews, didn't it? That much I know, but it is not what was carried forward, is it? All of this is a lie. A construction of good intentions, but a lie nonetheless. The mystery of Golgotha rests not in the final moments of the Christ, and the drama of his suffering, but in His gift to the dead, the spirits. Does it not?'

Guiscard looked shaken, taken aback by Esi's ruthless summary, and nodded slowly. 'There is much we do not understand, for it comes not in words or manuscripts, but in direct experience of the Divine.'

'That, I had figured out,' Esi responded gently. 'What we seek here is to step back through time to recover a knowledge brought to Alexandria from Jerusalem, a knowledge that reached the last pagan philosopher. One that cost her her life.'

Esi put her hands firmly at her hips and faced them squarely. 'In 869, at their Council in Constantinople, the Church ruled that we were no longer to have three natures, body, soul and spirit, but two. They banished spiritual man from the rites of the Church, but not from our nature. That is what we do here: recover what is lost. That which is so feared by both Church and Adversary. Both have worked together, one the master, the other the slave. The common agenda is to put spirit-man to sleep, forever.'

They all looked at Esi, open-jawed, overwhelmed by what she had just revealed, as if her words themselves would burst into flames and consume them. They were in no position to challenge what she said. She quickly snapped them out of their reverie. 'Come, let us go down from this hill, make camp and prepare for what is to come.'

Wordlessly, the four men turned and followed her.

CHAPTER 22
Friday the Thirteenth, 1307

Jacque was late to bed on the night of the twelfth of October, after a long day in Paris, accompanied by Geoffrey. He looked back at these eventful few weeks, satisfied that the alarm over King Philip and the interpretation of their meeting in Poitiers, had been misplaced. He turned around in his cot, chasing sleep. After all, why else would the king today appoint him as pallbearer at the funeral of young Catherine, the Latin princess of Constantinople? No, today I comforted the king, his brother Charles, and the royal nieces and nephews, over the untimely death of Philip's sister-in-law. I was one of the Capetian pallbearers selected by Philip to carry her.

He rolled over, wincing, on his shoulders which were still bruised from carrying the cortege which wound its way to the Cistercian abbey in the north-west of Paris. We are back in Royal favour, Jacque mused. The balance is restored; the moment of danger has passed. The Knights Templar will not rest until we are within the walls of Jerusalem. With that soothing thought, he fell into a deep, untroubled sleep.

*

At the western foot of Uisneach, Guiscard had set their camp, ready to push off towards the west if trouble blocked the way south. He had already plotted their exit, should events unfold as he feared. After a supper of rabbit stew with leeks, onions and mushrooms, he gave instruction: they were to rise in darkness, before dawn. This is the window, Guiscard explained, for spirit man, when the mind is no longer in deep sleep, yet not fully awake, the time when man connects with his essence. But a very calm state is required.

He gave Ultan and Rostan orders to patrol the slopes, and keep alert to any danger at dawn, using the elevation to spot any movement of men and horses. It was a clear night with an orange glow in the western sky, but Guiscard had lived on the island long enough to know that all four seasons could strike in the same day.

His focus was purely on Cormac, preparing him for what was to come. He wanted him to sleep soundly and be fully rested before he was tested, knowing that what he faced was not mortal. His mind needed strengthening; his body required sustenance and rest. Tonight, they had built a fire to warm Cormac, wrapping him in extra clothes to bring up his body heat, and had sprinkled lavender oil on his pillow and under his nose, to ease him into a deep sleep.

Guiscard explained to Esi that she would need to assist him, to keep Cormac calm once he went into a meditative state; that the measures they were taking now encompassed their rite in which to prepare a Templar nightwalker for the spirit world, just before the opening of the day.

*

At four in the morning, King Philip was wide awake, blood pumping through his veins, his mind bristling with the bright possibilities of a France free of the poison of the state within, the accursed Order of the Knights Templar. Their arrogance! Their piety! Their foolishness in supposing that papal power could protect them from his wrath! His long slender fingers grooved the rampart whenever he glared across the rooftops of Paris towards what he now perceived to be the Tower of Babel: the Enclos.

He had watched the Grand Master closely that day at Catherine's funeral, feeling the exquisite pleasure of the predator when the prey fails to perceive its danger, and parades in open field, blind to what lurks and watches, coiled, waiting. Today I will spring, he thought, and sink my fangs into your startled heart. Your last thought will be one of stunned betrayal by your senses. This is the greatest hunt of our time, he mused, settling onto the palace roof-bench, which he had ordered specifically to watch the beginning of the hunt for the biggest beast in Christendom. Here, today, the Order of the Knights Templar will be humbled, brought to ground and savaged. As above, so below.

Beneath Philip, in the palace courtyard, de Nogaret had assembled his host, fifty men-at-arms and a dozen royal knights, accompanied by handpicked Dominicans led by William of Paris, to oversee the interrogation. The king's confessor, he knew, could be fully relied upon to favour the intentions of king, not pope.

The Hound looked towards William of Paris, and smiled. There is nothing quite as pious, merciless and ruthless as you, he mused. You have that same intoxicating scent of heresy, idolatry and sodomy in your nostrils, do you not? He knew this to be the potent mix which would draw the lead Dominican swiftly past interrogations of the mind – the pope's weak limits – to the grinding torture of the body. There must be no delay. We must establish confessions from the heretics before the pope has a chance to interfere. I, the unchurched, will then lay the evidence at your feet, Aquitanian, look into your eyes and dare you, in all your pompous papal finery, to reject me, to reject my king. Bertrand de Got, I know you for who you are: a weak fool, just another politician of the Church, greedy to keep privileges and stature, a beacon for manipulation.

He sought one grey hood above all others, for his favourite inquisitor, through the silent gathering. The one he knew that, once unleashed, was unstoppable. The one with an insatiable appetite for cruelty, matched only by his own and the king's. He spotted Bertramanus swaying at the centre of the hooded habits. The Hound smiled at Bertramnus; their eyes met in silent understanding. Bertramnus, you appear to be in prayer like your brothers, but it is ecstasy which courses through your veins. Today you will savour new flesh. No longer the wizened remnants of the last of the *perfecti*, but the fresh white flesh of the highest Order of the Church, the untouchable and virgin flesh of the Templars.

He turned towards the gathering and addressed them in the low, powerful tone he had rehearsed since Poitiers. 'We go to fulfil the wishes of God, his Holy Church, and our great king. We go to root out the heresy, idolatry and foulness which deems itself to be beyond the reach of temporal authority. Today you fulfil a sacred purpose. Let no man fail in his duties to his master, nor hesitate in pursuing this holy task to its end. We go now, Church and State together, as one brotherhood, to look into the eyes of evil, and tell it we fear it not, for we are the instruments of heaven. We go, quietly, purposefully, silently, until we are upon our great foe.'

The huge gates opened. Above him King Philip squealed as the gates creaked, his bladder opening in excitement.

*

The group broke camp, and moved silently up Uisneach towards the burial-circle of the God of Light, an area which Cormac had selected. He chewed on some of the forest mushrooms Guiscard had selected, while Ultan and Rostan took up a rotating watch to monitor the perimeter. Both had been ordered to keep their posts no matter what occurred within.

They settled on the ground, which was damp with early dew. Cormac faced Guiscard. Esi stood quietly to one side, observing, as she had been instructed to do, holding the small drum which Guiscard had taken from his sack.

Cormac had not spoken since he had fallen into a half-sleep. He had already entered a trance-like state, his eyes half-closed, his head shaking softly, as if lines of hidden energy were beginning to massage it softly.

Guiscard began. 'Sit up, back straight, pulling from the gut. Draw in a deep, long, cool breath. Fill your lungs, to capacity, fill, fill. Now hold, hold, hold.'

Cormac's chest broadened, and his head arched while he held his breath, eyes shut, rocking to and fro in his seated position, as Guiscard guided him.

'Now, squeeze from the base of the pelvis, squeeze, drive the fluids of your spine, drive it up, up past your stomach, past your heart. Lift it, press, squeeze, and push the fluids into your mind, therein to fire up the third eye. Push, press, push. Now exhale.'

When Cormac's fully expanded chest deflated, and air rushed out of his nostrils, his whole body started to spasm. Esi watched, amazed at the transformation occurring before her.

Guiscard repeated the breathing cycle over and over for what seemed like an age. Each time, Cormac pulled in more air, sank deeper, the spasms intensifying as he exhaled. Guiscard, determining that the time was right, gestured for Esi to pass him the small drum. He drummed softly to the rhythm of a beating heart on the taut skin of the shallow circular drum, tuning into Cormac's heartbeat, bringing him lower, deeper, calming his breathing, slowing his heart-rate. His voice changed subtly, becoming uneven, like an echo, lifting, fading, his undulating emphasis on words giving his voice a musical quality. Then, Guiscard guided Cormac's mind towards the root of his spine, gently but commandingly asking him to open red petals of an energy-centre there. Guiscard's voice, quiet but powerful, beating in time to the drum, moved Cormac slowly, softly, to his sacrum, but changing the colour to orange, asking him to open its petals, prompting him to bathe it with breath.

Esi stood transfixed, amazed at the similarity between what she was watching and ancient religious ceremonies she had studied.

Guiscard guided up the body, through the yellow energy-centre of the stomach before pausing for a long time at the green petals of the heart's energy-centre. 'Open your heart, open your heart, let it flood with light, with love.' He emphasised love over and over, until Cormac's vibrations were almost violent, his hands open, palms facing upwards, as if pulling in energy from a field all around him.

When Guiscard guided to the throat, Cormac's chin visibly shifted, exposing his throat skywards, visualising washing it with blue light drawn downwards from above. Guiscard moved swiftly now to the head, opening the petals of the third eye and, finally, the crown of Cormac's head, and the area just above it, bathing it in violet light. Opposite him, Cormac's face was perfectly peaceful, his body calming, now swaying to the gentle drumbeat.

Guiscard whispered to Esi, 'He is deep in meditation now. He is past the veil of the mind to the great void. Beyond here, only pure hearts may tread.'

She looked at him quizzically, searching for logic, but finding none.

'Esi, he has moved to a different place, in space and time. What he asks for here – to recall memories of this place – will be heard, but you need to watch him very closely now, for this is also the vale of peril.'

Guiscard returned his attention, and drumbeats, to Cormac, 'Float in the void, the great blackness, before you, behind you, all around you. Become part of it, less of you, more of it, dissolve, fade, be one with the void, less of you, more of it.' Over and over, Guiscard guided Cormac to let himself dissolve. Each time Cormac breathed deeply, Guiscard slowed the drumbeat.

*

De Nogaret walked ahead of the host, across the stinking Seine, through the squalid narrow streets. Parisian night-folk scurried into the shadows at the sight. In his fist he gripped the king's parchment, as if it were a weapon. Behind him, in line, the hand-picked command marched in grim silence, eager to break their pent-up fury against the walls of the Villeneuve du Temple. They followed a diagonal line of march, staying off wider streets before spilling into Rue du Temple and the open ground in front of the Templar compound.

No assault was necessary. The doors through the walls circling the Enclos were lightly guarded; after a brief exchange, the sentries stood aside on the order of the king. De Nogaret smiled. His meticulous planning was paying off. We have the element of surprise, he thought in triumph, as they rushed to the Enclos in silence, surging swiftly past its guards; a great mass of armed men moving at speed through the castle to the rooms marked by the royal spymaster, to their prize, the bed-chambers of the most senior Templars.

Over and over, de Nogaret had rehearsed the plan with the king. It was simple: take the Enclos in one unexpected, overwhelming assault; find and isolate its leadership; do whatever it takes to extract confessions; mark it with Dominican inquisitors; and obtain the incontrovertible evidence to lay before Clement in Poitiers. It would be a lightning-strike against papal power. The first news from Paris should be the capture, capitulation and confession of the Templar leadership. Isolate, weaken and humiliate; reset the balance of power. Let no one remain in doubt as to who bows to whom in this dominion.

De Nogaret chose de Charney as his prey, leaving de Molay for William of Paris. He judged the Normandy Preceptor to be the hardest target. Crack these, he calculated, and the pyramid collapses from the top. As soon as word spread that its leaders had confessed, he expected resistance to crumble. Then the king could hoist his battle-standard, in the autumn sunshine. The golden flame will flutter in the sky over Paris this morning, this morning, he recited, as he reached the door of Geoffrey's chamber and kicked it open.

De Nogaret stood aside to let his men pass. They overwhelmed Geoffrey before he had had a chance to swing out of his cot. They pinned him roughly, pulled him upright and manhandled him towards the door. At a nod from de Nogaret, they stripped Geoffrey of his clothes, strapped his legs together, placed one foot over another and hammered a long spike through both, pinning the Templar's feet to the doorstep. Simultaneously his arms were forced upwards in an arc, both hands nailed left and right to the doorframe. Throughout the struggle, Geoffrey's resistance was met by brute force, the men clearly practised in what they were doing, anticipating his every response. The task was completed before the shock had registered with the Templar that he was being crucified.

De Nogaret then stepped forward and pressed a crown of sharpened thorns onto the Templar's head. He grinned as the horror of the arrest played across Geoffrey's face.

Geoffrey was in excruciating pain, and his eyes stung as blood flowed down his forehead. In the corridor, the men-at-arms parted, to let a hooded figure enter. It was Bertramanus. The Dominican uncoiled the only weapon he had brought: a leather lash commissioned from the royal armourer, bristling with coarse knots of sharpened sheep-bones weighted with lead to amplify the whiplash. The knots were designed to tear flesh off bones.

De Nogaret whispered in Geoffrey's ear, 'Templar, I foretold at Poitiers that you would burn for your heresy, but first you will know the scourging of Christ. Do you confess to denying Christ and spitting on his Cross?'

Geoffrey shook his head, the movement causing shooting agony.

De Nogaret smiled. 'I had hoped not.' He turned towards Bertramnus, before settling himself on Geoffrey's bed. 'This Templar does not confess. Let him know what Our Lord suffered; let him feel the pain of his unbelief and know the cost of purifying his soul.'

Bertramnus squealed, drew back and unfolded the first strike. It cracked through the air and wrapped itself around the exposed chest of the Templar, sending a spray of blood across the corridor, its teeth pulling skin away in chunks as the Dominican whipped it back to begin his second strike. He yelled in a high-pitched voice, trembling with rage. 'Templar, when you were admitted to the Order, were you led to a secret place? Did you deny Christ three times? Did you spit on His cross?'

Without waiting for a reply, he uncoiled the lash for its second strike, driving deep across the abdomen, causing Geoffrey to scream uncontrollably.

*

On the Hill of Uisneach, Cormac stiffened, the soft smile on his face giving way to alarm. His breathing switched to short and shallow gasps. His heart raced and he began to slump to one side. Esi moved swiftly, propping him up from behind by the shoulders and easing him to the ground. He started to vibrate violently again, but this time it was different. Great convulsions of energy without pattern pulsed through his body. His back arched, his limbs flailed out of sequence with his body.

Guiscard gestured to Esi to let him be, to let the event pass, but the convulsions grew in intensity. Esi jumped back, gasping, pointing down. Cormac's head and heels had sunk into the ground; the rest of his body appeared to levitate.

'Something is wrong. Something is wrong,' Guiscard repeated in alarm. 'He goes where no Templar has gone. There is no joy here, no peace, no bliss. He has not journeyed there by free will. Esi, he is being drawn!' he shouted, finally.

Cormac let out a primordial scream, a long, rising throat-filling howl of pain and horror which reverberated across the hill, renting the early-morning air in the flatlands below, and causing rookeries to empty, a great parliament of crows taking flight into the dawn sky.

*

Down the corridor, Jacque had been stripped, gagged and trussed, placed flat on his cot and rotated towards the fire, which had been stoked with bellows. His bare feet, extending beyond the edge of his cot, were coated in duck-fat. A metal shield framed in wood separated his soles from the fire, but through it he could feel the intensity of its heat.

He heard from up the corridor the sound of a whiplash, and judged it to be an assault on one of his brothers. He glared accusingly at the king's confessor, William of Paris, aware that the pope disapproved of torture. Strong arms pressed on him. He struggled, but no longer had the strength of the young Burgundian warrior he had been when he was sworn to the Order, decades before.

The Inquisitor leaned over him, cradling his Crucifix. 'On your initiation, did you deny Christ? Did you deny Him three times? Did you spit on His holy Cross?' Jacque looked aghast at William of Paris, and vigorously shook his head in denial. 'Did you, as Grand Master, cause brothers to lie with each other? Have you lain with fellow brothers?'

Jacque continued to shake his head.

'On initiating a new brother, have you caused him to kiss you on the navel, on the spine, on the mouth?'

Jacque this time shouted his denial through his gag.

William nodded to his assistants. The shield between feet and fire was removed; the cot was pushed towards the crackling flames and sparking embers. The duck-fat sizzled, sending great waves of agony throughout the nerves of Jacque's bare feet. He screamed as his feet blackened, and the room filled with the stench of burning flesh.

William signalled for the screen to be returned, and the cot pulled back. He began his questioning again. Through the agony and smell, the corridor suddenly filled with a cacophony of screaming. Jacque turned his head towards the sound, and at that moment knew he was to be the last Templar Grand Master. They were decapitating the Order. There would be no trial, no appeal. It would be one brutal and overwhelming strike. He had underestimated the king.

The bellows wheezed, the men grunted as the screen was removed again, the cot pushed forward. The second burning would be worse than the first.

*

Guiscard leaned back in shock at Cormac's sudden roar. The hair on the nape of his neck stood up, his face knotted in alarm. Cormac was gathering himself for another concussive roar when both Ultan and Rostan emerged at full sprint out of the dim light.

'Quickly, hold him softly that he does not injure himself. Do not resist his energy; let it flow out, flow through you.'

Both men took position at Cormac's hands and feet, immediately swaying with the energy and vibrations which flowed through them.

Esi looked towards Guiscard and shouted in alarm, 'He is being attacked, isn't he?'

'Yes, I fear so. I don't know how to rescue him. He cannot be awoken from this without risking his sanity. What will return might be but an echo of a man, but how can we stop the force that seeks to infect him from the other side?'

Esi rubbed her temples in concentration, as if searching for clues among all the knowledge she had accumulated under Astralabius. She then lay on the ground and wriggled close to Cormac, wrapping herself around him, moving with his convulsions as if forming one body, one mind, and shouted in his ear, 'Cormac, to whom did you call out in the corridor? To whom did you last speak? Who brought the seven colours? Who was it?'

She listened for a reply. It came faintly, through gritted teeth, but they all heard the name clearly, over and over. 'Michael. Michael. Michael.'

Esi gasped and drew back, releasing her hold. Then she straddled Cormac, sitting on his chest, staring down into his face. His eyelids blinked rapidly. She filled her lungs with air and shouted a command in pauses between Cormac's roars. 'Ahriman! Ahriman!' She looked towards the men gesturing, and they took up the words, sensing that it was a command. 'Ahriman. Ahriman.'

Cormac's convulsions intensified. His head swung violently from side to side; he was levitating.

Esi gripped him, forcing him to remain in position, and yelled, 'We must reach him! He must hear us. He must call out this name.' She leaned forward and squeezed the young Norman close to her bosom, cradling him, tears flowing from her eyes.

'Ahriman! Ahriman!' they chanted, in rising volume. A squall raced across the dawn sky, bringing a violent sheet of rain from the south-west. It advanced across the flatlands and raced noisily up Uisneach, tapping the ground as if it had been summoned.

Esi lowered her face, until she was nose to nose with Cormac, and shouted, '*Duor show, Ahriman, duor show.*' She pulled up and watched for response. There was none. She shouted again, '*Duor show, Ahriman, duor show, in rooh ra raha kon.*'

Again, it had no effect.

'Esi, we are losing him; his mind will fracture,' Guiscard shouted over the gathering power of wind and rain.

Esi grabbed Cormac's locks of red hair in her small fists, filled her lungs with air and roared: '*Duor Ahriman, duor show, in rooh ra raha kon, Ahura Mazda farman midahad. Ahura Mazda farman midahad.*'

It started to have an effect. Cormac began fighting for his voice, for control between waves of agony and convulsions. His body arched; his limbs cranked and stretched as if they had been racked.

Esi, sensing the shift, repeatedly shouted, '*Ahura Mazda farman midahad, Ahriman!*'

Suddenly, in the midst of a convulsion, Cormac screamed, '*Ahriman!*'

The cry echoed across the hill, as if driving back the wind and rain. Instantly the convulsion stopped. A powerful concussion of fetid air rushed past the group, flattening them, followed by a deathly silence. It was as if a great candle had been blown out, its energy spent. Cormac lay completely still, his breathing slowing. Nothing was left of the moments of violence, save for beads of sweat which dripped from his wet mane down his young face.

Bewildered, Guiscard turned towards Esi. 'What in heaven's name did you say to that thing? What language was that?'

She looked up, giddy with relief, and smiled weakly. 'That, Templar, was ancient Avestan, the language of the Persians, of the prophet, Zarathustra. I called the Adversary by its Persian name and commanded it to be gone, to leave Cormac's spirit, and I did so in the name of the Ahura Mazda, the Divine God.'

Esi lay next to Cormac. To her surprise, she found herself sobbing. She hugged him tightly, and began breathing in unison with him, in relief. She strok edhis head. 'I love you so, Cormac,' she repeated softly over and over into his ear, while her tears flowed freely.

Guiscard sat exhausted with barely enough strength in his voice to instruct Ultan and Rostan to return to their vigil.

*

Jacque had passed out in the middle of the third burning, his feet completely blackened, his bed-chamber full with the stench of burnt flesh. William of Paris decided to allow him to rest, before the next interrogation, if one was necessary. Jacque was carried out of the room still trussed up, and was manoeuvred down the corridor, lined with royal men-at-arms, who stared silently at the semi-conscious form of the great Templar Grand Master, some blessing themselves as he passed. He started to regain consciousness, feeling the cooler air.

Approaching Geoffrey's bed-chamber, he first noticed the blood spatters on floor and wall and then witnessed his old friend being released from his cruciform position in the doorframe. The tortured monk, still steaming with sweat and heat, was tumbled onto a fresh white linen shroud. Within the room, he saw the heaving hulk of Bertramnus, his hair wet with sweat from the effort of the scourging. The chamber floor was scattered with clumps of skin and blood. Behind him, de Nogaret waved a triumphant salute to the Grand Master.

Jacque blinked through searing pain, and whispered a solemn prayer for Geoffrey. *I am so sorry my old friend, I didn't listen.* The last Grand Master of the Knights Templar passed out again as another wave of pain flowed from his smouldering feet. He welcomed the moment of unconsciousness.

CHAPTER 23

Below the swirl of leaves, Esi carefully nursed Cormac, mopping his brow and squeezing drops of water onto his parched lips. He had remained unresponsive since the assault had ended, his eyes moving rapidly beneath their lids, his breathing slow and shallow.

Guiscard circled, muttering, 'He is clawing his way home, Esi, looking for the light, recovering his spirit-energies. I have no idea what is going to come back to us, but we must be prepared. You must be prepared, too, for a different person, a night-walker; enlightened or harmed, I know not.'

They waited.

The autumn morning had given up any semblance of calm as a stiffening Atlantic south-westerly started stripping the foliage from the great woods at the centre of Ireland. Leaves blew in the gusts, curling up and over the Hill of Uisneach. The autumn equinox had passed three weeks before and the land was settling in towards the liminal time of *Samhain*, marking the start of the darker half of the year.

Throughout the morning, Ultan and Rostan reported no unusual movement in the plains below. Towards midday, Cormac showed more signs of life: the vibrations that were occasionally visited upon him had subsided. He started to mumble.

Esi put her ear to his lips and looked up towards Guiscard. 'The words are incoherent, the language strange. It could be ancient Persian, but he is in conversation, judging from the pattern.'

Guiscard smiled. 'That is a welcome sign. My greatest fear was he would come back a mute. It has happened before to a night-walker.'

Suddenly Cormac's eyes blinked open, and he heaved in a great gulp of air under the grey sky. Esi rolled away, putting her hug from his memory, but remained kneeling at his side. She placed her hands over Cormac's face, peering deeply into his eyes. 'Cormac, are you back to us?' He nodded weakly.

'Can you tell us what happened. What do you remember? We thought we'd lost you.'

He tried to sit up, but failed. Esi turned to Guiscard. 'He's very weak. We must let him rest further, surely?'

Cormac rolled over onto his hands and knees and heaved, emptying his stomach as if expelling a toxin. The movement seemed to rally the young man. 'Esi, you fret too much. I'm coming around. It just feels like I've walked miles through mud and sulphurous fumes. Guiscard, it was the same as in the corridor: the same entity. I know it now. But it was chaotic, unstructured and unclear, as if a blanket of fog had been laid down to hide it from me.'

'Aye, lad, we know what it is now. I had expected it was the same horror, but you can thank this young woman's fast thinking: Esi saved you from its wrath. She named that thing, and it didn't like it one bit.'

Esi looked at both men. 'We did more than that. When Cormac identified the Amesha Spenta as Michael, I knew straight away what we faced. It is from ancient Persia, an entity of Druj of chaos, rage and destruction, the agent of the *Angra Mainyu*. This is the dark god called Ahriman. It opposes the *Ahura Mazda*, the good God and his seven *archai*.'

Cormac gasped, wild eyed with wonder. 'So, Michael, the Archangel of Judaism, Islam and Christianity, is the Amesha Spenta of my corridor?'

'Precisely.'

'But why did he not intervene this time?'

'Think, Cormac. What is the essence of Michael? What marks him out from all the other archangels?'

'He is chosen to eject the Fallen from heaven, to confront Satan?'

'Not entirely. Michael brings the impulse of free will. This is not his time, but when it comes, his era is marked by learning through acts of free will, free choice. He didn't intervene, because *we* did. We evolved. It is his way.'

Guiscard stared at Esi, dumbstruck. 'And how long were you intending to keep that one to yourself – or have you known all along?'

'You forget that I have been studying Philip of France, his growing manipulation of the Catholic Church, his exile of the Jews, and his control of the papal court. I fear that his real goal is to supplant papal power with regal power. What better way to influence the spiritual affairs of man than the conquest of man's Church? He means to separate spiritual man from God by denying him direct experience of Him, and replacing it with a church structure under Ahriman's control.' Both men were aghast at the picture Esi painted, of a Church under a malign impulse.

'To what end does he seek such control, Esi?' Guiscard asked. 'What does Ahriman crave?'

'His destiny is to convince man that he has no spiritual nature, that he cannot experience the Divine. There is no surer way of doing this than to sow his chaos, cruelty and corruption among the very structures man has established to combat him. When he controls the Church, he separates man from God. He does this by controlling powerful, spiritually vulnerable men. He seeks to set a new impulse for mankind, isolated, separated, alone. King Philip is his instrument, his creature.'

'Why then, assuming you are correct, does he fear us, fear what Hypatia spirited out of Alexandria all those years ago?'

'Bear in mind, Guiscard, your own words. In the void, there is no space and time. Hypatia lived and died today, in the now. We seek to unravel the mystery of Golgotha. What did the Christ achieve, not on the Cross, but in the spirit world? Why did the Church deny man's spirit in its councils? Why does Ahriman fear Michael so?'

Cormac pulled himself unsteadily to his feet and looked in the direction of the cat-stone. 'It is as Esi had guessed: in my walk, that boulder glistened. It was bathed in sunshine and not under dark skies, like today.' He looked across at Guiscard. 'Help me to my feet. I need to touch the stone, to reconnect, to remember.'

They walked the short distance to the Ail na Mireann, and stopped to leave Cormac circling it, caressing it with his hands, trying desperately to remember. When it was clear that nothing was coming to him, Guiscard whispered quietly to Esi, 'It is not surprising that he feels nothing. His mind has shut down to protect him, fearing what he might otherwise recall. It could be days, or years, before he sees anything again.'

Esi had been pacing around the stone in carefully measured steps. 'We are not finished yet. Here is how I see it. Two hundred years before Hypatia, this place was referred to by Ptolemy, the Roman mathematician, astrologer and map-maker. He died in Alexandria in 168 AD. Hypatia would have studied his works under Theon, her father. That is how she came to know it. He called the island *Iouerníā*, which derives from the Irish name *Éire*. That boulder was selected as a marker not just because it would transcend generations of time but also because the whole island was named after a woman, Ériu. She is said to be buried underneath the cat-stone, precisely where we now stand, according to Ultan's lore.'

Guiscard shrugged. 'Perhaps that is so, Esi, but even if Hypatia's box is buried somewhere, with the sacred boulder as a reference, we cannot know in which direction or at what distance, and we do not have time on our side.'

'Well, that's where I'm hoping you are wrong,' Esi said. 'Go back into Hypatia's mind. She was a mathematician, but also the custodian of knowledge from the Nasoreans. We know from the scrolls found under Herod's Temple that they contained quite specific drawings of Solomon's Temple. The measurements were deemed to be sacred to the Jews, thought to be based on esoteric measurements which went way back in time. Hypatia would have known.'

'So how does that help us?' Guiscard asked.

'Solomon's Temple was built from west to east, so its doors faced the rising sun, which flooded its first chamber with daylight. Its anterior chamber, containing the Holy of Holies, was in darkness. So, my guess is that the site we seek is facing due east from the cat-stone, which was itself the holy of holies to the people here at Uisneach in those times.'

'Yes, but it could be at any distance,' Guiscard interrupted, anticipating that Esi hadn't finished.

'Correct, Templar,' Esi said, pacing more quickly now. 'But the length of Solomon's Temple was sixty cubits, or about eighty-eight feet, and its width was a third of its length.'

Esi paced out due east from the cat-stone, drawing an imaginary line at the end of her walk, before turning. 'In both corners of the entrance here, left and right, stood the two bronze pillars, Boaz and Jachin, one represented the kingly line, the other the spiritual. These would have been facing north-east and south-east at the entrance. Hypatia's casket is under Boaz, I believe, just about here.' Esi stopped, and pointed at her feet. 'It will be at a depth of about three to four feet, like the Celtic souterrains which have been uncovered in the land-clearings Ultan has mentioned. We will find it by digging a trench through it, in line with the cat-stone.'

Guiscard laughed loudly. 'Let me guess. You figured all this out from an interrogation of the Gallowglass? Esi, do you ever stop?' With that, he turned and roared out for Ultan and Rostan. When they returned, he announced, 'Right, go and fetch the digging tools, and we will put Esi to the test. Now, where exactly does this trench of yours need to run?'

'*Ceann cac,*' Esi muttered, out of Guiscard's hearing.

Ultan burst out laughing. Rostan whispered, 'What was that one?'

'Shithead.'

Rostan giggled. 'Esi learns the language quickly.'

He unloaded the shovels, while Guiscard and Cormac marked out the area to be excavated with pebbles. Ultan and Rostan arrived back with an array of shovels, pickaxes and mattocks. The men stripped to the waist and attacked the ground, splitting the task of breaking and clearing, starting at opposite ends of Esi's trench-line. Ultan's strength and speed was impressive; with Rostan, he had soon reached a depth of four feet. They started to work their way towards Guiscard and Cormac. The ground was giving way, now that both teams had settled into the task, carving the sides of their pits and clearing out the debris with rhythmic ease.

Esi remained quiet, delivering cups of water for the thirsty work, and fearful of opening her mouth in words of praise, in case she interrupted what was becoming a competition for her attention between Cormac and Ultan. She was quietly enjoying the spectacle of steaming and rippling muscles glistening in the light rain, and the feral sounds men make when driven in labour. Her thoughts had begun to wander, when Cormac's pickaxe sparked. It was more than the sound of iron on small rock.

The ends of the trenches were now less than six feet apart; now all four of them concentrated on Cormac's trench, Guiscard clearing out the clay and stone, Ultan and Rostan working down from above. On they went digging, finding a new rhythm.

'There is something here!' Cormac cried in triumph. 'And it is not made by nature but arranged by man.' He clawed away at the earthen sides of the trench, to reveal two standing-stones, arched by a lintel-stone. He spun around, grinning, 'You are a gift, Esi, a gift.'

She beamed in reply, her face reddening.

'Right, steady now,' Guiscard called out. 'Let us slow the excavation. We don't want this structure to collapse and crush its tenant, do we?' Steadily they went, switching to short-handled shovels and picks as they cleared away the ground, revealing the opening and roof-stone of a small souterrain. 'Well, Esi, who should go first?' Guiscard asked.

Esi smiled. 'Well it won't be you, anyway. We'd need another week to make the opening bigger.' The group laughed. 'And it won't be you either, Ultan. That would be like sending in a minotaur. No, it will have to be Cormac: he's the lightest and most slender.'

The Gallowglass looked mystified by Esi's words. 'I'll explain later, lad,' said Guiscard. 'She has a wicked turn of phrase, that one.'

Rostan rigged a light rope around Cormac's bare chest and tested it before letting it out from above, setting himself across the trench. He poised, ready to pull the young Norman up if the stones started to give way.

Cormac began to ease his hands, then his head, through the narrow opening. Daylight followed him into the passageway for the first time in nine hundred years, but quickly lost its power in the gloom. Half in, half out of the opening, he shouted up, 'It slopes down but feels dry and sturdy. Pass through the candle, so I can see more clearly.'

Esi, cradling the candle, passed it through as she would a newborn chick. Cupped in her hands, she shielded it from wind and rain, its flame dancing and growing as it passed into the passageway. 'Beyond the passageway, Cormac, you should find it opens into a chamber at a lower level. It's not far; it should soon be visible.'

Cormac crawled gingerly over the dry stones. Esi remained at the entrance, feeding through the rope. Inside, Cormac felt the sides of the passageway, and called back, 'It is amazing to think that you and I are the first people here in hundreds of years, that something so simple could have stood, unguarded and untouched, for so long.'

'Cormac, bear in mind that this whole hill was sacred ground. No one was going to disturb it – not without trembling in terror of kings and gods.'

A minute passed before Cormac spoke again. 'Hold it, I've reached a circular chamber. The roof has large stone lintels, but the chamber appears to be empty.'

Esi called out into the gloom, 'Look closer, Cormac! Let your eyes adjust. In the western wall, facing the passageway, there ought to be a shelf, elevated off the ground, mirroring the inner sanctum where the Arc of the Covenant was held. Do you see anything?' Esi's question was met by silence. All she heard was the sound of shallow breathing and grunting. This started to fade as Cormac moved deeper. Minutes went by before the sounds started getting nearer again, then she saw the candle flickering proudly in the darkness, followed by Cormac's white teeth as he grinned, his eyes sparkling. Ahead of him he pushed a small casket, tarnished grey, unmistakably man-made. Even in the poor light, Esi could see it was a marvel of craftsmanship, alien to northern Europe.

We have found it, Hypatia, we have found it, Esi was about to shout in triumph, when she heard a yell of commotion from behind. Guiscard roared: 'Get out of there fast! We haven't a moment to lose. In minutes this place will be teeming with French and English. Just grab whatever you have. We have to run, now!'

As Esi and Cormac emerged into the daylight, cradling the casket, they spotted Ultan's great axe flashing silver on the south slope, and heard the sound of battle. Rostan had joined him, the combination providing savage strength and speed, forcing back the skirmish-line, the vanguard of a much larger body of men-at-arms emerging from the woodland below. Behind them were half a dozen knights in full armour, slowed only by having to push through the heavy furze that separated woodland from slope. Rostan and Ultan occupied a narrow gap in the shoulder-high furze, which could slow but not stop the oncoming tide of men.

Guiscard beckoned. 'Quick, to the horses. We cannot hold here. They are buying us time; let's not waste it.'

They turned to flee west, but stopped in their tracks a few feet past the catstone. Standing in a thin line across the Hill of Uisneach was a body of wild-looking warriors. At the head of them, Felim, his face painted, was holding his great Viking axe grimly. On his command, the wave of lightly armoured, grinning Gaels swept past them, wielding a gruesome combination of axes, long-swords and javelins, and yelling blood-curdling cries.

Guiscard shouted across the rush of men, 'Greetings, Felim lad. I take it your new friends are O'Kelly, then?'

'Well met, Guiscard. They have come east of the Shannon to the land of their cousins, craving more English blood after wiping them at the ford of Eascrach. Their chieftain, O'Kelly, dies from his wounds. Revenge is on their minds. It didn't take much, after I told them of French and English notions of martial superiority and the ransom for which a noble can be exchanged, as you suggested.' Felim laughed. 'You three, get out of here. We cannot long hold heavy armour on open ground, but we can distract them. I intend to draw them deeper west, where I have a surprise arranged. Now I must away, and not let Ultan have all the fun.'

Felim turned towards Esi, who was struggling to protect her precious find from the elements. 'Such a small thing makes such a big fuss?'

Guiscard cocked his eye at her, as Felim set off at a sprint. 'I don't think that lad was referring to your casket! It seems that he has you figured out, Esi.' He looked over his shoulder at the action and shouted, 'Quick, let us get to our horses!'

CHAPTER 24
The Béguinage, Paris

Marguerite's attention was drawn to the heavy front door. It wasn't the knock of a sister, but neither was it the thud of an unwelcome guest. She ushered the sisters to their dorm-rooms as she made her way to the entrance. Unbolting the door, she barely recognised Jean du Fay since he had first visited many years before, on a mission to take in the orphaned teenager who was to become her dear friend and collaborator. The monk was in the apparel of a street-trader, a nondescript tunic, with a deep hood, shading his face from enquiry. He had disguised his height and age with the limping shuffle of an elderly man.

'*Nom de Dieu*, Jean, you look like you haven't slept for a week. Come in quickly; get out of the street.'

He followed the mistress of the house to the kitchen, and flopped into a chair. 'It is a dangerous time, Marguerite. I rushed back to Paris from far south to find the city locked and the Enclos surrounded by a ring of steel. I got here too late. The king's standard flies from le Gros Tour. It is worse than I feared. My eyes were blinded to the mischief of the Hound, and my agents are scattered into the shadows of the city. What have you learnt from your spies in the nobility?'

'You will need the seat, Jean, for the news is grim.' The Templar spymaster sank into his chair, his shoulders slumped in resignation, anticipating what was coming. 'Yesterday the Enclos was raided. All of your senior officers have been arrested.'

'Jacque and Geoffrey?'

'Everybody. They have John of Tour, Hugh of Pairaud. They have even captured your Preceptor of Cyprus, Raimbaud of Caron. It is rumoured that throughout France hundreds from your Order are held captive, to be interrogated by inquisitor and state.'

He was aghast. 'What, all of the Knights Templar?'

'Many aren't warrior-knights, as you know, Jean. Many are over fifty years of age, and more are plain farmers, craftsmen and shepherds. The king seeks not to ring-fence the leadership but to capture the entire estate.'

Marguerite paused, to let the information sink in, handing Jean a cup of water, and some bread and cheese.

'It is the worst possible outcome then.' Jean turned towards his food.

'There is more, Jean. They have not waited to alert the pope. They have begun the torturing. It is led by William of Paris, but Jean, Bertramnus was also seen entering with a host of hooded Dominicans. He is not there as a scribe.'

'My God, do you know what this means? There will be no limits, no discipline, no quarter, no rest. They intend to extract by flame and *strappado*, that which cannot be extracted by Church examination. It is an abomination!'

'We both know that in Le Palais, at Îsle de la Cité, resides no king, but something much different, *n'est-ce pas?*'

The Templar fixed Marguerite with a stare, acknowledging the truth of her words. 'He is consuming the Order of the Knights Templar?'

'Yes, it seems so. It has been long planned, as I'm sure you have guessed. Clement has yet to learn the scope of the king's cunning. Already, preparations are being made for next week – next week, Jean! – for full confessions to commence at the Enclos, and they are to last at least a fortnight.'

'My God, they mean to take confessions from over a hundred in Paris alone. It is a crushing unmatched by anything before. It is breath-taking.' He sank into silence, then added, 'Both king and Hound have played their cards with skill, deceit and ruthlessness. I had expected a fulsome assault, in truth, but not the obliteration of the Knights Templar, wiping them from the face of the earth. They will seek written confession to heresy, and worse, but they will focus on heresy. There can be no way back for the Order, not if confession of heresy is extracted from the leadership.'

'That is so, Jean, but the forgiveness of the Church cannot hold if confessions, once made, are retracted. It then becomes a temporal matter, and that, I fear, is Philip's unstated wish. He seeks to burn them, to bring the field of flames to Paris.'

'Why do you say so, Marguerite? How can you know?'

'Because, Jean, you may have your agents within the Court, but we, the Sisters of the Béguinage, have women to whom we provide sanctuary. Women at every level of society, from courtesans to cleaners. Nothing happens without our eyes upon it, should we seek to open them.'

Jean sat up with a start. 'Can you get within the Enclos, to Jacque, to Geoffrey? They are isolated, but must be told what is happening beyond. I need to know what I must plan, what we must try to accomplish.'

Marguerite nodded. 'There is talk that they will be locked away at Chinon, where security will be much tighter, witwh fewer comings and goings. We may get a chance, now, as cleaners are sent in to remove the foulness created by the affairs of men; but it is not without great danger to the messengers.'

'Then I must craft a message, and ask you to risk having it delivered.' Jean looked at Marguerite. She responded by opening a drawer and passing him parchment, pen and ink. Jean wrote at speed, pausing between paragraphs, adding, 'We have already taken the precaution of removing our most precious and valued manuscripts and relics. It is where Astralabius is, now. But our plans must be made permanent.'

'How so?'

'The Order – what we hold as truth, much as you hold, Marguerite – is not fit for this time. We must fade but not disappear. We must separate the fate of the Order as a structure from what it contains, from its essence. That will require careful thinking. Jacque, Geoffrey and the rest are beyond my help. We must go to ground, but they may yet have a final duty to perform.'

'Jean, you will need to assume that the king's reach goes far beyond his kingdom. He has already petitioned throughout Europe for Templar arrests. Nowhere is safe.'

'Perhaps in time that may be so, but politics will play its part. The Templars of Tomar, our stronghold in Portugal, under Denis, the farmer and poet-king, is unlikely to bend to the will of Philip. The new King of England is another matter, for he is betrothed to Isabel and will seek to secure peace.'

Marguerite feared to learn more, in case she exposed information if she was arrested . 'There has been one other item of information that has come from Le Palais. The king's eyes move to Ireland, to talk of Templar treasure there. It is why he has sent an envoy to Edward, and a force to Ireland, a realm that the young king does not fully control. I assume that this concerns my visitors here, and Esi?'

Jean slowly nodded, sighing heavily, tension and exhaustion etched on his face as he absorbed the implications for everyone in his care. 'Esi and her companions are in great danger. They do not know what has happened here, and must not return to France. I must make preparations, then leave. There is so much to do, and so little time to do it. We fear that more is afoot from the lair in Le Palais, and that it concerns matters not purely of the physical realm.'

Marguerite stared at Jean. 'I was hoping not to hear those words, but fear that it may be so. We will pray for divine help for Esi, and for all of us.'

As Jean carefully folded the parchment for Marguerite, the kitchen reverberated with the sound of violent banging on the door of the Béguinage, loud voices shouting to open in the name of the king. Marguerite beckoned Jean to follow her. 'Quick, out of those clothes and into those of a Béguine. This is a routine search. All the sisters will exit as a group on to the street, while the king's men search our rooms.'

Jean nodded. 'Their eyes will only see what they expect to see.'

'Precisely.'

Jean was already half-dressed by the time Marguerite walked the corridors, calling on the sisters to assemble by the entrance. He was absorbed into their midst as they walked briskly past the waiting men. No one noticed the sister carrying a bag, who broke away silently, to disappear into the narrow back-streets of Paris.

CHAPTER 25

On the downward slope, at its narrowest point, Rostan had taken up a position to Ultan's left. The big Gallowglass was delivering powerful sweeps from right to left – or so he thought, until the back-swing nearly took out his side. He had skipped away just in time, as Ultan cut a swathe through the opposing ranks, forced together between the dense furze bushes.

The attackers, thin in number at their narrow front, were eager to make progress, until their way became blocked by dead and wounded comrades. When the ground became slippery with blood, they hesitated, their efforts becoming less certain.

Rostan sensed the shift in tempo and surged forward, slicing left and right with his arming sword, connecting each time through lightly armoured opposition. French and English voices could be distinctly heard as commands reached the vanguard, to hold and await reinforcements. That suits us; we can hold here just a little longer, he thought. Just then, Ultan let loose a roar, raising himself to his full height in battledress, his axe dripping with freshly spilt blood, sending a clear challenge to the French. The attackers shuffled backwards, uncertain, afraid, slipping on fresh blood.

'That's helpful!' Rostan shouted over the confusion. 'You must teach me that trick when we get out of this jam.' Just then, hearing a commotion to his rear, he turned to see the downslope filled with fighters. God almighty, that's as ugly a bunch as I've seen in my time, he thought. They are buzzing like angry hornets, spoiling for a fight. No wonder the French and English retreated.

On a silent command, the advancing fighters stopped and opened a path for their leader. Felim trotted forwards, grinning at Ultan. 'Greetings, Ultan, Rostan. I see you have them surrounded.'

The three laughed as the first wave of O'Kelly arrows swept over them towards the retreating enemy. Rostan couldn't help himself. His sides heaved with mirth. 'Where the hell did you come from?' he shouted.

'From west of the Shannon with this clan. Now listen. If you look beyond' – Felim pointed below – 'you'll see the enemy lines forming. They intend to use those knights to charge uphill and break our ranks. We cannot hold here, even if they are slowed by soft ground below and the uphill slope.' At that, Felim raised his axe in two sharp motions.

To the west could be heard an advancing line of war-pipes, screeching above the wind and rain. The knights below them paused to look left of their formation. At the edge of the woods, O'Kelly fighters appeared to form up, before disappearing from view and re-forming. All the while, the sound of pipes grew louder.

'Hope you like the spectacle, lads. There's only a few dozen of those lads, swapping tunics and playing the war-pipes. They're under orders to put on a demonstration of a larger force building in the trees. It seems to be working. Look.' He pointed.

Below, they could see the enemy force, numbering at least a hundred men and knights, begin to take a defensive stance, and form a circle. Expecting an attack, the men-at-arms were creating lines of spears, ready to part at a moment's notice to release cavalry. The wind grew in intensity, driving rain into their faces, masking the view of the open ground in between, causing the formation to slip. Atop Uisneach, several hundred feet above, the confusion in the ranks below could clearly be seen spreading.

'No wonder they are confused,' Felim said. 'They have force-marched here, not preserving their energy, not expecting to meet anything more serious than a handful of Templar monks. Now the whole countryside seems to be alive with menace, an attack imminent. Rumours of the massacre of the English will have them rattled. That's what I'm counting on.'

Felim grinned as Ultan smacked him on the shoulder.

Rostan gestured to his Irish companions as a rain of arrows started to fall on the retreat. 'See that fancy blue and red plume to the front of the armour? That's the French noble Simon du Merle.'

'Aye,' said Ultan, 'but what you can't see from here, Felim, is that his handsome young looks are spoiled by the flat nose that Rostan gave him as a gift in Kilkenny. It probably loosened his helmet.'

'Behind him – and mark this – rides Sir Gilbert de Bohun,' Rostan said. 'The reason he looks less than battle-ready is, I guess, because he is a reluctant companion to this hunt. He didn't strike me as a man who felt much love towards his French guests. He prefers Guiscard, and he'll recognise the war-pipes as those of O'Kellys.'

Below, the formation started to retreat carefully, in classic fashion, eyes to the front, hoping to open up more ground from the incoming threat and gain a better defensive position. The pipes grew ever louder and closer, the woods seeming to bristle with soldiery.

'Now listen carefully, lads,' Felim said, watching his plan unfold. 'Their eyes are to the west. We begin to back up, make it look as if we are going to outflank them to the east. Once we clear the top of the hill, out of sight, we bank west, and leave this lousy position.'

'How does the rest of your ruse work?' Rostan asked.

'When they find there is no attack or pursuit, they will return, but caution will slow them. We will draw them north of Lough Ree. The plan is to pull them into the soft bog and woods that drain the Shannon. Then we raid and retreat, drawing them north-west. The O'Kelly lads know how to sting, fast in and out, and we can retreat across the river on their small fleet of boats. Did you see any of those Frenchies carrying boats?' Felim laughed.

They both looked at him, grinned, and nodded. Ultan resumed his war-cries, turning the vanguard's slow retreat into a sprint for the safety of their closed ranks, out of range of arrows. They were unnerved by the sudden reversal in fortune.

At the top of Uisneach, the Kerns made a demonstration of fighters arriving at the breast of the hill, sweeping across it, and disappearing from view to the east – or so it would seem from below. Out of view at the top, they moved in a circle, swapping weapons, helmets and tunics before once again marching across the hilltop. From below, it looked like a continuous column of men skirting the hilltop. The plan was working. The knights were covering their exposed flanks from the threat of skirmishers as the enemy column started to retreat to the south, in good order to escape the jaws of a trap.

At the bottom of the western slope, Guiscard's group mounted and held horses ready for their companions. Ultan and Rostan came running, and quickly mounted. Rostan breathlessly recounted Felim's strategy, between heaves of laughter. 'That, behind me, walking in circles, is the great host of the Gael. See, thousands of them, with ever more arriving below through the woodland. Hear their war-pipes? The whole place is alive with them, a great host assembling to crush our pursuers.'

'But there is just a handful,' Esi said innocently, as she checked the ties which strapped the casket to her mare.

'Of course,' bellowed Guiscard. 'A masterstroke by the Gallowglass, but they'll be back as soon as the ruse is discovered. Sir Gilbert is no one's fool: he'll smell a Gael-trick, if he hasn't already. What do you think, Rostan?'

'Perhaps, Guiscard, but I observed your old friend from above, and he is not leading: he defers to De Merle. He is a fox, that one. My guess is that he won't be in any rush to let the Frenchman know of his suspicion, and even less of a rush to get drawn north, into wild country. He is a man I like, that Gilbert.'

'Right, then we go south-west to find the Shannon. Come, let us go through the woods and skirt the clearings until we are well out of here. Say farewell to Uisneach. We must away in haste. The opening of that box will have to wait.'

After following the retreating column for a couple of miles, Guiscard rode ahead to converse with Felim, before returning to signal his group to take advantage of a stream running west to mask their tracks. They shouted their farewells to the Kern and turned sharply, following the course of the stream, which took them towards the Ballynagrenia wetlands, halfway to the Shannon.

Guiscard, just as he had done across France, set a blistering pace, aiming to reach the Shannon crossing, ten leagues away, by nightfall, using the natural features of the landscape to full advantage. He plotted the course through a series of bogs to give their horses a plentiful supply of water, guided by Ultan's knowledge of pathways through the marshes, without which the journey would have proved treacherous.

At every pause, Ultan scouted the back path and reported no chase in sight. They pressed on relentlessly, pushing their steaming horses hard before crossing Mongan bog, to arrive at Clonmacnoise, the ancient capital of the Ui Maine, and the site of a monastic centre of learning.

Guiscard had decided that the Norman settlement and castle to the north at the bridge of Athlone was too risky a crossing. Further down the river, in an attempt to secure Clonmacnoise, the Normans had built a modest stone castle to replace their wooden motte and bailey, next to the site of the old monastic city. It had been destroyed by the Gael and had recently been abandoned, in favour of positioning Norman strength in stone at their stronghold in Athlone.

Night was closing in when the round-tower of Clonmacnoise filled the dimly lit horizon. They were nearing the banks of the Shannon, and moving out of Norman-controlled land. Guiscard chose to make camp in one of the abandoned thatched ruins near the old city.

As they settled, Cormac wandered off to see the Shannon with Esi. Rostan rose to follow, but Guiscard gestured to let them be, and pointed towards the casket. 'Whatever is in that, Rostan, is now your charge. No harm will come to Esi while she is in Cormac's company, not here, not on this land.'

At the banks of the Shannon, Esi and Cormac sat close together. She reached over and held his hand, which was warm and soft to the touch: still the hands of a child, not calloused from years of campaigning. 'Do you feel anything here, Cormac?'

'The Shannon feels like an old friend, Esi. Someone you would meet at the end of a long journey, who welcomes you with a hug. Clonmacnoise once rivalled Dublin and Waterford as a trading centre, did you know?' She let him ramble on, sensing that it concealed his shyness. 'This place was the busiest trading centre of the west. Ships sailed up the Shannon, bringing precious metals to craftsmen, coloured stone to be ground to make ink for illuminating manuscripts. Students came from all over Europe. It has been in decline since King John built the fortress at Athlone.'

Esi smiled at the detail. 'This place must have been trading with north Africa since ancient times. It seems that Hypatia knew of it from older records, from maps.'

Cormac turned to look Esi straight in the eyes, startling her with his sudden intensity. 'Esi, what is it you most desire? I don't mean this venture, but from life itself.'

She was taken aback by the profound question from one so young, and was unnerved by how it made her feel – a little out of control, the young man taking it from her in the most unexpected way. It is a philosophical question; he seeks to see into my heart, but that is unfamiliar territory even for me, she thought. 'Such a question from one so young, Cormac?'

'You are playing for time to think, Esi.'

Her face lit up in a broad smile. He's cheeky, but observant. 'Do you know everything I think, even before I do myself? Is that it, Cormac?'

'Esi, from the moment I met you on the beach, I knew you, and you knew me. It didn't much feel like a first meeting, did it? When you placed your hand in mine, just now, it didn't feel like the first time.'

He turned towards her, placing his free left hand gently against the side of her face, his thumb caressing her temple. 'And this isn't the first time I've done that, is it?'

Esi felt a surge of emotion, which confused and scared her. She was not ready for this; not now, not here, not like this. It was the unfamiliar feeling of not being fully in control, and something else she had never before felt: an ache deep inside. But there was too much at stake, too much still to learn, she was sure. She raised her hand to his, and softly lowered it into her lap, so that she was cradling both his hands. 'Cormac, you've asked me what I most desire. I am going to take my time to consider my answer, but yes, you are right. None of this feels like the first time.'

He smiled warmly, satisfied.

Esi looked at him, relieved. He had acknowledged her feelings, and was respecting her wishes. He would one day make a remarkable man, but a companion, or whatever else, to herself, she did not know. She had to be careful. 'Come, Cormac, let us return to the campfire and wait for the morning sun to reveal the contents of the casket to us. We can continue our discussion then.'

CHAPTER 26
Poitiers

'*Putain! Putain! Putain!*' the pope roared in bursts of anger. His bile rose; his temples throbbed. The emerald-encrusted goblet flew across the room, colliding violently with the twin doors as they closed. Its contents marked its path like a shooting star across the fine rugs of the private meeting room. Outside, the papal messenger ducked instinctively and hurried away, fearing the Holy Father's rising temper. He had just handed him, on the silver platter, the sealed parchment from Paris, passed through their Franciscan channel at the royal court. The Pope glared at the opening paragraph, spittle running out the sides of his mouth, his eyes dancing in and out of focus, his head spinning, his bowels, he knew, not far behind.

'*Putain de merde,* Philip! *Putain de merde!*' he spat, talking loudly, as if addressing Philip. 'You sat here with me at Poitiers, you king of sewer-rats, snakes, and all that slithers. You lied to me, who was your boyhood friend, and is now your Pope. You had planned this all the time. The invitation, the casual chat, the fake concern for my health. You piece of shit!' he shouted, as he kicked out at an imaginary foe. He read the paragraph again in disbelief. A month ago, it said, the secret orders had been issued throughout France. He read it aloud:

> They will place the persons individually under separate and secure guard, and will investigate them first before calling the commissioners of the enquiry, and will determine the truth carefully, with the aid of torture if necessary.

'With the aid of torture, Philip? From you, that is an open door to hell. There it is, see there, *par gehine se mestier est.* You will torture to get whatever you crave, won't you, you lying piece of shit, and you align me to your foulness.'

He sought the second paragraph and read aloud again:

They will be told that the King and the Pope have been informed by several very trustworthy witnesses in the Order, of the errors, and the buggery they committed, particularly on their entry into the profession. They will be promised a pardon if they confess the truth and return to the faith of the Holy Church. Otherwise, they will be condemned.

'There, you say it, you write it, you sign it. You give commands in my name. You subvert my power, you take my people, Philip, and you use them to take away my Order from me. This, I will not have. This, I will not stand idly by and accept. You have gone too far. It is an abomination of lies.'

He gripped the parchment, almost tearing it, as his eyes moved on, his voice rising in temper. '*Sainte Mère de Dieu*, William of Paris reports that Jacque is already breaking. The Grand Master himself! What have you done to the old man? He will accept the heresy but not the sodomy. He spat only once on the Cross, forty years ago during initiation, that he did so in body, but that he didn't deny Christ in mind. Dear God, Jacque consents to swear to heresy on the Gospel.'

The pope, aghast, paced the room, eyes glued to the paper, while continuing his conversation with himself, as if speaking the words out loud would lessen their agony. 'What, de Charney will swear to kissing the receiving master on the navel thirty-eight years past, denying Christ? But hold, look here, my God! Hugh of Pairaud? But Hugh is your ally, you scum. He, the most powerful Templar in England and France, has backed you in your condemnation of Boniface? You squeeze him most, don't you? He is the real prize, isn't he? Hugh is to admit to allowing brother monks to relieve the heat of nature with other brothers? To deny Christ once on entry to the Order forty-four years ago? He will admit to overseeing the whole foul ceremony – the kissing, the spitting, the denials of Christ many times – but not in his heart. Oh my God, he admits to worshipping a head, in Montpellier!

'The apex Templar in France, friend of the king, to swear himself a ringleader? Even the strongman, the preceptor of Cyprus, Raimbaud of Caron, to swear to the idol-worship, the sodomy, the foul kissing, spitting on the Cross, denying Christ?'

The pope's shoulders sank in despair as he read on. 'Raimbaud changed his testimony completely after being taken away by that foul Dominican, Nicholas of Ennezat, one of William's creatures. No wonder.'

The pope threw the parchment to the ground and paced around his room, throwing his hands in the air. Wild eyed, trapped, he was seeking a way out. I must take action, he thought. Yes, I must. I will call for the counsel of my cardinals. I will let Philip feel the wrath of the Holy Church. I will show him eternal damnation as an ex-communicant, see how he feels when he is denied the body and blood of Christ. No, I can't do that. Too many cardinals are in the favour of the king. I can push him, threaten it, surely? But remember Boniface, remember Anagni, remember the poisoned pope! Tread carefully here, de Got, or you too will feel the reach of the King.

I mustn't act in haste. I must let this settle for a few days, while I divine the best approach for the Holy Church. Maybe I will write. That's it: I will write to the King, to skilfully and delicately point out the error. That's it, an error in his understanding of ecclesiastical ways. I can do that. The words are important; the tone and structure will become subtle weapons of diplomacy. I am good at that: look how far it has taken me; here, to the seat of Peter. But I will not be a puppet pope. How can I manoeuvre myself out of this trap?

I will sacrifice the Templars. That is inevitable now. But I must save myself and the Holy Church. I must be seen, of course, to defend the monks, but not to the point of losing my life, or the papacy. No, I will issue a papal bull. That's it. I won't address it to Philip personally but to all kings – a timely reminder of the separation between the Church, its assets, its Orders, its ecclesiastical laws, and those of temporal man, including kings. I will write to all, but address but one.

That will help salvage the Order outside of France once those realms see me taking over the enquiry. I must be crafty. I will officially maintain an open mind on the matter of the Templars, pending Church enquiry. I'll drag that out, insert the Church in the process, thank Philip, but wear him down. I will contain it within our opaque procedures, establish a council, maybe, gather cardinals from far and wide. I'll make Philip feel that he has instigated a wide enquiry, saved Christendom. That will appeal to his piety, his hubris, his sense of omnipotence. I will address him as the bringer of light. He will love that.

The bastard.

Pope Clement found himself sitting, beginning to calm. He stretched out his silk socks, kicked off his emerald-clad slippers and reached for a glass of Fromenteau. He would await official reports, and feign surprise at their content. Now was the time for pretence, for acting. He would yet wrest something from this dreadful business.

The Templars were no more. But he had to look forward to new beginnings in the warmer winters of Avignon, further from the lair in Paris. He took another swig of wine, wiped the drops from his lips, and breathed slowly. Bertrand would know what to do, how to play it. Bertrand was his favourite name for himself, and the wine was delicious.

CHAPTER 27
Shannon ford, Ireland

The early morning brought a chill as the low-hanging autumn sky blanketed Shannonside, promising to brighten later in the day as the breeze began to stiffen from the south-west. Esi asked Guiscard to call for a council around their breakfast fire, which had been stoked with fresh wood. She removed the silver casket from her bag, placing it gently on the flat stone they were using as a table. In the dim early morning, despite the dancing firelight, the casket was dull. It revealed none of its secrets.

Guiscard said, 'It appears quite unremarkable really, doesn't it? It is heavily tarnished with age, and the locking mechanism is likely to be jammed. How do you think we should proceed, Esi?'

She asked Cormac to lift the casket so that she could examine its sides more closely. She gently ran her fingers over its surface. 'It is almost the size of a reliquary, a box from ancient times used to contain the bones of the dead. It is hard to say if the outside contains an inscription, a guide perhaps to opening it. I can feel an indentation underneath here,' she said, moving her fingers under it. She grunted as she took some of its weight. 'But I can't be sure if it is the result of age, or has been put there by its creator. I am fearful of forcing the lock: we don't yet know what lies within.'

'But surely, if it has lasted this long, there is no harm in opening it now?' Guiscard asked.

'The fear, Guiscard, is that sunlight may destroy the contents,' Esi replied. 'We do not know if it's hide or parchment.' She gestured to Cormac to place the casket back down on the stone. They all looked at it in silence, unsure what to do next.

'Perhaps we should ask the metalsmiths of Clonmacnoise to clean the box, so that Esi can see any inscriptions,' suggested Ultan.

Esi jumped up. 'Ultan, you are a marvel. Why didn't we think of that? It's so obvious, isn't it? I'm convinced Hypatia had it made for this purpose. It is not elaborate. No fancy ivory plate, no carving of figures or scenes describing the gods, nothing that signals down through the centuries. It was built so as not to draw attention to itself as a depository of power or treasure; even its appearance may have been deliberately altered to hide the fact that it is made of silver.'

'Unless anyone has a better idea, let's take it into the town. Put it back in its bag,' Guiscard ordered. 'Esi and Cormac, you two with me. Ultan and Rostan, stay apart from us, but vigilant, ready to intervene if needed. We are guests here, not enemies, so there is no need to crack heads. If anyone asks, we are crossing to go west to Connaught, on pilgrimage to the sacred mountain, Croagh Patrick.' Guiscard looked towards Rostan. 'That would be the Irish version of the Camino de Santiago.'

The town was bustling into life as they left. Boats were already arriving or departing to the south towards the mouth of the great river, where the castle walls of Viking Limerick stood in vigilance over the fast flow to the wild Atlantic.

It didn't take Guiscard long to find a metalsmith, a woman who had shared the task with her mother, and her mother before. She carefully examined the box. Once Esi had explained what might lie inside, she made up a solution of vinegar, lemon juice and salt. Using a delicate scrubbing brush, she demonstrated how to begin the process of stripping off the tarnish. Esi watched carefully, mesmerised by the skill of this woman, who described the steps carefully to her.

'It appears to be very tightly sealed, unlike anything I've seen or heard of before. It does not willingly give up its secret. But if you patiently apply my solution, it will begin to speak to you. Even its lock will eventually loosen its tongue.'

'Thank you. You don't know how much this means to me,' Esi said, before adding mischievously, 'The Templar here will pay you in French silver. Make sure you test it. Never trust the French not to debase their coin, nor a monk not to know the difference.'

The two women giggled as they examined Guiscard's coins.

Emerging from the workshop, Guiscard beckoned the group together. 'We have made progress. Esi can continue to work on the casket as we travel. We must hasten away from here, and head south along the river.'

Rostan, who was only half listening, pointed back the way they had come, his keen eyes scanning for unwelcome movements. 'Look to the distance, at the treeline between wood and open ground. There is movement. War-horses.'

The group turned in alarm and ran to their own horses. They mounted quickly, and headed towards the bridge which spanned the river to the south. Guiscard beckoned them across, then turned at the mouth of the bridge and drew his sword. He shouted to Rostan and Ultan, 'See them safely downriver to the great lake. If I do not return, and trouble follows, be prepared to cripple the crossing.'

Before anyone had a chance to object, Guiscard had turned his mare and was galloping towards the distant riders. The group paused at the other side of the river to watch the spectacle. In the distance, the riders had stopped. There were four of them. One moved forward at a trot. As the distance between them closed, they could clearly see that it was a knight carrying a white flag upon a lance, lowered to show that he had no violent intent. Guiscard had slowed. The two figures converged in the meadow and stayed facing each other for what seemed an age.

Suddenly Guiscard pulled his reins and galloped back towards the waiting group, crossing the Shannon at speed. 'We are away, south along the river. I will explain later.'

Esi was about to interject when he added, 'First, I have to think. Everything has changed.'

He wheeled his horse into the lead position and led them away from Clonmacnoise. Throughout the day they continued, stopping only to water horses and nibble at their diminishing food supplies. They would need to forage, later. They rode at pace, keeping the Shannon to their left, moving ever deeper south. After twelve leagues, it spilled into a great lake at Port Omna: 'the landing place of oak'. Guiscard called a halt to make camp, before foraging for kindling and game in the dense woods which ran to the sides of the great expanse of Lough Derg. He looked towards Cormac. 'How many days since we landed at New Ross. Nearly a week, I think?'

The young Norman nodded. 'That is my count.'

'Rostan, I need your keen young eyes,' Guiscard demanded. 'Look out on the lake. What do you see?'

The young Templar scaled a large rock at the shoreline and called back, 'A long way off, there are some boats, small, river-boats, traders; some with sail, some without.'

'Anything else, Rostan? Anything different?'

'In the far distance, there is a bigger sail. It comes in this direction, on a tailwind, or so it seems.' He strained to see more. 'It looks light in the water. Wait. It is becoming clearer. *Mon Dieu*, it is Fabian!' he cried with joy. 'It is the *Briganti*.'

Amazed, they watched the sail growing, and the unmistakable outline of the *Briganti* taking shape as if materialising out of the air over the great lake.

'Well, what are you waiting for,' Guiscard said, with a whoop. 'Stoke the fire, skin those rabbits and let's give Fabian's crew a hearty welcome. They will be ravenous.'

After they had made camp by Lough Derg, they had their first real rest in a week of hard travel. The group happily went about their tasks as the southwesterly pushed the *Briganti* to shore. Fabian luffed the sails, and beached the boat, before hopping off at the bow into the soft shale, with perfect timing.

Esi clapped, waved and hooted with glee. 'Well met, Fabian,' she exclaimed.

Guiscard pushed straight past the Templar's attempt at a formal French greeting and lifted him clean off the ground in a huge bear-hug. 'Thank God, Fabian, that you are safe. We have much to discuss, but first, sit and eat.'

Fabian nodded towards the Kern. 'They are good sailors. I could not have been in better hands since we spotted the French fleet breaching the mouth of Waterford harbour, the cogs in full sail, bristling with troops – as you suspected, Guiscard.'

'Indeed, Fabian, there is much to tell, not all of it pleasant.'

Ultan and Cormac had prepared a feast of hare and had made a stew from wild garlic, mushrooms and onions, flavoured with thyme Esi had found. They mopped it up with what was left of the bread and cheese they had brought from the boat, and sat back, their bellies full.

'It is time to tell our stories,' Guiscard announced. 'You first, Fabian.'

'The French took no notice of us,' Fabian began, 'presuming us to be a coastal fishing vessel. They seemed intent on gaining access at speed, and took the channel to Waterford city, as you anticipated. After rounding the headland, we first made good speed in a light easterly, until the breeze rounded to the south and became a stiff south-westerly. The next two days we spent tacking towards the shore, before we were just outside Cork harbour.'

'But still off Norman lands?' Guiscard offered to the listeners.

'Aye, still sailing off Norman lands. We sailed throughout the night, bearing away from the coastline and rocks, until we were nearing the isles of Carberry. By morning, the weather had worsened, but we found safe harbour where you said we would, in the inner harbour, protected from the Atlantic by Inis Arcain – known as Sherkin to the Normans. We made landfall at Baltimore. Its Norman castle is still being rebuilt by the O'Driscoll clan after McCarthy Mór emptied the land of the owners. There isn't a Norman now for many miles. We briefly treated with the O'Driscoll, who commands there for the Kingdom of Desmond, and found a welcoming host, happy to trade silver for sanctuary if required.'

'I thought you would,' Guiscard said. 'The kingdom crushed the Normans – a defeat that stopped further moves into the south-west corner of Ireland. My plan relied upon them for help. It is a wild outpost, quite beyond the reach of France or England, save for an overwhelming land and sea assault.'

'After provisioning,' Fabian continued, 'we sailed west into heavy seas, to complete the task you had set. The seas grew mountainous as we started to bear north-west, but the sail was in good shape to deal with the tempest. We were a little less exposed once we had cleared the high cliffs of Kerry, past the ancient monastic Skellig Islands, and we gathered speed to the mouth of the Shannon.'

'Aye, back off Norman lands once again, at Thomond.' Guiscard punched his hand in his fist, pleased with the report. 'So, how was it, passing through Limerick?' he asked eagerly.

The audience was riveted by Fabian's telling – especially the Kern, who were lovers of storytelling. At every pause, Ultan translated, helped by the Gaelic that Fabian had picked up on the voyage.

'Limerick was not easy. King John built a substantial fortress in the old Viking city. It stands over the Shannon. No army could take that city; not from the water, that is for sure. It could be besieged, but its walls will not fail it. But Guiscard, we were not stopped or searched by anyone; neither Norman nor Irish seemed too interested in a weathered trading boat.'

'As I had hoped, Fabian, you slipped past the walls of Limerick disguised as a trader eager to begin its voyage up the Shannon. That is significant: it means that the Normans of Limerick have not yet heard the news from France.'

All eyes turned towards Guiscard. 'What news?' the Templars asked in unison.

He looked slowly around the fireside. 'On the plains outside Clonmacnoise, I parleyed with Sir Gilbert de Bohun.'

'So that's who the lone knight was?' Esi said. 'Rostan, you seemed to have read him right on the heights of Uisneach. What happened?'

'Gilbert, as I suspected, did not fall for Felim's ruse – at least not entirely. He consulted du Merle, who was intent on chasing the O'Kellys into the wetlands, and convinced the petulant young knight to split forces, while he took his men south on our trail.'

'To what end?' Esi asked. 'Why did he choose to fail in his task?'

'He did not fail, Esi. He slowed the pursuit, figuring ut that we would head south-west to the kingdom of Desmond, where no Norman could go. He caught our trail along the stream above Uisneach, and sight of us at the ford of Clonmacnoise. Gilbert wanted to talk, not make war, which is why he rode out under the white flag.'

'But why, Guiscard? Would he abandon the instructions of his King Edward to assist the French?' Fabian asked.

'Because the young King Edward, who is obliged to assist his future father-in-law in order to secure peace with France, learnt of a planned abomination.' The Templar poised, to draw a deep breath. 'I am afraid the news from France, if the intelligence is to be believed, is grim. The worst kind, the unthinkable.' He paused to gather himself. 'Sir Gilbert says that the Order of the Knights Templar in France is being crushed in a single swoop by King Philip. All the brothers are to be arrested, their castles, farms and commands seized. All will be imprisoned and await trial by inquisition led by the Dominicans, under the heel of the Capetian. That is what Sir Gilbert imparted to me. If it is true, there is no place in France to which we can return. He says, however, that King Edward will take his line from Pope Clement, not the King of France. King Edward makes as if to support Philip, but actively seeks to undermine him. It is why we are still alive, why the English force at Uisneach stood without heart. Gilbert was obeying his king, not Philip.'

The group sat numbed by the implications, struggling to accept the possibility that the Knights Templar had been wiped off the face of France, without warning. Esi was first to break the silence. 'Templars, it is a shock to find that you may no longer have a home. Believe me when I say I know how this feels. But the grim news is not completely beyond expectation, not since the struggle at Uisneach with that thing, Ahriman.'

Fabian looked baffled.

'I will tell you about that later, Fabian,' she continued. 'It is evident from Cormac's first encounter that matters are afoot in both realms; as above, so below. This is a daring strike by the creature's vassal, who sits on the throne of France, but it is a long game, and there is much we can still do. So, Guiscard, if France is no longer home, where is?'

Guiscard paused before responding. 'It is much worse than the loss of the Holy Land after the fall of Acre. Then we had a homeland to which we could retreat. This is very different. I have been grappling with the dilemma since we left Clonmacnoise. In truth, I do not yet have an answer. What do you think, Fabian?'

'We have assets in Cyprus, Portugal, Spain, England and elsewhere, but the heart of the Order is France. If the centre is crushed, the limbs cannot hold. How quickly it collapses will depend on Pope Clement's reaction. He will play for time, then buckle under the triumphant Capetian. We need time to think, and get more information, from a place of safety. But Guiscard, you have worked that out already, haven't you? It is why you had me make landfall at Baltimore.'

'Aye, it is to west Cork, to the kingdom of Desmond, that we must go,' Guiscard said. 'We will regroup there, get messages to and from France, across what remains of our network, and find out truly what has happened. It will also be a sanctuary within which you can examine that casket, its only saving grace being that it compelled us to be out of France when the Iron King planned to snap shut the jaws of his trap.'

CHAPTER 28
Palais de la Cîté, Paris

Philip sat on his throne, alone, twitching with excess energy, impatient to hear the details of the capitulation. He was exhausted; sleep had only come in the early hours of the morning, after he had spent the night ruminating over his orders being carried out. He had toyed with the idea of slipping into the Enclos in disguise, but had ruled it out. It is so close, he thought, just there across the rooftops. The death of the Order. Yet I cannot see it. Such pleasures I'm missing. But just to see the white flesh of Templars, stripped and scorched, to watch them fall, as Lucifer fell from the heavens. Such a sight. But no, I must maintain indifference, let the Dominicans act as cover. Besides, I lower myself to no mortal, and they are now mere men, for I have stripped them of everything, as they have stripped themselves of Christ.

They stripped you, de Molay. You are now Grand Master of ghosts, like de Charney, Hugh of Pairaud, and all your foul kind. Your arrogance lies in ruins at your feet, written in blood. And not noble blood spilt on the alien battlefield against the Saracen. I will take everything. I will strip you of your manly energies, leave you nothing but a shell, nothing that Clement will see fit to resurrect. There is no Bethany here.

Renege, and I will cheer as you walk into my fires, smouldering, searing, excruciating. I will burn you again and again, burn your bones. There will be nothing left but ashes, nothing to put in a reliquary. You will be scattered, beyond the reach of shrines and the ignorance of pilgrims. I will destroy even the memory of you. You will leave the realm of man, forgotten, your blasphemy and heresy a footnote in history. The books of the future will glorify my name. My name, Templars! And that of my line, not yours. Yours will be the memory of the damned, erased as if I had sowed salt into the minds of men.

Philip had cleared the great hall, leaving it bare and hollow while he waited. He longed to relish the sound of footsteps marching along its stony length, the precursor to the report he had for so long craved. The door was opened from the outside, ushering in the king's Hound, side by side with William of

Paris. They walked in step, lawyer and enforcer, inquisitor and priest, pacing the length of the great hall, their footfall echoing across its huge floor, coming to rest before the king.

It was just as he had envisaged; every last detail was perfect. Philip raised his eyes slowly, and feigned a relaxed smile. 'Gentlemen, how goes the holy work of Church and State?'

Both men stiffened, knowing that the enquiry was the most loaded question the Capetian would put to them in their lives. De Nogaret deferred to William of Paris, continuing the pretence of an independent Church examination, as agreed by his master, and the Dominican played along, having long switched his loyalty from the pope to the king.

The priest cleared his throat. 'Your Highness, there is a Grand Master no more, merely a confessed heretic, a wreck of an old man, aged both in mind and body. He seeks to reconcile with God before his years decline.'

The king leaned forward casually, but his eyes blazed. 'Jacque will formally confess?'

'He will, my king. I have arranged for his confession to be heard by the full panel of inquisitors on the twenty-fourth. It will begin what I expect to be two weeks of confessions, each echoing the other.'

'How many?' the king asked.

'Almost a hundred and forty. It is now a matter of words and rehearsal – with occasional reminders to cooperate.' The king smiled, amused by the coded words of the Dominican. 'Tell me, Father William, how the Templar leader chose to confess. How his world was rent from him; how he fell from his heretical throne; how he must have felt. Leave nothing out.'

'Yes, Highness. We took the Grand Master by complete surprise: he was still in his night-clothes. He had no chance to reach for his sword or arm himself. His resistance was feeble. I had handpicked the men for the task, including from among our hardy Dominican stock. He was stripped of all clothing, fastened to his bed, with feet exposed, towards the fire we had stoked.'

'Did he resist? Did he scream? What did he say?'

'Until I was ready to put questions of faith to him, he was gagged, so his protest was unclear and could not affect our work.'

'When, Father William – and this is important to my learning – when was the precise moment that he realised he was Templar no more, that he was flesh and blood, that he was to be examined just like any common heretic?'

'Your Highness, that would have been the moment that I ordered his bare feet to be brushed in duck-fat, the screen removed, and his feet extended into the smouldering fire.'

'Why that moment, priest?'

'Because your Councillor and Keeper of the Seal, standing here at my side, asked me to record the moment. I looked down into de Molay's eyes and watched the realisation dawn on him, that he was of mortal flesh, that he was not under the control of his Order, but in my grip.'

The king shifted to the edge of his chair, riveted. 'Yes, yes, and what did the window to his mind convey?'

'Your Highness, I saw not the sparks of defiance, but instead saw the emptiness of desolation: lifeless, flat, resigned. Before the fat boiled and pain screeched through his body, along every nerve, the Grand Master surrendered the Order and everything it stood for. This I knew, for I have done this much before.'

'So be it, William of Paris. The most senior Templar crumbles before the fire, in trepidation of God, his Holy Church, and in fear of the King of France. Did he fully confess on the first cycle?'

'He stumbled much, incoherent with pain. He did not fulfil my requirement for complete confession, which I would normally meet with a respite, and time for reflection. Instead, I burned him again and again, until he offered me the words, and then passed out, your Highness.'

'Thank you, Father. You have performed your task with consummate skill, and saved much time and expense for the realm. By confessing the Grand Master so swiftly, you have destroyed resistance throughout Paris, throughout France, once the news has been released.' The king then looked towards de Nogaret. 'Make it so. And what of your prey?' the king asked. 'Did you make him eat his words at Poitiers?'

De Nogaret bowed slightly before answering. 'Your Highness, it was always to be the case that the Preceptor of Normandy would be hewn from sturdier stuff. It is why I brought Bertramnus –with whom you are familiar, I believe.'

The king grinned, enjoying the careful understatement from his Hound, knowing he was familiar with the king's peccadillo, as he saw it.

'We followed your Highness's suggestion to the letter, that he be stripped, crucified and flogged. Upon his head I placed a crown of thorns. Bertramnus flew upon him, scourging him from shoulder to groin, deeper with each lash, affording him little time to confess, until his body flowed with blood and had lost flesh from crown to feet.'

'The flagellation Our Lord would have experienced from Pilate?'

'Indeed, your Highness; worse, because of his crucified position. Bertramnus even squeezed vinegar from a cloth to his lips when he cried out for water. De Molay broke early; de Charney did not. Again and again, he was scourged; each time, he was asked whether he would confess. He did not, would not, until he was told that the Grand Master had broken. The iron will then departed from him, as a gust blows out a candle. He gestured that he would confess just when his body was streaming from the scourging. We removed the spikes and wrapped de Charney in cloth to preserve him for later.'

'Excellent work from you both. What now remains to be done?' the king asked.

De Nogaret continued, 'With de Molay and de Charney broken, Father William and I concur that Hugh of Pairaud will next break and confess. So will all Templars, for there is no hope of escaping the flames without doing so, their leaders, their Order, their homes, the foul things of heresy, all destroyed.'

'So it will be, but heed. Each Templar must confess without equivocation, without stumble, without hesitation. Each confession must be presented as if purely by examination, the manner of its extraction kept within these walls,' the king said.

'Your Highness,' de Nogaret concluded, 'there will be no room for games of ecclesiastical complexities, nor scope for an ill-conceived response from Clement. I have already seen to it that the pope is made aware of his predicament. He receives reports which, he believes, come from his spies. In fact, they come from the hand of this humble excommunicant, your Highness.'

King Philip then did something he had never done in the great hall: he stood up, startling both men, put his hands to his hips, and roared with laughter. The king's glee boomed around the room, echoing from stone to rafter, scattering the pigeons on the roof, and into the skies over Paris.

CHAPTER 29
Baltimore, west Cork, Ireland

The seagulls basking at low tide scattered, protesting, as the lookout ran across the slippery rocks towards Dun na Long castle. Built on the site of an Iron age promontory fort on Inis Arcáin, the castle overlooked the narrow eastern entrance to Baltimore harbour. In the distance, rounding the next headland, a large vessel in full sail came into sight, set against the rocks of Kedge Island to the east. The lookout could see she was a big galley, beating into the stiff south-westerly which hurled huge waves towards the west Cork coastline.

The lookout reached the island, alerted the company of O'Driscoll's men to the oncoming danger, then lit the torch-fire to signal Dun na Séad castle on shore. On the battlement, despite the dim winter light, the fire flickered its warning across the harbour to the lookout at Baltimore, where Guiscard's party had sought sanctuary.

In the great hall, the guests had gathered to share brekfast with their host, clan chieftain Eoin O'Driscoll, who looked as if he hed been hewn out of wind and rock, his face carved by the Atlantic. The O'Driscoll, swarthy, square shouldered and barrel chested, looked, as always, as if he wanted to be somewhere else, except when he was drinking whiskey distilled from local grain. Cera, his bookish middle-aged wife, stood taller. Fair haired, with an attentive and sparkling personality, she was popular with the local children for her storytellings during the long winter nights. She was held in awe by the local church as a biblical scholar and was regularly consulted by the clergy who travelled from throughout Munster to debate the Gospels with her.

Esi escaped into Cera's company as soon as they arrived. Both women shared a love of learning and ostensibly played chess until it was dark, by candlelight, leaving the menfolk to their revelry and stories. But Cera, whom Esi had sworn to secrecy, was in fact helping to gently prise the secrets of

Hypatia's casket from the ravages of age. Esi relished Cera's detailed knowledge of the Bible; her insights had helped fill gaps in her own knowledge as she went about her work. It was a delicate and patient task, peeling away centuries from the casket before challenging its lock to reveal what lay inside. Esi had pushed aside persistent enquiries from the Templars on her progress: this was to be her work. She was going to do it at the pace it required, and nothing would be revealed until it was done.

Neither had the men dared challenge either woman to a game of chess, for fear of being soundly beaten; none could decide who was the weaker of the pair. Esi and Cera came and went as they pleased, disappearing for days to take long walks along the dramatic coastline, while immersed in debate. They teased through their findings, keeping their conclusions private.

Across the dining tables of the great room that ran parallel to the harbour and afforded a bird's-eye view of it from east to west, the guests mixed with the Irish, indulging in intense discourse. Below, nestled in the safe berth within the inner harbour, was the *Briganti*. It had been more than three months since Guiscard and his company had sailed out of Lough Derg, caught a fast-flowing Shannon filled with autumn rains, and powered under the walls of Limerick to the open Atlantic, and south to freedom.

In the intervening time, the group had grown very fond of their hosts. Christmas had helped. The Templar monks brought added devotions to the birth of the Christ – much to the delight of the devout locals. Guiscard and Fabian had used the opportunity to familiarise themselves with the politics of the kingdom and its military preparedness, should the Normans sally west again and test its strength. Rostan had used the time to teach Cormac more of the art of combat, and had earned for himself a large following among the younger members of the clan – much to the delight of the O'Driscoll, who had helped set up a small school. Already the O'Driscoll could see improvements in formation, both in attack and in defence, and marvelled at the fun the young men were having with the Templars. The training helped bond the relationship beyond that of the French silver which covered the costs of their unexpected guests.

Felim had made it south through the early January snows from O'Kelly country, far to the north. He had reported that the French pursuit had fizzled out after crossing the Shannon, where they had been met by an onslaught from the local clan, who had been primed for their arrival. He described an escalating series of skirmishes as the O'Kellys deployed their advantage in boats to great effect, outflanking their opponents and hitting them from the rear, sowing confusion and demoralising them. The arrival of winter had helped by catching the wet, cold and miserable French and

English in the open flood-plains. Unable to get to grips with an elusive enemy, which hit hard and appeared to dissolve into the freezing mists, they eventually gave up. Felim described how he had admired the French pluck in their organised retreat south-east, but they had been unprepared for the Gael's instinct for warfare; de Merle was lucky to escape with his life. The French knight was harassed all the way to the midlands before he eventually found safety at Dun na Masc, his route of retreat marked by his dead. Once the enemy had been safely bottled up, the O'Kelly dispersed, returning to winter quarters across the Shannon, while Felim made his way south by foot and boat.

From Baltimore, the Templars had sent coded messages to France and Portugal, via trading vessels going along the south coast, but had heard nothing in return. The risks were minimal. Guiscard and Fabian had concluded that a French or English incursion was highly unlikely, given the terrain of west Cork and Kerry, which lent itself instead to the raiding warfare favoured by the MacCarthy Mór. The Normans had unwisely judged that the Kingdom of Desmond would not be able to face a battle on open ground, and had paid for their error at Callann, with the loss of their leadership – and of their control of south-west Munster. It was most unlikely that they would try again.

Guiscard watched across the babble in the great hall as a servant brought news to Eoin O'Driscoll, noting the change in his features and the stiffening of his huge shoulders. The movement had also been caught by Fabian, who nodded towards the sea. The O'Driscoll rose from his seat and addressed both men, out of earshot of the rest of the guests. 'Come, my friends, let us to the battlements. We have an unexpected arrival in these waters. A galley approaches. It is alone, and has not enough strength to mean mischief. It is something else; I know not what, for we have received no word to expect a ship of this kind.'

Guiscard followed close behind. 'Perhaps, Eoin, she comes from the Ostman and Norman of Waterford to discuss a peaceful settlement of your differences?'

'Unlikely. There has been too much bad blood between our fleets. Besides, they would first send a single messenger, not risk a galley.'

The three men stood at the highest point of Dún na Séad and watched as the tip of a mast bisected the channel between island and mainland.

Eoin leaned forward over the battlement, eager to view the arrival. 'She is very big. That mast looks well over a hundred feet tall, which puts her beam at maybe thirty feet. By God, she is a Venetian cog! They will have to trim sail shortly. I once saw something like that, but a little larger, in southern waters:

the *Roccafortis*, a Venetian which pulled more than two hundred tons, and averaged six knots.'

'She looks too big for this harbour,' Guiscard said. 'She resembles one of those big Genoese galleys off Acre. Some of those could take up to a thousand souls, but could not dock. Smaller boats had to ferry in and out through the waves.'

'It will be the same here. She is slowing, to drop anchor,' the O'Driscoll noted. 'She will look for a ferry. This is going to be interesting.'

The men turned, to find their way blocked by Esi and Cera, who had followed them up to the roof, curious about what was happening. They, too, were transfixed by the scale of the ship now nestling in the harbour, dwarfing the O'Driscoll's ocean-going fleet, which was dotted around the harbour in safe berths.

'That flag at the stern, there.' Esi was pointing it out to Cera. 'It is familiar. It goes back into antiquity. It is not of any nation. It is from the death-rites of the Pharaohs; the staff and flail cross diagonally beneath the head.'

'That is the skull across two leg bones,' said Guiscard. 'It was once a hidden Templar symbol, to remind us that our nature is understood only by contemplating our mortality.'

Esi fixed Guiscard with one of her stares. 'You never told me that before, but only now, when it flies in the harbour? When, old bear, were you going to reveal a connection between Templar and Pharaoh? What else have you Templars been keeping from me?'

Guiscard stepped forward, put both hands on her shoulders and said softly, 'Esi, as soon as you open that damn box, we will connect everything. Nothing will be withheld. I knew nothing about the origin of the skull and crossbones. Trust me, please.'

Below, a ferry-boat was already pulling out from the pier towards the broad beam of the galley, which shifted at anchor into the wind, displaying its full girth and length to the seasoned sailors ashore. They watched in silence as the ferry-boat shrank beside the scale of the galley, and watched a nimble single passenger disembark and stand square as he was rowed ashore.

'Sweet God in heaven,' Fabian said. 'It is Le Grincheux! I'd recognise that pinched, snarly grimace from a mile away. He is alive, but how in heaven's name did he pull off that stunt?'

Offshore, as if on cue, the figure waved up to his audience and gave a slight bow, prompting a ripple of laughter.

'Who is this Grincheux?' asked the O'Driscoll.

'That, Eoin, is someone you will get on with like two flies on fresh dung. Jean is the Templar spymaster. You two are a match well made,' Guiscard said.

He turned towards Fabian and shrugged. 'At least we will get the intelligence we require, and can decide what to do next.'

'Aye, Guiscard,' Fabian said. 'But Jean flies under the skull and crossbones, not the Templar banner. This seems to confirm Sir Gilbert's grim warning. I fear what tidings he may bring.'

CHAPTER 30

The Templar reunion on the stone pier abutting the castle, was interrupted by a fast-moving squall which barrelled across the standing stones of Cape Clear and Sherkin islands, before breaking on Baltimore.

The skies to the west darkened with angry, low-hanging clouds which could be clearly seen racing ashore, pushed by powerful winds. Outside in the harbour, the galley tightened rigidly into the onrushing gusts as the temperature dropped, presaging rain.

The O'Driscoll, shouting over the sudden winds, beckoned everyone back into the shelter of the castle. The run back made for some merriment as it turned into a race for the castle, the menfolk giving way to Cera and Esi, who had both taken off at a fast clip.

Fresh bread, cheese and warm milk were promptly served from the kitchen, as the group assembled in the great hall, pride of place being given to Jean. Once the excitement had died down, Guiscard conferred with the O'Driscoll, then called for attention. 'Ladies, gentlemen and brother monks, first let me introduce you to Jean du Fay of the Poor Fellow-Soldiers of Christ and of the Temple of Solomon. The O'Driscoll, with whom we have shared what we know of affairs in France, and who have provided such valuable sanctuary from French mischief, are most welcome to stay to hear Jean's news.'

Cera rose, and nodded towards her husband. 'Guiscard, that is kind, but there are Templar matters which may require to be shared without limits, and beyond our understanding or right to know.'

She beckoned towards the O'Driscoll, who promptly rose. 'My wife is correct. We will vacate the hall for you. After you have considered your reports, please let me know what your conclusions are.'

The O'Driscoll clapped his hands and gestured for the staff to exit the room, leaving the Templars huddled around the great fireplace, where flames crackled, drawn up by the squall passing the mouth of the chimney above.

The room settled into silence as Jean stood up to speak, preferring to pace across the open hearth as he organised his thoughts. The fire surged as the Templar spymaster began. 'Brothers, Esi, so much has happened. Although Guiscard has told me of his warning from Sir Gilbert, there is much that you do not know. I am afraid that things are considerably worse than we expected after you fled Paris.'

The group shifted uncomfortably as Jean struggled to find the right words, 'On the morning of Friday the thirteenth of October, the King of France raided every Templar location, sparing nothing.'

Esi shot up. 'That's the morning that Cormac was attacked when night-walking! Guiscard, is this to be deemed coincidence?' She glanced at him in query, but he remained silent.

Jean continued. 'By my calculation, there have been more than six hundred arrests. It was highly organised, lightning fast and, I am afraid to say, hugely successful. In Paris, all senior Templars were arrested and immediately tortured.'

Fabian interrupted hotly, 'But surely not! How can temporal authorities inflict torture on Catholic monks in a Catholic country, without the sanction of the pope?'

Guiscard gestured for the Templar to calm, and re-take his seat. 'Brothers, we have much to discuss, including Esi's report. Let us first hear all, and then consider our position.'

Jean continued once more. 'The pope was not informed. William of Paris led the Dominican inquisition without papal authority. He acts for the kingly, not the priestly, pillar. His oaths to serve God are a fiction, his robes a disguise for his purpose. Unhappily, the charges levelled against the Order are egregious, and mounting. This includes denying Christ, spitting on the Cross, practising idolatry, and committing carnal acts, including sodomy. It is in keeping with what King Philip has previously alleged against his enemies. False testimony had been sworn, oiled by royal silver; it is clear that the Order had been infiltrated by de Nogaret's agents.'

Guiscard raised his hand to seek a pause. 'Jean, has everyone and everything been taken?'

'No, we also have agents at the royal court, and took the precaution of dispersing our most treasured documents and relics. Many fled to Portugal, including Astralabius, but there, I'm afraid, the news is very sad. His old heart eventually succumbed to the calling of Our Lord, just as he arrived at Tomar.' Jean removed a wax-sealed letter from his coat and gently handed it to Esi. 'Astralabius sent this. It is his final letter. He requested that it be given to you in person, Esi.' The room went silent as the monks bowed in prayer for their fallen brother.

Sobbing openly, Esi broke the seal and read the letter quietly through her tears. She then caressed it softly in an act of farewell, and gently folded it, to re-read in private at a later time.

Jean waited for her to finish, then pressed on. 'The galley sailed from Lisbon, where King Denis is establishing a new navy, using Genoese expertise, with which to protect the southern flanks from Muslim Spain. We have established our main sanctuary at Tomar, under his protection. He does not accept the allegations against the Order; besides which, he needs help to build his country and protect his realm, which lies on the frontiers of Islam.'

Guiscard shuffled uncomfortably in his seat. 'So, what of Jacque and Geoffrey, and what help, if any, from the Holy Father?'

'Brace yourself, brother. Jacque's feet were scorched, and Geoffrey was crucified and scourged. Jacque's confession to heresy, followed by that of Hugh of Pairaud, broke whatever resistance could be mounted in isolation from each other. By the time a cardinal reached Jacque, a month later, and he retracted his confession, it was too late.'

'Can nothing be done, Jean?' Guiscard asked incredulously.

'To save them, nothing: our military strength is gone. But I managed to slip notes to both of them through Marguerite's contacts. It was my final report. I gave each of them my assessment: that the only thing left to be defended is the legacy of the Knights Templar, that the Order's light must shine through history, and that the manner of their deaths was the only currency left.'

'You have guided them to retract their confessions?' Guiscard asked, ashen faced. 'But a relapse into heresy will mean a public death in Philip's fires.'

'Yes, because we must be seen to fight. The Knights Templar must have meant something for the ages. The pope has slowed down Philip by issuing a papal bull, *Pastoralis Praeeminentiae*. It is an attempt to establish papal control over the rest of the Templar inquisition, but the damage is irreversible. He can only slow Philip; he cannot stop him. On the heels of the pope's intervention, in the past few weeks, every Templar within the reach of Edward II has been arrested – although I do not expect them to receive anything like the brutality meted out by Philip. Naples and Cyprus have followed, and arrests are expected even in Dublin.'

'How has Philip reacted to Clement inserting himself into his inquisition?' Fabian asked.

'He galvanises his power. He has pressed on all university scholars of theology and law to find in his favour. They cannot, of course, because he acts outside church law, but they grovel and praise him for his zeal, implying that his allegations are so serious as to warrant his action on behalf of the Church. He is gathering evidence with which to overwhelm the papal court.'

'It is a dismal report, Jean. You have had much more time to think on these matters than we have. What do you advise?' Guiscard asked the question which hovered on everyone's lips.

Jean sighed. 'The Knights Templar is finished. It ended when Philip acted to crush it. That the confessions will be retracted will have little impact on the outcome. What remains is to disperse, with our knowledge intact. Disperse, I mean, into new structures.'

Fabian raised his hand to speak. 'In the kingdom of Desmond, we are safe, but the clans could not long resist an invasion by both kings, if Edward acts as a proxy for Philip. This cannot be a permanent home. The alternative to Portugal is to head north-east, to Scotland.'

'To Scotland?' Esi asked, startled. 'Why Scotland, in heaven's name?'

'There is a new king,' Fabian replied, 'Robert the First, who has soundly beaten King Edward's knights in open battle in Ayrshire, at Loudoun Hill. He makes Scotland into a fortress, and raids southwards at will.'

'Aye, Fabian has a point,' Jean agreed. 'I like the look of this Scottish king; he descends from Aoife, the warrior-princess of Leinster. Also, in our favour, he was excommunicated by Pope Clement for the sin of killing his rival, John Comyn, at the altar in Greyfriars Kirk, so he, too, is outside the Catholic Church.'

'It makes sound sense, if we are to go underground, so to speak, to cast our efforts across kingdoms and lands,' Fabian continued. 'Besides, this Robert will welcome former Templars, to sharpen his swords and bolster his battle tactics. Longshanks' son will not lightly give up claims over Scotland, nor the pope his excommunication of its king – certainly not with Edward marrying Philip's daughter, Isabel.'

Guiscard rose and walked the length of the hall in thought, before returning. 'There is much here to consider, but we must know what it is we are defending, what we nurture and keep safe.' He looked towards Esi. 'When will you be ready to impart what you have learnt from that infernal box?'

Esi, her face wet with tears, fought to compose her reply. 'Now is as good a time as any. The silver casket has been revealing its contents of thin copper plates imprinted in several languages. Ancient Greek is known to me. Another, ancient Persian, less so. It has been a delicate task, cleaning and separating the sheets. Cera has been vital, not just for her dedication to the task, but for her knowledge of the Bible. May she join us?'

Guiscard looked towards Jean, who replied, 'I see no reason why not. The Order is no more, but our knowledge remains. Oaths and secrets protect us no longer, here.'

The rain and wind continued to grow in intensity, battering the windows and rattling the roof of the castle, while outside, the light darkened. As Esi left to fetch the casket and call Cera, she felt Cormac's arms envelop her from behind.

'You loved that old man like a father, Esi, that is clear, and I sense that you are overwhelmed at his loss.' Her shoulders shook as she sobbed. Cormac turned her gently around and hugged her, allowing her to give in to her grief. She sobbed uncontrollably, her body shaking in waves, before recovering her poise.

'Your deep loss is not the only thing I have felt, Esi. There is another presence here. I have sensed its malevolence before, in the corridor of my dreams, and on the hill. It is uncoiling nearby, watching, listening. It is unfolding its hatred.'

He placed his hand over her heart. 'I felt its loathing, as real as I feel your heartbeat here. Cold hatred surged against you the instant you promised to open that box. It was marking you out, Esi. I know it. I will not stand for that.'

Esi looked at him, startled. 'What are you saying to me? Do we thwart this thing by belaying the revelations from our study?'

'No, Esi, that is the most dangerous road to take. It is only when that box speaks that you will be safe, but I fear its assault is imminent. It knows what you intend to do, and its intention will be to kill you for it. I cannot let that happen. I must face it again, Esi. It is the only way I know to protect you and all who are here.'

She looked into his eyes, stricken with fear, but saw a flash she had not seen before, a swirl of colour. 'How can you hope to wrestle with that thing, Cormac? It seeks your eternal despair.'

'It failed twice, and I believe that to have meaning, I must trust in that feeling. There is no other way. You will find me on the balcony overlooking the great hall when this has been done.'

CHAPTER 31

The meeting restarted after a short break, while the storm gathered its main strength offshore and coiled, waiting to unfold itself onto the land. Cera joined them, carrying books and notes. Esi walked behind with the casket and its treasure of copper plates, indented with alien script. Both women now took control of the meeting, the men rearranging the seating near the fire to give the women the top of the table. They moved instinctively closer to the great hearth, which was becoming the stronger source of light in the long room as the sun began to weaken outside.

*

Above them, in shadow, Cormac relaxed quietly in a seat, his arms resting gently on its wings. He faced them from behind, eyes closed, a candle burning low on the bench next to him, his back to the stained-glass window, which gathered light from the highest point in the sun's arc across the horizon, and cast it along the great hall. Outside, the winter storm continued to tap its fingers on the castle roof. He breathed deeply, each cycle of inhaling and exhaling slowing his mind, bringing it to rest on the present moment. Each time his thoughts sought attention, distracting him with the storm, he gently but firmly returned to emptying his mind. Each time he returned to his breath, to not thinking, to allowing his mind to reach a state of calm, ready to receive. His breath slowed, until we was taking just a few breaths each minute, from deep from within his abdomen. He was ready.

*

Esi looked nervously over the huddled group, and began slowly. 'We had to proceed carefully and cautiously, the task slow and delicate, so as not to damage the precious contents of the casket.' She lifted it up, so all could see. 'You will see that it is quite plain, except for here.' She gently caressed the polished surface at the front of the open casket. 'Here you will see a symbol which is perhaps familiar to you.'

Leaning forward, they all clearly recognised an unpretentious sign in the silver. 'This symbol, we know, was used by the first Christians: the sign of the fish. What does that tell you?'

'Let me guess, Esi. It is not what is on the casket, it is what is *not* on it that intrigues you.' Jean noted.

'Precisely. The earliest symbol was not the Cross but the sign of the little fish, the *Nasrani*, in Arabic. The cross and its symbolism, as you will see, followed later,' Esi replied, nodding towards Cera, who took up the cue.

'We know that the earliest practice was to mark important locations with this simple sign of the fish, not the Cross. But by whom was this started? In the writings of Epiphanius, the Bishop of Cyprus, the Nasaraioi was a Jewish sect which considered its members to be as little fish.'

As Cera spoke, Esi angled the casket and pointed. 'See here, it is not the only symbol we found as we cleaned the casket. We slowly revealed other symbols which Hypatia must have had inscribed to announce its antiquity.'

They leaned forward, following her fingers as she traced the workmanship on the casket. 'You will see here, the T-shaped cross. This is a reminder not just of the shape of the Cross upon which the Christ was crucified, but is also the symbol painted on doors at Passover by the Jews, before the Exodus from Egypt. It is not the only hint of what is contained herein. There is a remarkable symbol at the top of the casket, see?' Esi held up the lid and turned it slowly, sketching a clear outline.

They each studied the shape that emerged: a symbol known to them from the Catholic hierarchy.

Fabian commented, 'But why would Hypatia put a drawing of a mitred bishop holding a cross on her casket? It makes no sense.'

'Because, Fabian, that is not a Christian bishop at all,' Esi replied. 'That which you have all assumed to be Church regalia, is not. It is an ancient Egyptian form which I believe means "amen", and the crucifix-type cross being held in the hand is also Egyptian writing. It means "saviour".'

Outside, the wind had grown further in strength, whistling over the roof of the castle, drawing great tongues of fire from the dry logs at its base, while rain lashed at the narrow windows. The hall seemed to crackle with energy.

*

Above them, Cormac's body started to vibrate, his eyelids flickering. He was night-walking. His breath was now barely perceptible. In his mind, he was walking slowly through huge, grey-barked trees, which soared upwards to a forest roof. Everywhere there was life: water sparkling on leaves glistening in rays of sun which reached through the canopy, bees and other insects busy about their tasks, and small birds flickering between flowers and shrubs. He was at peace. Through the leaf-cover he could make out a tall dry-stone wall. He ran his hands along its length, eventually discovering a door. He gently pressed down the latch and pushed it open, to reveal stone steps leading to a field of green rushes. He stepped through, feet bare, and entered the field. His hands, reaching out gently, caused the rushes to fall away, as if blown by a breeze. They were weaving to and fro with his breath.

He arrived at some large grey stone slabs of heavy rock, which paved the way to a ledge that hung above an ocean, far below. Hundreds of feet down, great rollers curled lazily. He walked calmly to the edge, curling his toes over the lip of the stone slab. He breathed slowly, and the ocean responded, the great waves clawing and receding, as if he were breathing them in and out, in and out.

*

Esi pressed on, her audience staring at the silver casket as if it had, itself, come alive to speak to them. 'Look, all this is much easier if you accept one simple truth: that the world as we know it today, partially dominated by Christianity, and to the south by Islam, did not begin in the days about which we have been told. It is much older; its traditions and conventions run deep into human history.'

Esi watched the audience stiffen. This would not be easy for them, despite the knowledge they already held. She realised she needed to provide some context, or she would lose them. 'On the hill, I interrupted the attack on Cormac with ancient Persian, addressing that thing, Ahriman, by its name in Zoroastrianism.'

The windows and roof erupted, the wind violently lifting loose debris, and hurling it at the castle. It seemed angry at the defiance of the stone structure, craving entrance, seeking attention, willing the revelations to cease. The temperature dropped further outside, darkness deepening to purple; still the storm gathered power, forcing Esi to raise her voice to compete with the din. 'That Persian religion most likely predates Moses and the Exodus,' she said. 'It relies upon the sacrifice of a saviour who mediates with God. Heaven and hell, resurrection, living a godly life, and the last day of judgement: it is all there, long before events in Egypt, and events much later in Judaea. The virgin birth, which you believe is central to Christianity, is everywhere. Zoraster was born of a virgin, but this was also the case for more distant religions: Buddha and Krishna were also born of virgins.'

*

Cormac first felt it as a pressure, coming in from all sides. He continued to breathe the huge waves in and out, in order to be in command of the sea. He sensed a compulsion to step from the cliff. He looked down. Hundreds of feet below, he could see white seabirds flying to nests clinging to the face of the cliffs, and below them, greened rocks and spray. He raised his foot out over the edge, and took a step. In his mind, he held an image of Esi. Instantly he was elsewhere, inside, in the dense darkness of a stone-lined space. He sensed he was in a shrine of sorts, devoid of windows. Before him rested a great stone altar. This is not just a shrine, he realised. It is a *lair*. Then he felt the anti-life filling the space around him with its pulsing presence: *Ahriman*.

*

Seeing the impact of Esi's words on the men before her, Cera held aloft her Bible, worn from years of study. 'The name itself, Jesus Christ, is a later Greek title given to our Saviour, whose real Jewish name is absent from the Bible. It is upon this book that we rely, but it has been subject to much rewriting, including Constantine's Council of Nicaea, which chose what was heresy and what was not.

'What Cera is really telling you is to brace yourself for what I am about to reveal,' Esi said pragmatically. 'Hypatia was constrained by the material available to her in those days, capable of carrying messages over the ages. She chose copper scroll, and clipped it for purpose. The writing style is concise, like a set of conclusions from many years of study. We do not have the source material, simply the summary of her findings. This is its strength and also its weakness. But it talks to us with the voice of the last great pagan philosopher, mathematician, and scholar, a woman not captive to religious superstitions or conventions.'

'You admire this Hypatia.' It was Ultan, who rarely spoke. 'But do you *trust* her?'

It was a question none had thought to ask, awed by Esi's firmness of thought. She was startled by the bunt astuteness of the question. 'Gallowglass, I should have expected that. It is an issue that Astralabius also raises in his last letter to me.' She paused. 'Hypatia is impressive, in both her knowledge and her courage, but do I trust her? That requires my instincts, precisely what Astralabius has asked that I use more often, because gaps in knowledge first need to be filled with informed conjecture. But isn't all religion a conjecture? Can we know God?' She looked upwards towards the balcony, and could not see Cormac in the gathering gloom there. This worried her greatly. 'There is much yet that I need to learn if I am to fill in those gaps: much which is not written, but experienced. It does, however, fit together with the echoes from Alexandria. I cannot be certain about Hypatia's conclusions, but merely report and interpret on what I know of them. Does that answer your question, Ultan?'

The big man shrugged his shoulders. 'It will have to do. Because these men's lives depend on your judgement, woman.'

She recoiled as if she had been struck. *La vache!* she thought. He is right. In her desire to know, she had not fully considered that the words she spoke might condemn a man to death if they were uttered in the wrong company. She looked to Cera for support, and found in her eyes the courage and understanding she sought. She could not control the future, but she could bring light to the past, to help them steer a better course.

'It is evident from what Hypatia secreted in the casket that she was engaged in studying the records of the remaining Ebionites, the Nasorean sect which fled Jerusalem after the failed uprising. This was but one aspect of her studies; heaven knows what else she had access to in the remnants of the Great Library of Alexandria. The Jewish sect to which she was drawn was led initially by John the Baptist, whom the Nasorean saw as their priestly pillar, descending from the Levi line. Hypatia tells us there was not one messiah, but two, represented by the two pillars of Solomon's temple. The other pillar is the kingly line descended from the house of David. Both pillars, the priestly pillar representing righteousness, and the kingly pillar representing judgement, were overarched by Shalom, by God.' Here, Esi paused to let them absorb her words.

'But John the Baptist was beheaded, so ended the messiah in one swift act?' Fabian asked, as the gathering pulled blankets tighter around themselves against the creeping cold in the long room.

'It was not that simple, Fabian,' Cera said, pressing her hands closer to the fire for warmth. 'We know from Matthew, from Mark and from Luke that John the Baptist was imprisoned for some time. The Jewish historian Flavius Josephus tells us why: it was because of his power among the people and the possibility of rebellion. It was why Herod Antipas, the tetrarch of Galilee, had him in a cell. He knew that people believed he was the messiah. John the Baptist gave Herod the excuse he needed to execute him. He criticised the Galilean king for divorcing his wife and marrying Herodias, his brother's wife. To please his stepdaughter, Salomé, as a gift for her dancing, he brought her the head of the Baptist.'

Jean shuddered and pulled his stool closer to the heat, raising his hand to make a point. 'As I recall, John the Baptist plays only a small part in the New Testament; his primary function appears to be to validate the Christ by symbolic baptism, is that not so?'

'It is, Jean,' Esi said. 'He is presented as a character on the fringe – although it is what Hypatia sees in the baptism of the Christ at age thirty-one, his acceptance into the Nasorean sect by John the Baptist, and what happens after his decapitation by Herod, which is important. What Hypatia tells us is that the Nasorean sect lived in the desert near the Dead Sea. Herod's mighty fortress, Machaerus, which soared thousands of feet above, was situated on its eastern slopes. It was here that John the Baptist was put to death in 32 AD, bringing an end to his leadership. Do you see the significance? This put the Christ's ministry at just one year. You have in the Templar scrolls which were unearthed beneath the Temple Mount, the drawing of heavenly Jerusalem, containing both pillars. Consider those pillars, for they are vital. John the Baptist is replaced by J'acov, which translates from Hebrew to "James". That means James the Righteous, whose ministry lasted more than twenty years. James is brother to the Christ, but he is not the only one.'

Esi paused, spotting Fabian about to interject again, and put up her hand to signal him to hold. 'Hypatia's scroll speaks of Didymos Judas Thomas. In Aramaic, Thomas means "twin". He wrote of the sayings of the Christ in the Gospel of Thomas.' She quoted:

> *The disciples said to Jesus, 'We know that you will depart from us. Who is to be our leader?' Jesus said to them, 'Wherever you are, you are to go to James the Righteous, for whose sake heaven and earth came into being.'*

Fabian jumped to his feet. 'But that is not one of the Gospels accepted by the Holy Church, and what you are saying flies in the face of everything that we have been told! Anyway, what about His life of miracles among the people, and the manner of His death? What about the fact that He was the Son of God?'

Fabian's outburst silenced the long room. The temperature continued to plummet, and the unseated half of the room darkened, the candlelight losing its battle against the encroaching darkness, which appeared to be twinned with the cold.

Esi used the silence to wait for Fabian's eruption to cool, before replying calmly, 'The words of Hypatia reach us across the centuries from her enquiries. The Nasorean, the Gnostics, the Arian church, which includes the Irish Christian church, and even the Koran, did not require Jesus to be the Son of God for the mystery of Golgotha to shine. Hypatia has evidently studied the Bible carefully, in light of what she learnt from the Nasorean, and it begins to make sense.'

Fabian, still upset, continued, 'You say a ministry of one year, in which John the Baptist and his brother James were regarded by the Nasorean as the priestly messiah? So, what about the miracles, like raising Lazarus or turning water into wine at Cana? How do you explain these?

'It is how the words are used. The Nasorean was a Jewish sect. It was based in the desert near the Dead Sea. Membership required initiation, and unbroken service according to its rules. Those who are not yet members, and have not turned to the *wine* of the Nasorean, are called *water*. At Cana, Jesus the Christ was recruiting new members, turning water into wine. At the Sermon of the Mount, He was listing the rules of Nasorean membership required to gain access to the kingdom of heaven. At Bethany, He caused Lazarus to rise not from physical death but from his death to the Nasorean: that is, from his lapsed membership of the sect. He brought him back to life, the life of the Nasorean, as opposed to the death of being an outsider. Hypatia shows that the people the Nasorean referred to as dead, were simply those who had not yet converted, or those who had lapsed. Once you understand the use of the language, all becomes clear.'

Esi turned to Cera. 'Reveal what references you have found.'

Cera took over, giving Esi a chance to catch her breath. 'The idea of resurrecting through initiation is not at odds with the Bible. Bringing people in from the dead, raising them up, standing up, all fits, as does those who lapse being regarded as falling down, buried or dead. In Mark, 4:11, we have a clear reference: *And he said unto them, Unto you it is given to know the mystery of the Kingdom of God: but unto them that are without, all these things are done in parables.* In Mathew 8:21–22, Jesus is asked by one of the disciples for permission to attend his father's burial: *And another of his disciples said unto him, Lord, suffer me first to go and bury my father. But Jesus said unto him, 'Follow me; and let the dead bury the dead.'*

Cera slowed, glanced around to let the group absorb the significance of her words: that the Gospels could be read more simply. The other end of the long room was now fully shrouded in a purple darkness, compressing the heat and light to the smaller space near the fire, around which they huddled tightly, the better to hear the speakers over the bedlam of the raging storm. She continued. 'There is clear reference to a falling out of the sect in Acts 5:1, when a husband and wife are admonished by Peter after the Crucifixion for holding back money from their collection. *But Peter said, 'Ananias, why hath Satan filled thine heart to lie to the Holy Ghost and to keep back part of the price of the land?' And, Ananias hearing these words fell down, and gave up the ghost: and great fear came on all them that heard these things. And young men arose, bound him up and carried him out and buried him.*

Peter, who was clearly part of the sect, repeats the expulsion to the wife, Sapphira, who *Then fell down straightway at his feet and yielded up the ghost:*

and the young men came in, and found her dead, and, carrying her forth, buried her by her husband. And great fear came upon all the church, and upon as many as heard these things.'

'Precisely, Cera. There is no death or burial here, and "young men" means the initiated members of the Nasoreans,' Esi said. 'Employ your intelligence. Are we to believe that Peter, the rock of the Church, is ordering death by being buried alive, for the act of holding on to some money? Was Saint Peter a cruel and vile murderer? I don't think so. Neither did Hypatia. We come to the key moment as Jesus the Christ is condemned to death.'

*

Cormac sat motionless in the dark, isolated, abandoned and alone with *it*. The space was freezing cold. There was no joy there. This was its shrine. It pulsed with darkness. His breathing ran shallow, pushing against his mind's desire to surrender into terror, readying to flee. He shifted his mind and tried to return to calming his breath. He could barely make out the outline of a shape: its back was turned; a man, perhaps, but without clear edges, like a shadow, sculpted from blackness, and from the stone altar. He sensed it waiting, coiled, unhurried, its attention elsewhere, as if he were an insignificant fly, held captive in its black web, a meal to be consumed later. Again, despair and terror rose, but he immediately shifted his mind towards Esi. In a flash of determination, he pushed his mind across the space between them and concentrated on one thought only. 'Ahriman, I see you.'

*

Beyond the castle windows, the storm suddenly stopped, as if it had paused to eavesdrop. Gone was the incessant banging from debris pockmarking the rising roar of the wind. The suddenness caused Esi to wait until the group had settled. The darkness intensified as if day had turned to night, and cold raindrops started to freeze on the windows. Inside the long room, everyone looked towards the ceiling, expecting a revival of the din at any moment, assuming that they were in the eye of an uncommon winter storm. The quietness extended, but the freezing descended into the air, inside the long room. Outside, the boiling sea flattened as the wind vanished, to be replaced by an impenetrable fog. It rolled across the islands towards Baltimore, curling its dark fingers across the moorings, separating the fleet from land, and then boats from each other. Visibility fell to just a few feet. Candles were lost in the gloom.

Esi caressed the casket as if, by doing so, she was drawing strength from Hypatia. She looked towards the balcony; she did not know why she did this, only that it helped her to draw on her courage. She continued her report.

'Pilate washed his hands, remember? Hand-washing is a ceremony in the Jewish tradition: one for after death, and never before. It is a poor insertion, made later. It was made to absolve the Romans. The release of a common criminal at Passover is another cover-story, but for what purpose? The Romans had no such tradition, and anyway, it is illogical. Why would the Jews choose a common criminal over a holy man, unless the tale was later constructed to absolve the Romans and blame the Jews for the death of the Christ? The Jews are still suffering for that lie today, including under Philip. No, Hypatia's explanation makes more sense: Pilate had two saviours captive, two Jesuses, one kingly, whom we know as Jesus the Christ, and the other priestly, his brother James. Pilate and the Sanhedrin feared the crowd, but knew that the priestly messiah was deemed more valuable to the Jews. That is why the crowd chose to release Barabbas. He was not a common criminal; he was James the Righteous. Barabbas is not a name but a title: Bar means 'son of' and Abba means 'father'.

The intake of breath in the room was audible – and visible – in the cold air. The air was freezing quickly now. Esi stopped mid-flow and looked over the group slowly, stressing her conclusion. 'Jesus *did* sacrifice himself. The mystery of Golgotha, however, is not in His death but in His passage through the land of the dead before resurrection, and what Jesus achieved in the spirit-world. He was not the Son of God; neither was James nor John the Baptist; but they were *of* God, and form part of a lineage. That is the true mystery, isn't it, Guiscard? But you knew about John the Baptist and about James, so none of this is a surprise to you, is it?'

Startled by the sudden thrust by Esi, the group spun towards the old monk, catching his nervous glance towards Jean. Esi then addressed both men directly. 'There are circles within circles, are there not? When were you going to tell us of the Johannite church? Hugh de Payens, one of the two knights on the horse, became a John, didn't he?'

Guiscard squirmed visibly and chose his words carefully. 'He did: he became the seventieth in a line back to John the Baptist, the priest-messiah of the Nasorean.'

'And this occurred in the Holy Land, when some of the founders of the Order were initiated into Johannism. But by whom?' Esi asked.

'By Theoclete, the patriarch of the Johannite church,' Guiscard responded.

'It is why the Templars continued to excavate under the Temple Mount for more artefacts put there by the Nasorean, is it not?' Esi asked.

Guiscard nodded. 'How did you know?'

'Because Hypatia studied ancient Jewish documents from the first century, which claim to be the last testament of Moses, Prince of Egypt. These give his successor, Joshua, clear instructions to conceal the sacred books of knowledge in what Hypatia believed to be the holy of holies – which means, under the Temple Mount. She also relies on the Jewish text, the Tosefta Shebuot, which dates from this tumultuous period, when Judaea seethed under Roman rule. It makes direct reference to a race to the altar between two brothers who were priests, and to Rabbi Tsedeq, the priestly messiah, announcing a death on the steps of the Temple Mount. It can only have been James talking about his brother's death. You also registered no surprise at Hypatia's conclusions, because you already had some of this knowledge, did you not, Jean?'

The Templar spymaster did something he did rarely: he smiled. 'Touché, Esi. The allegation of denying Christ, while grossly exaggerated by Philip to suit his twisted purposes, is, in part, true. We do not deny *Christ*, but the basis upon which the Catholic Church has been grounded.'

'Ah the sweet, clear sound of truth! It chimes like the perfect bell, does it not? That brings me to the one the Ebionites describe as the spout of lies. Let us deal with him next.'

Esi nodded to Cera, who looked at her notes. 'After the death and resurrection of the Christ,' Cera paused momentarily, 'we find Saul of Tarsus on a journey to visit James the Just in Acts 22:14. *And he said, 'The God of our fathers hath chosen thee, that thou shouldest know his will, and see the Just One, and shouldest hear the voice of his mouth.'* So, the Roman Jew from Turkey converts on the road to Damascus; but what I conclude this means, is the road to the Nasorean initiation.'

*

Cormac sensed a gale of venomous attention suddenly upon him. He felt black fingers envelop his spine, curling around it, preparing to wrench it from his body. He felt his heart being compressed, as though between two great anvils. He felt desolation. In that moment, against his will, he was suspended above a teeming mass of what first looked like black ants devouring their prey alive, but then transformed into the black robes feasting on their victim in the Caesareum. He could see beneath them, writhing pale flesh which gushed sprays of red as the frenzy of black robes carved, cut and slashed, stripping, removing and discarding the skin of their victim. He was drawn to look down through the black robes, into a familiar pair of green eyes, which pleaded at him in terrified agony as the head was being scalped. It is Esi! I cannot allow this again. I must stop it.

*

Below him, Esi added, 'What really jumps out, the most striking finding from Hypatia, is the venom reserved by the Nasoreans for Paul. He has lied. He lied about his training, as a Nasorean, just as he had lied about his training as a Pharisee, when he had been an agent of the High Priest. It is why apostles were sent to challenge his authority, and his teaching. Paul denounced them as servants of Satan, and false apostles. It is clear from his own writing that there were two opposing views about the mission of the Christ: that of James, his brother, and that of Paul, who never knew him.'

Esi slowed, looked towards Fabian, who was clearly still struggling to reconcile what he was hearing with what he had been taught. 'Fabian, remember from your Bible, Paul writes that he made himself a Jew to the Jews, to win the Jews, that he made himself all things to all men, that he was free of the law – which was how he intended to win. In other words, the end justified the means. It is why James called him the spouter of lies. In Romans 13:1, we see that Paul did not confine himself to constructing a religion for Hellenistic tastes, but openly sided with, and courted, the Herodian rulers of Jerusalem, proclaiming: *You must obey the governing authorities. Since all government comes from God, the civil authorities were appointed by God.* Paul openly describes himself as 'the architect'. That is his choice of word, and he describes Christ as the 'cornerstone'. That is his word too. He made up what we call Christianity, and built the weight of the story around the sacrifice of Christ, and not his descent into the spirit-world. This is the first heresy. It could not be any clearer why Hypatia chose to send it to a time which was more open to enquiry, and why she was slaughtered by the Christians.

*

Cormac twisted and vibrated violently. He felt nauseous, almost overcome with dread and desolation. But this time he refused to succumb. Instead, he reached out his mind to Ahriman. 'You seek to strip us of love, but we are loved, we are all loved because we are of the Divine. What we have to do is to remember. This is what you most fear, isn't it, Ahriman? Our memory. It is why Christ's mission was never to create a church of stone and rules, but a community of love in direct communion with God. This is what you fear: that we will remember that we are, all of us, angels.'

The dark shadow instantly recoiled, and its outline began to lose definition, to fade. The sides of the stone shrine dissolved into sun and sea. Cormac still stood at the cliff, sensing Ahriman's loathing behind him. He chose not to turn his head, but instead said, 'You too are loved, Ahriman. There is no love like the Divine. You are on your own journey back to Him.'

Below him, instantly, the sea first flattened, and then was almost rent in two, with the force of cold fury that exploded outward from the cliff-face and carried out to the farthest horizon.

*

In the castle, the sun suddenly poured through the stained-glass window, splintering into colours. In the harbour, a rainbow formed across the retreating black clouds.

Esi stopped to let them take a breath at the profound implications of what she had just revealed to them. After the room had settled, she continued in a gentler tone. 'Remember, it is Paul who provides the name, *Christians*, the Greek translation of the Hebrew word for 'messiah'. He sees actual events in the parables, and applies the Hellenistic view of the man Jesus Christ.'

Fabian shrugged. 'Does it matter how he appeared? Surely that is of little relevance to the substance of the man?'

'Indeed, you are correct,' Esi responded. 'But it might explain a few quotations, and why he died quickly from breathing difficulties when he was crucified. Hypatia chased down a physical description at the time of his arrest. Described in works by Josephus, the Jewish historian, Jesus was small in stature – three cubits high – and hunchbacked, a shape that could not have sat easily with the Graeco-Roman view of a god. It may not be accurate, Hypatia concludes, but in the Acts of John there is another reference to small stature, and again in Luke 19:3, when Zacchaeus *sought to see Jesus who he was; and he could not for the crowd, because he was low of stature.*

Fabian, who had ceased shaking his head in disbelief, asked, 'What happened to both men?'

'Based on a Gospel which didn't make it past the Council of Nicaea, James, probably in full regalia, wearing the mitre of the first bishop of Jerusalem, followed in his brother's footsteps, and forced his way into the Temple. He was stoned to death by the Jewish priests. I believe that it was one of those events which added to the boiling pot that erupted into the war with Rome and the sack of Jerusalem. Several years after James's stoning, Paul was beheaded in Rome by Emperor Nero, who had chosen the Christians as the scapegoat for the great fire which swept the city.'

'God in heaven, Esi,' Fabian proclaimed, slumping into his chair. 'This is all beyond shocking.'

'Aye, it is shocking but not unsurprising, brother,' said Guiscard softly. 'Strip away all the confusion, and the mission of Christ is clear: to connect us directly with the Divine, to help us remember, and to show us the path to Him, to ascend. He did not come in order to build a church to get in the way.'

It is time to finish, Esi thought. The cold and dark has retreated. A joyous light again grows outside, and Cormac's eyes are open. I have relayed Hypatia's message from across the centuries as best I can; my purpose here is ending. 'Templars, you are no more: you lose an Order, but you gain a new understanding of Jesus, part of the Divine, begotten by God. Jesus ascended in the spirit-world after his death, and lit the way for humanity. The mystery of Golgotha was not in his physical death, but in the new life he brought to the dead, to all of us, turning water into wine. It is why the old Adversary fears him so.'

Esi sat, exhausted.

Guiscard rose and paced the room, as if in doing so he could help drive away the gloom which had enveloped it. Outside, the fog had blown through, a gentle breeze pushing it inland, giving way to blue skies. 'We have heard much, and witnessed much, this day. All must reflect on what has been revealed. The first heresy – for it is surely the first, if it is true – questions the very foundation of the Catholic Church, its position as an intermediary to God, and implies that it has been infiltrated. Hypatia's words down the centuries reinforce the need for a great remembering, a great longing to go home, for personal experience of the Divine.'

Guiscard ceased his pacing at the door to the long room, which was now bathed in sunlight. 'But the information cannot leave this room, not without risk to all, until we are decided on our next steps. I will consult with my brother monks on what is best, and then we can reconvene. But for now, I have a blinding headache, trying to keep pace with these women! I do not think I could bear another revelation. This meeting is over.'

CHAPTER 32

After the room had emptied, Esi looked for Cormac. She sensed him, and needed to connect with him, to hear about his night-walk. He was quiet after the others had gone: hard to read, as if transported elsewhere. Then the young Norman slipped away. No one had spoken to him; she was curious, and a little troubled. He was much more than he appeared. Young, vibrant, curious; now there was something else, but what? Then she realised. He felt ancient. That was it: not aged, but ancient beyond his years, and it was to do with his night-walks.

Part of her loved him, she knew that now, and part of her wanted desperately to learn more about his visions. Her instincts flared with connections yet to be made, her learning of the physical world, his of the mystical. Just like the twin pillars, she thought, or the staff and the serpent. It was an idea, still in formation, in her mind. It had something to do with a law of opposites, and she thought Cormac might be the path to understanding it.

By mid-afternoon, the sky had fully cleared to the south-west, bringing with it a sudden calmness, with a glorious low-hanging sun arcing across the horizon. It was as if the sun itself had chased away the yammering wind and rain, and the strange fog which had followed. It is a rebirth, she thought. Just then, she spotted Cormac on a huge horse, rounding the hill which overlooked Baltimore. He waved to her.

Her heart leapt. She felt her face flushing, and found herself clapping. Why did I clap just now, like a little girl? What was that? He is just a boy. But she found herself running towards him as he gently eased the horse down the steep decline, coming to rest at a small boulder.

'Esi, jump up. I want to show you something sacred, something nearby, as the sun sinks; someplace safe from that thing.'

Then he did something he had never done before: he winked at her. It is a mischief, she thought, and caught herself getting excited. She loved the mystery of it. She mounted behind him, and put her arms around his strong, narrow waist. 'Where are we going, Cormac?'

'Not far, Esi. Be patient. I'm taking you to a sacred place. I've been going here quite a bit on Eochaid here, the O'Driscoll's favourite mare. You'll see why, soon. She knows her way around these hills, like a spirit of the woodland, and she's gentle. Feel her rhythm.'

Esi let herself move rhythmically with Cormac, quickly finding that Eochaid became one with them both as they cantered over the brow of the hill.

'See there, Esi?' Cormac pointed to a high mound of wood which had been transported by the clan to the highest point overlooking the bay. 'That is the great fire they will light tonight. It is one reason why I brought you here.'

Esi scanned through her knowledge as she stared at the bonfire, trying to make the connection. 'Tomorrow is one of the four great Celtic festivals, isn't it? The festival of Saint Brigid. How could I have forgotten?'

'Aye, Esi, it is *Imbolg*, the first day of February. The turn of winter, and the run into the vernal equinox. It will be a beautiful night. The storm has cleared, so I am taking you to a sacred place of rowan and willow, which is a very special sight. Why is rowan and willow important, Esi?'

She paused, hugging him close. She loved this kind of conversation. 'Let me see: rowan is for protection, according to the ancient beliefs of this land, and willow, Cera told me, is their connection to knowledge and healing.'

'This, you will see, is a sacred place, secure from the malign. Both trees are sacred to the priestly caste which predated Christianity. The druids were the philosopher-teachers and judges who held nature to be part of the Divine. Unlike Hypatia, they chose not to write down their knowledge, but to pass it on after twenty years of study, to their students, and so on down the generations.'

'Imagine what secrets they must have known, Cormac!'

'They were not secrets, Esi, they were night-walkers who experienced the Divine at a time when the connection was much easier, the veil thinner; when dreams were visions and mankind spoke to great spiritual beings. I will explain in a while.'

Esi marvelled at the transformation. It was as if Cormac had emerged, like a butterfly from a cocoon, and was treating her as a woman, and an equal. She hugged him tightly at the thought, even though Eochaid's gentle movements did not require it.

They crested the next hill inland, and moved steeply down its side before taking a narrow woodland track, where the tall trees almost blocked out the sun. Cormac guided the mare upwards again. She took easily to the slope, familiar with the ground, powering her hind-quarters while she pulled more air into her huge lungs.

He stopped in a grove surrounded by rowan trees, and dismounted, before helping Esi down from the large mare. At the centre of the clearing lay a flat boulder, above which a willow tree swayed, its long thin branches fluttering, as if welcoming guests. 'Esi, we are safe here. I found this grove after talking to some of the local people about the olden days. They believe it was a place where druids would go to meditate, to take their night-walks. I have spent much time here, and have learned much – which is the reason why I brought you.' He turned, and took her by her hand. 'Come, we ascend from here to the top of the hill, above the treeline.'

They started up the path, pressing past the trees to the rocky pathway, as daylight started to fade from the west and the clear night sky announced itself. Suddenly they crested the hill, and Esi gasped at the vista. Below her was a lake thwhichat seemed to blend into the sea. But how could it, she thought. She could almost sense power flowing from the grove up to the ceiling of stars, as if birthed by Brigid herself. She turned towards Cormac, could see his warm smile as he watched her silently absorb it all.

She sat on Cormac's blanket. 'Below you, Esi, is Loch Oighinn, a lake like no other. It drains its freshwater into the sea and seawater back into the lake, ebbing and flowing over the rapids with the tide, and around it, springs life in trees and plants that are unique to this place. It is sacred, which is why the druids chose it; or it chose them, as it did me.'

Cormac paused, and looked deep into her eyes. 'It is secure from the Adversary.'

She looked at him curiously. He was leading to something he wished to share. They lay flat on the blanket, staring up into the first starlit sky of spring.

'See there, Esi, all the twinkling lights which go on forever. They are always there, only masked by the brightness of the sun. Everything is connected, from the tiniest plant to the brightest stars. Everything vibrates and moves. The world, as you see it through your eyes, is limited, not just by eyesight, but by a change in the connection of mankind to the Divine.'

Esi, mute at the scale of Cormac's opening comments, resolved to tiptoe softly through the next few minutes, not wanting to interrupt with her usual pointed questions. 'How do you know these things, Cormac?'

He reached out and held her hand. 'Let me show you, Esi. I have been practising night-walks, without guides or drum; just myself and all that is here – which seems to nurture it. It is hard to describe, but my mind opens with a tingling at the top of my head, and immediately the vibration begins. Can you feel it?' He closed his eyes. Through her fingers, she felt his whole body gently vibrate with energy, which ran through her too. It was not alien, not cold, but natural and warm. She felt safe. 'Here I begin,' he continued, 'as though I am in an outer ring and softly entering a void where I feel things. It is not like sight; it is feelings, Esi. First it was hazy, distant, indistinct, until I stopped concentrating, and learned to see myself as an infant taking its first steps. By not trying, by clearing my mind of all thoughts other than just being, I enter. Here it is, opposite your world of research, facts making connections by logic, by deduction.'

'As I did today?'

'Precisely. It is why I brought you here, Esi: to fill some of the gaps for you from what I have felt, even though I have no manuscripts, no years of study, and no time-casket from Hypatia. There is no proof here, Esi, just knowing. Do you understand?'

'I think I do, Cormac, but it is difficult, because my mind has been trained to ask, to probe, to prove.'

'For everything, there is an opposite. One cannot be without the other, just like your twin pillars, and how you found the casket. Even the Divine has an opposite. It is a being called Sorat. We are not separate, but part of the Divine. Our soul is part of him, and he of us. Each of us has a higher self: our spirit.'

'Is that why the Church sought to extinguish that part of our nature?'

'Yes, precisely, but we have no need of intermediaries, Esi. We just need to remember. We are on a journey back to the Divine across multiple lifetimes. Our pathway requires us to evolve, to become less of this world and more of that one.' Cormac pointed to the stars. 'We will evolve into beings of pure spirit, and lose the need for physical bodies, Esi, in ages to come. That journey requires us to lead lives of goodness, of love, of solidarity, such that we no longer just see the pain of others, we feel it. And then, we will not inflict hurt without hurting ourselves. What we feel, all feel; what we know, all know.'

'Why are we required to make this journey, Cormac? What stands in our way?'

'This is the gift of Jesus Christ, Esi: transformation. He chose the physical death and suffering of the Cross, not to lead to the creation of an intermediary Church, but to show us how we are to enter the world of the spirit at a pivotal point, how we are to ascend. He did so by confronting powerful opposing forces, to give us the gift of ascension, but the price of evolving means more separation from the Divine, before we finally no longer think *I* but *Christ in me*.'

'I don't understand, Cormac. Why would we not simply ascend like Him, if that is the destination?'

'Because it may not be the destination for all; not for those who succumb to the forces that seek to take us on different paths, paths that lead away from the Divine across multiple lives. The gift of Golgotha was freedom to think, free will. But to reach out to the Divine, we must first become more separated from Him. Jesus came to free mankind. He provided an example of how life ought to be led, and he entered the spirit world to reset it. But in doing so, we have found it harder to feel the spirit. It is the price of evolving.'

'So, Ahriman looks for what was taken by the Nasorean, by the Christ. That is from your first walk?'

'For everything the Divine is, Sorat is the opposite. The Divine created all you see above and around you. It all vibrates with His love. Everything is spinning and growing, as his universe expands. Sorat opposes this. It is quintessentially destructive, chaotic and hateful, yet serves a purpose. Sorat relies on two pillars, twin horns: powerful beings that seek to separate us from the Divine. Ahriman seeks to convince us that there is no Divine, that we are separated, alone, mechanical. His influence is growing as mankind learns more knowledge of the material world. This is his time to mislead man into believing in his omnipotence, his hubris, his power. It is why he chose Philip. Ahriman will eventually be able to penetrate the veil which separates us from the spirit-realm.'

'You mean that he will incarnate, as Jesus did?'

'His time has not yet come, but it matches the next epoch of Michael, six to seven hundred years from now.'

'That was the Amesha Spenta in the corridor?'

'Yes, but unlike other archangel epochs, Michael's is characterised by the giving of free will. It is through the exercise of free will in the midst of temptation to take other paths, that we evolve. It is why Ahriman hates him so.'

'When does Ahriman come?'

'He will incarnate to establish his followers when man reaches his most powerful control over nature through his invention, through knowledge. It is the same distance into the future that Hypatia's death was into the past.'

'The twin horns resonate with the vision of Saint John, in the Book of Revelations. Who is the other?'

'It is the Bringer of Light, Lucifer, a being who craves adoration, who yearns for souls to see him as the Divine. He is the opposite of Ahriman: he seeks not to disconnect from the spirit-world but to *be* the world itself, a world of sensual pleasure where entry is not earned. Both beings are an essential part of our evolution; both threaten to disconnect us from the Divine; but in doing so, they perform His task. It is by being in peril that we find how not to be. I know it is difficult, but it is the nature of it.'

Esi sat up and stared at the stars while she gathered her thoughts. 'It is so hard to understand this, with our grasp of time and space, Cormac, but it doesn't contradict the common threads which weave across all religions I have studied. How long have we been on this journey?'

'Hundreds of lifetimes, Esi, in many other worlds as well, and the end of times is not the end but a crossing over into pure spirit. This is what Jesus brought. It is as far ahead in time as the Great Flood is in the past. Not everyone will cross over; many will return, to start again. Ultimately, even Ahriman and Lucifer will return. All are loved; there is no love like the Divine; it is beyond measure or description in our world.'

Esi got to her feet, unable to still herself, her mind reeling with fresh connections which Cormac's words had fired. He watched her walk in circles, while he sat still. She turned, and offered her hand to him. 'Cormac, where do we go from here? I overheard the Templars plotting a voyage to Scotland in the late spring, and after that the galley will sail to Lisbon. There is even talk of a land to the west in ancient records.'

'Esi, you have a sharp mind, and a sharper tongue, but you are no warrior.' Cormac laughed aloud, filling the hilltop with his young voice, bringing Esi's pacing to a halt, as she joined in with him.

Then suddenly she felt tearful, as the truth escaped from her lips. 'But I cannot bear being away from centres of learning. I must follow across the universities of Europe, to Coimbra in Lisbon, to Bologna, Naples, Padua, and even across the Mediterranean, if I can get safely to the great Islamic centres that survived the Mongols. Maybe even over the mountains to India, and further. It is in my bones to do so, but I cannot explore these places, not without you.'

Cormac swung up to his feet, still chuckling, pushed back his red curls and spun around in a circle, just as the night-sky started to glow and flicker as the great fire of *Imbolg* was lit on the hilltop to welcome Brigid, the goddess of rebirth. He took both her hands in his and turned her slowly in a circle, to watch the hilltops light up one by one as far as the eye could see, mirroring the heavens.

'As above, so below!' he shouted with joy, his breath warm, gentle and fresh. 'It looks like we are stuck with each other again, in this life's journey, Esi.'

EPILOGUE

The dense blackness turned, coiled about itself, a thing of pulsating energy, darker than its black surroundings, an eternity of blackness. It felt; it thought; it watched. Not alive, not dead, but undead, housed in a realm like no other, from which it searched the far reaches of the universe, sending out its thoughts, probing, violating with its alien energy. No particles vibrated within it; instead, it consumed energy, sucked it into its maw, but no matter how much it consumed, it felt unfulfilled, unsated, alone. It had an infinite, ravenous appetite to hate; it loathed everything it touched, perceived, or imagined, because it was part of Him.

Still, it felt its power growing; it sought souls at the thin veil between dimensions, caught them in the in-between, those not yet stripped of their memories of the physical world, still being purified, vulnerable. Confused souls, unclear about the nature of the universe, unclear about Him. Souls with the footprints it sought, especially hate. It loved sweet hatred, especially when it was carried from below by souls who had chosen paths of chaos through lives, souls that were static, not evolving, but learning to hate, to tear down, to destroy, and were revelling in it.

It glorified tyranny, mass murders, destruction, lifelessness, a barrenness of nothing. At its centre was a vacuum, a great emptiness. The emptier and more alone it felt, the more powerful it would become.

The becoming will come, it thought. The veil will thin, I will step through, and be able to tolerate the light, the life, the energy-signals that I loathe so. It is just a matter of waiting, growing, readying for the ecstasy of incarnation. It visualised the moment of erupting into the world of mankind, sheathed in its disguise, ready to spring upon the flock of men, and consume souls alive. Not between realms but in the realm below, revelling in the extinction of eternal life. It cast its darkness outward in great waves of blackness which grew in strength, swelling, before breaking in every direction, announcing its hatred, its venom; displaying its power.

At the far reaches of its realm, it felt the presence of the eternal sentinel, Michael, Amesha Spenta. I feel you. I am becoming. You have nothing to stop what will unfold. Can you not feel the change, feel it now as I roll it towards you? It focused its attention behind the great wave it sent flooding in the direction of the flickering light, and waited, revelling in every moment. All around it, at every interface of its realm, it now perceived the infernal light flickering; it was everywhere. The darkness responded by spinning in circles wreathed in hatred, glaring, daring, challenging.

In the distance, the light grew, all around the horizon. The colours changed, no longer blue white, but flashing red, orange and yellow, before pausing on a pulsating green. It hated green most of all, the colour of their hearts. Green faded to blue, indigo, then violet. The colours danced, pulsed, joyfully flashing back to blue-white, before bursting into the seven colours again, sending a wave of bliss, joy and love which bit into it, generating pain, so much pain, the unbearable pain of being separated. From Him.

Before retreating in on itself to balm its wounds, it flashed its intent out to the very extremes of its realm. I am coming during Aquarius, the next age of Michael. You will feel the pain, emptiness and hatred which I have prepared for millennia.

For I am becoming.

Fictional Characters

Leon (1), personal slave and lifelong companion to Hypatia of Alexandria
Cormac Fitz Stephan (2), Norman Irish youth
Esi Benoit (3), aka Esi Akiba, Persian scholar, advisor to the Knights Templar
Guiscard Carrel (4), retired Templar warrior-monk
Bertramnus (5), Dominican monk and inquisitor
Astralabius Bazin (6), Templar monk and librarian
Jean du Fay (6), aka Le Grincheux, Templar monk and spymaster
Fabian D'Airelle (6), Templar monk and military strategist
Rostan D'Arcy (6), Templar monk and martial expert
Ultan (12), Gallowglass warrior
Felim (12), Gallowglass warrior
Simon du Merle (19), French knight, son of the Marshal of France
Eoin O'Driscoll (29), chieftain of the O'Driscoll clan, in the Kingdom of Desmond
Cera O'Driscoll (29), Biblical scholar and wife of Eoin O'Driscoll

Historical Characters

Hypatia of Alexandria (1), born c. 350–370, died 415; pagan philosopher, astronomer and mathematician, who lived in Alexandria, Egypt; member of the Neoplatonic school in Alexandria, taught philosophy and astronomy

Saint Cyril of Alexandria (1), patriarch (archbishop) of Alexandria; 76–444; protagonist in Christian heresies; held Jesus to be the embodiment of God; expelled the Jews from Alexandria; inflamed tensions against Hypatia, who had supported Orestes, the Roman governor of Egypt, with whom he clashed over religious encroachment on secular matters

Orestes (1), appointed governor of Roman Egypt (*praefectus Aegypti*) just before Cyril was appointed Christian patriarch; clashed with Cyril on the issue of secular versus church power; supported by Hypatia; following her murder, he left Alexandria.

Theon of Alexandria (1), c. 335–405; father to Hypatia; Greek scholar and mathematician; wrote about the works of Ptolemy the geographer, mathematician and astrologer, and established a school of learning in Alexandria

Peter the Lector (1), leader of the Parabalani brotherhood, an early Christian group which buried the dead, cared for the sick and acted as a violent arm to bishops when required; volunteers were recruited from the lower strata of society

Marguerite Porete (3), died 1 June 1310; Beguine and Christian mystic; author of *The Mirror of Simple Souls*, which explored the personal experience of divine love. The Beguines were single women in a lay order who lived semi-monastically, basing their lives on imitating Christ's life, caring for the sick and the poor in a life of voluntary poverty, much like St Francis of Assisi. Unlike nuns, Beguines took no vows and could come and go. Members were drawn from all strata of society. The Beguinage, founded in Paris in 1264, had four hundred residents. Written in Old French, rather than Latin, Marguerite's book described the union with God through the annihilation of the soul. The work was deemed a threat to the intermediation of Catholic Church rituals in connecting to the divine. She was held to be a heretic, tried by the Dominican inquisitor of France, William of Paris, and burnt at the stake on 1 June 1310 for refusing to renounce her teaching at the Place de Grève, now the Place de l'Hôtel de Ville.

Archangel Gabriel (3), one of the archangels; appears in the Hebrew Bible, Book of Enoch and Christian Bible as messenger to Mary, mother of Jesus, and throughout Islam as Jibril, messenger of Allah to the Prophets, especially to Muhammad.

Prophet Muhammad (3), *c.* 570–632; the founder of Islam, regarded as the last prophet, visited age forty by the archangel Gabriel in a mountain cave; he then began his preaching of revelations, which would last twenty-three years and was written down as the words of Allāh in the Koran. He united Arabia into a single Islamic entity. He died on 8 June 632 in Medina, his head resting in his wife's, Aisha's, lap, his last words: *O Allah, to Ar-Rafiq Al-A'la* ('Exalted friend, highest friend in heaven').

Al Biruni (3), *c.* 973–1050; Abu Rayhan Muhammad ibn Ahmad al-Biruni, an Iranian Muslim, a multi-talented scholar and polymath, regarded as the first anthropologist; studied comparative religions, mastered maths, engineering, astronomy and languages; travelled extensively in modern-day Afghanistan and in India, where he explored Hinduism

Haluga Khan (3), *c.* 1215 to 8 February 1265; Mongol ruler, grandson to Genghis Khan; conquered Persia, ending the Islamic Golden Age with the fall of Baghdad 1258

Caliph al-Musta'sim Billah (3), *c.* 1213–58, the thirty-seventh, and last, Abbasid Caliph; ruled from 1242 until his execution by the Mongols on 20 February 1258, after the fall of Baghdad

Avicenna (3), *c.* 980–1037; Ibn Sina, a Persian mathematician, physician, geographer, astronomer, philosopher and poet; regarded as the founder of early modern medicine; believed to have published four hundred and fifty works

William Marshall (4), First Earl of Pembroke, 1146 or 1147 to 14 May 1219; Anglo-Norman soldier and statesman under five English kings, he was the most powerful noble of his period. At age forty-three, he married seventeen-year-old Isabel de Clare, daughter of Strongbow (Richard de Clare) and Aoife Mc Murchada, princess of Leinster. On his deathbed, he was invested into the Knights Templar and is entombed in the Temple Church, London.

Constantine the Great (4), *c.* February 272 to May 337; sole ruler of the Roman Empire in 324 after civil war against Emperors Maxentius and Licinius. He oversaw the First Council of Nicaea in 325, held to standardise Christian teaching, and was baptised a Christian on his deathbed.

Philp IV (5), Capetian king of France *c.* April 1268 to November 1314; also known as Philip the Fair and the Iron King; ruled from 1285 to 1314; disputed territory in south-west France with Longshanks, King Edward I of England, and warred with the Flemish, losing heavily at the Battle of the Golden Spurs (1302), before eventually supressing the rebellion of Flemish cities. In the Treaty of Paris of 1303, he made peace with Edward I, promising his child Isabella in marriage to the Prince of Wales, a marriage which was celebrated at Boulogne on 25 January 1308. King Philip expelled the Jews and crushed the Knights Templar. His conflict with Pope Boniface VIII led to the capture of the pope at Anagni 1303, and the pope's subsequent death. Pope Benedict XI was hastily elected as Boniface's successor but his reign was very short lived. This reopened the papacy to a fresh contest, which ended with French clerical support electing a French pope, Clement V. Clement moved the papal court first to Poitiers, then to Avignon. Philip died at Fontainebleau on 29 November 1314, weeks after sustaining a brain injury during a hunt.

Pope Celestine V (5), *c.* 1215–96; born Pietro Angelerio, also known as Peter of Morrone; a hermit Benedictine monk, and the last pope to be elected without conclave, after a two-year impasse. He was pontiff for just five months, to December 1294, before resigning to return to his hermit life. He was imprisoned by his successor, Boniface VIII, at Fumone Castle in Lazio, where he died aged eighty-one in 1296. He was canonised by Pope Clement V on 5 May 1313.

Pope Boniface VIII (5), *c.* 1230–1303; elected pope on 24 December 1294. Born Benedetto Ceatani, he promulgated claims to strong temporal power, interfering in political affairs in France, Sicily, Italy and Scotland. He appears in the eighth circle of hell in Dante's *Divine Comedy* for simony: selling church offices, roles and relics for money. He clashed bitterly with King Philip IV of France after the king imposed taxes on clergy, issuing the papal bulls *Ausculta Fili* and *Unam Sanctum,* which held that kings were subordinate to the pope, both spiritually and in temporal matters. After Philip burned the bull in public in 1302, Boniface excommunicated him; the king then sent troops to the pope's residence in Anagni in the hills south-east of Rome on 7 September 1303, captured and beat the pope over three days. The pope died a month later, on 11 October.

Pope Clement V (5), *c.* 1264–1314; born Raymond Bertrand de Got in Aquitaine, was a subject of the King of England but a childhood friend of Philip IV of France. He was elected pope in Perugia after a year of conclave, on 5 June 1305, following the death of Benedict XI in 1304, after eight months as

Pope. Clement V chose Lyon in France for his coronation and withdrew Pope Boniface's bull *Unam Sanctum,* which asserted the primacy of papal authority in temporal matters. In March 1309, he moved the papal court from Poitiers, where it had been held for four years, to Avignon. He disbanded the Knights Templar and violently suppressed the Dulcinian sect in Lombardy, dying on 20 April 1314. Allegedly, his body, while lying in state, was destroyed in a lightning-strike.

Guillaume de Nogaret (5), *c.* 1260 to 13 April 1313; Keeper of the Seal and leading statesman to King Philip IV of France; was born in Saint-Félix-Lauragais, Haute-Garonne, in south-west France, a village which had previously been used for Cathar councils. He was elevated from Professor of Jurisprudence at the University of Montpellier, to become a member of the royal court in Paris in 1296, where he found favour with King Philip; he formulated the plan to seize Pope Boniface VIII and take him to France before deposing him. He led a band of sixteen hundred men which included bitter enemies of Boniface's family, led by Sciarra Colonna, to Anagni on 7 September 1303, retreating three days later after facing popular resistance locally. Pope Boniface, who was badly beaten during his captivity, died in October 1303. The death of his feeble successor, Benedict XI, in July 1304, paved the way for intrigue to place a Frenchman on the papal throne. Bertrand de Got, Pope Clement V, succeeded thanks to French clerical support; during his reign, de Nogaret was central in assembling evidence against the Knights Templar. Nogaret died in 1313 with his tongue horribly thrust out, according to French abbot and medieval chronicler Jean Desnouelles.

Arnaud Amaury (5), died 1225; Cistercian abbot, also known as Amalric, took a lead role in the Albigensian Crusade to crush the Cathars. He was selected as papal inquisitor in 1204 to deal with the Albigensians and ordered the massacre of Béziers in July 1209, killing twenty thousand Catholics and Cathars alike. At the siege of Minerve in July 1210, he insisted on burning 140 *perfecti* at the stake for their refusal to return to Catholicism. He was appointed Archbishop of Narbonne in 1212 and died on 29 September 1225.

King Louis IX (5), April 1214 to August 1270; ascended the throne at Reims aged twelve; was canonised by Pope Boniface VIII, the only French king to be sainted. He reformed feudal laws, banned trial by ordeal, introduced the presumption of innocence, and created new structures in administering laws. He led two Crusades to the Holy Land, when he was in his mid-thirties and in his mid-fifties, dying from dysentery on his last Crusade, in Carthage. He was renowned for his devotion to the Catholic faith and his charity: feeding beggars, administering to lepers, and founding hospitals and sanctuaries for reformed prostitutes.

Pope Benedict XI (5), 1240–1304; born Nicola Boccassini in Treviso; was Pope for eight months from 22 October 1303 to his death on 7 July 1304, following which he was succeeded by Clement V. He was beatified by Pope Clement XII in 1736. He was appointed Cardinal by Pope Boniface VIII, whom he defended during the attack at Anagni in September 1303. After Boniface died, Benedict was elected by conclave to be pope; he was not hostile to Philip IV of France, whom he released from the excommunication placed upon him by his predecessor. Pope Benedict excommunicated Guillaume de Nogaret, and all those involved in the attack at Anagni. He died suddenly eight months into his pontificate from suspected poisoning.

Jacques de Molay (5), *c.* 1240 to 18 March 1314, twenty-third and final Grand Master of the Knights Templar, the Order dissolved by Pope Clement V on 20 April 1312. He is thought to have become a Knight aged twenty-one, in 1265. He was burned at the stake by King Philip IV in Paris on 18 March 1314 after seven years' imprisonment. He succeeded by election as Grand Master from Thibaud Gaudin, the twenty-second Grand Master, who had fled to Cyprus after the fall of Acre 1291 to the Egyptian Mamluks, dying in 1292. He spent much of his period as Grand Master attempting to rebuild the Knights Templar and gain European support to retake Outremer and the holy city of Jerusalem, including forging an alliance with the Mongol Golden Horde, who threatened the Mamluks from the south. In 1305, Pope Clement V sought views on a new Crusade, and on merging the Knights Templar with the Knights Hospitaller in advance of a meeting which was delayed until 1307 due to the pope's gastro-enteritis. De Molay resisted attempts to merge the Orders, favoured by King Philip of France, who was in debt to the Knights Templar. He was arrested in Paris on 13 October 1307, tortured and imprisoned by King Philip on charges of heresy and sodomy between warrior-monks, to which he first confessed but later recanted. King Philip burnt fifty-four Templars at the stake over two days in May 1310, effectively crushing resistance to his will; on 22 March 1312, at the Council of Vienne, the Knights Templar were abolished by papal order. Jacque de Molay was burned at the stake, along with Geoffroi de Charney and two other Templars, in March 1314. In 2001, a document, known as the Chinon Parchment, dated 1308, confirmed that Pope Clement V had absolved the leaders of the Knights Templar of the charges against them. According to accounts from the execution, de Molay cursed both king and pope from the pyre, stating that they would account to God within a year. Pope Clement V died on 20 April 1314, and King Philip later that year.

Hughes de Payens (5), *c.* 1070 to May 1136; with help from St Bernard of Clairvaux, founded the Knights Templar and its code of conduct, the Latin Rule, which was confirmed by the Council of Troy (1129) under Pope Honorius II. He was the first Grand Master for twenty years, and obtained approval from King Baldwin II of Jerusalem to entrust the Temple of Jerusalem to the care of the Order.

Geoffrey de Charney (6), died March 1314; burnt at the stake with the last Grand Master of the Knights Templar, Jacques de Molay. He was the Order's Preceptor of Normandy. He was arrested on 13 October 1307 and faced charges of heresy, sodomy and blasphemy, similar to those levelled against the Templars and Pope Boniface by King Philip IV. After confessing under torture, he later recanted and was executed as a relapsed heretic, burned slowly to death on Île aux Juifs, a small island in the Seine in Paris. According to contemporary accounts, he went fearlessly to his death.

Horus (6), the leading ancient Egyptian deity; the Eye of Horus is a symbol of health, protection and royal power intended to ward off evil and safeguard souls in the afterlife. The symbol is still commonly painted on boats today throughout the Mediterranean.

Vercingetorix (6), *c.* 82–46 BC, leader of the Arverni of his native region of Auvergne, he united the Gauls in revolt against Julius Caesar's rule, but was defeated and captured at the Battle of Alesia in September 52 BC, facing Julius Caesar and Mark Anthony. Gallic losses were thought to be 250,000. Paraded through Rome, he was publicly executed by strangulation after five years of imprisonment.

Amaury de la Roche (6), in Grand Commander of the Knights Templar 1261, close friend to King Louis IX, grandfather of King Philip IV

Guillaume de Beaujeu (6), *c.* 1230–91, was the twenty-first Grand Master of the Knights Templar; he died leading the defence of Acre during the siege of Acre in 1291. He was the last Templar Grand Master to preside over the order in Outremer, and was killed by an arrow-strike under his armpit, from which he bled to death.

Thibuad Gaudin (6), *c.* 1229 to 16 April 1292; the twenty-second Grand Master of the Knights Templar, succeeding Guillaume de Beaujeu after his death at Acre in 1291. He fled the city on the eve of its fall to Sultan Al-Ashraf Khalil, eventually reaching Cyprus, where he was elected Grand Master in October 1291.

Peter de Severy (6), Marshal of the remaining Templars at the siege of Acre in 1291, in which he died, in May 1291. Peter de Severy held out for ten days at the Templar fortress at Acre; he was captured and executed during negotiations by the Sultan Khalil, after which the fortress fell on 28 May 1291. Losses at Acre, where 15,000 defenders faced 200,000 Mamluks, are estimated to have been 100,000, including civilians.

Sultan Al-Ashraf Khalil (6), *c.* 1260 to 14 December 1293; the eighth Mamluk sultan, from November 1290 until his assassination in 1293. He ordered the execution of remaining defenders and civilians after the final fall of Acre in June 1291. The sultan then took all remaining Crusader strongholds along the Syrian coast: Tyre, Beirut, Haifa, Tartus, Sidon and Atlit.

Longinus (7), the Roman soldier who pierced the crucified Jesus with a lance, later converting to Christianity. His name may derive from the Greek word *lonche*, for lance.

Maxentius (7), *c.* 283 to 28 October 312; Roman Emperor from 306 to 312; defeated at the Battle of Milvian Bridge outside Rome in 312; died by drowning in the River Tiber during a crushing retreat at the hands of the forces of Constantine, who condemned Maxentius to *damnatio memoriae* (condemnation of memory), erasing all his laws, projects, depictions, inscriptions and documents

King David (7), *c.* 1000 BCE; appears in Christian, Jewish and Islamic written and oral tradition as the shepherd-boy who slays Goliath and takes the throne after the death of King Saul, becoming King of the Israelites in Judah

Charlemagne (7), Charles I or Charles the Great, 2 April 748 to 28 January 814; united western and central Europe as a Frankish state under the Carolingian Empire; canonised by Antipope Paschal III, known as *Pater Europae*, father of Europe; entombed in his imperial capital at Aachen Cathedral

Geoffrey de St Omer (8), co-founding member of the Knights Templar in 1119; thought to be one of the two knights sharing single horseback in the Templar seal, the other being Hugh de Payens

Lambert Canon of St Omer (8), *c.* 1061 to 22 June 1125; French Benedictine monk, scholar and chronicler; studied n music, theology, grammar; known for *Liber Floridus* (Book of Flowers), completed in 1120, an encyclopaedia covering geography, theology, philosophy and natural history

Zoroaster (8), also Zarathustra, founded Zoroastrianism, one of the oldest continuous world religions. He was an ancient Persian spiritual leader thought to have lived on the eastern part of the Iranian plateau between the seventh and sixth centuries BC, but may date much further back, to the second millennium BC. Zoroaster perceived human struggle between *aša* (good) and *druj* (evil), overarched by human free will, the purpose of mankind being to align with *aša* through thoughts, deeds and words. Zoroastrianism perceives an uncreated supreme deity of wisdom, *Ahura Mazda* (Wise Lord). Its features, such as messiahs, judgement after death, heaven, hell and free will, flow through all subsequent religions: Judaism, Christianity, Islam, Greek philosophy, Buddhism and the Bahá'í faith. In the Gathas, the poetic texts of Zoroastrianism, the Ahura Mazda works through spirits known as the *Amesha Spenta*. Druj, or destructive, chaotic spirit, comes from *Angra Mainyu*, later referred to as Ahriman, over which *Ahura Mazda* will triumph, leading to *Frashokereti*, when time ends, and all souls, including the dead, reunite with *Ahura Mazda*.

Arius (8), c. 250–336; priest in Alexandria, Egypt; preached the theology of Arianism, holding that God the Father is unique, and Christ his subordinate. This was the centre of the debate about the relationship between God and Jesus. Arianism opposed the Trinitarian view of the godhead in Christianity. The Arian theological controversy led to the first ecumenical council, which adopted the Nicene Creed in 325 and, after heated debate, rejected Arianism. Opponents of Arius accused him of heresy, denying the divinity of the Son and being Jewish in his thinking. The Nicene Creed affirms the co-essential divinity of the Son, and a later version refers to the Holy Spirit as worshipped and glorified with the Father and the Son.

Eusebius of Caesarea (8), c. 260–340; biographer of Constantine the Great; historian, interpreter of scripture, and scholar, notable for blaming the Jews for the Crucifixion of Jesus while pleading for their forgiveness

Thomas of Aquino (8), 1225 to 7 March 1274; Italian Dominican friar, priest, philosopher, theologian and scholar; proponent of Aristotle's teachings, reconciling these with Christianity. Widely regarded as one of the great Western philosophers, many accounts attest to his levitations and ecstasies. Half a century after his death, Thomas Aquinas was pronounced a saint by Pope John XXII in Avignon.

Aristotle (8), 384–322 BC; Greek philosopher and scholar; teacher of Plato; tutor to Alexander the Great; founder of Aristotelian tradition; huge breadth of writing, covering physics, economics, biology, logic, music, politics, psychology and metaphysics, his influence has spanned over two millennia in the physical sciences and philosophy

Reginald of Piperno (8), *c.* 1230–90; Italian Dominican; closest companion to Thomas Aquinas, who dedicated several of his works to Reginald, with whom he began to teach in 1272. Reginald attended Thomas Aquino's deathbed, heard his confession and delivered his funeral oration in 1274.

St Francis of Assisi (8), *c.* 1181 to 3 October 1226; founder of the Franciscan Order; Italian friar, philosopher and mystic; canonised on 16 July 1228 by Pope Gregory IX. Received stigmata, the wounds of Christ's Passion, during religious ecstasy on 14 September 1224; arguably the most beloved of the Catholic saints, for his dedication to reliving the life of Christ, his focus on the poor, and the warm response he inspired among people and animals alike.

Paul Aurelian (11), Saint Pol de Léon, born in Wales, died 575 as Bishop of the Diocese of Quimper and Léon; said to have been a vegetarian

King Edward I (13), *c.* 17 June 1293 to 7 July 1307; also known as Edward Longshanks; king of England from 1272 to 1307. He suppressed rebellions in Wales, warred with Scotland under King Robert I and France under King Philip IV, and died after signing peace with France, but leaving war with Scotland unfinished. His son Edward II would be routed at Bannockburn seven years after Longshanks' death. King Edward I expelled the Jews from England in 1290, an edict which remained in place until 1657. He participated in two Crusades, allied to King Louis IX of France. He died from dysentery en route to Scotland to face Robert de Bruce's Scottish army after it had defeated the English at the Battle of Loudoun Hill in February 1307.

Fra Dulcino (13), *c.* 1250–1307; leader of the Dulcinian movement; took over the reins from Gerard Segarelli, who was executed by the Catholic Church in 1300. The Dulcinians, inspired by the teaching of Saint Francis of Assisi, opposed the feudal system, but their teachings in northern Italy about liberty and practising lives of poverty were deemed heresies. The Dulcinians responded to attacks by Catholic troops with raids, a medieval form of guerrilla warfare, plundering and killing their opponents in what was later considered to be one of the earliest socialist rebellions. Fra Dolcino, once captured, was not tried by the Church under Pope Clement V but castrated, torn to pieces and burned by the public executioner.

Margaret of Trent (13), died 1 June 1307; concubine to Fra Dolcino, joined the movement in 1303 and is described in contemporary accounts as a woman of immense beauty. After Pope Clement V declared a crusade against the movement in 1306, the couple took refuge in a fortified position in Val Sesia, in the mountains near the current Swiss border with Italy, where she was captured. Pregnant, she was torn to pieces before Fra Dolcino's eyes, before he was killed in the same manner. Their remains were then cremated. Other historical references suggest she was burnt at the stake.

Esquin of Floyran (14), from Béziers, was a prior at the Abbey of Saint Martial in Limoges, central France; promulgated rumours about the Knights Templar from a confession he had allegedly heard from a Templar monk. He alleged idolatry, sodomy and blasphemy by spitting on the Cross, and sought payment for written testimony, including from James II, King of Aragon, in 1305.

Baybars (15), c. 1223 to 1 July 1277; also known as 'Baibars'; Mamluk Sultan of Egypt. He defeated the Seventh Crusade, led by King Louis IX of France in 1250, and also substantially routed the Mongol army at the Battle of Ain Jalut (Spring of Goliath) in 1260, establishing the primacy of Mamluk power in the region.

St Bernard of Clairvaux (15), 1090 to 20 August 1153; French Cistercian Abbot; established a monastery at Clairvaux in 1115. He was appointed secretary to the Council of Troyes by Pope Honorius II in 1128, to settle disputes and regulate the Church in France, at which time he formulated the Latin Rule, the code of conduct for the Knights Templar. He advocated widely for the Second Crusade and preached against Catharism.

Pope Formosus (15), c. 816–96; born in Rome, he became pope on 6 October 891. His body was famously disinterred and put on trial in the Cadaver Synod. After his death, his successor, Pope Boniface VI, was pope for just fifteen days before the election of Pope Stephen VI, who, bowing to pressure, established the Cadaver Synod. Formosa was disinterred, clothed in papal regalia, seated on a throne and prosecuted for his unworthiness to have sat as pope, following which a *damnatio memoriae* was applied, nullifying all his acts as pope. His papal clothes were torn from his body, three fingers of his right hand were removed (those which had conferred blessing) and his corpse thrown in the River Tiber, before being retrieved by a monk and reinterred in Saint Peter's Basilica.

Pope Stephen VI (15), died August 897; became Pope on 22 May 896; established the Cadaver Synod in January 897 to prosecute Pope Formosus posthumously. The controversy caused by the Cadaver Synod ended in Pope Stephen's imprisonment and death by strangulation in August the same year.

King Edward II (16), 25 April 1284 to 21 September 1327; King of England, 1307–27; married Isabella, daughter of King Philip IV of France, in 1308. Edwards II was alleged to have been a lover of court noble Piers Gaveston. He was heavily defeated at Bannockburn in 1314 by the Scots. Isabella returned from France in 1325 with the exiled Roger Mortimer; she launched an invasion in 1326, with the aim of protecting the crown for her son, eleven-year-old Edward III, and captured, imprisoned and deposed Edward II. The dethroned king was allegedly murdered on 21 September 1327 while in captivity, although this was never proven; on 29 November 1330, his son, Edward III, executed Roger Mortimer.

Piers Gaveston (16), c. 1284–1312; First Earl of Cornwall; born in Gascony, son of a Gascon knight, Arnaud de Gabaston, he was the favourite companion to Edward, Prince of Wales, who became Edward II. He was banished from the royal court by Edward Longshanks to punish his son. On the death of his father in July 1307, despite Longshanks' deathbed wishes, Edward II recalled Gaveston from exile in Aquitaine, making him Earl of Cornwall. While in France in January 1308, to marry Isabella, daughter of King Philip IV, Edward II appointed Gaveston as regent, inflaming tensions. Parliament, in April 1308, demanded Gaveston's renewed exile; this had the support of King Philip, who was concerned about Edward's treatment of his young wife. The English king exiled Gaveston to Ireland as Lord Lieutenant. In August 1309, Gaveston returned to court after Edward II secured deals with the nobility, and Pope Clement V agreed to raise the threat of excommunication against Gaveston, should he return. In 1311, he was again forced into exile, reluctantly, by Edward II, under pressure from his nobles, during which time he was excommunicated. He returned once again, at Christmas that year, to be reunited with Edward II in January 1312. Captured by a group of nobles at Scarborough in May 1312, he was executed on 19 June on the lands of the Earl of Lancaster.

William of Paris (16), died in 1314; Dominican priest and theologian; confessor to King Philip IV of France from 1303; closely involved in intrigue against the Knights Templar, he oversaw the trial and burning at the stake of Marguerite Porete, the Beguine.

Pope Celestine I (17), Bishop of Rome from 10 September 422 until his death on 1 August 432

Palladius (17) of Poitiers, died *c.* 461; the first bishop of Ireland, preceding Saint Patrick. Before becoming a priest in 415, Palladius was married with a daughter, whom he put into a convent in Sicily where he lived around 408, moving to Rome between 418 and 425. After ordination as a bishop by Pope Celestine I, Palladius landed in Arklow, County Wicklow, and preached for a time there before being banished by the king of Leinster. He retreated to Britain, leaving two companions behind: Sylvester and Solinus. Palladius is thought to have organised the Scottish Christian Church until his death near Aberdeen.

Donough Muimnech Ó Cellaigh (19), died 1307; known to the English as Donough Ó Kelly, king of Ui Maine (Hu-Many); chief of the O'Kelly clan, 1295–1307; regained independence from the kings of Connaught; inflicted a heavy defeat on the English at the Battle of Ahascragh in 1307, in response to the sacking of Ahascragh by Lord Edmund Butler. Within weeks, the O'Kelly chief was dead, the kingship passing to his nephew Gilbert O'Kelly.

Edmund Butler (19), *c.* 1268 to 13 Sept 1321; Earl of Carrick and Justiciar of Ireland in 1303; knighted by Edward II in London 1309; died in 1321 in London, after going on pilgrimage to Santiago de Compostela.

Fineen McCarthy (19), died 1261; also known as Fineen of Ringrone; king of Desmond, 1251–61; inflicted a heavy defeat on the Anglo-Normans of Munster, and the Geraldines, in 1261 at the Battle of Callan, securing Gaelic control of the kingdom of Desmond in south-west Ireland for the following three centuries. Fineen, using his experience in fighting the Normans, chose his battleground carefully where rivers meet near Ardtully Castle, negating the advantage of Norman heavy cavalry, and killing eight barons and fifteen knights, including the Geraldine leadership.

William de Dene (19), justiciar of Ireland, died from wounds inflicted at the Battle of Callann in 1261.

Sir Gilbert de Bohun (19), seneschal (governor) of Kilkenny; inherited Kilkenny county and castle from his mother in 1270; was outlawed by King Edward I in 1300; was reinstated in 1303 and held the castle until his death, following which it was seized by the Crown and sold to the Butler family in 1391.

Foulques de Merle (19), died 1314; marshal of France; served both King Philip III and King Philip IV; was made marshal of France in 1302 after the Battle of the Golden Spurs, in which he fought. He fought alongside King Philip IV in the field at the Battle of Mons-en-Pévèle. From 1311 to 1312 he represented the king at the ecumenical Council of Vienne, in which King Philip put pressure on Pope Clement V to suppress the Knights Templar – which he did by papal bull on 22 March 1312. The council also disbanded the Beguines. Du Merle died in 1314, while leading the French army in Flanders.

Catherine I (20), 25 November 1274 to 11 October 1307; also known as Catherine of Courtenay; empress of Constantinople and daughter-in-law to King Philip IV after marriage to his son, Charles of Valois, in 1301. She died two days before the nationwide assault on the Knights Templar.

Claudius Ptolemy (21), *c.* 100–170; renowned geographer, astronomer, astrologer and mathematician; lived in Alexandria under the Roman Empire.

John of Tour (24), Knight Templar, banker and treasurer, based in Paris; oversaw loans to King Philip IV; worked closely with royal accountants in the Louvre; acted as financial advisor to the Crown.

Hugh of Pairaud (24), Visitor of the Temple (second highest rank in the Knights Templar); contested the election of Jacque de Molay as Grand Master; supported King Philip IV in his clash with Pope Boniface VIII in 1304; arrested in October 1307 in Poitiers while waiting to see Pope Clement V; sentenced to life imprisonment on 18 March 1314. Hugh's confession was regarded as holding very high value, due to his prominence in French affairs; he was inducted into the Order in 1263.

Raimbaud of Caron (24), Preceptor of Cyprus; arrested in Paris, October 1307; interrogated after Hugh of Pairaud by Dominican Nicholas of Ennezat. Initially rejecting the charges, he was taken away and returned later in the day, a broken man, ready to accept them. Thought to have died in prison in Chinon Castle before the imprisoned Templars were moved to Gisor's Castle, 1310.

King Denis of Portugal (24), 9 October 1261 to 7 January 1325; known as 'the Poet King' and 'the Farming King', he ruled for forty-six years, during which time he reformed and modernised Portugal and its economy, and established its navy. He created the Order of Christ in 1319 as a Portuguese military power, effectively continuing the Knights Templar by securing for it, from Pope John XXII (who succeeded Pope Clement V), the right to Templar property and assets.

John de Grey (24), died 18 October 1214; returning from Rome to England, he served as Justiciar of Ireland from 1209 to 1213 under King John, who attempted to elevate the Englishman from bishop of Norwich to archbishop of Canterbury, but was stopped by Pope Innocent III in 1206. After King John's expedition to Ireland 1210, the king ordered de Grey to build three castles, one of which was at Athlone.

Nicholas of Ennezat (26), Dominican inquisitor; deputised for William of Paris in overseeing the interrogation of Templar knight Hugh of Pairaud on 9 November 1307. Nicholas adjourned the hearing, and had the Templar removed; when he later returned, Hugh confessed to worshipping a four-faced idol in Montpellier.

King Robert I (30), 11 July 1274 to 7 June 1329; Robert the Bruce; King of Scotland from 1306 to his death in 1329; led Scotland during the First War of Independence; descended on his mother's line from Aoife Mac Murrough, princess of Leinster. He killed his rival to the Scottish throne, John Comyn III, in February 1306, for which he was excommunicated by Pope Clement V; he seized the throne one month later. After hiding following a defeat by the English at the Battle of Methven on 19 June 1306, he emerged to defeat the English at the Battle of Loudoun Hill on 10 May 1307, thereafter waging guerrilla war across Scotland. On 23 and 24 June 1314, he soundly defeated King Edward II's forces at the Battle of Bannockburn, and subsequently launched raids into the north of England, and invaded Ireland, as part of a force led by his brother Edward. In 1320, the Declaration of Arbroath, submitted by Scottish nobility to Pope John XXII, declared Scottish independence, and Robert I its king. Following the death of Edward II, his son Edward III concluded the Treaty of Edinburgh-Northampton, renouncing English claims to Scotland.

John Comyn III (30), also known as Red Comyn; Scottish baron; acted as guardian of Scotland following the forced abdication of King John Balliol, his uncle, in 1296; was killed by Robert the Bruce at the altar of Greyfriars Church in Dumfries on February 1306.

Epiphanius (31), c. 310–403; bishop of Salamis, Cyprus; a polyglot and robust advocate of the conventional Church; composed a list of heresies, including against unorthodox images, and travelled widely to combat heresies.

John the Baptist (31), late first century BC to 31 or 32 AD; Jewish preacher recognised in Christianity, Islam and Mandaeism; anticipated the coming of a messiah; may have been a relative of Jesus Christ; applied baptism as a holy sacrament; was arrested and beheaded by Herod Antipas after he had criticised Herod divorcing his wife and unlawfully marrying his brother's wife. According to the Gospels (Mark 1:11), John the Baptist baptised Jesus in the River Jordan.

Titus Flavius Josephus (31), c. 37–100 AD; contemporary Jewish historian; born in Jerusalem as Yosef ben Matityahu; led resistance to Rome by Jewish forces in Galilee during a Jewish uprising; surrendered in 67 AD, becoming a slave and interpreter to Emperor Vespasian, before being freed to become a Roman citizen and advisor to Vespasian's son, Titus, who besieged Jerusalem in 70 AD.

Herod Antipas (31), c. 20 BC to 39 AD; tetrarch (ruler) of Galilea and Perea; son of Herod the Great, who ruled during the birth of Jesus Christ and who died in 4 AD, making Antipas tetrarch, a post he held for forty-two years. A ruinous war followed with King Aretas IV of Nabatea after Herod Antipas divorced his first wife, Aretas' daughter. Herod beheaded John the Baptist according to Matthew and Luke, under pressure from Salomé, his stepdaughter, as a reward for her dancing at his banquet. After the death of Emperor Tiberius on 16 March 37 AD, Caligula was persuaded by his nephew Agrippa that Herod Antipas was plotting against him. The emperor responded by passing Antipas' land and assets to Agrippa, and exiling Herod to Spain, where he died.

Salome (31), c. 10–60 AD; described as stepdaughter to Herod Antipas in the New Testament, she married twice, first to her uncle Philip the Tetrarch, until his death in 34 AD, then to her cousin Aristobulus of Chalcis, becoming queen of Chalcis (near Damascus) and Armenia Minor.

St Peter (31), died c. 64 AD; known as Simon Peter; regarded as first bishop of Rome; may have been crucified under Emperor Nero. He was a fisherman in Bethsaida; most prominent of the Apostles, and the first to whom Jesus appears after his Crucifixion. Recognised, along with James the Just and John the Apostle, as the pillars of the Church, he may have been the intermediary between James the Just, bishop of Jerusalem, and Paul, who saw himself as Apostle to the Gentiles. Peter is believed to have founded the Church in Antioch before travelling to Rome in later years, where, according to Church tradition, he was crucified upside down.

Thomas the Apostle (31), also called 'Didymus' or 'twin'; one of the Twelve Apostles, referred to as Doubting Thomas for initially doubting the Resurrection, he is thought to have travelled to Kerala, India, in 52 AD and was martyred in 72 AD near Madras, according to Syrian Christian tradition. In December 1945, the Coptic Gospel of Thomas was discovered near Nag Hammadi Egypt, dating from 60 AD. Comprising of 114 sayings of Jesus, it is a non-canonical gospel, the twelfth one, and credits the leadership of the community to James the Just, not Peter. Scholars do not hold that the gospel was written by Thomas; there is general agreement that it is a key gospel.

Barabbas (31), in Aramaic *Yeshua Bar Abba,* meaning 'son of the father' or 'son of the teacher'; according to the New Testament, a criminal freed by Pontius Pilate at Passover, in preference to Jesus Christ. The custom of freeing prisoners at Passover appears only in the synoptic Gospels, Mark, Luke and Matthew, the last having the crowd retort to Pilate *Let his blood be upon us and our children.* There is no historical record of any tradition in Roman rule that frees prisoners at the time of a Jewish celebration. Early manuscripts of Matthew 27:16-17 refer to 'Jesus Barabbas'.

James the Righteous (31), died *c.* 62 AD; also knowns as James the Just; brother of Jesus, and leader of the early Christian community in Jerusalem. The Dead Sea Scrolls refer to James as 'the Righteous Teacher'. The Gospel of Thomas refers to Jesus' response to questions from the Apostles before his Ascension: *We are aware that you will depart from us. Who will be our leader? Jesus said to them. No matter where you come, it is to James the Just that you shall go, for whose sake heaven and earth have come to exist.* According to Josephus, the brother of Jesus, James was executed by stoning. Christian writer Hegesippus (*c.* 110–180 AD) states that the Scribes and Pharisees had placed James at the pinnacle of the temple, then threw him down before stoning him, killing him finally with a blow to the head with a club.

St Paul the Apostle (31), *c.* 5 BC to 67 AD; Hebrew name Saul of Tarsus (an area in Turkey); founded Christian communities in Europe and Asia Minor; initially persecuted the followers of Jesus, before converting on the road to Damascus after a vision of an ascended Jesus. Nearly half the books of the New Testament are attributed to him. Citizen of Rome, born to a Jewish family, but claimed independence from the church of Jerusalem. Travelled extensively on missionary journeys; in final visit to Jerusalem in 57 AD he narrowly escaped being killed by a mob, by surrendering to the Roman military; after this, he was transported to Rome to stand trial as a Roman citizen. He was shipwrecked en route on the island of Malta. He arrived in Rome in 60 AD, spent two years under house arrest, preaching while awaiting trial, and is thought to have been beheaded under Emperor Nero, who persecuted the Christians after the Great Fire of Rome in July 64 AD.

Emperor Nero (31), 15 December 37 to 9 June 68 AD; Roman emperor, 54–68 AD; his uncle was Emperor Caligula; at age sixteen he succeeded Emperor Claudius on his death in 54 AD. Claudius is thought to have been poisoned by Agrippina, his wife, and Nero's mother. Nero killed his mother, Agrippina, in 59 AD. His rule was characterised by extravagance, tyranny and taxes. The Great Fire of Rome in July 64 AD is attributed to him, as an attempt to clear away old buildings for a palace complex. He blamed the Christians for the tragedy. After a revolt among his army in Germany, his praetorian guard deserted him, and Nero fled Rome for the coast, later returning to an empty palace. He then fled Rome a second time, to a country villa where he failed in an attempt to commit suicide, forcing his secretary Epaphroditus to assist him by sword. Epaphroditus was executed by Emperor Domitian many years later, in 95 AD, for failing to prevent Nero's suicide; a year later, Domitian was stabbed to death by a servant in retribution for the killing.

Events and References

Vernal Equinox (1), two moments yearly, when day and night are of equal length, and the sun is exactly above the equator.

Ebionites (1), means 'poor ones' in Hebrew; a Jewish Christian sect which saw Jesus not as God but as a man who became the adopted son of God through baptism, resurrection and ascension, a sinless prophet chosen by God. The Ebionites placed emphasis on voluntary poverty, lived in communes and adopted asceticism; they are regarded as the closest followers of the teachings of the historical Jesus; they rejected virgin birth, saw James, the brother of Jesus, as his successor, not Peter, and denounced and opposed Paul as a false prophet.

Mandaeans (1), refer to themselves as Nasurai or Nasoreans; followers of Mandaeism, indigenous to southern Mesopotamia, a gnostic and pacifist religion with a single God. The Mandaeans practise baptism and are thought to have lived around Jerusalem and the River Jordan rver in the first century; they especially revere John the Baptist; they have a dualist view of existence, the light world ruled by a heavenly father, the king of light, who is opposed by the lord of darkness, representing chaos. The Mandeans hold that the body of the first human, Adam, was created by dark beings, but his soul by light beings. Accordingly, repeated baptism is deemed to be central to redeeming the soul.

Parabalani (1), the black-robed volunteer military arm of Cyril, Bishop of Alexandria.

Uisneach (1), Hill of Uisneach; covers two square kilometres and is 182 metres above sea level, in County Westmeath, Ireland. It is an ancient sacred site of pre-Christian Ireland, regarded as the centre of Ireland. It includes enclosures, burial mounds and a megalithic tomb, and is the legendary burial location of mythical figures including Lugh, the god of light. It is associated with the festival of *Bealtaine*.

Orion (3), a constellation named after Orion, the hunter in Greek mythology. Orion is widely depicted in art, from prehistoric carvings onwards, in several cultures.

Betelgeuse (3), one of the brightest stars, a supergiant in the night sky; part of the Orion constellation, estimated to be 530 light-years from the sun.

Currently dimming, it is expected to go supernova within the next hundred thousand years.

College of Sorbonne (3), founded in Paris in 1253 by Robert de Sorbon, master of theology at Notre Dame de Paris; confirmed by King Louis IX of France two years later.

Mamluks (3), originally slave soldiers who grew to become a warrior class under Muslim rulers. One of the strongest became the Mamluk Sultanate in Egypt, 1250–1517, and defeated the Mongols at the Battle of Ain Jalut on 3 September 1260, in the Jezreel Valley, in south-east Galilee, ending its incursion eastwards; they forced the Crusaders from the Holy Land after the capture of Acre on 18 May 1291.

Fall of Acre (3), 18 May 1291; the fall of the capital of the kingdom of Jerusalem brought an end to the Crusades in Outremer, resulting in an estimated 100,000 casualties. The Mamluk forces were led by Al-Ashraf Khalil, and the defence of Acre by a coalition which included Guillaume de Beaujeu, the Templar Grand Master. The defenders were outnumbered twenty to one. The siege commenced on 6 April 1291. Despite the arrival of modest reinforcements from Henry II of Cyprus, at dawn on 18 May the city was stormed after undermining operations collapsed key defensive towers, forcing the defenders to retreat through the city to inner defences, and begin a chaotic evacuation by sea. By the end of the day, the only redoubt left was the Templar fortress at the western edge of the city, which fell on 28 May; it is thought to have been collapsed by the remaining thirty Templar knights upon its occupants and attackers.

Fall of Baghdad (3), 10 February 1258; followed a thirteen-day siege by the Ilkhanate Mongol army, bringing an end to the Islamic Golden Age, and the fall of the Abbasid Caliphate. It resulted in a huge death toll among its fifty thousand defenders and eight hundred thousand civilians. It was the defining military engagement in the region in the thirteenth century, leaving Baghdad depopulated and in ruins. The Mongols destroyed Baghdad's mosques, palaces, hospitals, and thirty-six public libraries containing priceless books, historical documents and artefacts.

Fall of Aleppo (3), 24 January 1260; followed a six-day siege within two years of the Mongol capture of Baghdad. Mongol forces led by Hulagu Khan, and supported by Christian troops from Antioch and Armenia, stormed the city after a barrage of catapults had weakened its defences. It was followed by a methodical massacre over six days of Muslims and Jews, and the enslavement of women and children.

Kingdom of Cyprus (3), 1192–1489; ruled by the French House of Lusignan. The island was conquered by Richard I, King of England, during the Third Crusade in 1191, and later sold to the Knights Templar, who crushed a local rebellion before returning it to Richard. The Crusader offered the Kingdom of Cyprus to Guy de Lusignan, his vassal. His ancestor, Henry II, ruled Cyprus from 1285–1324. It remained a key Templar base until the Order was crushed by King Philip IV of France, and was later disbanded by Pope Clement V.

Bactria (3), the ancient central Asian region to the north of the Hindu Kush mountains in modern-day Afghanistan, Tajikistan and Uzbekistan. Bactria was Islamised, along with the remains of the Persian empire; previously, its principal religions had been Zoroastrianism and Buddhism.

Hindu Kush (3), thought to translate as 'Hindu killer', is an eight-hundred-kilometre-long mountain range thwhichat runs through Afghanistan, Pakistan and Tajikistan, its highest point being Tirich Mir, at 7,708 metres above sea-level. The Hindu Kush marked the passageway to invade the Indian sub-continent for Darius I of Persia, and later for Alexander the Great. Al-Biruni, the Islamic scholar, lived for fifteen years in the region from 1017, studying local culture, languages and religions.

Tigris (3); the river, together with the Euphrates, which defines Mesopotamia, flowing 1,750 kilometres from south-east Turkey's Taurus Mountains through modern-day Iraq and Baghdad to the Persian Gulf.

Levant (3); refers to an area which combines the eastern Mediterranean with parts of western Asia, including much of Turkey, Syria, Lebanon, Israel, Palestine and Jordan, and includes islands in the eastern Mediterranean, including Cyprus and parts of Greece and Libya

Frankish Kingdom (3); the kingdom of the Franks is the predecessor to the modern states of Europe, France, Germany, Holland, Belgium and Luxembourg. The Kingdom was founded by Clovis I, who was crowned king of the Franks in 496, setting up the Merovingian dynasty, which included Pepin of Herstal, Charles Martel, Pepin the Short, the legendary Charlemagne (who was crowned Holy Roman Emperor on 25 December 800), and his son Louis the Pious. The Merovingian dynasty continued until the early ninth century, when it was superseded by the Carolingian dynasty.

Knights Templar (3), founded in 1119 at the Temple Mount in Jerusalem; suppressed in 1312 by Pope Clement V in the papal bull *Vox in Excelso*; the Poor Fellow-Soldiers of Christ and of the Temple of Solomon was a Catholic military order that grew to become the wealthiest and most powerful of the Crusade period, skilled in combat, strategy, engineering fortifications and banking.

Milky Way (3), the galaxy which contains our solar system; estimated to contain between one hundred billion and four hundred billion stars, and thought to extend 200,000 light-years in diameter. It appears in the night sky as a long, indistinct band of light which covers thirty constellations, including Sagittarius, and extends north to the constellation of Cassiopeia and south to the constellation of Crux.

Battle of Montgisard (4), 25 November 1177; kingdom of Jerusalem forces led by a heavily bandaged sixteen-year-old King Baldwin IV, suffering from raging leprosy and comprising of eighty Templar Knights, routed Saladin's Ayyubids from the Sultanate of Egypt, despite being outnumbered five to one. Saladin fled the battlefield and was chased, late into the night, barely escaping capture. Ten years later, he would crush the twenty-thousand-strong Christian army at the Battle of the Horns of Hattin.

Council of Nicaea (4), 325 AD; an ecumenical convention of bishops in Nicaea (modern-day Turkey) called to reach consensus on the Christian creed; amongst other things, it settled the controversy surrounding the divinity of Jesus.

Pillars of Hercules (4); name from antiquity to describe the Straits of Gibraltar, the northern pillar being the Rock of Gibraltar

Amesha Spenta (4), in the Avestan language, one of seven immortal beings emanating from the supreme being in Zoroastrianism, the *Ahura Mazda*

Ad Extirpanda (5), papal bull issued in 1252 by Pope Innocent IV, in the wake of the killing of Saint Peter of Verona by a pro-Cathar group, which allowed for the limited use of torture during inquisition

Ausculta Fili (5), papal bull 5 December 1301, issued by Pope Boniface VIII to Philip IV King of France, it was politely critical of the king's behaviour and suggested that he ought to mend his ways and do penance. When ignored, it was followed by another papal bull, *Unam Sanctum* on 18 November

1302, grounding the supreme authority of the pope and the requirement to be a member of the Church in order to attain salvation. When King Philip IV refuted the bull, he was excommunicated. The French king responded with twenty-nine accusations against Pope Boniface VIII, including heresy, idolatry and being responsible for the death of Pope Celestine V, and gained the support of five archbishops and twenty-one bishops.

Anagni (5), hillside town 475 metres above sea-level, south-east of Rome, chosen by popes in early medieval period to escape Rome for healthier air; location of the assault on Pope Boniface VIII on 7 September 1303, led by Guillaume de Nogaret, French royal agent, and Sciarra Colonna (1270–1329), whose family disputed the pope's election. The pope was assaulted, and imprisoned for three days without food and drink; the palace was plundered; the band of mercenaries retreated after the population rose against them.

Albigensian Crusade (5), also known as the Cathar Crusade; a twenty-year genocide, a military campaign ordered by Pope Innocent III in 1209 to wipe out Catharism in Languedoc, southern France.

Castle Montségur (5), Cathar stronghold defended by a hundred fighters; was besieged for nine months by a royal force of ten thousand from May 1243, before surrendering. Civilians who renounced Catharism were to be allowed to leave, but around two hundred defenders and *perfecti*, Cathar 'pure ones', led by Bishop Bertrand Marty, marched to the field of pyres, mounted the pyres and voluntarily burned to death on 16 March 1244. Prat dels Cremats in Occitan language means 'Field of the Burned'.

Béziers massacre (5), 22 July 1209; at the beginning of the Albigensian Crusade, Béziers was besieged by a Crusader army under the command of Cistercian abbot, Arnaud Armaury, the papal legate. The town collapsed after a botched attempt to launch a sortie against the newly arrived Crusader army backfired on 21 July, exposing the town to invasion and plunder. Despite a list drawn up in advance of the fall, of over two hundred Cathar *perfecti*, it is claimed that twenty thousand inhabitants were slaughtered, including many Catholics. The papal legate chose to kill everyone rather than risk Cathars masquerading as Catholics escaping his grip. He is recorded as ordering: '*Caedite eos. Novit enim Dominus qui sunt eius.*' ('Kill them all. God will know His own.')

Aragon Crusade (5), 1284–85; declared by Pope Martin IV against King Peter III of Aragon after he had conquered Sicily, and because the pope disputed King Peter's right to the Aragon throne as a papal fief, favouring instead Charles of Valois, son of King Philip III of France, who invaded in 1284, taking Girona. Following the defeat of the French fleet at the Battle of Les Formiques, north-east of Barcelona, and an outbreak of dysentery, the hundred-thousand-strong French army retreated across the Pyrenees, suffering a heavy defeat in the mountains at the Battle of Col de Panissars, before reaching safety. King Philip II died from dysentery at Perpignan shortly afterwards.

Battle of the Golden Spurs (5), 11 July 1302, part of the Franco-Flemish War, 1297–1305; victory by Flanders over the royal French army, in the south-west of modern Belgium, near Kortrijk Castle, resulting in the rout of 2,500 French nobility, leaving five hundred pairs of spurs from defeated French heavy cavalry on the field. The spurs were offered in thanks by the Flemish to the Church of Our Lady in Kortrijk.

Fall of Acre (5), 1291; effectively ended the Jerusalem Crusades; heavy defeat of Frankish forces by the Cairo-based Mamluk Sultanate. Casualties and deaths estimated at one hundred thousand. The siege, pitting ten thousand defenders against two hundred thousand Mamluks, began on 6 April 1291. The walls of Acre were breached on 18 May, leaving the Templar fortress at the western corner of the city as the last redoubt. It held out for ten days before being breached and collapsed on 28 May; a small party escaped Acre by sea to Cyprus.

Bealtaine (6), 1 May, Gaelic festival midway between the spring equinox and the summer solstice, it is one of four festivals: *Samhain*, 1 November (Halloween); *Imbolc*, 1 February; and *Lughnasadh*, 1 August. At *Bealtaine*, 1 May, bonfires were lit as protection to people, crops and cattle, and hills throughout Ireland would await the first fire on Uisneach before lighting their bonfires, followed by households.

Battle of Milvian Bridge (7), 28 October 312, a decisive clash in northern Rome near a bridge over the River Tiber, between Emperor Constantine, coming south, and Emperor Maxentius, sallying out from Rome, with estimated forces of twenty-five thousand on both sides. A crushing victory for Constantine, putting him on the path to become sole emperor. According to Constantine's chronicler, Eusebius, he had his soldiers' shields painted with the first two Greek letters of Christ's name, Chi Rho, after a vision of a light in the sky which he interpreted as telling him: 'With this sign, conquer'.

Capitulatio de Partibus Saxonae (7), Charlemagne's law, established *c.* 782–95, in an attempt to Christianise the Saxons during the Saxon Wars, 772–804, it included death for failing to be baptised. Contemporary records report that 4,500 Saxons were killed for this reason at Verden in northern Germany in October 782.

Testament of Moses (8), also known as the Assumption of Moses; Jewish document of revelations dated from the first century, presenting the prophesies of Moses over twelve chapters, passed to Joshua, his successor, before his death, and through him to the Israelites.

Arianism (8), early Christian belief that Jesus Christ was not God but begotten by Him, and thus subordinate to Him, a belief attributed to Arius of Alexandria.

Trinitarianism (8), opposing view to Arianism, adopted by the First Council of Nicaea, and a central tenet of the Catholic Church, holding that God is three eternal, equal and indivisible beings in one essence.

Mirror of Simple Souls (9), a book of Christian mysticism about the divine, written in Old French by Marguerite Porete at the beginning of the fourteenth century. Marguerite was burned at the stake in 1310 for not renouncing its contents. The book charted seven stages to oneness with God through love, and the annihilation of the soul through oneness.

Vita Apostolica (9), means 'apostolic life', mirroring that of the Apostles by following a path of poverty and preaching the Gospel.

Sancta Camisa (10), which means 'holy shirt', is a relic said to be the tunic worn by the Virgin Mary at the Annunciation by Angel Gabriel and at the birth of Christ. It is twenty feet long, and made of silk, and dates to the first century.

Routiers (12), violent mercenary foot-soldiers organised in bands common to France from the twelfth century.

Gallowglass (12), descended from Norse Scots of west Scotland, they were heavily armoured, highly trained warriors who moved to Ireland to join powerful Gael families as professional warriors to stiffen resistance to the Norman conquest. Renowned for standing and fighting to the death.

Kern (12), light infantry local militia skilled at guerrilla fighting, the Gael warrior which, in larger numbers, accompanied groups of heavily armoured Gallowglass.

Birlinn (12), very similar to the Irish galley or *longa fada* (longship), powered by up to sixteen oars and a square sail amidships, it originated in western Scotland, influenced by Viking design. It was clinker-built, single mast, typically of oak.

Dulcinians (13), religious sect founded in 1300 in northern Italy; originated from another sect, the Apostolic Brethren, whose leader was burned at the stake, paving the way for Fra Dolcino to revive the sect. It retreated with 1400 followers into a fortified mountain position after three Dulcinians were burned at the stake.

Garderobe (13), originally referred to a storeroom in a medieval castle, but most commonly used to describe its toilet. It comprised of a holed seat which discharged waste to an external cesspit, a moat, pit, pond, river or the sea.

Camerarius Domini Papae (13), the papal chamberlain, a member of the Curia, deals with finances of the papal court and its revenues. The lead position is the *camerlengo*.

Clericis Laicos (13), papal bull issued on 5 February 1296 by Pope Boniface VII to prevent kingdoms confiscating or taxing Church revenues without the express approval of the Pope. It was specifically aimed at King Edward I of England and King Philip IV of France.

Treaty of Paris (14), 20 May 1303; peace treaty following war between King Edward I of England and King Philip IV of France; it returned the territory of Gascony to England, and reconfirmed the betrothal of Philip's daughter, Isabella, to Edward's son, the Prince of Wales, later Edward II.

Battle of Zierikzee (14), naval battle involving more than ninety ships, which took place on 10 and 11 August 1304, near the town of Zierikzee, during the Franco-Flemish war. The result was victory for France, leading to the capture of Zierikzee; this was followed a week later by a French victory on land at the battle of Mons-en-Pévèle.

Battle of Mons-en-Pévèle (14), 18 August 1304, between French forces led by King Philip IV, who was seeking to restore his personal honour after the defeat at the Battle of the Golden Spurs two years before, and Flemish forces. During the battle, Philip narrowly escaped a surprise Flemish attack on his tent, during which the Oriflamme flag was captured, but rallied to lead a decisive counterattack with the Marshal of France, Foulques du Merle, prompting a Flemish withdrawal.

Treaty of Athis-sur-Orge (14), signed 23 June 1305 by King Philip IV of France and Robert III of Flanders, ending the Franco-Flemish War (1297–1305). It returned three cities to France and established harsh yearly war reparations, paid by the Flemish to the French Crown.

Oriflamme (14), meaning 'golden flame'; the medieval battle-pennant of the King of France, which signalled no quarter to be given. It is thought to have originated when Charlemagne carried it to the Holy Land, but its first documented use was by King Louis VI in 1124, and its last was at the Battle of Agincourt in 1415.

Cadavar Synod (15), started in January 897; a posthumous seven-month trial of the exhumed body of Pope Formosus, conducted by Pope Stephen VI, on counts of illegal election to the papacy, and perjury. The guilty verdict nullified all acts by Formosus. His mutilated corpse was cast into the River Tiber.

Damnatio memoriae (15), meaning 'condemnation of memory'. It signifies oblivion, and requires the person's name to be erased from all official records, statues and place-names. It is a practice as old as the Pharaohs, dating at least from the fourteenth century BC, commonly used by the ancient Romans and throughout medieval and recent history, such as in the removal of statues of Stalin.

Baucent (16), black and white Templar war-flag, two knights seated on a horse, later emblazoned with the Templar red cross.

Tuatha Dé Danann (17), meaning 'people of the goddess Danu', the mystical race of otherworld deities in pre-Christian Ireland, prominent among which is the Dagda, but which also includes Brigid, Lugh, Nuada and others, including Ériu, after whom Ireland is named. They deposed the Fir Bolg at the first Battle of Magh Tuireadh. At the second Battle of Magh Tuireadh, the Fomorian leader, Balor, kills Nuada. He is then slain by Lugh, the champion of the Tuatha de Danann. After fresh invasions of Ireland in the second millennium BC, the race retreats into the mystical otherworld, establishing modern-day fairy lore.

Shillelagh (17), traditionally a strong, knotted Irish blackthorn walking stick with a large knob on top, used also as a weapon, sometimes lead-weighted to increase its power when used for striking.

Cúlán (17), medieval Gaelic Irish hairstyle consisting of tightly shaved head, high at the sides, and long hair grown from the crown to the back, and forward to the eyebrows.

Souterrains (18), underground passageways; stone structures, lined with stone and wood, used for storage and hiding; found throughout Iron Age Europe, from Gaul to Ireland; in Ireland, often found close to ring-forts.

Dál Birn (18), ruling line of the Irish kingdom of Osraige (Ossory), modern-day Kilkenny, and western Laois, a kingdom from the first century to the Norman invasion of the twelfth century. The Osraige occupied fertile lands between the Rivers Nore, Barrow and Suir, known as the Three Sisters.

Battle of Ahascragh (18), 1307, in Gaelic *Áth Eascrach,* ford of the River Esker, a tributary of the River Suck in east Galway. The battle is referred to in the medieval chronicles the Annals of the Four Masters, compiled in the seventeenth century from earlier annals, as the location of a strategic defeat of English forces by the O'Kelly clan.

Battle of Callann (18), August 1261, near Kilgarvan in south Kerry; a significant defeat of the Lordship of Ireland forces led by John Fitzgerald, the First Baron of Desmond, and Maurice John Fitzgerald, his son, by three Gaelic clans led by Fineen McCarthy, King of Desmond, and comprising of his kinsmen the O'Donoghues and O'Sullivans. Eight Norman barons and fifteen knights lost their lives, together with an unknown number of foot-soldiers.

Libros de los Juegos (19), in old Spanish *Book of Games,* influenced by Arab scholars but sponsored by King Alfonso X of Castile, and completed in 1283. It is a colourfully illustrated manual dealing with board-games including chess, dice and backgammon, with links to astrology and astronomy.

Balor (20), in Irish mythology, an evil giant cyclops, leader of the supernatural Fomorians from his base on Tory Island off north Donegal. He is killed by his grandson Lugh using a slingshot to the eye, before Balor could unleash its destructive power.

Solomon's Temple (23), the porch was held by two pillars, Boaz and Jachin. It was the first temple in ancient Jerusalem, according to the Hebrew Bible. Constructed by King Solomon, it was destroyed by Nebuchadnezzar II after the fall of Jerusalem in 587 BC; it had stood for more than four hundred years. Dedicated to Yahweh, god of Israel, it is said to have housed the Ark of the Covenant.

Roccafortis (28), derives from 'strong fortress', one of the largest Venetian ships of the thirteenth century, thought to have been constructed in 1268 for King Louis IX of France for the Eighth Crusade in 1270. Its overall length was believed to have been thirty-four metres, with its forecastle and aft castle being twelve metres high.

Pastoralis Praeeminentiae (29), papal bull issued by Pope Clement V on 22 November 1307, ordering the seizure of Templar assets and members on behalf of the Church.

Aramaic (31), the language of Jesus; originated in ancient Syria; a written language for more than three millennia

Johannite church (31), emanates from an indeterminate early Christian sect thought to have emphasised the teachings of Jesus by focusing on the Gospel of John.

Tosefta Shebuot (31), second-century rabbinical text recording the story of the Jerusalem Jews after the fall of the city to the Roman siege in 70 AD; part of the Tosefta, a gathering of Jewish oral law written in Hebrew and Aramaic

Sorat (32), the sun-demon, the opposing force to God, which stimulates the evil forces in humankind to push against the force of good and deflect souls from uniting with the divine.

Lucifer (32), 'Bringer of Light', is associated with the planet Venus, the morning star. Cathars viewed Lucifer as an angel, a brother of Jesus, who fell from heaven to establish a material world, his kingdom, where he trapped souls, and that Jesus descended to earth to free them. Many conventional Christian beliefs place Lucifer as the fallen angel, as Satan, although this is disputed elsewhere, including by Rudolf Steiner.

Acknowledgements

In recent years I decided to study life after death, which took me to the works of Rudolf Steiner (1861–1925): his lectures and some of his books, including *Occult Science: An Outline* and *Theosophy*. The lightbulb moment was on a weeklong meditation course in Malta in 2019 with Joe Dispenza, when I was prompted to make the leap and start on the plot. I opened the laptop just as Covid-19 lockdowns unfolded, and started typing.

First, I want to acknowledge and apologise to my long-suffering, loving family, for their dad prowling the house in the early hours and thumping the keyboard in rapid single-finger style, and also to those readers in my circle upon whom I relied for feedback on rougher drafts. Thanks so much for the searing, honest and tough feedback. I won't ask you again! I'd also like to thank the kind staff at the Embassy of the Islamic Republic of Iran in Ireland for their translation of a number of phrases into ancient Persian.

Notable recent book-sources include Goddard Henry Orpen's seminal work *Ireland Under the Normans*, published in 1911, and Dan Jones's excellent 2017 book *The Templars: The Rise and Fall of God's Holy Warriors*. For its investigation into early Christian times, I returned to one of my long-time favourites, *The Hiram Key* (1997), by Chris Knight and Robert Lomas, and *Michael and the Two-Horned Beast* by Bernard Nesfield-Cookson – a keen student of Steiner's works – which appeared the following year. *The Secret History of the World* by Jonathan Black (2007) is another source: a romp through eclectic information you won't readily find elsewhere.

Along the way, I've dipped into an endless supply of philosophy and history, since being inspired by an outstanding historian in the 1970s in secondary school, Brother Dominic of the Presentation Brothers. I always have a few books about history and the philosophers on the go, and listen to little else when walking or in the gym. This time it included *Freedom's Sword: Scotland's Wars of Independence* by Chris Brown (1998) and *King and Outlaw: The Real Robert the Bruce* by Chris Brown (2018), and the BBC's fabulous In Our Time archive.

In particular, I want to acknowledge the explorers of guided meditation I met along the way, who helped me open my mind to possibilities, and use it gently in wonderful new ways.

Eddie Hobbs